Finished with Life

But Unable to Die

The *Unable to Die* Series Omnibus

To Donna,
I hope you
enjoy the read!

Scott Bartlett

Mirth Publishing
St. John's

FINISHED WITH LIFE BUT UNABLE TO DIE

Cover art by: Rebecca Weaver (rebeccaweaver.com)

Edited by: Laura Kingsley (laurakingsley.wordpress.com)

Library and Archives Canada Cataloguing in Publication

Bartlett, Scott

Finished with Life but Unable to Die / Scott Bartlett ; illustrations by Rebecca Weaver.

ISBN 978-0-9812867-3-0

To you, the reader, without whom none of this would be possible.

{ 1 }

Finished with Life but Unable to Die

Much of Michael Haynes's life was dim to him now, though there were parts of it that remained so bright it hurt.

Being ninety-one could do that to you. He remembered shades of happiness, and ample sad hues, too. Blurred faces who had jostled him one way or another, or tried to. Car trips, back and forth across the island endlessly.

The dimness that shrouded his past reminded him of how old photographs faded with the years. He'd started working in a dark room at the age of fourteen, and both his children and grandchildren had joined him there during their youth for long hours filled with fascination. None had followed in his footsteps—thank God. Digital photography had killed his old profession as surely as video had done for radio stars. Now he was the one fascinated, by the strangeness of the new machines, which his descendants toted everywhere and treated with the same carelessness as the rest of their possessions. Michael had only ever owned three cameras in his lifetime, which he'd tended and serviced with care. Parting with each one had hurt with a deep-down ache. But times had changed, and he knew acceptance was the wisest course. *You'll never understand the new ways, and that's fine,* he told himself. *Also: just because you don't understand them doesn't mean they're wrong.* He often had trouble with the last part.

The present had taken on dimness, as well. The world had blurred to his eyes. Colours weren't as sharp as he remembered. Food didn't taste as good. He moved more slowly, deliberately, fearful of the consequences a misstep could have.

With his grandchildren mostly grown, Michael welcomed the sickness when it came. It started as a cough that wouldn't go away. In its third week, he expelled a small amount of blood into his favourite handkerchief. He developed a wheeze, and started losing weight, despite that he was eating as healthily as he ever had. A few medical exams later, the doctors told him he had a stage four small-cell carcinoma of the lung. It was inoperable, and at his age he could expect to survive another few months at most, though they did prescribe him a combined regimen of chemotherapy and radiation. Michael didn't exactly see the point, but he supposed he should undergo it, for his children.

If he was being honest, it had surprised him when he didn't pass away shortly after Linda did ten years before. Old couples who loved each other as much as they had tended to go more or less together. But Michael had carried on, and the pain her death had left him with never diminished, not one bit. She'd been nine years his junior.

Now he hoped to join her, leaving this troubled world behind. She'd been a devout Catholic, and he'd grown much more devout since she passed. If Jesus was truly as forgiving as the Bible and the Church represented, he just might end up where Linda had surely gone.

But that wasn't his only reason for wishing to die. It wasn't even the biggest one. Two of his children had stumbled into deep financial trouble, and selling the large tracts of family land they'd inherit upon Michael's passing would give them opportunity to regain their footing. He was willing to just give them the land now, but they were far too proud to accept it. They insisted on waiting until his death before inheriting anything.

Then there was Esther, his youngest daughter, to whom in a perverse way he felt he owed it to die. His death would put a lot of things right for her, he was certain.

After hearing about the cancer his children said they wanted him in St. John's, to which most of them had migrated at a young age, leaving their native Corner Brook and crossing the island for a new life on the other side. "If you want me there, come and get me," he told them, so they did, travelling westward on the Trans-Canada Highway in a five-car convoy, carbon dioxide emissions be damned, apparently. Back to where they were born.

Once there, they spent a week packing up what Michael wanted kept, while he held court in the living room, berating them cheerfully. "Be careful with that carving, whippersnapper," he said to Luke, his youngest offspring, who was forty-two. "It's not one of your game controllers, to be tossed about whenever you lose a one up."

"You don't *lose* a—" Luke shook his head, thick glasses flashing in the lamplight. "Do you realize how old using the word whippersnapper makes you sound?"

Michael laughed. "Good. I am old!"

Luke was always quick to criticize, but he came by that honestly. Michael didn't like to admit it even to himself, but he'd been hard on Luke over the years. As the youngest child, Michael had seen him as his last chance to create a truly formidable individual. He'd always expected perfection from him, and as a result Luke had been a quiet, serious kid. Overly serious. And in his early twenties he'd gone through a delayed rebellious stage, cutting off all contact with his parents for a time, and dropping out of the engineering program Michael had encouraged him to pursue. By the time they finally began speaking to each other again Luke had used his programming skills to get a job with Healthr, a technology company devoted to life extension. Michael had always called programming a hobby, and he knew Luke took pride in having turned it into a living.

Luke could be prickly, but for the most part they all took the light-hearted needling in stride. Of course, Michael didn't dare needle Esther. At forty-three, she went about life with shoulders always hunched forward, her long brown hair pointing straight at the floor. She was a brittle woman, and prone to crying at the slightest upset. She'd been that way ever since she was eight.

As they worked, Michael thought he saw his children eyeing some of his belongings with an interest that went beyond sorting and packing it. They were sizing up what they wanted, he realized. It was a bittersweet thing to behold. It meant they wanted things to remember him by—most of the objects they paused to stare at could only hold sentimental value, though Craig did seem drawn to things that would sell. It also meant they were preparing for a world that no longer had him in it.

His temper flared a couple times during the week, followed immediately by an awkward silence, and his offspring exchanging furtive glances. He didn't apologize, but he felt badly, and though they gradually regained their easy banter he knew they would talk about it later when he went to bed. Michael hated letting his temper get the best of him, but an aged body filled with aches and pains made it difficult sometimes. The littlest thing could set him off. Despite the medications he'd been given, his cough was almost as bad as before. It had a ragged edge that made his children wince.

They finally finished loading everything aboard the vehicles, leaving a space for Michael in the passenger seat of Stephen's car. Stephen was the oldest, and he owned a print and frame shop in St. John's. Michael maintained that he had no favourite child, but he sometimes found himself thinking that maybe he did, and if so it was probably Stephen. Unfortunately, he was one of the two offspring struggling financially—him and Craig. The print and frame shop had fallen on hard times, and Stephen's taste for bigger and better didn't help things.

After dropping off the leftover odds and ends at the Salvation Army thrift store, they set out on the eight-hour journey, which would probably become a ten-hour one with the frequent pit stops necessitated by having an old man along for the ride. They didn't drive in a convoy on the trip to St. John's—instead the others went at their own pace, which would probably be much quicker than Stephen and Michael.

"I won't miss this trip," Michael said. "Eight hours of nothing."

"You should have brought a book to read, Dad," Stephen said. He liked to keep the driver's seat as far back as possible, to make room for his big belly.

Michael grunted. His eyesight had been too poor to read for years, now, even the large print versions. Luke kept telling him he should get an eReader so he could jack up the font as much as he liked. But he was damned if he'd stare at a screen till his eyes fell out.

Stephen knew his way around a silence. He felt no pressure to maintain the constant babble young people seemed inclined toward, and he exerted no such pressure. Michael appreciated that. Esther had quietly wrapped a fleece blanket around him before their journey began, and now he felt his eyelids droop. Soon, he drifted off.

In his dream he knelt in the middle of a vast graveyard, imploring the sky with his hands clasped together. He knew that if he begged convincingly enough, for forgiveness, for salvation, he would be plucked up by some celestial force, and he would rise.

"Please," he sobbed, tears streaming down his face. "Please. I didn't know. I couldn't have known. It seemed like make-believe. Like a game she was playing. And I couldn't believe it of—"

Suddenly gravity's downward pressure was diminished, and he felt his knees leave the ground, then his feet. Suspended several meters over the ground, he laughed through his tears, with joy. He would be let in. He would be forgiven.

But the celestial hand had only been weighing him, gauging his worth. It found him wanting. Undeserving. It dropped him. His kneecaps cracked off the ground, shattering.

Michael woke screaming.

*

When they arrived in town they reconvened briefly at Stephen's house, where they sat around his sumptuous living room with mugs in hand. Stephen suggested waiting until the morning to move everything inside, which struck everyone as a good idea. Michael requested a stiff whiskey drink, and received it. No one told him he shouldn't have one, given his health, and he didn't expect them to. His children had always respected him, and they were more likely to avoid him than question him. He got his stiff drink. He liked that they didn't baby him, as he'd seen being done to others his age.

Luke was the last to arrive at Stephen's. When he did, he suggested a late dinner at his place, which drew uncomfortable glances from his siblings, and an outright glare from Valentine, the eldest of Michael's daughters. "Look at Dad, Luke," she said. "Look how tired he is after that drive. Do you think he's up for being trucked downtown to your apartment?" Her gel-spiked black hair made her seem angrier than she probably was.

"Geez," Luke said. "It was just a thought."

"It's fine, Luke," Michael said. Everything was fine with a stiff drink in hand. Most things, anyway. "I appreciate the offer."

His son gave a half-smile, and that was the end of the matter. They were all tired, with frayed nerves. "Time for bed, I think," Michael said when he'd drained his glass.

"I'm for that," said Craig, revealing his big straight teeth with a grin.

Michael didn't remain at Stephen's for long. Even with the chemotherapy and radiation, his condition deteriorated more rapidly than the doctors had anticipated, and soon he found himself occupying a hospital bed in the intensive care ward.

He was ready to go. After, when his children spoke of his death, they would append the phrase "but he lived a long life." And he had. More important, he'd straightened out his last will and testament decades ago. Stephen would execute the will, and Michael didn't expect there would be any hiccups. He trusted his son to treat his siblings fairly. Michael did have some savings, as he'd always been frugal. And then there was the land, back in Corner Brook. It had been in the family for generations, but now it would be parceled out equally to his six children. A lifeline for Stephen and Craig. Even Doris would get her share, despite having eloped to England in her twenties and barely ever calling. They told him she was headed home now, given how ill he'd become. He wondered whether she would make it in time.

The number of people who came to visit surprised him. Michael always made a point to be friendly, but he hadn't anticipated there being so many people who cared enough to go out of their way just to wish him well. They brought him cards, flowers, balloons, and candy, which of course he felt too sick to eat. But he appreciated the gestures. All of them. It seemed that even here in St. John's, he would be well remembered. He'd never been the sort to speculate about what his funeral attendance would look like, but it occurred to him now that the church might well be packed.

He wondered whether that counted for anything with the Lord. Probably not.

At any rate, he was rarely without someone at his bedside. His children took turns staying with him in six-hour shifts, though Luke couldn't contribute as much since he worked a lot of overtime at Healthr.

"I'm going to run to the cafeteria, Dad," Stephen said, whose shift it was. "Do you want anything?"

"I'm fine." The hospital fed him, and his son could do without the extra expense.

"Okay. Be back in a few."

A grey-haired man appeared at the door a mere thirty seconds later, leaning heavily on a cane, hesitating. For a moment Michael mistook him for a patient, but of course he wore regular clothes, not the green dress in which they clad the sick. Straining to focus his gaze, he soon realized the man's true identity. He felt all warmth drain from his face, fixing the man with a cold stare.

"You dare," he said, but couldn't finish.

"Brother," Horace Haynes said. "It's been so long."

"Why are you here? You waited for Stephen to leave, didn't you?"

"Please. Don't be this way with me. I'm your little brother."

"You're no brother of mine." Michael had disowned Horace the same time their parents had. "What if my daughter had been here, and seen you? Did you consider that? You scum." One of the machines to which Michael was connected began to beep more rapidly.

"Hear me out, Michael. I'm changed. I changed a long time ago."

"You've gotten wilier, maybe. More insidious. Are you here about my will? Our parents took you out of theirs, and I'll be damned if I'll ever let you back onto the family land, except maybe as the trespasser you are."

"I'm here to ask your forgiveness."

"Never."

"Aren't you afraid to die?" Horace's eyes looked moist. "I am. I still believe in God. Now, more than ever. I'm terrified where I'll end up."

That gave Michael pause. The fact he shared something with Horace. But it only served to stoke his anger even more.

"Get out. Don't come back. Don't come to my funeral. And never contact my family."

"Please, Michael—"

"You won't get a penny when I die. Everything goes to my children, you bastard." He started pressing the buzzer that lay near his hand at all times. "Nurse!" he shouted. "Nurse! This man won't get out of my room. Nurse!"

Horace's mouth formed a hard line, and he turned, disappearing down the hall. A young nurse appeared in the doorway, the pretty one with her black hair in a bun, dividing her attention between Michael in the bed and Horace as he receded down the hall. "What's the matter, Mr. Haynes?" she said. "What did he do to you?"

"Near pestered the life out of me," Michael said, trying to make light of it with a weak joke. He suddenly felt deeply tired. More than he'd ever felt in his life. "Don't worry, though. I think you chased him away."

She gave him a smile, and returned to the Nurse's station.

*

That night, around midnight, he abruptly fell apart. His doctor ordered his morphine dose increased, but before that happened Michael wanted to speak with his children one last time, even with waves of excruciating pain racking his system. Doris had arrived three days ago, and so soon enough all his progeny were assembled around his bed. He'd long considered what he would say when this moment came, and now he said it.

He told them all he loved them very much. He wanted that to be the first thing they remembered about him. Then he started with the specific things he wanted to say to each offspring. To hear the rasp his voice had become, each had to bend low over his mouth as he whispered to them. First, he beckoned Doris. He told her that even though she'd been the one farthest away geographically, she'd remained as close to his heart as any other. She smiled and turned away, her eyes glistening.

Next came Craig. He told him to never let go of his good humour. That his jokes had helped Michael get through some tough times, and they would help others too. Of course, Craig's jokes could get a little personal too, sometimes bordering on outright gossip—an alarming trait in a psychologist. But Michael didn't feel like bringing that up just then.

He also asked Craig to start inviting Stephen to come out with him on his morning jog. "He runs himself ragged with that shop, but never takes time for himself. He needs others to help him with that." Doing so would also take Craig's mind off the marital problems plaguing him.

Michael told Valentine not to worry that she'd never found a man right for her. "Much worse would have been if you'd stayed with any of those assholes." That made her giggle, which he loved. "You don't need a man. You're a fiercely independent woman. But if you decide to try out another one, keep doing as you've been doing. Don't stay with him if he isn't right." Valentine hugged him, dampening his shoulder, and stepped away. Michael felt confident she would keep the family together once he was gone. She'd always been their de facto leader. As a child she would play 'School' with the others. When she lined up all her siblings in front of her plastic chalkboard she would dispense a level of knowledge very few children possessed. The others looked up to her, and when disputes arose Valentine quickly got to the heart of the issue, not only resolving it but also making both sides feel like they'd been treated fairly.

To Luke he said gently: "You've been alone too long, son. It seems like you haven't really tried to find a wife, and I think you're someone who could use a woman to keep him on an even keel. What about that dating program you told me about? Think that might do it?"

His son had trouble forming meaningful connections with other people, probably because he was always criticizing other people in his head. That wasn't entirely his fault. Michael had been very demanding of him in his youth, and now Luke was demanding of other people.

Luke drew back, and fixed him with a tight smile. "Thanks Dad. Sage advice." He stepped away.

He didn't have much to tell Stephen, which made sense. Michael's favourite memories of him were times they'd shared a silence, completely at ease in each other's company.

"Take care of yourself, son. You need to pay more attention to your diet. You'd better not end up in a bed like this for a good long time. If you do, I'll give you a right old ass-kicking once you get to heaven."

"I love you, Dad."

"I love you. And you should probably consider downsizing, you know? If you're honest with yourself I think you'll realize you don't need a big house and fancy cars to be happy."

Last came Esther. When Michael tried to speak a lump formed in his throat, and he found himself battling tears of his own. Esther looked down at him, expressionless, hands clasped at her waist. “Father?” she said at last.

But he couldn’t. He couldn’t speak. His carefully prepared words had crumbled to dust.

“I’m sorry,” was all he could manage.

Esther opened her mouth to say something, but closed it again, the corners turned downward. “Thank you, Father,” she said, her voice so devoid of emotion it came off as cold. She returned to her corner of the room.

Then they called the nurse, who increased his morphine drip. Soon he began to drift in and out of consciousness. Mostly out. His children never left his side, except for Stephen, of whom there appeared to be no sign. That might have been the delirium, though. Sometimes his children were joined by apparitions. Friends from Michael’s childhood, long-forgotten teachers, old co-workers.

His parents. Shaking their heads sadly as they looked upon their dying son. After a while they linked hands, turned, and left, exiting through the wall.

At one point he rose to consciousness, or what seemed like consciousness, to find only Esther in the room, sitting beside him, holding his hand. He tried to speak, but his voice was reduced to a death rattle. She leaned in closer, her flat expression never changing. Giving away nothing.

Speaking was the hardest thing he’d ever done. He managed to croak out four syllables: “Have I been good?”

Several moments passed, and finally she nodded. Paused. And nodded again.

Darkness engulfed him, for the last time.

*

Bright, white light. Shining through his eyelids. Making him squint, even with his eyes closed.

He tried to open them, and couldn't. "Where am I?" he rasped.

Rustling, to his left. A hand gripped his knee through a blanket.

"You're in ICU, Dad. With us." Luke. "You're still with us."

Trying again, he managed to open his eyes. Valentine and Stephen were there as well. "How?"

"The cancer is gone. You're a survivor."

Michael felt his facial features draw downward. *No,* he yelled inside his head. *No, no, no.* "That doesn't make any sense."

"I've been working on this ever since you got sick," Luke said. "I didn't tell you about it, or anyone, because I didn't want to get hopes up. But when I mentioned your cancer to a colleague, the first day I found out, she told me about a new procedure that was almost ready for human trials. I got in touch with the researchers and convinced them to take you on as their first trial patient."

"How on Earth did you do that?" This was wrong. This was all wrong.

"Luke has some high-up contacts in the government," Stephen said. "He had them put in a good word."

The two brothers' eyes met, and annoyance flashed across Luke's face. Then he turned to face Michael again. "That wasn't all. Normally a ninety-one-year-old man would never be accepted as a trial patient, let alone the very first one. They want people in their prime, to increase the probability the procedure will work, which makes it more likely to be adopted as standard medical practice. But these researchers were unusually confident. Animal tests weren't just promising—they were mind-blowing. I convinced them that if they could cure a cancer-ridden old man, everyone would pay attention. Their procedure would be sure to change the world. Plus, you've always kept pretty healthy. So they agreed." Luke's glasses magnified his calm eyes, framing his half-grin below.

"How do you feel, Dad?" Valentine asked, a distinct note of uncertainty in her voice. Stephen seemed uncomfortable, too. Unlike Luke they sensed their father's distress. *The cancer was supposed to fix things. It was supposed to deliver me to Linda.*

But here he remained, with his children, two of who looked very upset. He couldn't bear to see them unhappy. He would pass off his torment as a joke. He would lie.

"You brats," Michael said, and pain in his chest made him pause. Stephen winced.

"You brats don't get your inheritance yet."

They all chuckled, then. "That's a shame," Stephen said. "I've had my eye on that ratty old couch you made us haul over from Corner Brook."

But it wasn't just a ratty old couch, and this disaster was no joke. Dying would have meant giving his sons a leg up out of their financial messes. Knowing his children they would continue refusing any land or money from him. Why couldn't they see what was best for them as well as he could? He might have cursed.

Instead he told them he needed to sleep, as cheerfully as he could manage, and they left. Wrapped in the sensation that everything in the world had spoiled, he sunk into slumber, praying he would not wake.

*

The miraculous procedure had involved sending microscopic structures into Michael's body to deliver chemo drugs directly to the cancer cells. Within hours his terminal, stage four small-cell carcinoma of the lung went into remission. As Luke predicted, everyone paid attention. The media clamoured to get access to Michael, but they were kept away until he felt well enough to leave, which took weeks. He didn't understand their eagerness to speak with him. What could they possibly learn? He knew nothing about the particulars of the technology itself. They couldn't learn anything by just looking at him. He looked like any other ninety-one-year-old. He wasn't the pioneer, the researchers were, and judging by what he saw on the TV in his hospital room they weren't spending nearly enough time talking to them.

They wanted his story, he supposed, which ultimately meant nothing in the grand scheme of things. His story wouldn't change history. The procedure would. At any rate, he wouldn't give them his real story no matter how many times they asked. It went like this: he was ninety-one and ready to die. He'd made peace with it long before the cancer. He longed to be with his wife, and ultimately he felt his death would solve many of his family's problems. His son had unknowingly robbed him of that chance, for God knew how long. Michael could never say that to Luke, or anyone else. It would make him appear ungrateful, abominable, and it could crush Luke. But that was his story. The true one.

When he finally did leave the hospital, and reporters swarmed him just outside the entrance, he fed them platitudes. "Yes, of course it's amazing to still be alive. Of course I have a new lease on life. I'm thinking of all the extra books I'll get to read." Chuckle.

"Are you aware that your operation could mark the beginning of an era of life extension? That with drug delivery methods having become so advanced, human life expectancy might be set to increase rapidly?"

"No," Michael said. "I was not aware. Is that how it is?"

His children had decided that Michael would stay with Stephen until fully recovered, at which point the choice could be made about whether he would return to live in Corner Brook. They called staying with Stephen a suggestion, but Michael knew it for what it was: a decision on how he would conduct his life, made without him. For the first time his children were presuming to steer him like he was a child, or a horse. He would bear it silently as long as he could, though he didn't expect that to be very long. He wanted to seem grateful. But it tasted bitter.

"Martha's making scalloped potatoes tonight, Dad," Stephen said as he helped Michael into the Mercedes. "Your favourite. Excited?"

"Overjoyed." *Uh oh. Not sounding very convincing.*

He fell into a silence as they drove out of the hospital parking lot, which he hoped his son took for fatigue instead of the sullenness it was. Michael felt angry, at his children, at the world, and at himself. He felt helpless, too. When did he lose control over his own life? He'd always prided himself on his independence, at such an advanced age. Now he might as well be his own children's child.

Finally his irritation got the better of him, causing him to speak his mind more freely than he normally would. "You know, if you owned a less flashy car you probably wouldn't be in such deep shit when it comes to money."

He regretted it immediately. Stephen reddened, not answering, and the silence continued, tense and full of shame on both their parts.

Looking out the passenger window to conceal his emotions, Michael's eyes widened, and his frown became a rictus of fear. "Stephen," he started to say, but never got to finish the word. The pickup truck smashed into them, flipping the Mercedes over and sending it into oncoming traffic.

*

Stephen's orphans were sending fire balloons out over Adam's Pond.

They shouldn't have been doing it—the latex would end up in the water, and maybe inside some fish's stomach, if the pond still held any fish. But no one bothered to stop them. The oldest, Samuel, picked up another balloon and lit the alcohol-soaked cotton ball sitting in the attached basket. He gave it to his brother Daniel to release. The little brother thrust his hands forward, and at first the balloon went down toward the water, the basket rocking back and forth, looking like it would be caught and sunk. It found its lift at the last possible second, and rose up into the air, into the clear, hot day. Daniel squealed with delight, and Samuel watched it go too, equally rapt.

"Do you think it will float on forever?" Daniel said.

"No," Samuel answered. "That's stupid."

Stephen had had children rather late in life, after a couple decades of trying. Eventually he and Martha had gone looking for a surrogate mother, after undergoing tests that showed Martha was infertile.

Sam and Dan weren't technically orphans. Martha was still alive somewhere, presumably. She'd vanished shortly after the car accident, having apparently decided the single mom life wasn't for her. She hadn't checked in with anyone since. The boys lived with Valentine. So did Michael.

Gravel crunched in the driveway behind, and Michael twisted around in his wheelchair to look. Luke had arrived, in his DeLorean. He got out, smiling, and walked over, hand extended toward his father. Michael regarded it coldly. Luke's smile wavered, and after a couple seconds he put his hands in his pockets.

"Happy birthday, Dad."

Michael said nothing.

Luke cleared his throat, pulled his hands out again, and sat at a nearby picnic table, leaning back against it. "Fire balloons," he said, nodding at the children. "Ray Bradbury would be proud."

"Who?"

"Never mind." He twisted around and grabbed a fistful of chips from one of the bowls on the table. Over the last nine years, Luke had developed a gut to rival his dead brother's. After he finished cramming the chips into his face he rubbed his fingers against his shirt before scratching his eye, which caused grease to get on his glasses. He removed them, wiped them on the same spot he'd wiped his fingers, and replaced them. Then he grabbed another fistful of chips. "So," he said through a mouthful. "Triple digits today, hey?"

"I don't want to talk about it." From someone else, that might have been a joke. But Michael truly didn't want to discuss it, especially not with Luke, whose fault it was that Michael remained alive.

"I just hope I live that long."

"Your mother used to say that neither of us would last long without the other."

Luke stopped chewing for a moment.

"How wrong she was."

"Mom would be happy for you, Dad."

"Can't see why."

"Now why do you say that? You're one of the luckiest people alive, and your bellyaching isn't helping anyone. Least of all yourself."

Michael brought a shaking hand up to wipe his nose, which had started to drip. "It's not natural for a father to outlive his son. How is *that* lucky? My oldest son killed in his prime, and here I am a dried-out cripple. Nine years later, I still can't understand how a ninety-one-year-old fresh out of hospital survives an accident that kills a fifty-year-old with no health problems. How? The truck hit us on my side. How did I live while he died?"

"Luck, Dad. You're very lucky. Like I said. Also, modern medicine. You weren't far from the hospital, and they zipped you right back."

It hadn't been any fancy magic procedure that saved Michael's life, the second time. There were no strings for Luke to pull. He simply didn't die. Paralyzed from the legs down, his collarbone broken, and his arm. His shoulder shattered, and his hip. Coma for months. And one day he woke up again, back in the hospital, where they spent another year rehabilitating him till he could operate a motorized wheelchair. Then Valentine took him home. Stephen's wife had been long gone by then, so returning to that house wasn't an option.

The extra year in hospital had driven him nearly insane with boredom and frustration. During that time he often thought about the miraculous stories he'd heard over the years, of people who went from full paralysis to being able to walk around and do everything they used to do. Those people always had amazing attitudes, and worked at their rehabilitation every minute of every day. Michael had none of their optimism. He didn't even have the will to live. He wished for death constantly, and a few times he considered trying to see to it himself. But his children came to visit all the time, and working together with the hospital staff they cheerfully goaded him into recovery. Why wouldn't they let him die?

Daniel ran up clutching some gadget in both grubby paws, holding it toward Michael, the screen pointing at him. "Check out my new app, Pop! It turns Lacy into a lizard, or a big scary monster, or anything!" He pointed the thing at Valentine's dog, Lacy, as though he intended to take a photo of her. But instead of Lacy, an orange rhinoceros appeared on the screen, moving around in exactly the same way Lacy was moving in real life. She stuck out her tongue, panting, and the rhino did too.

"See, Pop?" Daniel said. "You can feed her and everything." He tapped the screen and a cartoon muffin appeared, which Dan dragged toward the rhino, causing it to open its mouth. There was a chomping sound. Lacy had not opened her mouth.

"If that was all we fed to Lacy, she'd starve," Michael said.

Daniel frowned. "Yeah, but it's still cool."

Michael grunted, and looked away, out over the pond.

"Show me, Danny," Luke said. "Poppy's not into that kind of stuff." Daniel passed him the phone. "Hey, cool. A guy showed me this at the con last year."

"What's a con?"

Luke grinned. "It's short for convention. Sci-Fi on the Rock is the biggest one in the province. All kinds of cool nerdy stuff. It's been happening every year for eighteen years."

Daniel's mouth dropped open. "That's older than me."

"Way older. If you're good, I'll take you there this year. If I have the weekend off."

"Okay!" Dan ran off to brag about it to his older brother.

"Cute kids," Luke said. He glanced over and saw the way his father was looking at him. "What?"

Michael pressed the chair's knob left, so that it turned him around to face the house. "And I used to wonder why you've never had a girlfriend."

Luke's grin soured. Michael told the chair to carry him forward, and it did.

The media had made much of his surviving a car accident mere minutes after being interviewed by reporters about undergoing the historic new procedure. They called him the "Luckiest Man on Earth," a phrase Luke liked to dredge up *ad nauseam*, even nine years later.

A couple talk shows invited him to come on, but he'd had zero interest. He was too old to be caked in powder and dragged onto TV. He wanted as little attention as possible.

Finally, after months of foolishness, the media attention had tapered off, and they left him alone. But now they'd returned in full force. Thousands of people had undergone the procedure since he did, and now most of them were dead, or dying. He was by far the oldest among them, by a matter of decades. It seemed that the drug used in the procedure, delivered in such a highly concentrated way, sped up mitochondrial activity in the lungs, which caused them to fail in less than a decade. But not Michael's. If anything, his mitochondria appeared to function slower than usual, according to his doctors, anyway. No one knew why, but everyone wanted to. Only two others responded to the procedure the same way he had, but of course they were of no interest to the media, because they weren't nearly as old as him. "It's remarkable," one of the doctors said to him. "Your body is the closest thing to a holy grail for life extension science I've ever seen."

Though he probably should, Michael didn't care about any of it. Researchers wanted to run a series of tests on him, but he was a hundred years old, and had no interest in spending any more time inside hospitals than was absolutely necessary. Only one thing remained that concerned him: making sure his children got their inheritance soon. But that entailed dying, which he appeared utterly incapable of doing.

His wheelchair rolled up the ramp to the back deck—one of several Valentine had paid to have installed within a week of his moving in. Esther sat there, hunched forward, sipping an iced tea. Her eyes met his momentarily over the rim of her glass, expressionless as ever. They'd barely spoken since that night in the hospital room nine years ago. But she'd shown up for this, his hundredth birthday party. The one he'd told his children he didn't want to have.

It's important to them, a faint voice admonished him from the back of his head. He thought it might be Linda's voice. He pushed it farther back. Why didn't anyone ever ask what was important to him? When did that cease to be a thing anyone did?

The other day, Valentine told him Esther was seeing a new therapist. The two sisters went out for coffee most every week, so Michael did keep updated on his youngest daughter's doings, despite the lack of communication. Valentine also said that Esther cried nearly every time they met. Even now, her eyes were rimmed with red.

"How does it feel to hit a century?" she said, almost knocking him over backward in his chair with shock. He couldn't remember the last time she'd initiated a conversation. Possibly never.

"Um, okay," he said. "I guess." He turned his chair to face the pond again, feeling awkward, without a single clue about how to proceed in a conversation with Esther. He needn't have worried, though. The conversation stopped there.

The party had been Valentine's idea. She'd noticed his worsening lethargy, and recognized it as more than just the usual symptoms of inhabiting a decaying shell for a body. "Where did my chipper father go?" she'd asked him. "What happened to the man who joked and teased and smiled all the time?"

"He didn't go anywhere," Michael had said. "That's the problem. He was supposed to die from cancer, but instead his son sent tiny robots spelunking under his skin, and he turned into the bitter old git you see before you." He never bothered to sugar-coat anything for his children anymore. *It's good for them to get a dose of realism every now and then,* was how he justified it to himself.

"I'm tired of hearing you talk like that."

"How else am I supposed to talk? My entire family's in disarray. Craig's marriage is on the rocks again, and his money problems are worse than they've ever been. Esther's psychological issues only seem to get worse, and she's not flush with cash either, with her cats' constant vet bills. Luke is a pompous know-it-all who thinks he could solve everybody's problems if only they let him. And you have your own finance issues, now that you're caring for Stephen's children, not to mention me. You certainly don't have time to be worrying about an old man's feelings. You should let me help out with the costs at least."

"Nonsense. I'm not going to chip away at my brothers' and sisters' inheritance just to make things a little easier for me."

"And this is the other thing," Michael said, pointing a finger in Valentine's face. "None of you will accept the slightest bit of money from me, or advice, or even help. I'm just a lump to you. Clearly I've failed as a father. Everyone will be better off when I die—I truly believe that."

Valentine sighed, laying a hand on his knee. "Dad, that's ridiculous. You're not a lump." She gave a little chuckle, to show how silly the idea was. "You're our father, and we love you. You dying won't make our lives better. It will leave a gaping hole. Know what I think? I think you need to start taking advantage of the time you have left. You *can* help your children, you know. By being there for us. Being fully present, and with us. Esther would be a great person to start with. I think there a lot of things between you two that have gone unsaid for too long."

He frowned, considering.

Valentine's eyes lit up. "I just had an amazing idea. Your hundredth birthday is coming up. We're having a party, and inviting the whole family."

Michael raised his hand again, this time to hold a palm up. "No. No, Valentine. Don't you dare. I hate being the center of—"

She sprang to her feet and went to the phone. "I'll start inviting people now. This'll be so much fun, Dad!"

"*Valentine!*"

So here they all were, gathered at Valentine's house for his centennial. Except for Doris, but that didn't surprise him. Michael hadn't been very optimistic about the chances she would fly over from the UK just for this.

Now Valentine emerged onto the deck, cordless phone in hand. "Craig's not coming," she said. "Says he has a client in crisis. Can't possibly leave him."

"He's probably fighting with Sandy again," Luke said from the bottom of the deck's steps. He'd taken a bowl of chips with him from the picnic table, cradling it in one arm as one would an infant wrapped in swaddling.

"I'm surprised you were able to make it, Luke," Valentine said. "Didn't Healthr just land another major contract with the government?" A couple years ago Luke had been promoted to CEO of Healthr.

Luke gave his trademark grin—half smarm, half condescension. "Wouldn't miss Dad's birthday for the world." He cleared his throat, and met Michael's gaze. "Also, I wanted to ask his thoughts on the proposal I brought to him last week."

"Out of the question," Michael said.

For the second time today, Luke's grin dropped away. This time a glower replaced it. "I don't understand you, Dad. You've been given more amazing opportunities than everyone I know combined, yet you're still as stubborn and negative as ever. You have the chance to help make history. To better the human race."

"Living longer does not better anyone. God gave us lives with natural ends, so that we appreciate our time on Earth. Living as long as I have doesn't serve anyone. Trust me."

Valentine looked at him with sadness, and Esther's eyed filled with tears. He'd never spoken this way in front of them before, he knew, but his restraint had all been used up. Perhaps he'd reached a threshold of tolerance for the kind of nonsense Luke kept spouting. He felt bad for upsetting Esther, but he'd had enough.

"Dad," Luke said, and his tone spoke volumes: *You've failed utterly to grasp the situation.* "I can't believe you're serious. God gave us natural lifespans? What about the third world countries where the average life expectancy is under forty? Is that natural?"

Michael had no answer for that.

"In terms of humanity's basic genetic material," Luke went on, "you've lived an unnaturally long time. So have I, for that matter. That's the effect modern medicine has had, and unlike you, most people tend to celebrate it. But this isn't just about increasing the average life-expectancy. And it isn't just about you. The government has offered to finance your cryogenic preservation because of your unique response to the procedure that cured your cancer, and because of your body's unique resistance to aging. They think studying you could be of immense help at a later, more critical stage of research. It would help others with deadly diseases survive, too. That's what you're saying no to. That's what you're taking away."

"He doesn't want it, Luke," Esther said, her voice ragged. "Can't you see that?"

"You're being awfully controlling," Valentine said.

At that, Luke truly began to lose his cool, which happened rarely. He removed his glasses, his face turning red, sweat beading on his forehead. "*Controlling?*" he said, his voice squeaking with anger. "I think we all know who's controlling, and it certainly isn't me. Why did we all move away from Corner Brook in the first place? Every single one of us?"

"Excuse me?" Michael said.

"You tried to micromanage every part of our lives, Dad. And you wouldn't listen to Mom when she told you to lay off. Where we went, what we did, who we saw, what opportunities we pursued. Criticizing us for not pursuing what you thought we should. You had to know everything, and you had an opinion on everything. Even when we moved to St. John's, you never stopped calling, telling us how to live our lives. I for one had to start screening my calls."

"Oh, did you now?" Michael said, becoming every bit as enraged as Luke seemed to be.

"Luke," Valentine said. "This is no kind of conversation to have with your father who just turned a hundred." Beyond Luke, Samuel and Daniel had stopped in their play, and were watching the altercation.

"This is exactly the conversation to have," Luke said. "This is the conversation we should have had years ago. You're a stubborn, overly-opinionated man, Michael. Stephen always said so."

That struck at Michael's heart. "Stephen? He said that?"

"He couldn't believe it when you said goodbye to him by telling him to lose weight. That was it—your profound parting remark, in addition to rubbing his financial trouble in his face. Just like the way you're always telling me to get a girlfriend. Mind your own fucking business."

"Luke!" Valentine had gone pale. None of them enjoyed confrontation. In fact, it was normally the Haynes way to avoid it at all cost.

"Worst of all is what you let happen to poor Esther. None of us have forgiven you for that, and I doubt we ever will."

At that, Esther fled inside the house, sobbing. Valentine fell into the seat her sister had vacated, as though no longer able to support her own weight. As for Luke, he marched back to his DeLorean and screeched out of the driveway.

Michael brought a hand to his face. It came away wet. He stared at it.

"Happy birthday," Valentine said, her tone flat and dead.

*

With his latest trip to the doctor came the revelation that he now weighed forty pounds heavier than he had when he first started using the wheelchair. They'd given him a diet outline to follow, and up until a few months ago he'd been good about it, with Valentine's help. But lately he found himself just sitting in front of the TV in his chair, overeating, and feeling useless. Too tired to try any of the exercises the doctor had suggested to him.

He watched game shows, and when none were on he watched the news. That didn't improve his mood any. Luke's company, Healthr, was getting talked about quite a lot. According to one report he saw they were now "the number one provider of devices and apps for tracking health and fitness data globally." Independent studies estimated that their products had led to countless early diagnoses of conditions that would otherwise have been life-threatening, if left undetected long enough. Their latest product, a machine-washable undergarment playfully named Bionic Undies, tracked hundreds of metrics about each user, and sent them alerts if it picked up on anything out of whack. Bionic Undies were incredibly cheap—at twenty bucks each, most people bought enough that they had a clean pair to wear every day of the week. The company boasted tens of thousands of lives saved so far.

But that wasn't why they were in the news. An employee had recently blown the whistle on Healthr for sharing customer data with the government wholesale, without asking to see a warrant, without any restrictions whatsoever. If the government wanted it, they got it, no questions asked. The whistleblower had leaked a number of emails, internal presentation slides, and private policy documents that detailed these practices. She said the government was particularly interested in the personal data of environmental activists, who they consistently referred to as 'radicalizers.'

Healthr was pressing charges against the employee for breaking a nondisclosure agreement she'd signed. She claimed not to remember signing such an agreement, but she had—it was a clause that had always been present in Healthr's job application form, and it applied to everything from the job interview onward. Michael expected she would see jail time, and a fair amount of it. Leaks like this were punished very harshly, nowadays. Healthr, however, wouldn't even get a slap on the wrist if things played out the way they normally did. No doubt the data sharing with the government would carry on completely unchanged.

Luke had tested plenty of his company's prototypes on his father over the years, and was always trying to convince him to start using Healthr products regularly, so he'd have a better chance of preventing illness. They'd always been too newfangled for Michael, though. Now he was glad of that. He wondered how much data Luke had collected on him, just from his use of the prototypes.

The government wanting to cryogenically preserve him for study only served to creep him out even more. He couldn't understand why they couldn't just run tests now, and keep the results for future analysis. Why did he have to be frozen?

The next news story was about some controversial legislation that the Canadian government had managed to re-enact, after it had been passed around a decade ago and then repealed shortly after because it was considered unconstitutional. Now it was back, thanks to a number of underhanded parliamentary tricks. It would again allow operatives working for government agencies to enter any Canadian citizen's home without a warrant if they were suspected of terrorism. Such a person would not be entitled to see the evidence used to conclude they were a terrorist. The government could seize their property at will, and detain them indefinitely, without notifying friends or family. It made Michael think of the government's desire to stick him in a freezer. Of course, this new law wouldn't allow them to do that without his consent—he certainly couldn't be considered a terrorist. Still, it worried him.

When she got home from work, Valentine often took in the evening news with him. Her favourite was the weather segment. She liked how the weather reporters put on a jaunty façade as they discussed extreme weather event after extreme weather event while never once mentioning climate change. "Wow," a young man said tonight, grinning a flawless aw-shucks grin into the camera. "We sure are getting hammered tomorrow morning. We have a big thunderstorm on the way, and it looks like we could be set to break another record in terms of rainfall."

"He's scrubbed so clean you could eat off him," Valentine said.

"I think he's a bit young for you, sweetheart." She stuck her tongue out at him, and he winked.

Valentine avidly followed climate change news online, and she frequently spoke to him about the current state of things—essentially, that society had moved past the point where climate change might have been prevented, and now could only hope to mitigate its effects. The longer society went without doing that, the worse things would get. As it stood, not nearly enough was being done.

In her youth, Valentine had been quite the environmental activist. Nowadays, knowing that environmentalists were among the most closely surveilled citizens in society, she kept her thoughts on the subject to herself, except during private, in-person conversations with friends and family. Her profession as a lawyer meant keeping a low profile. She couldn't risk inviting the threat that surveillance posed to attorney-client privilege, the protection of which she took very seriously. As it stood, she spent hours every week tutoring her clients in how to protect their correspondence from prying government eyes.

But Michael knew that worrying about climate change kept Valentine awake many a night. Whether she was overestimating the danger or not, she believed there would be widespread disaster within a matter of decades. And she wasn't certain human civilization would survive it.

"Can you teach me to use the computer?" Michael said.

That sent her eyebrows crawling up her forehead. "Um, okay? My laptop, you mean? I kind of need that for work..."

"Right. Well, maybe I could buy my own."

She shook her head in wonderment. "A hundred-year-old man learning to use a computer for the first time. That's a local news story right there."

He waved his hand dismissively. "I've made bigger news."

"Well la-te-da." Now it was her turn to wink. "We'll find you a computer to use somewhere. What brought this on, anyway?"

"I want to learn more about this cryogenic process Luke keeps talking about."

Valentine raised her eyebrows. "Are you considering going ahead with it, now?"

He shook his head as vehemently as he could muster. "Hell, no. But I'd like to know what it entails. What, exactly, the government is proposing. And I'd like to know where I stand with regard to my rights, too. It seems like a new law gets passed every week, now—who can keep track of what the government is and isn't allowed to do to you, anymore?"

She nodded. "Is that all?"

It wasn't, of course, and his daughter could sense that. She always could.

"I..." he began, but trailed off for a moment to collect his thoughts. "I've been thinking on what you said, about how I should talk to Esther. And I'd like to do some research on how best to go about it."

"What sort of research?"

"Just...how people are affected later in life, by going through...what she went through. The sort of things I should say to her." He shrugged, and gave a small chuckle. "I'm at a loss for how to talk to my own daughter."

"You talk to me just fine." Valentine's eyes crinkled at the corners. "Computers have actually become extremely easy to use in the past few years. This might not be too hard, even for an old geezer like you."

He smiled. "Michael Haynes, welcome to the twenty-first century."

After the birthday party, Valentine hadn't brought up what Luke had said, about him being controlling, and about his children never having forgiven him for his behaviour toward Esther. That hurt him more than they could know—it almost made it seem like Luke had spoken the truth. Was the idea they hadn't forgiven him all that surprising, though? He'd certainly never forgiven himself.

And the thought that he'd hurt Stephen dragged on him like a weight hung from his sternum. Poor, solemn Stephen. Michael had thought he'd had such a good relationship with his son. With him, and with all his other children. Apparently not.

Nevertheless, they all pitched in to buy him a brand new laptop. "Something to keep his mind active," he overheard Valentine saying to Craig over the phone. "It'll be good for him."

Learning to use the damned thing proved much more arduous than Valentine had suggested. His first challenge was turning the contraption on. He'd expected to just be able to press a power button, but in the last few years power buttons had gone the way of the VCR. Now you told computers to come on by using your voice, or by pressing your finger onto a fingerprint scanner. But the thing had trouble recognizing what he said in his thin old rasp, and he found the fingerprint thing way too creepy. So he stuck with talking to it. Sometimes ten minutes passed before the screen finally came on.

"Cursed machine," Valentine was apt to hear him mutter whenever she walked by his chair, where he hunched over, pecking at keys, bifocals perched on the end of his nose. "Damned piece of trash."

"Keep at it, Dad," she would say. She showed him how to search for information using a 'search engine' inside a 'web browser.' "Can a search engine help me find my dignity?" he asked. "I can't remember where I put it."

"Very funny, Dad."

According to her, search engine AI (which stood for Artificial Intelligence, he learned later, by searching it) had improved enormously in recent years. You no longer had to know all the little tricks that used to be necessary to actually find what you wanted. Now it was virtually impossible to type in a query and get anything other than what you were looking for.

He managed it, though. Time and time again.

"I'm achieving the impossible," he said to her, straight-faced.

"I'd say."

Another day: "How do I make this bigger?"

"What, Dad?" She was folding up laundry. He'd begun to detect some exasperation creeping into her voice, whenever he asked her one of his many daily questions.

"The web browser. It shrunk on me."

She came over. "You need to maximize it again. Click this, up here. In the corner. The one with the squares."

He clicked, and the browser vanished. "What? What happened? Where did it go? I had ten different tabs open! Do I have to make all those searches again?"

"Calm down. You just minimized the window."

"I whatted the what?"

She rolled her eyes, and brought the cursor down to the bottom of the screen. "Minimized windows are down here on the taskbar. Look." She clicked, and the browser reappeared. He started breathing again. Valentine brought the cursor back up to the corner, hovering over a button with a hyphen on it. "Dad, meet the minimize button. Minimize button, meet Dad." She returned to the laundry, chuckling.

Despite his joking, and his frequent cursing on the machine, Michael felt immensely proud of himself. Grappling with technology at a century-years-old. He honestly had not felt this alive in many years.

Michael's offspring were mostly delighted when they received their first emails from him, but that was for novelty's sake. His true success came from gaining a better understanding of how Esther's trauma had likely affected her in the long-term. As a child, she'd shown such promise. Without a doubt, she had been the brightest among her brothers and sisters. But all that changed after what happened. Her grades plummeted, and she shied away from her friendships, allowing them to melt away until she had none.

He read that many children who were abused suffered from anxiety and insecurity for the rest of their lives. That certainly fit Esther. In adulthood, she'd fulfilled none of the promise of her youth. She was a work-from-home employee of a call center. She'd never gotten into drugs and alcohol, which many victims apparently did. But she continued to be stunted socially. She'd never dated, and still didn't have any friends.

One day, he looked up from his morning coffee, which had gone cold while he stared into it. "Okay," he said to Valentine. "I'm ready to talk to Esther."

She inclined her head. "I'll call her and see when she's free."

*

"Dad?"

He woke slowly, half-wondering whether the voice was part of his dream.

"Are you getting up?"

Blinking. His head sunk deep into the pile of fluffy pillows he liked to sleep on. The bedroom door stood open a crack, through which Valentine had poked her head. "I'm surprised you aren't up yet," she said.

"Can't an old man sleep in once in a while? I've been retired for over thirty years for Christ's sake."

"She has to work in the afternoon," Valentine said. "If we don't get a move on we'll have to go see her another day."

He stared at his daughter from within his pillow cocoon, hoping his consternation didn't show on his face. There was something he was supposed to be remembering. He sensed that. He could feel the contours of the gap it had left in its mind. Who was Valentine referring to? Who had to work in the afternoon? And why were they going to see this person?

"Dad?"

Unable to dredge up the information he knew should be there, he gave up. "What do we need to get a move on for?"

Valentine's brow wrinkled. "Esther, Dad. We arranged to visit her today. To have the talk."

The talk. He couldn't remember a talk. Why would he talk to Esther? They'd barely spoken ten words to each other in years.

"You don't remember, do you?"

Slowly, he shook his head.

"You've spent weeks researching for this, Dad."

"Oh!" he said with a start. "Yes, of course." He remembered. "Come here, hurry. Help me into my chair."

She studied him a moment longer, worry still etched across her brow. Then she walked over and helped him roll out of bed, into the chair that waited beside him every night as he slept. Once he was situated she fished his false teeth out of the glass where they soaked in solution, passing them to him. He popped them into his mouth.

Breakfast was a banana cut up into porridge with cinnamon sprinkled on top. It suddenly occurred to him that she'd been feeding him mostly soft foods for quite some time now. He had his fake chompers; they chewed well enough. Was she afraid he would choke?

"It isn't the first time this has happened, Dad."

"What?"

"Forgetting things like that. I'm beginning to worry. Do you think it's a good idea to go do this today?"

"We have to go. What else have I forgotten?"

Valentine took a sip of orange juice, and stared down at her placement. Then she met his gaze. "You forgot Doris last week."

"What? How do you mean, forgot her? Was it her birthday? Did I forget to call her?"

"You *forgot* her. That she existed."

He felt light-headed, then. Gripping the arms of his chair, he tried to steady himself, accidentally pushing the button to go forward and shoving the table toward Valentine a couple inches. “Oops. Sorry.”

“Are you all right?”

“Yes. Just—can I have some water? This orange juice isn’t cutting it.” *A stiff scotch is what I need.*

When she handed him the glass he found he lacked the strength to raise it to his lips. Instead, he began to cry.

“Oh, Dad. Oh.” Valentine knelt beside him and put her arms around him, rubbing his shoulder, patting his back. “It’s okay. It’s okay.”

“It’s so funny,” he said, his voice nasally. “For so long I’ve felt at peace with knowing I’ll die someday soon.” He’d *wanted* to die, in fact. “Right now, though...” He sniffed, trying to fight back another wave of tears. “I just feel scared.” He broke down again. Suddenly, the thought of leaving his family forever felt dreadful, in a way it never had before. The thought that he might play a part in helping Esther to finally find peace...it made him want to stick around. But how much time could he possibly have left?

A half hour later he’d composed himself. He considered wearing a suit, but decided that would be silly. Why dress so formally for a visit to his daughter? Even one with whom the silence had gone on so long. He did shave, however, and combed his hair, and dabbed on some cologne, which he hadn’t had reason to do in years. He smiled at himself in the mirror. “Not bad for a hundred years old," he whispered to himself under his breath.

Valentine helped Michael into her minivan, which she'd traded for after he moved in, so that he would have lots of room whenever she brought him places. He tried not to curse when his shoulder scraped against the doorframe, or when a jolt of pain shot up his torso from landing on the passenger seat at a bad angle. It had started drizzling a couple hours before, which had transformed into a torrent of cold droplets. The damp always got inside Michael and made him ache even more than usual.

Once he was seated, Valentine dismantled his wheelchair and arrayed it neatly in the trunk. His daughter took better care of him than he deserved.

Esther lived alone in the east end of town with seven cats. She'd been alerted they were coming out for a visit. Michael thought she would have likely come up with an excuse for why they couldn't come today, if such an excuse was possible. But nothing would be believable. Esther never did anything with her days, except talk to her cats. The only possible reason she wouldn't be able to have Michael and Valentine in her house would be that she didn't want Michael and Valentine in her house. Actually, probably just Michael. She didn't seem to mind having Valentine around. He couldn't blame her.

But he put such thoughts aside. Today was a new day—a new beginning, hopefully, for their relationship. He wanted them to be close again. He wanted to see her light up, laughing like she had as a young child when he teased and tickled her.

Esther's house was a bungalow, which was lucky. Otherwise he probably wouldn't have been able to gain entry in his chair. He doubted Valentine had the strength to lug it backward over any steps, not with him in it, and he was certain Esther didn't. But the doorway had only a small rise to conquer, which he helped with by putting the chair in reverse as his eldest daughter pulled it up and over.

Immediately, the ammonia smell hit him. Cat piss, and lots of it. Over a decade had passed since he was last in Esther's house. He didn't remember it being this bad.

He motored his hundred-year-old husk into the living room, his face twisted up in disgust. "One of your cats is dirty." He sniffed. "Smells like more than one, actually. They've been pissing around everywhere, haven't they?"

Esther had already folded herself into an overstuffed armchair as though attempting to disappear between its crevices. As always, her head hunched over farther than her body. At this point Michael didn't know if she could straighten up even if she tried.

She raised her head a little, though, to look at him through a curtain of stringy brown hair. "There's no such thing as a dirty cat," she said softly. "There's always a reason why they aren't peeing where they're supposed to. Sometimes it's the kitty litter."

"Have you tried changing the kitty litter?" he asked.

She gave a barely perceptible nod. "It didn't work."

"They're dirty, then."

Valentine cleared her throat. "Did we come here to talk about Esther's cats, Dad?"

Michael frowned, momentarily unable to overcome his irritation at the state they'd found Esther's house in. Then he made himself relax. "No," he admitted. "We didn't."

"What did you come here about?" Esther asked.

Michael looked down at his lap, where his hands had clenched into fists involuntarily. He uncurled them, studying the multitude of wrinkles, and the thick, sickly-losing veins. Once, his hands had been strong. He'd used them to beat his brother till they were slick with blood and Horace lay unconscious on the floor.

"I think we need to talk about what happened to you when you were eight," he said.

What little colour Esther's face possessed naturally drained, and her eyes widened. She looked at Valentine, and then at Michael, and then back down at her hands clasped over her knees. Watched as they trembled.

"That was over thirty years ago," she said.

"That's why it's so overdue," Valentine said, and Michael felt immensely grateful for the show of support. This wasn't a half-baked notion cooked up by a half-senile centenarian. Valentine considered it important, too.

"I see a therapist regularly," Esther mumbled. "You know that."

"And I'm sure that's extremely valuable," her sister said. "But I think you'll find nothing can compare to the closure this conversation will bring you both."

Silence, then, and in the midst of it Valentine looked at him meaningfully, eyebrows raised a millimeter. It was time to say his piece. Esther's head was still down.

"Horace was a taker," Michael began. "*Is* a taker," he amended—the monster still lived, after all. "He was always willing to do a favour, for anyone. Always willing to help out when help was needed." Here Esther did look up, confusion in her eyes. He pressed on: "What I failed to realize was how Horace saw every favour as a down payment for something he would take later on. Whatever he decided he was owed, he collected it at his leisure, whether he was truly welcome to it or not. We all loved Horace, back then. Before what he did to you. We had no idea he was capable of betraying that love so completely. You were a child, and children must trust the adults that care for them. They have no other choice. Children are powerless, and it's the job of adults to make decisions on their behalf, without their consent, that benefit them. Making them go to bed on time, making them eat healthy food, sending them to school, getting them vaccinated. But Horace violated that ancient, sacred pact between adults and children. He violated our trust in him, and our love—yours most of all."

He paused, and into the quiet Esther's tears burst forth, along with gasping sobs that were torn out of her despite her efforts to stop them. Michael had put a lot of thought into what he would say today, and he had more. He continued.

"I loved Horace," Michael said. "And you children did, too. He'd take you wherever you wanted to go. To the movies, to a hockey game." Esther cried even harder. Valentine's eyes were moist too, and she leaned toward her sister as if she wanted to go to her, to hold her. "He would sit on the carpet and engage you on your level, becoming fully immersed in whatever fantasy world you created with your blocks and dolls. Your mother and I were charmed by how Horace could enter the mind of a child and seem to exist there comfortably. We didn't hesitate to leave you all with him—you loved your uncle. So when your mother opened the invitation to her friend's wedding, we called Horace right away, to see whether he was free to look after you. He agreed, as always. But when we got to the church, we found out the couple getting married had had a terrible fight that morning, and the wedding was called off. We headed home. I had no idea then how lucky we were that those two people decided not to get married. If they had, we wouldn't have uncovered what we were about to uncover. And it might have gone on for years."

Esther tears had stopped flowing for the moment, and she was making eye contact now, with lips that trembled still. She looked like she had something to say, but was waiting for him to finish. Which he appreciated. In truth, he felt frightened to hear how Esther would respond to all this.

"We came home to find your brothers and sisters sitting in the living room, unattended. Missing from the picture were you and your uncle. We asked the others where you were, and Luke told me you weren't feeling well, so Uncle Horace had taken you into your bedroom to try and make you better again. We opened the bedroom door. And, I—" He sobbed now, and fought to control the tears that wanted to spill down his cheeks. He cleared his throat. "I can't describe the emotions that ripped through me, Esther. There you were, eight years old, stripped naked on the bed. Horace was naked too, from the waist down. And he was all over you. He obviously hadn't expected us home so soon, and he still hadn't heard us come in.

"I don't know how much of this you remember. But when I saw what he was doing to you, I walked over and grabbed him from behind, throwing him to the floor. I put my knee on his chest, and I hit him until his face was a bloody ruin."

It wasn't possible to continue without taking a moment to compose himself. He rooted in his pocket until he found his handkerchief, using it to dab at his eyes. Then he covered his eyes with it and cried.

Esther was crying again, too, fat tears beading on the tip of her nose and falling onto the floral skirt she wore. Each tear caused him physical pain. Valentine was also crying. No one spoke.

Michael had run out of things to say. He'd conveyed everything he'd intended to. But this silence was unbearable. What was Esther thinking? What did she truly think of him? He spoke again: "We'd noticed you acting differently before, but we couldn't explain why. Once, you were a bright, chipper girl, sharp and full of life. After what happened, you seemed uninterested in everything. You let all your friends fall away. You—" he broke off, and stared at her, pleading with his thoughts. *Please. Please just say something.*

"I remember the change in you, too," Valentine said. "How withdrawn you became. It happened gradually, over the months when he used to take you into the bedroom and shut the door. Like all the life in you was trickling out, drop by drop."

A cat leapt into Esther's lap, and she automatically raised a shaking hand to stroke its back. It purred, arching at her touch. At last she spoke, her voice barely audible. "His face still haunts me. I see it in my dreams, almost every single night. Leering. A patronizing little grin. That's how he used to look at me, when he did what he did. Like I was a worm."

"I—" Michael said. *Sorry. Say you're sorry.* But he couldn't talk.

"Why didn't you press charges, Dad?"

He swallowed. Glanced at Valentine for some support. But Valentine avoided eye contact, now. He was on his own.

"My father—" he said, haltingly. "Your grandfather. He was a strong man. Cared deeply about family honour—about the Haynes name. He said it would mar our reputation forever, for people to know that a Haynes was a pedophile. He insisted that your mother and I keep what Horace did to ourselves. And we agreed to. God damn it all, we agreed." He felt his face bunch up again, but he forbade himself to cry any more. "I wish we hadn't, Esther. I'm so very, very sorry. Your grandparents struck Horace from their will. They completely disowned them. But it was a much lighter punishment than he deserved. I should have defied my father's wishes. I'm sorry. Do you—could you ever find it in yourself to forgive me?"

His daughter's hand moved back and forth over the cat. She was looking down again, and refused to meet Michael's eyes again. "I don't know, Dad. I—I don't know."

Michael's heart felt like it had fallen apart into countless jagged shards. The pain was physical—so much so that he brought a hand to his chest, and Valentine's gaze snapped toward him, concern etched across her forehead.

"Okay," he said. "Okay." And he wheeled himself slowly toward the door. Valentine stood and followed.

Outside, a burgundy SUV screeched away down the road as his daughter helped him through the doorway. Michael squinted after it. "Do you recognize that car?" he asked.

"No," she said.

*

Michael spent the week after his talk with Esther feeling listless, slumped in his chair, staring at the TV but never really watching it. He seemed to be sliding backward—feeling again that his family would be better off without him. Valentine tried frequently to cheer him up, in between ministering to Daniel and Samuel, the latter who was rapidly approaching adolescence and whose life grew rapidly more complicated, accordingly.

An email wrenched him out of his funk, but not in a good way. It was from Horace. He hadn't checked his email in a while, and the message had been sent two days before.

It read:

Michael,

I know you haven't heard from me in nine years, with an even longer gap before that. But never think that I have forgotten about my family. I have no one in my life. You and your children, ghosts that you are—you're all I have left.

I'd like you to stop being ghosts. I want you to be real people in my life again. I said it to you in the hospital nine years ago, and I'll say it again: I have changed. I repented for what I did to Esther a long time ago, begging the Lord for forgiveness, with whom I have known a close relationship for decades. Now I beg you: please give me the chance to seek Esther's forgiveness, and also the forgiveness of her brothers and sisters. I am an old man—not as old as you, mind, but still very old. I want nothing more than to be reconciled with my family before I die.

I await your reply with trepidation.

Your brother,
Horace

Michael shook with anger. How had the bastard gotten his email address? He pounded out his reply with as much force as his arthritis-ridden hands could muster:

Absolutely not. My children want nothing to do with you. Stay away from them, and from me.

It didn't occur to him to ask his children whether this was the case. He moved the cursor over 'Send,' and slammed his finger down onto the left-click button, as soon as he could master his trembling hand enough to stop the cursor from wobbling around.

He glared at the screen, trying to figure out who could have given Horace his email address. Only his children had it, so one of them must have made contact with his brother. Why? And why would they put him in touch with Michael? How dare they?

As he sat there trying to suss out a solution from his muddled thoughts, another email from Horace appeared. He clicked it open.

Michael,

It saddens me to think you have forgotten all the things we shared in our youth. I understand that you're still upset with me, but how could you have forgotten all these special family memories, which you yourself captured?

With regret,
Horace

Underneath the signature he'd included a link, which Michael clicked after a moment's hesitation. He gasped. The link led to a website that contained nothing but hundreds and hundreds of photos, which Horace must have scanned, since they'd been taken long before digital cameras.

Michael had taken them all. They were from Horace's childhood and adolescence, and showed him posing with their parents at his high school graduation, throwing a Frisbee around during a family trip to the beach, helping their father build a shed, goofing around with his food during a meal. Being held in his mother's arms as a newborn—Michael would have been eleven, then. There was a significant age gap between them.

The early shots were all in black-and-white. Back then it was somewhat unusual for a family to have so many photos. If it wasn't for Michael's avid interest in cameras, and for the fact that his parents were reasonably well off, Horace wouldn't have been able to make this crass, manipulative play to worm his way back into the family.

At the bottom of the gallery, the following words were displayed in bold text: "Are these the photos of a man who deserves to be exiled from his family forever? Or do they show a man capable of redemption?"

If Michael had been angry before, now he was livid. His brother had ruined Esther's life, and caused the rest of the family untold suffering. And charges had never been laid. The bastard had gotten off Scot-free, and now he expected to be welcomed back with open arms, just because he scanned a few pictures? He would get nothing. Michael wished him only ill.

"Valentine!" he called, and the distress in his voice brought her running through the house.

"What?" she said, breathless. "What is it?"

He showed her the emails, and she read them with a hand pressed to her lips, slowly shaking her head from side to side.

"What are you going to say to him?"

"I already told him to stay away from my family. That's all he gets. What I want to know is how he knew where to send the email. You and your brothers and sisters are the only ones who know it."

"Sam and Dan too," she said. "Haven't you exchanged emails with them too?"

"Yes, but they've never met Horace. It has to be one of my offspring. But who—?" Then it struck him. Which of his children were the least stable right now? Which of them would be prone to doing something this insane? "It's Craig," he said. "I'm sure of it."

Valentine's brow furrowed. "Why do you say that?"

"His marriage and financial problems have had him behaving very strangely. Plus he's a psychologist. He's probably developed some bizarre ideas about reconciling with Horace being good for our mental health."

"I really don't think Craig would give Horace your email without asking, Dad."

"I want to go ask him myself. Will you bring me?"

"All right. But I don't think it's a good idea."

"It's what we're doing, Valentine."

"You're obviously very upset by what Horace sent you. Maybe we should wait to go on a day you're feeling calmer?"

"It has to be now."

"Dad, please. You're making me worry about you. How do we know he's even home right now?"

Maybe she was right. He suddenly felt exhausted. His eyelids drooped, and he sagged in his chair. "All right," he said. "But I don't want to go any later than tomorrow."

"I'll call right now and see what time he'll be there."

The next day it was raining, but Michael still felt determined to go. Valentine helped him aboard the minivan without him getting too wet. Craig lived in Mount Pearl, more or less equidistant between Valentine's and Esther's. They rode in silence for most of the way, but five minutes into the drive his daughter glanced at him. "I have to say, Dad, giving Horace your email really doesn't seem like Craig."

"I'm sure it's him. I'm positive."

"You should ask him gently, okay? You shouldn't accuse him."

Unlike Esther, Craig did have steps leading up to his front door, a lot of them, but he also had a large piece of plywood, which he dragged from his shed and laid over them. Michael simply drove his chair up, with Craig behind to steady him. With that, he was in. It was still raining, and he said, "Should we dry off my wheels before I go across the carpet?"

His son went to fetch a rag and spent a minute wiping down his father's chair, as well as his face. "Thank you," Michael said, suddenly feeling bad about the conversation he intended to initiate.

Soon they sat in the spacious living room, each holding a teacup, with a plate of biscuits also on hand.

"You look tired, Dad," Craig said.

"So do you, actually." It was true. Dark spots shadowed Craig's eyes, and his face sagged, as expressionless as Esther's normally was.

"I haven't slept. Sandy left me last night."

Michael's mouth hung open, whatever words he'd intended to say with it now lost. *Say something*. "Oh," he said. "I—I'm sorry, Craig."

Craig waved it away. "What did you guys come for? Valentine said you had something you wanted to discuss, but she wouldn't say what."

Michael looked at Valentine for strength. Her mouth drew downward at the corners, and she exhaled loudly.

"Craig," Michael said. "Did you give my email address to Horace?"

"What?" His son looked more alert, now. He squinted, eyebrows drawn down. "Horace?"

"I received an email from him yesterday, asking forgiveness for what he—" Michael cleared his throat. "Someone had to give him my email. Did you do it?"

Craig slammed his cup on the coffee table so hard tea slopped out. Valentine winced. Craig leapt to his feet. "I can't believe this," he said. "I can't believe this is happening."

Michael felt his hands trembling. The sensation of awfulness had multiplied so that he could barely stand it. Still, they'd come this far...

He said, "I'm only asking a—"

"What about her?" Craig said, pointing at Valentine. "Why couldn't she have given him it? Your sweet, innocent Valentine? Or—" Craig jammed a finger hard against his own temple. "Here's a brain wave. How about Luke? He's constantly meddling in all our lives, convinced he knows how to solve everything. And he learned that tendency from you."

"I don't know what you're talking about," Michael said, his voice low. "Your mother and I always—"

"Don't play dumb. Luke told me he confronted you about this at your birthday party. He said he felt bad about it, but you make him so mad, with the way you are. He got the worst of it, growing up. You tried to control everything he did, and when he was young he actually let you. Then he finally broke away from you, and now he believes he has all the answers, even more fervently than you ever did. He thinks he knows what's best for the entire human race. You created a monster with him, you know."

Michael was getting angry, but instead of inflaming him his anger formed a cool ball in the middle of his chest. "Did you give Horace my email address, then?"

His flippant tone had the desired effect. Craig's face went completely red, and he took a step closer.

"Are you going to hit me?" Michael asked mildly.

"*Get out!*" Craig screamed. "Get him out of here, Valentine!"

Valentine did, calmly collecting her purse from an end table, straightening her blouse, and taking the handles of Michael's chair. She shot Craig a cool stare.

Her phone rang, then, and she removed it from her pocket, reading the screen. "It's Luke," she said, and answered it. "Hello?" She listened, and her mouth fell open. "Okay. We'll be right there. Text me the room number." She hung up, and looked up from her phone with wide eyes. "It's Esther," she said. "She's tried to kill herself."

*

Luke had found Esther collapsed on her bathroom floor, a bottle of pills strewn across the linoleum. She was still breathing—shallow breaths, her chest barely rising. But he got there in time. He called an ambulance, which arrived in short order, her house just ten minutes from the hospital—six or seven minutes if you were a speeding ambulance with your siren on.

She was stable in a matter of hours, and conscious too. Her brothers and sisters were gathered around her, except for Doris, who was still in the UK. Michael was there too. They all wanted an explanation, but no one wanted to press her for one.

Eventually, they got it. She told them how, since Michael had visited to talk about Horace molesting her as a child, she couldn't stop reliving it, in both her dreaming and waking life. Every detail more vivid than memory should allow. Michael had forced Esther to dredge up old pain, long-buried.

Luke had been right, clearly, and Craig. He obviously did try to exert too much pressure on his children to conduct their lives the way he thought they should. *I need to change.* But could he? He was so old...

A little over a week after Michael's visit, Horace came to Esther's house. She answered a knock on her door, opening it to reveal her old tormentor. She froze, completely at a loss for what to do. He asked to come in, and she said nothing. Just stared at him, wide-eyed.

Horace started talking. About Michael. As he listened to her relate his brother's words, rage boiled through his veins. But he didn't speak.

Horace told her Michael was always very jealous of their parents' affections. In his version of reality, Michael resented even their smallest displays of affection toward his brother. Afterward Michael would beat him, according to Horace. Until he promised not to tell their parents what had happened. "Your father abused me regularly," the filthy liar had said to Esther. "I lived in terror of him, right up until the day he moved out. When I did what I did to you, I was carrying on that cycle of abuse. I don't say that to justify or excuse my behaviour—not the slightest bit. But I want to try and help you understand."

With that Esther had closed the door in his face, and locked it. She watched through the curtains as he got into his burgundy SUV and beat the steering wheel with his fists. Eventually he drove away, leaving her an emotional mess. After decades of therapy, slowly building up a life that had been burned to the ground when she was eight, she felt like all her progress had been erased. She couldn't bear it. So she tried to kill herself.

Finally, Michael spoke. "Did you believe him, Esther?" he asked. "Did you believe that I abused him?"

Her lips tightened, and she refused to look at him. They all sat there in the strained silence a while. Then Michael commanded his chair to take him out into the hall, where he waited until Valentine came to collect him.

*

They got lunch in the hospital cafeteria. Halfway through Valentine went to use the restroom, and almost immediately

Luke appeared, accompanied by a man wearing a suit. "This is Agent Peele, Dad. Agent Peele, Michael Haynes."

"Nice to meet you," Peele said, and they shook hands. Peele had close-cropped blonde hair, and two small blue eyes that huddled around a sizable nose. He towered over Luke.

"Likewise." He still had an awful feeling in the pit of his stomach from hearing Esther recount Horace's visit, and it made him bitter, and catty. Plus, what right did Luke have to introduce him to some stranger from the government at a time like this? "To what do I owe the honour?" he said sarcastically.

"First, I'd like to tell you sorry for my behaviour at your birthday," Luke said. "I haven't had the chance to do that yet, but I was very rude, and you certainly didn't deserve it. I'm sorry."

Michael felt a potent mixture of surprise and suspicion at the apology. It was unlike Luke to say sorry for anything he did. He had a slightly haughty way about him, which seemed to imply that anything that went wrong could only be the fault of the less intelligent people surrounding him. But now Luke had apologized to him in front of a government official, someone in front of whom he'd be extremely hesitant to lose face. *I didn't expect that.* But the fact it was so out of character made him wonder what Luke really wanted.

He soon found out. After a couple minutes of strained small talk, Luke said, "Dad, I think you should take the government up on their offer to pay for you to be frozen. A lot of eyebrows are being raised at the fact you won't. It's very selfish of you. And besides, it doesn't make any sense. Why wouldn't you want to journey into the future with your family? There's no guarantee this offer will always be on the table. Soon they may decide they no longer need you. You should let them freeze you now, before it's too late."

Michael shook his head. "Why are you skirting the truth with me, Luke? I started researching cryogenics online the moment Valentine taught me to use a computer. They can't freeze you until you're dead. They'd have to kill me first."

"I'm not trying to trick you, Dad. That *used* to be the case—they couldn't freeze you alive, because the liquid in your body would expand and tear up your cell membranes. But things have changed. They've found a way around that."

"Have they found a way of bringing people out of it?" Michael asked. "Has anyone survived cryogenic freezing?"

"Not yet. But—"

"Then it's still effectively murder. Would you care to tell me the Canadian law that permits someone to undergo it before they've actually died?"

Peele answered him, this time. "Actually, they recently updated the Dying with Dignity Act to allow individuals to choose to attempt cryogenic preservation, if they're going to perish soon anyway. That appears to be the case with you, Mr. Haynes."

Luke shuffled awkwardly, and Michael returned Agent Peele's level gaze with one of astonishment. "That was frankly said."

"Dad, I can't fathom why you aren't leaping at this opportunity. The science is advancing rapidly, and there's a good chance you could live to see what the world looks like decades from now. And you'd be helping countless people. Agreeing to this could save millions. You'd go down in history. Besides, we all want you to do it. Your children."

"Esther doesn't want me to do it, I'm sure."

"Esther loves you, Dad. She's going through a horrible time right now, but I can guarantee we would all love to keep you around for as long as possible."

"What's going on here?" Valentine had returned from the restroom. She noticed the man in the suit, and then glared at Luke. "What is this?"

"If I give you what you want," Michael said, "my children won't get their inheritance for decades. Maybe not ever. I know that means nothing to you, moneybags. But I want to leave something behind for my children. It's the natural way."

Luke opened his mouth to speak, but Michael talked over him. "Let's go home, Valentine." He directed his chair toward the exit, leaving his lunch half-eaten.

But remembering everything he'd seen on the news, he realized it would only be a matter of time before the government got what it wanted. In the end, governments always did.

*

The sun was an angry blister on the day Agent Peele came for Michael.

Five months had passed since that day in the hospital, and Michael's mind had steadily deteriorated. He was aware it was happening, but never discussed it with Valentine. Forgetting things caused a burning shame that made his skin prickle uncomfortably. At least, *realizing* he'd forgotten something did that. Sometimes it took him a day to realize he'd had a lapse, or weeks, and he was certain there were things he'd forgotten that he would never remember again. It was an awful way to descend into one's final days. He prayed for the end.

When the doorbell rang Michael carted his sorry carcass to the front porch. Normally he didn't even answer the door, leaving that to Valentine. But she was in the bath, and he was bored.

"*You,*" Michael said when he opened the door, his heartrate increasing. He hadn't forgotten Agent Peele. The man's blonde hair had grown out a bit since they'd met, but Michael still recognized him.

Peele smiled. "Come on, Mr. Haynes. It's time."

"It's time for you to go piss on an electric fence. I'm going back in to watch *Jeopardy.*" Incredibly, Trebek still hadn't retired.

"You're coming with me. It isn't an option anymore."

"You can't just take me from my home. I know my rights."

"Your rights have changed. Given your refusal to cooperate, and your apparent willingness to let millions of people die needlessly, you are now considered a terrorist, under legislation that passed just last week."

"I want my lawyer."

"You aren't entitled to legal counsel. You aren't entitled to see any of the evidence collected against you. You aren't even entitled to a phone call." Peele grinned. "Come."

Instead, Michael tried to get away. He commanded his chair backward, and it crashed into the wall. "Valentine!" he screamed. "They're trying to take me!" The chair began to turn, so that he could return to the living room and fetch the baseball bat he kept under his favourite chair. Peele knelt and ripped the battery from his wheelchair. Michael clicked forward, but all movement had stopped.

The agent forcibly wheeled him around and through the open door, toward the road, where a black limo waited. "It's wheelchair accessible, Mr. Haynes. We keep it around especially for old cripples like you."

Without warning, Michael rocked forward, pushing back against the armrests. He would throw himself out of the chair, and hopefully perish in the fall.

Peele grabbed him by the shirt and yanked him back.

In the end, he failed to mount much of a struggle. Within thirty seconds he was sitting in the back of the car. Luke was there, too. Looking back at the house, Michael saw Valentine standing in the door, wrapped in a towel, confusion and fear written across her face. Then she left the house, running down the driveway, waving and shouting. Peele dashed around the car, jumping into the front passenger seat. "Go!" he told the driver. They went.

Michael turned to face Luke with a withering stare.

"Nice day for it," his son said.

He chose the vilest words known to him, and hissed them at Luke through clamped teeth.

Luke winced, but Michael could tell he wasn't actually upset, not even a bit. "You're extra feisty today."

"How much did they pay you to deliver me to them?"

"I didn't deliver you to anyone. They took you themselves. Or didn't Agent Peele explain that?"

"You brought me to their attention, though. Didn't you?"

"I am guilty of that. But I never accepted a penny from the government."

"Why have you done this to me, then, Luke?"

"Well, I want life-extension technology to advance, because I'll want to use it myself someday. But I'm also helping you, Dad, though I know you'll never believe that."

"You aren't helping me. If you freeze me, my children won't get their inheritance."

"That won't happen anyway. You don't get to die. No one does."

Michael squinted at him. "Come again?"

"Your sister's tailing us," Peele called from the front seat.

"Jesus," Luke said. "Is it going to be a problem?"

"No. We'll deal with her when we get to the facility."

"I don't want her harmed."

"Of course."

"What did you mean?" Michael said. "You said no one gets to die."

Luke sighed. "Explaining this to you will be pointless—your brain's not in the best condition nowadays, but I doubt you'd have gotten it even back when it was. But I'll explain it anyway, because that's the kind of son I am."

If Luke had hoped for some kind of reaction to that last remark, he was disappointed. His self-satisfied smile stayed the same, though, and he kept talking. "You wouldn't happen to be familiar with quantum physics, would you?"

"Not very."

"Multiverse theory?"

Michael shook his head.

"I'll keep this as basic as I can. There's this idea, taken seriously by a significant number of physicists, that has been derived from the implications of both quantum theory and multiverse theory. I believe that it's how the universe really works, and I think it explains your unusual, death-defying longevity."

"What is it?"

"No one ever dies."

"You said that. How is it possible?"

"Like this." Luke spoke very slowly and deliberately. Michael both hated him for it and felt grateful. "Whenever a quantum event resolves itself, the universe splits into several universes, one for each possible outcome. But according to quantum physics in order for a quantum event to resolve there must be an observer. And it's impossible for you to observe your own death. Therefore, every time an event occurs that might have caused you to die, multiple universes are created, and you'll always end up in one where you survive. No matter how unlikely. In all the other universes you might be dead, but in your universe, from your perspective, you're alive. Forever."

Michael thought back to the ground-breaking operation that had come out of nowhere and rescued him from terminal cancer. He thought about the hideous car accident, which had killed his son but left him alive, against all odds.

Luke leaned over and opened a mini fridge built into one of the seats, fetching a bottle of Coke out of it, which he combined with some rum from a rack near the roof. Then he leaned back and watched Michael try to grasp the implications of what Luke had told him.

"Impossible," he said at last. "I don't believe it."

"That doesn't surprise me at all. But it doesn't matter. You'll believe me when you're three-hundred."

"Why is the government so dead-set on freezing me?" Michael said. "Why can't they just run tests on me now?"

"Oh, they will. But they also want you around for when new tests are developed. Besides, it's not just about your value to life extension science. I've convinced my friends in government to take this immortality idea pretty seriously. And they share my view that in this universe, you're the one who's going to live forever. Or at least, one of the ones. And that makes you invaluable. They're thinking that maybe this whole phenomenon can be harnessed, somehow. The possibilities are literally endless."

The car stopped in a tiny parking lot. "We're here."

Valentine pulled up as they were getting Michael out, wearing her housecoat and slippers. She looked ridiculous, and Michael had never loved her more than he did right now.

"What are you doing with him, Luke?"

"Saving him. From himself. Do you want to watch?"

She stepped forward. "I'm taking him home."

Peele and the limo driver turned to face her, their bodies taught with readiness. Eagerness.

"These men are government agents, and they will arrest you if you obstruct them. It's not worth it, Val. You can come in, though."

She cursed at him. And they all went inside. A woman with long brown hair was sitting in the lobby, waiting, hunched over and staring at the floor.

Tears sprang to Michael's eyes. "Esther?"

"I called her," Luke said. "To ask if she wanted to say goodbye. Craig declined. He's still mad at you. And Doris is still in England."

"What about me?" Valentine said. Her forehead was flushed, which happened whenever she got angry.

"I knew you'd cause trouble, so I left you out. I'm sorry. I really am."

They were about to continue deeper inside the facility when more government agents entered the lobby, escorting someone else. It was Horace. He smiled broadly at Michael.

"What is he doing here?"

"Oh," Luke said. "They're freezing him too. My idea. He hasn't had your string of near-death experiences, but as your sibling he shares fifty percent of your DNA. So they're freezing him as a control, for comparison. He didn't require as much persuading as you did. Barely any, actually."

Michael turned to Esther, who looked as stricken as he felt.

"You're the one who gave him my email address," he said to Luke. "Aren't you?"

His son nodded. "I thought it might make it easier to convince you to be frozen if we could clear up some long-standing family drama. But with these laws, that's no longer necessary. It's happening regardless."

They didn't give Michael a chance to argue further. The agents ushered him down a series of corridors, to a room where men and women in long lab coats waited next to what resembled a dentist's chair. "They'll sedate you here," Luke said. "And that's it. Say your goodbyes."

"I can't believe you," Valentine said to Luke.

"I knew you wouldn't understand. History will, though, Val. And that's what matters."

Michael did not want the agents and Luke to see him cry. But it was unavoidable. "Thank you, Valentine. For everything you've done for me. I've been a tremendous burden on you, though I know you'll never admit it. I would have been lost without you. I love you."

"I love you, Dad."

They embraced, for a long time. "Please tell Craig and Doris that I love them too," he said when they parted. She nodded.

Valentine left the room, unable to watch him go. Luke left too, since Michael refused to speak with him any further. Before going, he said, "I love you too, Dad. That's why I'm doing this, you know. I'll be waiting for you when they bring you back."

Michael maintained his silence. Finally, Luke turned and exited the room.

Only Esther remained.

"I'm so sorry, sweetheart," he told her through his tears. "I know that can never be enough. But I am. You'll never know how sorry I am."

She had tried to tell him what was happening, many times. "Uncle Horace is mean," she'd say. "He does bad things."

And he would hush her. Esther had always been such an imaginative child. The idea that his beloved brother, who he'd trusted more than he trusted himself, would do anything to harm his children was as absurd to him as the rest of Esther's fancies. He hushed her. And he had lived with the guilt ever since.

Now, she held his hand while they put him under. As the world faded, and his mind became even more muddled than it already was, she leaned down until her mouth was just a couple inches away from his ear.

"I forgive you," she whispered.

And he slept.

*

He woke to warm sponges wielded by disembodied robotic arms. And immense pain. He tried to cry out, but his voice came out in a faint creak. The sponges dabbed at him briskly, applying only the slightest pressure. A young man in an orange blazer stood nearby, staring into space, moving his arms around in the air like a mime who'd encountered an invisible wall. Michael thought he must be crazy.

Again, he tried to speak. Again, the alarming creaking sound, slightly louder this time. The man looked over, saw that Michael had woken, and approached after performing one last midair gesture. He held a finger in front of Michael's mouth. "Go on."

He could only speak in a low rasp, but his voice was amplified far louder than it should have been. "I feel like shit," he said.

The man glanced down at his body, and back at his face. "I suppose you would. Don't worry, though. We'll be performing a head transplant within the hour. Do you care about the gender?"

"What?"

"Your new body. Do you care what gender it is?"

"I don't want a new body." The idea made Michael feel even more nauseous than he already was.

"Well, you don't want to upload, do you? There are some people that think it's not actually you when you do that. The ones who do it say that they're still themselves, but they would, wouldn't they?"

"What are you talking about?"

"Oh! I guess you wouldn't know about uploading, would you?" He chuckled.

"I'll be keeping my own body. Thanks."

The man gave him a strange look. "We can't have you walking out of here in this one. I'm sorry sir, but you're due to get a new, healthy body. It's been ordered by the government in your case, and they've even paid for it."

"Where is Luke?"

"Luke? Who's Luke?"

"Luke Haynes. He said he would be here."

"I don't know who that is, sir."

"He was CEO of Healthr."

"Healthr? Hold on, I'll look him up." The man frowned. "I'm sorry, sir. Looks like he died five years ago. Yep. Nanocrime. Untraceable, of course. I'm very sorry."

Michael didn't answer. He stared at the ceiling as the sponge-wielding robots went about their work, and tried to fight the regret welling up inside him over refusing to tell his son goodbye.

He needed to get out. To find the rest of his children. To make sure they were alive, and safe.

But that would have to wait.

{ 2 }

Finished with Faith

Michael could walk again.

After he'd woken, into the year 2046, from what he was learning to think of as cryosleep, it didn't take the clinic's staff very long to check all his vitals and declare him fit for surgery. The operation would be fairly straightforward, and non-invasive, other than an extremely large incision at the neck. Michael was getting a head transplant. Or, depending how you thought about it, a body transplant. The latter seemed more accurate.

"We could easily regenerate the nerves in your old body's legs, restoring their functionality," said the technician who'd been present when Michael had come out of cryogenic preservation. His name was Barf. "But why do that when you can have a brand new body, without all the problems your old one had?"

"What about the problems my head has? Before being frozen I was starting to forget things, and even now my thinking feels cloudy."

"I'm afraid the government has only supplied enough funds to cover the head transplant, not neuroplasticity therapy. You're on your own for that."

When Michael asked the young man why his mother had named him Barf, his mouth quirked in amusement. "She didn't. My generation has a lot of resentment toward our parents, for failing to address Earth's problems when it was still possible to address them, and for keeping us under such close surveillance all the time. A lot of us changed our names on social media to the terms for bodily fluids, to embarrass them. The new names just kind of stuck."

"What problems?" Michael said.

Barf laughed. "Where do I start? I don't really have time to give you the rundown, Mr. Haynes. Sorry about that. We have more clients to process today."

By late afternoon on the same day, they were ready to give him his new body.

"Where did he come from?" Michael said as he lay on the operating table, looking at the young man lying perfectly still on a similar table across the room. "Why am I getting his body?"

"He's a suicide, tragically," the chief surgeon said as she arranged a number of tools that were utterly foreign to Michael. "Drug overdose. Prescription meds. We've cleaned the toxins from his body, and he's ready to go. Perfectly healthy, other than being dead."

"Why do I get his body, though? Didn't he want to be buried?"

The surgeon took a deep breath, as though answering questions from people whose last memories came from decades ago was among the least favorite parts of her job. "Burial plots are extremely expensive," she said. "And people get healthcare rebates when they sign up to be body donors."

"Healthcare rebates?" he said. "But Canada has free healthcare!"

"Time for the anesthetic, Mr. Haynes. Open wide." She held a small spray bottle in front of his mouth. Michael opened it, and she spritzed his tongue with a bitter-tasting solution. Darkness enclosed him.

He awoke around two hours later, and when he did he lay on the same table the young man had. The table he'd occupied before going under was hidden under a grey, plastic covering. "Is that me?" he asked, feeling only a little bleary from the anesthetic.

Just Barf remained in the operating room, and when Michael spoke to him he turned from where he stood in the corner, making the weird midair gestures he'd been performing when Michael first woke from cryosleep. Barf approached him. "No, Mr. Haynes," he said, poking him in the chest. "This is you. That's just your old, discarded body over there."

Michael felt very odd. His pectoral barely gave way at all under Barf's finger—it was made of hard, unyielding muscle, whereas his old chest had been saggy and soft. He brought his new hands in front of his face. This body's skin tone was significantly darker.

"Why don't you try getting up and walking a few steps? Careful. Things will feel very different for a while."

His first attempt brought the floor rushing up to meet him. The only thing that prevented him from injuring his new body was Barf's swift response: he swiftly knelt, catching Michael with outstretched arms. *My hero.*

"Told you," Barf said. He helped Michael regain his feet.

"Everything feels wrong," he said, wobbling.

"It will, at first."

The weight of the young man whose body he'd inherited was distributed differently from his old one. Evidently this body had spent long hours at the gym. It was very top-heavy. Every movement he tried to make went farther than he'd intended—he hadn't had this level of responsiveness and strength in decades, if ever. Not to mention the fact that he'd been wheelchair-bound for a decade before being frozen. The simple act of walking felt like a very uncertain affair.

"I don't suppose you have my old wheelchair kicking around here somewhere?" he asked. "I could use it till I get used to these legs."

Barf shook his head. "It would have been scrapped long ago. At any rate, you'll have the next couple of days for rehabilitation. We'll have you one-hundred percent comfortable with your new body by then."

"What happens after that?"

"After that, you'll be leaving us."

"Where do I go?" He wanted badly to know whether his family still lived, but no one here seemed to have any time to help him out with that. Barf had looked up Luke for him when he first woke, and informed him his son had been murdered—by who, no one knew. But after that, Barf was too busy to do any further research for him.

Barf shrugged. "That's up to you. We really can't provide any guidance, beyond administering the services covered by your funding. Here, come look at this, Mr. Haynes." He helped Michael hobble over to a mirror.

He watched his own eyes go wide, and brought a hand up to paw at his cheek. The skin it encountered was smooth, taught, flawless. "What did you do to it?"

"Standard tissue regeneration. Otherwise you'd have an old-looking head on a young body, which makes for a somewhat jarring effect. Trust me, I've seen it in customers whose funding didn't cover a facial do-over. You're lucky."

They'd even changed his face's skin color, to match the body's olive tone. And his hair was as black as night, whereas once it had been a dark brown. Would his children even recognize him?

*

The cryogenic clinic's staff had been friendly and accommodating during the three days it took for Michael to wake, get transplanted to a new body, and learn how to use it. But in the end it was just as they said: they could only help him as much as his funding allowed. Their farewells as he left the clinic did not seem warm, or even authentic. They were a routine part of the process. He even sensed that they felt a little glad to see him go.

Funding crises haunted many of the clinic's customers. The global economy was in turmoil, he'd gleaned from the employees' chatter, and currencies fluctuated wildly. Sometimes inflation ate through customers' funding so fast that before anyone knew it, they didn't even have enough to cover the cost of being revived. Unless they had families still living who were able to help, those patients' bodies were simply thawed—which was different from being revived—and discarded.

Michael had been protected from that fate since the Canadian government had guaranteed it would fund his revival. They'd learned much from studying blood and tissue samples they'd harvested from his body before freezing him, and apparently they'd unfrozen him once in the interim to take more samples, using advanced techniques. They'd kept him under sedation for that, though, so he had no memory of it.

Thanks to Michael, life extension technologies had advanced significantly. They rewarded him by bringing him back to the world, even though there was nothing left to be learned from him, and even though they'd forced him into cryosleep. Apparently they'd changed their minds about him being a terrorist, which was how they'd justified strong-arming him into doing this in the first place. So that was something.

"All the best, Mr. Haynes," Barf said to him in the clinic's lobby. "I hope you find that you still have some family living in the year 2046. Here." He passed him a tiny bottle, which turned out to contain sunblock. "I'd recommend putting some on. It's

May—a much hotter month than it used to be in Newfoundland. Reapply every hour."

"Thanks," Michael said, and did as Barf suggested. When he finished he slipped the bottle into his pocket. He hesitated then, afraid to leave—afraid of what he'd find in the future, and what he wouldn't find. He couldn't stomach the thought that something might have happened to any of his family. To have made it this far only to be denied seeing them would be awful.

"Goodbye," Barf said, a little pointedly.

An armed guard nodded at Michael as he left the building. He raised his eyebrows at that. There hadn't been any guards when he'd been frozen, in 2024.

He stepped out into the clinic's parking lot, which was still just as tiny. Right away he felt the full force of the sun beating down on him, warmer than he ever remembered it being. Was that mostly because of his newly youthful senses, or had it really gotten that hot? Climate change had been ramping up with frightening speed before he'd undergone preservation, especially if you considered the scientific models, which Valentine had often discussed with him. But he wasn't prepared for this stark contrast. He felt like an egg in a frying pan. Sweat coated him within seconds of arriving outside.

Looking around, he couldn't make sense of the city's geography. He assumed the streets themselves hadn't changed much, even in two decades, since that would involve massive reconstruction and the money wouldn't be available for it in a teetering economy. But none of them looked familiar. It would take three hours or more to walk to where Valentine had lived, but he didn't know which direction to go, even if he'd been willing to risk the journey in this heat just to see whether she still lived there. Michael didn't know whether his inability to figure this out was due to the way St. John's had changed or due to his aged brain, which had not enjoyed the same rejuvenation his face had. He stood at the end of the parking lot, looking all around him, blinking.

Was this really the future? Old boards covered the doors and windows in most of the buildings he could see. Even the ones still in use looked rundown. In the few minutes since he'd left the clinic, the surrounding pockmarked streets stayed empty. There were no planes overhead. No sound. Nothing.

Back when he'd been frozen, St. John's had been riding the crest of an oil boom. Michael had known it couldn't last, of course, but he hadn't expected the fall to be so hard. This area looked abandoned. And yet he stood in the parking lot of a cryogenic clinic—a facility that must be very expensive to maintain. Given the extreme contrast with its surroundings, the presence of an armed guard made sense.

In the end he chose a direction at random and started walking. After a couple minutes he encountered the first sign of life, a scrawny cat who eyed him as he approached and fled between two houses when he drew near. Trudging onward, he noticed the number of boarded-up buildings gradually declining.

Soon, he began to ache. Walking felt strange in this body, and he would need time to adjust. His new arms were set forward more than his old ones, and the shoulders hunched in a way that reminded him of his daughter Esther. Michael suspected the body's previous owner had spent too much time on one particular type of weightlifting exercises, while neglecting other important muscles. Barf had suggested researching a workout routine that would help balance them out.

An immense sadness washed over him. Since waking he'd been too shell-shocked by the parade of new, alien things he was experiencing to really process his emotions. But now he began to, and realized how alone he felt. How lost. Payphones had been all but extinct in his time, and there surely wouldn't be any left now. Even if there were, he wouldn't know what number to call, and anyway he didn't have money. Did people even use phones to communicate anymore? He didn't feel like approaching any of the ramshackle buildings. They looked unwelcoming, even menacing. That he would get a positive reception by explaining he was from the past, and therefore had no clue about anything, seemed dubious.

That said, other people shared the sidewalk with him now. Not many, but they were there. He appeared to be entering a more active part of town.

He reached a bridge spanning a river, which he didn't recognize. Much of it had dried up, it seemed—several rocks poked up through the water. The current moved slowly. Michael stopped to lean against the bridge's guardrail. Even with his lithe new body, he was drenched in a disgusting amount of sweat.

"Hey Dad," someone said.

Michael gave a start, nearly tumbling forward over the rail. He looked around. Passing on the sidewalk behind him was a young lady who looked to be in her early twenties—unless she'd had a body transplant too. She noticed him staring at her and quickly looked away, quickening her pace.

But it hadn't been her. The voice had been male.

"Who's there?" he whispered, not wanting to appear insane to the man who'd just passed the girl, walking in the opposite direction, and now drawing closer to Michael.

"It's your son. The same one who told you that you'd live forever. Looks like you're off to a good start."

Michael gasped. "Luke? They told me you died."

"I did. Someone flew a microscopic robot up my nose and used it to trigger massive hemorrhaging in my brain. I died within seconds. It happens enough that there's a name for it: injuries and deaths inflicted using nanobots are called nanocrimes."

Michael looked all around him, trying to pinpoint the source of the voice. "Are you a...ghost?"

Luke sighed. "No, Dad. I'm an AI."

"A what?"

"An Artificial Intelligence. Every month, I used to have my brain scanned and uploaded into a database, to be activated upon my death. I've been an AI for five years."

"Why can't I see you?"

"Because you don't have any Smartans. You look great, by the way."

"What are Smartums?"

"Smart*ans*. You wanna grab a beer?"

"How do I grab a beer with an invisible robot?"

"I'm not a robot. More a computer program than anything. Come on. I'll give you directions to a place you can get some Smartans. They give them out for free. I'll be your personal GPS."

"Will you tell me what they are, first?"

"Walk fifty meters, then turn right."

Michael sighed, and continued along the bridge. He couldn't imagine a device that would make his son any less invisible. It sounded miraculous. *And they're giving them away for free?* Forty feet beyond where the bridge ended, he turned down the road that Luke had indicated.

"How are you talking to me right now?" he said, his brain feeling muddled again. *Senile is what I am. Or getting there. Might as well call it what it is.* He was a senile old man in a twenty-five-year-old's body.

"The ground is littered with microscopic sensors, roughly one per every square meter, which also function as broadcasters capable of beaming sound to a tiny, specific location. Your ear, for example. That's why none of the passersby are paying any attention to me. They can't hear it. Only you."

"Wow."

"The future may not look very futuristic to you yet, but trust me, you'll see. Just wait till you get your Smartans."

"How long have you known they unfroze me?"

"I knew immediately. I signed up to receive a notification when it happened. I've been watching you since you left the clinic. I might have known I'd find you wandering aimlessly."

Michael gave a sardonic laugh. “So I take it you’re still convinced about your pet immortality theory?”

“It’s not my theory,” Luke said. “I didn’t come up with it.”

“If no one ever dies, how do you explain the fact that you did?”

“Wow.” Luke chuckled, which sounded authentically human enough. “I knew you wouldn’t get the concept, but I didn’t expect you to misunderstand quite so thoroughly. The theory holds that when something happens that might have caused your death, the universe splits into all possible outcomes, and you end up in one where you survived. So when I died in this universe, another universe split off in which I didn’t die. I’m still in that universe, alive. Just because I’m dead in this one, from your perspective, doesn’t mean the theory’s wrong. It doesn’t mean anything.”

“Huh.”

“Besides, if you think about it, I didn’t really die in this universe, did I? I’m still here, talking to you.”

Michael pondered this for a moment. “A technician at the cryogenic clinic mentioned something called uploading. Is that what you did?”

“Yeah. I’m an upload.”

“He said it’s not actually still you when you do that.”

“A lot of people say that. They might be right. If so, I guess I really must be alive in some other universe. But I think they’re wrong. For one, I feel like me. I remember being the flesh Luke Haynes, and honestly being digital Luke Haynes isn’t all that different. I've merely lost a few physical limitations, and gained some other types of limitations."

"But when they scanned your brain they were just creating a copy. Even an exact copy of you still wouldn't be you." The buildings he passed now, while still somewhat dilapidated, looked sumptuous compared to those he'd left behind. He guessed they were headed downtown.

"Why not? Even in biological bodies we become copies of ourselves over time. Every seven years the atoms in a human body completely regenerate with all new atoms. Hell, you just received an entirely new body from another person. Do you still consider yourself you?"

Michael hesitated. "Yes," he admitted. *Because I still have my head.*

"There you have it. I'm still me, despite what the navel-gazing naysayers might say."

"Bet you can't say that three times fast." Michael still wasn't convinced Luke was the same person that had been his son. Not intellectually convinced, anyway, But he was willing to behave like the AI was really Luke, and he even found himself responding that way emotionally—getting annoyed at Luke's know-it-all attitude, and feeling the same undercurrent of love he'd always felt toward him, despite the aggravation.

"Either way," Luke went on, "You're definitely still you. And if I'm right about you living forever, which I am, you're going to want to be very careful here in the future. It's a dangerous place, but you can make a big difference to whether it stays that way. Remember: the one thing that's certain is that you'll be around indefinitely. There's a lot of power in that. If you set your mind to it, you could end up ruling this universe. Or you could experience endless torment. Or anything in between."

All Michael wanted was to protect his family, and help them in any way he could. He steeled himself to ask the question he'd so far felt too terrified to ask. "What about your brother and sisters? Are they alive?" The idea that any of them were lost to him forever, while he lived on, was nearly unbearable.

A heartbeat of silence from Luke, and then he said, "Doris has passed. Just a couple years ago."

"Did she refuse life extension treatment?" He couldn't blame her if she did. That's what he would have done if given the option. The thought saddened him, and he would mourn her deeply, but he understood the decision.

A longer pause from Luke this time. At last he said, "I'm worried about your mind, to be honest, Dad. You haven't had any neuroplasticity therapy yet, and I'm afraid that overloading you with a lot of emotionally-charged information—"

Michael stopped in his tracks. "Tell me, Luke. Or we go no further."

"Fine. Doris and her husband moved to Paris a decade ago. A little under three years ago, France became a failed state. The protests that had already been going on for years turned ugly. The government went under, and the riots began. Doris was trampled to death on her way home from work."

The news hit him like a cement truck. Luckily Michael stood within a couple feet of a metal bench, which he managed to stagger to. Otherwise he would have collapsed onto the ground. He covered his face with his hands.

"I told you, Dad."

"Shut up, Luke," he said through his sobbing.

"I'm sorry. It's horrific, I know." His son let him weep in peace for a time.

After a few minutes a soothing female voice began whispering into his ear. "You've been sitting on this bench for three minutes now. You must be tired. Tell you what. Take the Metro down to Water Street, and come into the Cool Beans Café. I'll be waiting for you, along with a host of other lovely baristas, eager to make your beverage just the way you want. Cool Beans Café. Join us."

Ten seconds later another voice chimed in. "Tired of being on your feet? Pop on down to Andy's Used Cars—"

"What is that and how do I make it stop?"

"Hmm?" Luke said. "What is what?"

"I'm hearing voices that are reading commercials to me."

"Oh. Shit. They're coming from the bench, and they won't stop as long as you're sitting there. Come on, Dad, let's get going again. The commercials aren't helping, I'm sure, and more walking will be good for you. Come on."

Michael complied, putting one foot in front of the other, feeling like he was made of wood. "What about the others?"

"Valentine, Craig, and Esther are all still alive. Craig lives in Montreal, now. Valentine moved to Mount Pearl, so she's close by. And Esther—well, you'll see."

"What do you mean? Is she doing okay?"

"Oh, she's doing more than okay," Luke said with a cryptic chuckle.

He decided not to try and decipher that just now. He was already suffering from informational overload, not to mention emotional. "My grandchildren? Samuel? Daniel?"

"Dan lives in Ottawa, working as a contractor. Sam's in the UK, teaching."

They were getting pretty close to downtown St. John's now—Michael had begun to recognize some landmarks that still remained from his time. Everything still appeared down on its luck, though, except for the giant, modern-looking buildings, which he saw had multiplied rapidly in the last twenty years. "What are they?" he asked, pointing.

"Condos, mostly. For the wealthy."

They reached the core downtown area in another twenty minutes of walking. Luke directed him down George Street, which was still just as crammed with bars as ever. "Some things never change," Michael said. "Looking pretty dead right now, though."

"It still looks fairly dead by night. It's the Smartans that make it really incredible-looking."

And Michael was finally about to find out what the hell they were. They left George Street for Water Street, and soon came to a tiny shop with a dull-looking sign over it that simply said "SMARTANS."

"After you," Luke said, which Michael assumed was a joke.

"Good morning," said a man sitting behind a counter at the rear of the store. "Are you here for a replacement?"

"Hmm?" Michael said. "I'm here for, uh, Smartans."

"Right," the man said, giving him a strange look. His name-tag said "Spit." His hair contained so much product it looked like he'd dumped a bucket of spit all over it. "Well, feel free to browse our models." Spit gestured at the walls.

Michael looked at them, and then turned back to Spit. "They're blank."

"They're which?"

"The walls are blank, Spit."

"I assure you they're not," Spit said. "They're displaying all our very latest models."

"He's here for his *first* pair of Smartans," Luke said. Spit's attention turned to a space in the air a couple feet to Michael's right.

The clerk mouthed the words slowly, like he didn't understand them. Then he said them out loud. "His first pair?" He looked at Michael again. "You've never *had* any Smartans?"

"That's right."

"But—how—how have you *existed?*"

"He just woke from cryosleep," Luke said. "The last year he remembers is 2024."

"Oh my God," Spit said. "What model do we give him?"

"Give him a starter pair. Low intensity. Do you have any in stock?"

"You have money, Luke?" Michael asked.

"They're free, sir," Spit said. "I'll go out back and check to see if we have any starters." He left them to stare around the blank room. Michael stood with his shoulders slumped, feeling like a freak, an out-of-place lump of muscle and confusion.

"They don't charge for the basic models," Luke explained. "Some of the premium Smartans cost a bit, but even they're not that much."

"How do they make their money?"

"Advertising."

"Wonderful."

Smartans turned out to be flexible transparent discs the size of contact lenses, and they slipped inside your eyes exactly the same way. Spit gave him a case to go with them, and a bottle of cleaning solution, which he said should never run out since you never actually had to change out the solution. It contained nanoparticles that broke down any dirt that got on your Smartans and then vented it into the air, through hundreds of holes in the case that were big enough to release a gas but too small for liquid to fit through.

When Michael put them in his eyes everything changed. The bare, white walls became paneled with mahogany, and a number of floating screens displayed various multi-colored scenes, with an informational panel below each paired with a price tag. He turned around to find that Spit had disappeared, replaced by a well-muscled medieval knight wearing tight-fitting chainmail and a helm that sported an overlarge red feather.

Spit noticed Michael's expression, and shifted uncomfortably. "It's my *Destrier* character," the knight said in Spit's voice, with a hint of defensiveness.

Michael decided not to ask what that was.

There was someone else standing in the room—someone who hadn't been there before. It was Luke, looking as young as he had when Michael entered cryosleep. No, younger. He looked not a day over thirty-five.

"Son," he said, overcome with emotion. Michael moved to embrace him, and his arms swept through the air, colliding with each other. Now he occupied some of the same space as his son, which felt awkward. He took a couple steps back.

"No touching," Luke said, wearing a sad smile. He had his hands in the pockets of an expensive-looking red blazer. Below were matching pants, and black shoes so shiny they shone. He still wore his thick glasses too, though Michael was certain they were unnecessary in digital form. He supposed everything about his appearance was. Still, he felt glad for it.

"It's so good to see you," he said.

"You too." Luke extended an arm toward the door. "Shall we?"

Spit cleared his throat. "Uh, will he be wanting a Fingertip Chip?" He appeared to have switched to speaking exclusively to Luke, having apparently given up on effective communication with Michael.

"No thanks. I think the Smartans themselves will be more than enough for him to adjust to, for now."

"What about earbuds?" Spit said, speaking a little louder, as they had each taken a step toward the exit.

"Oh, yes. He'll want those."

Spit reached below the counter and slapped a slim box down onto it. "Here you go. They're complementary as well."

"Thanks," Michael said. They left the store.

Outside, the streets had gotten much busier, with nearly twice as many people walking down the sidewalks. "Many of them are digital," Luke said when he noticed Michael looking. "It's still considered impolite to walk through them, though. You walked through a few on our way here, but I didn't say anything. It couldn't be helped."

"Oops."

"You got a few dirty looks. Nothing major."

Water Street had been completely transformed by the Smartans. For one, the drab "SMARTANS" sign was a pulsing light show, shooting a rainbow's worth of pencil-thin light beams in all directions. As well, the buildings no longer looked worn-down. Instead they were colorful, pulsing, futuristic. The sort of structures you might expect to find in the 2040s. Overhead, he saw that several businesses had gigantic mascots that loomed over their respective stores, appearing to stand in the street behind them, beckoning customers inside. "Jesus," Michael said, and Luke glanced at him askance. Michael never took the Lord's name in vain. But it was extremely disconcerting sharing the street with these multi-colored colossi.

"The mascots?" Luke said, and he nodded. "Yeah. The first time I saw them I thought they were pretty freaky too. They're only in the default skin, though. You can avoid them by buying a different one."

"Skin? What the hell is that?"

"It's just the sort of world you see when you're wearing Smartans. Each skin will superimpose different images and text onto your environment. You can customize them. There are almost a thousand skins available now for St. John's. Hundreds of thousands, for bigger cities."

"Why do people want to see things that aren't true? I mean, it's one thing to go see a movie, but to walk around inside a fiction all the time...." Michael shook his head. "I saw what those buildings really looked like. St. John's is falling apart."

"It's not just St. John's, Dad. It's everywhere. People willingly hide the truth from themselves. They put in their Smartans when they wake up, and they don't take them out again until they're going to bed. People want to pretend they're living in a world that isn't on the way out. If that means big businesses can sell to them more effectively, then so be it."

*

Luke brought him to a bar called Sing Twice, which he said catered to all ages. Michael would have assumed 'all ages' denoted a much narrower range than it once had, but there were still old people, according to Luke. Not everyone could afford access to life extension technology, or they could but couldn't afford the cosmetic features. It didn't matter. No one could tell what you could and couldn't buy, because everyone wore Smartans, and therefore anyone could look however they wanted for fairly cheap. "It's a leveler, really," Luke said. "Makes people more equal "

"It makes them *appear* more equal," Michael said. "And it allows the rich, the ones who caused all the problems, to hide in plain sight." Nothing had truly changed, from what he could see so far. Other than getting worse.

There were plenty of celebrity lookalikes walking around. On their way to the bar he'd seen Taylor Swift, looking around thirty, which was about how old she'd been when he was cryogenically preserved.

"Is she still popular?" Michael asked his son.

"More than ever. Getting near her late fifties, and still going strong. She still looks like that, too."

"Isn't the future grand?" He'd meant the comment sarcastically, but he enjoyed looking at the beautiful young pop star more than he would have expected at his age. An electric-blue box popped up a foot in front of his eyes, making him jump. "Your heartrate has increased," it said. "Press to receive more alerts like this. Swipe away to turn off." He reached until his hand touched the blue rectangle floating before him, and flicked it, causing it to slingshot out of his field of vision in a way he found rather satisfying. *I'm getting the hang of this.*

Dusk had nearly fallen when they reached Sing Twice, and through the Smartans Michael saw a George Street that already looked like the interior of an enormous bar. The sky had been replaced by a giant black dome, on which twenty or so gigantic screens played commercials for the various clubs. As he and Luke waited in line to get into Sing Twice, he found himself watching an ad featuring a woman with flowing brown hair and gorgeous mascara-accented eyes, beckoning him with a crooked finger. "Hey, handsome," he heard her say. "You look like you hit the gym a lot. I want to run my fingers through that jet-black hair while we grind on the dance floor. I wanna grab that ass. Come find me at Lust, or someone like me. I want you."

Michael quickly averted his eyes, his cheeks heating. His gaze fell on another giant commercial, this one featuring a broad-shouldered, bluff-faced man with his shirt rolled up to his elbows and a cowboy hat sitting at an angle on his head. He was cleaning out a glass with a rag. "Hey there, buster," he said in a southern accent. "You want a real drink, you come on down to The Tavern. We got the finest country tunes, and of course, the finest country women. Or maybe you prefer a tumble in the hay with a nice strong man. I've been known to partake myself, from time to time. What is your speed, anyway, cowboy?" Another rectangle popped up, this one looking like it belonged on an old-timey saloon wall. It asked, "Which do you prefer? Tap your selection. Cowboys or Cowgirls."

He decided not to watch the commercials in the sky anymore, instead keeping his eyes firmly locked onto the entrance of Sing Twice. Luke was looking at him with some amusement. "A commercial just asked me whether I'm gay," Michael whispered.

"You'll get that sort of thing a lot at first. You're a new user. A clean slate. They're hungry for data on you, so they can sell to you better. They'll keep asking till you tell them."

"They already know enough. One of them knew I'm muscular, or my new body is anyway, and that I have black hair, and—"

"That stuff's easy. Anyone can see that. They want to know the things about you that people can't see. Dietary preferences, taste in music, political leaning, sexual orientation. And they'll find out soon enough."

Michael grimaced. "What are the earbuds used for, if I can already hear what they're all saying?"

"Playing your own media. For when you want to block out the ads. Of course, you'll still hear commercials between pretty much anything you listen to."

There was no bouncer at the door, just a metal gate. When he reached it a box popped into his vision telling him to stand still. After a second it disappeared, replaced by another one: "Please confirm your age. Are you 25?" He pressed "Yes," not wanting to give them accurate information. The bar admitted him, and he waited inside while Luke stood raised his digital hand (to press on the alert presumably) and was admitted as well.

"Couldn't you just walk straight through the barrier?" Michael said.

"No, actually. I can't physically go anywhere without those microscopic sensors I told you about. And the bar won't let me access theirs unless I pay."

"Really? It didn't ask me to pay."

"They'll get your money when you order a drink. They can't sell drinks to me. Instead, they charge AIs for access."

"What's the point for you, then? Why do AIs even come to bars?"

Luke frowned. "Don't ask other AIs these types of questions, okay? They're awkward."

"Oh. Sorry."

"It's fine. I'm just letting you know." Luke's digital shoulder rose and fell as he took a deep, digital breath. "AIs come to bars to share a social space with non-AIs like yourself, and with other AIs too. We don't want to be segregated any more than we already are. And it would look weird if AIs just hung out with each other out on the street."

"Fair enough."

"Here. Let me order you a drink." They walked over to the bar and the woman behind nodded at them, unsmiling. "A beer for my friend," Luke said.

"What kind?"

"Surprise me," Michael said, not recognizing any of the brands. She slammed the most generic-looking beer bottle imaginable onto the bar top. "Thanks."

"Come on," Luke said, walking toward a corner booth.

"We didn't pay."

"Sure we did." Luke looked over one shoulder with his trademark half-smile, glasses flickering in the dim light.

Once they were sitting across from each other, Michael in the plush booth seat and Luke in a chair across the table, his son performed a little flourish with his hand, and a beer bottle appeared. He slid it across the table, bringing it next to Michael's bottle. "Look. My beer's bigger than yours."

So it was. Twice as big at least.

"Cheers," Michael said, knowing the bottles would pass through each other. "Oops," he said when they did. Luke's self-satisfied grin turned down a notch, which was fine.

A stage area in the center of the bar lit up, a solid column of white light flashing rapidly. It stopped the moment Michael looked directly at it, and then a pole appeared in the stage's center. A hole opened in the ceiling and a woman slid out, fit, tanned, and skimpily clad. The hole closed again as soon as she hit the stage. She began twirling around the pole, gradually removing articles of her already minimal clothing. In the corner of his vision a box appeared that said "Tap here to change your preferences."

Luke twisted around, following his look of shock to the stage, and then turned back. "What? What are they showing you?"

"A striptease. Am I the only one seeing it?"

"What did you tell the bar your age was?"

"Twenty-five."

"Yeah, the bar's algorithms will generally assume a male in his twenties wants to see naked women."

"Why wouldn't they ask me first? How do I stop it?"

Before answering, Luke tipped his drink up for a healthy gulp. He wiped his digital mouth. "You can change the gender or appearance of the dancers, but you'll have to approach the bartender about stopping it. Bars are pretty touchy about the atmosphere they try to create. You'll probably get a weird look if you do ask them to change what you're seeing. I doubt they've had anyone ask to see less nudity in a long, long time."

A young girl who'd entered the bar a couple minutes ago approached their table carrying a luminescent drink. She slid past Luke into the booth, so that she was sitting between them. Michael looked from Luke, to her, to Luke again, his brow furrowed. Did they know each other? She looked all of nineteen years old. Why would Luke know a nineteen-year-old?

"Hey," she said.

Luke just smiled.

She brought a hand up in front of her face, flicked it, and then looked at Michael, her eyebrows shooting up and her mouth going wide. "Oh, wow. Wow. He really looks like that now?"

"Yeah," Luke said. "He's not wearing a skin. He hasn't downloaded any yet."

As for her she wore a skin-tight, beige-colored dress that was cut open to reveal a diamond-shaped portion of her taut belly. Black wire wrapped around and around fluorescent yellow stockings, and devil horns poked out of her shining brown hair. They looked like they had really grown from her skull.

Michael would soon be one-hundred and one, not counting the frozen years, and he felt a little uncomfortable sitting at the same table as this teenager. He glanced around the bar to check whether anyone was looking at them. Would people think they were a couple, with her sitting right next to him? He was a little old for her.

Then he remembered: if anyone looked at him they would see a twenty-five-year-old. A six-year age gap was a lot less shocking than an eighty-one-year one.

He decided it would be rude not to speak to her. An awkward silence had already settled over the table—though Luke still looked amused, and the girl did too, come to think of it.

Clearing his throat, he said, "So, uh, I'm Michael. What's your name?"

At that she broke into peels of high-pitched laughter that rang out across the bar. A few heads turned then, and Michael noticed more than a couple of gazes that lingered on her.

"Dad," Luke said. "This is Esther."

His eyes went so wide it was surprising they didn't tumble from their sockets and land, *plunk plunk*, on the table. That only increased her laughter's volume.

"Wh—" he said, and tried again: "Wh—"

She laughed harder.

"Why?" he finally managed.

Esther reigned in her mirth long enough to answer him. "Why what, father?"

Where did he start? Before his cryosleep, Esther had been a total homebody, never going out, never doing anything. She'd paid zero attention to her appearance, and had always sat with her shoulders hunched forward, staring at the ground. Now she sat perfectly straight, meeting his eyes with a directness that bordered on confrontational. "Why are you dressed like that?" he said. "Why do you look nineteen?"

"Why do you care?" she said, and the question gave him a potent dose of vertigo. He actually felt like he was the parent of a teenager again.

"Esther and I live together," Luke said.

At that, Michael felt apprehension twist his features, and the skin on his back began to crawl. "You—you aren't—you don't—

do you?" How much *had* things changed in the last twenty years?

"No, Dad," Luke said, rolling his eyes.

"Oh my God," Esther said. She jerked a thumb at Michael. "Has he had neuroplasticity therapy yet?"

"No. This is his first day unfrozen. Whatever was going on with his brain in 2024 is still very much a thing." Luke finished off his beer, and the empty bottled vanished, replaced by a fresh, unopened one. When he twisted the cap off Michael heard it hiss. "Dad, think about the question you just asked. Besides the fact that it would be incest, I'm digital, and Esther's still biological. Like, how would that even work?" Esther giggled again. "We're just roommates," Luke went on. "I crash on her couch, so to speak. Not that AIs need sleep. But if she didn't let me access her apartment's sensors overnight I'd have to spend my nights out on the street. Which would be pretty embarrassing."

"Why would you have to stay on the street?" Michael said. "Can't you just get your own place?"

"AIs can't own property."

Knowing the barely-dressed teenager sitting next to him was his daughter made him even more uncomfortable. But he tried not to let it show. "So, do you still have cats, then?" he asked her. In 2024, she'd had seven of them.

"Just the one," she said, still wearing her mocking smile, which was beginning to remind him of the one Luke had taken to using when he was actually the age she appeared to be.

Abruptly he decided to stop beating around the bush. He was her father for goodness' sake, and there was no point in refraining from asking what he really wanted to know.

"Are you okay?" he said to her. "You're a completely different person from the Esther I knew. I'd like to know why."

His offspring exchanged glances, and then she sipped from her glowing drink, which looked like it was made out of light. Luke spoke.

"Esther made the same realization I've been trying to help you make," he said. "That none of us are ever going to die. And after she realized that, she decided she didn't want to live forever in the shadow of what certain members of a mostly bygone generation did to her. She decided to enjoy forever instead. To put the past behind her, and come out of her shell. It took her years of hard work, but she did it." Brother and sister shared a warm smile.

While Luke spoke, Michael had hit a limit in his tolerance. He stood. "You have no right to speak to me like you are. Not on this subject. I might take it from Esther, but I won't take it from you anymore. You don't have the right."

"Sure I do. And Esther has the right to live her life however she wants. She's decided to be a club kid, and she's proud of it. She takes home a new guy every night. I think it's awesome. She's come so far in the years you slept in a freezer."

"Stop it. You're turning my stomach."

"What are you gonna do? Spank my digital ass?"

Esther laughed, and took another sip from her drink, this time quite a long one.

"I'm leaving," Michael said.

"Aw, come on, Pops. Where are you gonna go without my help?"

"How do I contact Valentine? Put me in touch with her."

"Why? So you can burden her for another ten years?"

If Michael could have punched him then, he would have. He truly would have.

"Do it, Luke," Esther said. "If that's what he wants."

"Fine." A chunky rotary phone appeared on the table, vibrating as it rang, eliciting yet more laughter from Esther. "You know how to operate this technology, right Dad?" Luke said. "Go on. Pick it up. I connected you—it's calling Val."

He picked up the receiver and brought it to his ear, feeling foolish with his hand curled around empty air that happened to resemble an obsolete phone. As soon as he did he heard ringing. "Hello?" a woman said once it stopped.

A lump formed in his throat. Her voice was just as he remembered. He was near tears, he realized, and fought to hold them back. "Valentine?"

A pause. "Who is this?"

"It's Michael. Your father."

Loud clattering filled his ear, and he winced, jerking the ethereal receiver away from his head. Then, Valentine again: "Dad? Sorry. I just dropped my dinner onto the counter. Oh my God. It's so good to hear your voice. How did you know to get Smartans?"

"Um, how do you know I have them?"

"It's the only way anyone communicates. When did you leave the clinic? I was supposed to get a notification when you did."

"This morning."

"Ugh. Luke. I bet that bastard pulled some strings to block me from the clinic's alert system."

Michael made eye contact with his son. He wondered whether Luke could eavesdrop on their conversation. His expression didn't seem to have changed at Valentine's remark. "Why would he do that?"

"Because he's a manipulative asshole. Where are you? Do you want me to come get you?"

"Yes, please. I'm on George Street."

"Wow. Your first day and he drags you onto George Street. At your age. I'll be right there. Meet me where it intersects with Water Street."

"Thank you, sweetheart."

"I love you, Dad."

"Love you. See you soon."

He hung up the phone and it promptly dissolved. Esther and Luke still stared at him, identically amused expressions intact. "I hope you're wearing more clothes the next time I see you," he said to his daughter. He ignored Luke.

Then he turned and left the bar, averting his eyes from the stage, where two men with unicorn horns sprouting from their foreheads were making out.

*

The green lawns on which the city of Mount Pearl had once prided itself were no more. What grass they did have was brittle and brown. Several front yards contained only dry, hard-packed dirt.

Last night he'd mentioned a desire to take a walk today, and Valentine had suggested going in the early morning, since the closer to noon it got the more scorching the sun became. He couldn't get over the differences he saw in this city. Several houses had been reduced to rubble, some charred. Most were boarded up. He saw one with boards over its windows and a row of rusted bicycles chained up in the driveway, guarded by a very vocal Rottweiler. People still lived there.

That was without the transformative magic of his Smartans turned on, of course. Val had taught him how to properly control the things last night, which was done via a combination of midair gestures and simply thinking of whatever you wanted to happen. Smartans had microscopic EEGs built into them that could scan your brain waves for what you wanted them to do. After that lesson, she showed him how to navigate the Skin Store.

There were twenty skins available for Mount Pearl, all but one of them free. Now he activated the official skin produced by the Mount Pearl City Council. The lawns of decades past returned instantly, with a diligently tended flower garden gracing every third property or so. Bumblebees buzzed from plant to plant, butterflies fluttered, and everywhere you looked children were yelling and playing. Ghost children, who would vanish the second he turned off the skin.

Valentine called Smartans "vile things." A "necessary evil."

Despite the close bond they'd once shared, Valentine and Esther barely spoke to each other anymore. They'd become so radically different, she told Michael, that there seemed to be nothing left to discuss. According to Valentine, Esther not only looked nineteen, she acted it.

"I shouldn't say that," Valentine said. "Not all nineteen-year-olds are unreliable, flighty, and emotionally immature. But that's the stereotype, and Esther fits it."

Valentine had availed of life extension technologies herself, but the age she'd chosen seemed more reasonable: she looked to be in her mid-thirties. Even that made Michael a bit uncomfortable, though. He now looked ten years younger than his oldest daughter. *Weird.*

Another reason conversation between the sisters had withered was Esther's living situation—in an apartment downtown with Luke. Valentine had a dramatic falling out with him a few years after they froze Michael. Luke still had a physical body, back then. The trouble started when Healthr experienced another huge leak of internal documents. This time the trove included emails Luke had exchanged with Michael's brother Horace, and with government officials, about how best to go about securing their 'research asset.'

"It was you, Dad," Valentine said. "You were the research asset. Because of how you survived that nanotech operation when barely anyone else did."

He shook his head. "How can Esther be on such good terms with Luke?"

His daughter shifted in her chair. They sat at the kitchen table, each with an untouched mug of tea, which had stopped steaming some time ago. "I think she's always been bitter that no one ever pressed charges against Horace. She says she's put it all behind her, but...." Valentine took a sip of her tea now, and grimaced, likely because of how cold it had gotten. "I hate to say it, but I think she's angrier at you, and at Gran and Pop, than she ever will be at Luke."

Hearing that broke his heart anew. But it made sense. And he couldn't say Esther was wrong to feel that way.

"What about Horace?" he said. "Where is he now?"

"Dead," Valentine said. "As far as anyone knows. They unfroze him a decade ago, since he was younger than you and there was a good chance they could keep him alive with the level of technology back then. But there was a boating accident, and no one heard from him again. His body was never found."

"Hmm." He took a sip of his own icy tea. "Do you think Luke still has his government connections?"

She shook her head. "I'm pretty sure he lost them when he died and became an AI. He lost his CEO position at Healthr at the same time. AIs aren't permitted to hold influential positions like that. But he still works for the company as a consultant, and I'm pretty sure he still effectively runs it. They bring him in on every major decision. And he has quite a lot of Healthr stock." She'd drained her tea, even chilly as it was. She got up and set her empty mug on the counter above the dishwasher. "I'd avoid Luke as much as you can, Dad. He's only gotten more conniving since uploading. Way more."

"Why does the government put so many restrictions on AIs?"

"Well, AI experts started getting really riled up in the 2030s, warning that AIs posed a threat to humanity, a more severe one than even climate change. And given all the crises we're already experiencing, the government takes new threats pretty seriously nowadays. AIs can't hold property, can't hold positions of influence, can't run in parallel—thankfully, we'll never have to deal with two Lukes. Most of all, they're forbidden to improve their own intelligence. That's where the main risk stems from. All AI brains are stored in Intellitech servers at a secret location. Intellitech is the corporation that patented the uploading technology. They run constant IQ tests on the AI brains, thousands every second, and if an AI is caught getting smarter they format it immediately. Permanent deletion."

"So no one really trusts AIs."

"And rightly so. Even with all the restrictions, they're still way beyond us. Their intelligence itself is within the human range, but they can think a thousand times faster than we can. Conversations with Luke are infuriating. He's a smarmy jerk, and for every second you have to think of a comeback, he has the equivalent of over fifteen minutes. Are you done with your tea?"

"Yeah," he said, and passed her the mug, which was only half empty.

"I'm pretty sure the government has gone from collaborating with Luke to thoroughly distrusting him. Not just because he's an AI—he's also an advocate for allowing AIs to improve their intelligence. He says it's the only way for the human race to survive this century."

"Do you think he's right?"

"Maybe. But if I have to choose between no future and one where I'm lorded over by Luke...well, I don't know which I'd pick."

Michael heaved a sigh. "No wonder I felt so out of my element around him."

"Well, I can't believe he got you Smartans and dragged you onto George Street straight away. That place is worse than Times Square was twenty years ago. A bit overwhelming for your first day in the future."

"I'm impressed by how well you've grasped everything, even given the time to process it. I mean, you're technically in your eighties."

"Don't remind me." Valentine grinned. "I've had neuroplasticity therapy in addition to life extension. I don't have a muddled old brain like yours. But soon you won't either. I've booked your first appointment with a neuroplastician for tomorrow afternoon."

"Oh, gosh, Valentine. I don't want to be a burden on you—"

"It's no burden. The real burden would be having you gradually turn into an unresponsive vegetable inside my apartment." She was teasing, but he supposed that was what really would happen, if they left his brain alone. "Besides," she said, "nothing happened to your money while you were frozen. So I'll put it on credit, and you can pay me back." She smiled.

Having neared the end of his morning walk, he switched off the official City skin for a last look at his desolate surroundings.

He never wanted to lose touch with reality, as so many here in 2046 seemed to have. The ghost children vanished.

Upon his return he enjoyed a modest lunch with Valentine, consisting of crackers and cheese dip. She turned on the news while they ate.

"...the German government fell this morning," a newscaster was in the middle of saying, eliciting a gasp from Valentine, "after months of sustained protests and riots. This comes after the government took numerous precautionary measures, including closing its borders to neighbor countries whose governments had all collapsed, and extensive quantitative easing policies administered by the German Federal Bank. In the meantime, stocks in North America are taking a heavy hit as a result of plummeting investor confidence that our own governments will be able to inoculate our economies from the ripple effects of major economies collapsing all around the globe. The direst predictions have the Canadian economy collapsing within a few months at most, and analysts from China are saying—"

Valentine switched off the TV. "Sorry, Dad," she said. "Not the best introduction to 2046."

She smiled, but her eyes stayed worried, and Michael could understand why. For his part, tension was building in his chest, and he could hear his blood rushing in his ears. *What if Luke has it right? Am I really about to live forever in this mess?*

With lunch eaten, they went out into the driveway Valentine shared with the house's upstairs occupants and got into her car. Even as a successful lawyer, Valentine could only afford to live in a basement apartment now.

When his daughter got in the passenger's seat instead of the driver's, and instructed him to sit in the back, he stood still for a moment, his head tilted to one side, as though momentarily malfunctioning. "Um, why?"

"Oh, sorry. Forgot to tell you. I've ordered us a driver."

He looked around the dilapidated neighborhood. No one was in sight.

"All right, then," he said, and got in.

They waited.

After some time a strange woman materialized in the driver's seat, giving Michael a start. "Sorry I'm late," she said. "I was finishing up with another client. Times like this I wish they'd let us run a second iteration. For work purposes only, you know? Just one more iteration!"

Valentine chuckled politely. "You aren't very late at all, dear. Only twenty seconds or so."

"Oh, I suppose you're right. Felt like twenty-thousand to me, is all." They exchanged smiles.

The car started without any apparent input from anyone, and then he saw the AI press the gas, steering left. The pedal and wheel responded to her touch.

"Excuse me," Michael said. "I don't mean to be rude—I'm new to the future—but how are you able to turn the wheel like that?"

"New to the future, eh? Aren't we all." The AI laughed. "I'm not actually steering with my hands, love. The car's internet-connected, and Val here's given me access to send it commands that way. Me pressing the pedal like this, and turning the wheel, that's just a comforting illusion, for both you and me. Believe it or not, AIs are just as partial to the trappings of biology as anybody."

Valentine's face popped up in front of him, next to a line of text: "A lot to learn, hey?"

He reached out to try and tap the text, and nothing happened. He tried tapping her face. Nothing. He frowned.

Another message came: "Just think to type, Dad. Remember?"

Right. "I just remembered something," he answered back. "The way I accused Craig of giving Horace my email address. He must hate me."

A couple seconds' delay, and then her reply came: "Actually, he's very remorseful about kicking you out of his house and then not talking to you until you were frozen. He's been looking forward to the day you woke for a long time, so you guys could reconcile."

That stretched the corners of his lips upward. So the future did have some happy parts after all.

"Craig doesn't talk to Luke either, by the way," Valentine messaged.

They made it to the east end of town, where the neuroplasticity clinic was located, in under fifteen minutes. The AI vanished soon after they parked, since Valentine planned to do some shopping in this area during Michael's appointment. First she led him inside, and then to the correct floor. He felt good about getting this done. His mind's deterioration was the source of a lot of stress, before and after cryosleep. He'd been afraid that the next stage would be forgetting his own children, and he didn't think he would be able to forgive himself for that sort of lapse.

The neuroplastician was a young woman named Sputum.

"I'm Michael," he said.

She had him sit in a chair that reformed itself around the contours of his body, and she told him to remain calm as she lowered an enormous helmet connected to an articulated metal arm over his head, blocking out his vision. Then the helmet began to whir as though something inside it were spinning around and around its rim, circling his head, at top speed. This went on for about ten minutes, which he determined by calling up a time display on his Smartans. It felt like a lot longer than that.

"Your brain shows the standard symptoms of an aging mind," Sputum said a couple minutes after the scan completed. She hadn't left the room—he supposed the machine must have sent the results straight to her own Smartans. "The therapy I'll recommend is completely uninvasive. If Alzheimer's had showed up, or something equally severe, we'd have to pursue nanotherapies. But your issues can be resolved with only the nerve receptors we already have access to, which we'll use to essentially reprogram your brain. Sound good?"

"Um, sure," he said. "What nerve receptors will you be, uh, reprogramming me with?"

"The ones on your tongue, chiefly. The human tongue has over fifteen thousand sensory receptors, making it ideal for neuromodulation."

"Uh huh," he said. "When do we start?"

"Right now." With her gloved hands, she picked up a piece of film from a nearby tray and handed it to him. "Place that on your tongue. And please give me access to your Smartans' brain scans. They'll provide me with enough data to ensure the process is going smoothly."

"How do I do that?"

"Just think it."

Before he left his first session with the neuroplastician she sent him some information on a local support group for people who'd undergone cryosleep for a long time. "There's more to mental health than just neuroplasticity," she said. "A lot more. Adjusting to a new time period is rough, even for a fully plastic brain. It's not just learning to use new technologies, because social norms have changed, too. Talking to others who have been time displaced can help a lot. The group meets every Thursday."

Before leaving the clinic he hesitated. "Should I, uh, feel any different? After the session?"

"Not right away. Those around you will often be the first to notice a change, especially for people with a brain as old as yours. But you'll find it gets easier to acquire new skills and learn new things, especially after we've had more sessions. I expect you and I will be doing around ten in total."

He thanked her and walked out to the elevator, shooting Valentine a message on his way down to let her know he was finished.

That night, back at her apartment, he called his son Craig. The process reminded him of using Skype in the 2020s, which he'd done once or twice at the prodding of his family. Except now no webcam was necessary, as there were sensors all over Valentine's house which, using footage from various angles, put together a composite that looked exactly like him, and did exactly what he did, so that it looked to Craig like Michael was sitting in his living room with him. As for Michael he felt like he was there, too. His Smartans made it so, showing Craig's house instead of Valentine's apartment.

They spoke well past midnight. (Michael's rediscovered ability to stay up that late still surprised him.) Craig looked not much older than Valentine—he'd availed of life extension too, of course. He'd remarried, to a woman who was authentically in her thirties, and he worked for an advertising agency, writing copy targeted at companies looking to buy ad space in popular skins for Montreal.

A lot of the things Craig told Michael about his life nearly made him wince. He didn't know how he felt about Craig dating a woman so much younger, and from what his son told him about the advertising job it sounded somewhat cynical and exploitative. But then, advertising had always been so. At least Craig seemed to have overcome his financial woes.

"You should visit, Dad," Craig said toward the end of the conversation. "Air travel's gotten quite expensive while you cryoslept, but we can help out with the cost. I'd love to see you again."

"I'd like that too." He'd never been to Montreal. "If you don't think I'll be too much of an imposition."

"Of course not. It's settled. You'll come out and spend a couple weeks with me and Rose. I can't wait for you to meet her."

*

The people he met at the support group for the time displaced were some of the least adorned he'd met since waking up in 2046. They'd barely altered their personal skins at all, which Michael confirmed by instructing his Smartans to show him the real view of the world. The first time he'd ever done that the things had displayed an alert: "Are you sure? But SmartWorld is so much cooler than the boring normal world!" An animated winky face emoticon accompanied the text. He reached out and pressed the "I'm sure" button. A fair number of the controls for Smartans were tactile, mostly those used for tasks that could easily be disrupted by stray thoughts, like indicating a preference.

Despite their lack of digital plumage it wasn't hard to tell that most here were exceedingly wealthy. Besides all the expensive clothing on display, almost everyone looked like smooth-faced twenty-year-olds, meaning they'd been able to afford cryopreservation, life extension, cosmetic surgery, and presumably neuroplasticity therapy. Michael had only had access to that because of the government's interest in him, and possibly some cash infusions provided by Luke.

The meeting's structure was familiar to him, based on what he knew of support groups from movies made decades ago. Everyone sat in a circle of chairs and took turns introducing themselves, followed by swapping life stories.

"I died from multiple sclerosis in 2019," one woman named Elizabeth said. "At the age of seventy-nine. Instead of burying me my three children used some of their inheritance to have me cryogenically preserved. When they brought me back, around this time last year, at first I thought I'd gone to hell."

That spooked Michael. He'd assumed much the same thing when the first person he saw after waking up informed him that his son Luke had died.

"All three of my children are dead," Elizabeth went on. "After freezing me they took a cruise to celebrate my life, since they figured, correctly, that a funeral was no longer necessary. Stupid idea, that. The ship sank at midnight, with them all passed out from an inordinate amount of alcohol. They all drowned."

"My family never had any respect for me," said the man whose turn it was next, as he peered around at those assembled. His name was Francis. "I entered cryosleep in 2030 to escape their constant judgement."

"What sort of judgement?" the meeting's leader asked.

"They didn't respect my efforts to grow as a person. I changed, and I changed, but nothing was ever good enough for them. I didn't notify any of them that I planned to be frozen, and I certainly haven't gotten back in touch now that I'm thawed. I'm sure they're capable of leading their miserable lives without me. God help them if they run out of money for life extension treatments. They'll get no money out of me."

After the group discussions everyone stood up and mingled over hors d'oeuvres. Michael ended up talking to Francis. Most of the hors d'oeuvres had come from a 3D printer. "They're easy to make," Francis told him. "You just fill the extruder with goop and the machine does the rest."

"Extruder?"

"That's the part that does the actual printing." Francis took a bite out of a spherical 3D-printed pastry snack, which had mushrooms and lichen-looking stuff growing from it. He held what remained aloft. "This is more delicious than it looks. You should try one."

"Yeah, okay." Michael could resist newness all he wanted, but he doubted it would make life any easier. Things were never going to change back to what he was used to. Time to try getting used to the way they actually were.

He popped an entire pastry into his mouth, chewed a couple times, then grinned at Francis with his mouth filled with masticated mush. Francis burst out laughing. Michael thought they might become friends.

"Do they still have church, in the future?" he asked. "I haven't gone in, oh, around twenty years. About time I went back."

His new friend nodded. "They do, but it isn't as popular as it once was. Turns out there are atheists in foxholes. A lot of them. I go every Sunday, though. What denomination are you?"

"Roman Catholic. You?"

"The very same. You should come with me this week. The congregation's sparse, and it's mostly old people, but at least they don't look old anymore."

"As long as you have your Smartans turned on, that is."

Francis gave him an appraising look. "I never turn mine off anymore. The world's gotten far too ugly."

"I like to keep in touch with reality. Such as it is."

"Respectable, I suppose. Will I pick you up Sunday morning?"

"It's a date. Do I need to give you my number, or something?"

"Nah. We've both been added to each other's contacts just by having this conversation."

Sunday morning came, and Michael got up bright and early to iron and dress in the suit he and Valentine had gone shopping for the day before. He could have just relied on a skin for his formal wear—plenty of people did, transposing it over a less impressive outfit—but this was important to him, and Valentine sensed that. She didn't suggest it was foolish or unnecessary. Instead she helped him pick one out, and gave him her thoughts when he tried on each one and emerged from the dressing room to show her.

When Francis arrived Valentine peered out the ground-level window, parting the blinds with a finger. "He has a nice car," she reported from where she stood on tiptoe. "And he's driving it himself. That's daring." Nowadays it was considered much safer to have an AI drive you, and fairly cheap, too. "Oops!" Valentine released the window and plastered herself against the nearby wall, looking at Michael sheepishly. "I think he saw me."

He smiled at her, gave her a kiss on the cheek, and made for the door.

"Enjoy yourself," she called after him.

"I'll see you later. Have a good morning."

Francis drove a Cadillac, which was apparently still 'a thing,' as the younger folks said. Or at least his octogenarian children said it. Michael opened the passenger door, bade Francis good morning, and sat. They rode to church in silence, which he enjoyed. It reminded him of spending time with Stephen, his son who'd died so many years ago. Stephen had known his way around a silence too.

Michael hadn't felt this peaceful since being revived from cryosleep. Maybe this life wouldn't be so overwhelming after all. As long as he could find like-minded souls as Francis seemed to be, still attend church and develop his relationship with God, he thought that maybe he could get by. Since his wife Linda had died the thought that he would one day join her in heaven had provided him the comfort he needed to get through day-to-day life with a body that was slowly falling apart. Now, even after being rejuvenated physically, his belief in God allowed him to think that he still would join her one day. That Luke was wrong—that he wasn't a prisoner in this body, this world, this life. That there was a chance one day he would ascend to be with Linda and the Holy Father, having cleansed himself by begging forgiveness for his many sins.

In the meantime he would try to be happy and help out his family however he could.

Francis had told the truth about the paltry attendance. The lack of interest seemed to infect the priest himself as he navigated the rituals of Mass and delivered an uninspiring sermon. It didn't diminish Michael's enjoyment. He found that he remembered the rote utterances of the call and answer. The faith-affirming words bolstered and energized him. He felt reborn, in a way that attending church had never made him feel before.

The possibility struck him that maybe he felt this way because of the obvious lack of interest in church. He felt like one of the early Christians, who were few in number, marginalized, but galvanized in their certainty that Christ would return soon. Given the current fortunes of the world he would not be surprised to learn that the last days were almost upon them.

Afterward he and Francis went for coffee at the Cool Beans Café, which Michael remembered from the park bench ad he heard on his first day. Their conversation soon turned to the foibles of the younger generations, a topic Michael admittedly took some pleasure in, though not without a slight tinge of guilt. "It's no wonder the economy is in the toilet," Francis said. "Young people today waste their time on completely unproductive activities. Cultivating their social media presence, endlessly tweaking their personal skins, and complaining constantly. They whine about the way the world is, and meanwhile our entire society is geared toward them. The younger market is by far the most lucrative, mostly because they're so adept at siphoning money from their parents, and advertisers know it. They point everything at them, all those personalized commercials, everything."

Michael wrapped his hands around his coffee mug so that they soaked up its warmth. "It is pretty off-putting how self-obsessed they are," he said. "I made the mistake of allowing my son to bring me to a bar on my first day here. The way I saw these youngsters staring at each other, without a trace of shame or modesty..."

Francis had a way of making eye contact for uncomfortably long periods. It lent him a fervency that he probably didn't actually possess. Now his gaze intensified even more. "The thing I hate most about this time period is how unforgiving it is. Your mistakes, which in the past would have been briefly lamented over and forgotten, are dragged into the public arena and lynched. Missteps follow you around forever. The pressure is enough to make someone snap, and it often does. Gun crime is on the rise, and now we have nanocrime, which is even scarier. Enough to make someone snap, I tell you."

Michael nodded, not replying, seeking to lapse into the easy silence that had characterized their car ride to church. The word 'nanocrime' jogged something in his memory. Wasn't that how Luke had been killed?

They did resume the sort of quiet that Michael so cherished, and they mostly maintained it until pulling into Valentine's driveway. "This was fun," Francis said. "Thanks for accompanying me."

"My pleasure. Can I give you some gas money?"

"No need. This baby's one hundred percent solar powered."

"Wow. Marvelous."

"It's ridiculous all cars aren't solar. I, at least, like to keep it green. Someone has to. Give the planet some breathing room, know what I mean?"

"Makes sense to me. Same time next week?"

"Same time next week, friend." Francis reached out a hand, and Michael clasped it. Then he got out of the car and walked up the driveway, turning back to wave once. Francis saluted him as he pulled back out onto the road.

Michael could have jumped into the air and clicked his heels. Finally, he seemed to be easing into a comfortable groove where he could exist in contentment. The new technology was opening itself to him, and he'd found a new friend. Maybe he could even find a way to make himself useful to his offspring. That brought a smile.

He found Valentine leaning over the counter, tears falling into the sink. Michael crossed the kitchen and laid a hand on her shoulder. "Sweetheart. What is it?"

She turned to him. Her eyes were bloodshot, and the area beneath them was swollen. She'd clearly been crying for a long time.

"It's Craig," she said. "He's dead."

*

For the next couple of days Michael didn't have an inclination to do much of anything, other than pore over the details surrounding his son's death as they came to light.

He spent a lot of the time crying. He'd now outlived half his children. It seemed so unnatural, and it made him even more fearful that Luke's immortality theory would turn out to be true.

Craig's wife returned home from work that day to find her husband sprawled across their living room floor, pale and motionless. A few inches from his hand had been a snack he'd printed using their 3D printer, which he'd purchased a year ago to speed up meal making. Work had followed Craig home a lot, and he valued the ability to whip up something to eat just by sending the printer a command.

But something had gone wrong. The 3D printer had multiple filament chambers, some containing organic, edible matter, and others holding inedible plastics, metals, ceramics, and so on. Unbeknownst to Craig and his wife their plastic filament had contained an unusual amount of cyanide, way above regulation. That wouldn't have been a major issue, except for some reason the printer inserted a significant amount of plastic filament into the pastry it had made for him, switching back and forth between the two chambers during the printing process, inserting enough cyanide-laced plastic to kill him but not so much that he would detect it immediately and stop eating. It didn't seem like an accident. It seemed carefully designed.

A few days ago Valentine had helped Michael to set up an account on Britely, a popular social media service, and now he watched as everyone buzzed about what had happened. People had died from weapons made using 3D printers before, but this was the first time someone was poisoned by a printer they owned, inside their own home. He watched a lot of fearful posts flit across his feed. Companies that sold 3D printers saw their stock prices plummet.

Three days after Craig's death, Michael received a visit from two government agents who were conducting an investigation. They asked Valentine to find something else to do outside the apartment. She cast Michael an anxious look, but she put on her shoes and did as she was told. What else could she do?

The female agent introduced herself as Agent Jada McQuaid, the male as only Agent Peele. The latter name, along with the young man's face, caused an uneasy stirring in the back of Michael's mind, but he couldn't discern why.

"To what do I owe the pleasure?" he asked after offering both of them tea, which they refused.

"You haven't figured it out?" Peele said.

There. It was the snippy attitude that brought it back for him. "You," Michael said, pointing. "You're the one who forced me into cryosleep."

Peele nodded, and he actually looked abashed. "Yes. I owe you an apology for that, Mr. Haynes. I treated you brashly that day, and there wasn't any need for it. I do believe what I did benefited Canadians, and humanity in general. But I didn't offer you the respect an upstanding gentleman like you deserves. For that, I am deeply sorry."

Michael blinked. A heartfelt apology from a government official? He thought he'd seen everything in his century's worth of life. "Thank you," he said. "I accept. Is that why they sent you in particular? Because you know me?"

Again, Peele nodded. "I normally don't do much field work nowadays. But it was agreed that since I had prior dealings with you it would be best for me to come. I'm sorry if my visiting stirs up painful memories."

"It's fine. But I'm curious as to why I'm being visited by agents at all. What could I possibly have to tell you about my son's murder? He lived in Montreal. I can't possibly be a suspect."

"Not you," Agent McQuaid said. She brought a hand in front of her face, tapping the air, flicking it, and then making a smooth semicircle. That done, she re-established eye contact with him. "Someone you spoke to very recently."

"Your son's death has all the markings of an AI's work," Peele said.

"Hmm." Michael drummed his fingers on his knee. "Someone hacked Craig's printer. Couldn't that have been anyone?"

"It wasn't just hacking the printer," McQuaid said. "The attacker also hacked the factory where the plastic filament was made, to increase the cyanide content of one specific batch. Whoever it was knew that batch would be sent to Craig, among other customers. They performed the tampering covertly enough that the company didn't realize what had happened till the batch had been shipped to customers' homes. The company issued a recall, which was successful, except that the notice sent to your son's Smartans was intercepted. Only then did the perpetrator hack your son's printer, and waited till the moment he used it to make something to eat, carefully distributing the cyanide throughout the food so that your son wouldn't detect it until it was too late."

Peele sniffed. "Security measures have become incredibly refined since the day you entered cryosleep, Mr. Haynes. To avoid the factory's intrusion detection systems, the hacker would have had to be incredibly nimble."

"As fast as an AI," McQuaid finished.

"You suspect Luke," Michael said.

They both nodded.

"But he lives here in Newfoundland. Craig died in Montreal."

"AIs can travel anywhere there are sensors. Instantaneously. Besides, he could have easily performed the attack remotely, from anywhere he wanted."

"What would his motive have been?"

"We don't know yet," Peele said. "But murder victims are far more likely to have been killed by a family member than a stranger. And we suspected your son was a sociopath when we dealt with him during his tenure as CEO of Healthr. Since he uploaded, we believe he's gotten much worse. It's possible Craig knew something damning about Luke. Something that would result in him getting shut down."

Michael shook his head. He didn't believe Luke had killed Craig. He couldn't believe it. But that wouldn't mean anything to the agents. Instead he said, "You thought he was a sociopath, and you used him to achieve your own ends. What does that make you?"

"The government avails itself of whatever tools are necessary," said McQuaid.

"You don't have to tell me twice. I'll ask you again. Why are you here?"

There followed another ten minutes or so of dissembling and preventive ass-covering. Finally, Michael learned what they wanted: for him to give them access to his Smartans, so they could see what he saw and hear what he heard, and to pay Luke a visit. Engage him in conversation, about Craig and about other things. Learn whatever he could.

"We'll be waiting in a vehicle nearby," Peele said. "In case you run into any trouble."

"If I'm going to do this for you I want you to be straight with me, for at least a second. This isn't about access to my Smartans, and to suggest as much is insulting to my intelligence. You can access my Smartans any time you want. You can access anyone's. What's important is that I go see Luke, right? The conversation we'll have is important. Access isn't an issue for you."

Peele and McQuaid wore identically bland expressions. "We're not at liberty to discuss that with you."

"You won't give an old man even one second of honesty, before he goes and does your dirty work for you?"

"Like I said. We're not at liberty."

"Very well. Let's get this over with. When do you want to do it?"

"Now would be good."

"All right."

He sent a message to Valentine telling her the house was free, and that he would be gone with the agents for a while. "Don't worry about me," he said. "I'm not in any trouble." He considered telling her not to message him until he got back, since his Smartans would be under increased scrutiny from the government, but decided against it. That would look suspicious, and anyway he expected Valentine already knew enough not to do that.

Michael might have had his conversation with Luke right there in Valentine's basement apartment—after all, as an AI his son could teleport there in less than a second. Except, Valentine had permanently blocked her brother from ever accessing her home's sensors. Michael felt certain that the relationship between brother and sister had been irreparably damaged.

Halfway to Esther's apartment, the agents told him to come up with a pretext for visiting Luke. He couldn't just show up and start asking about Craig's death. That would obviously rouse his son's suspicion. By the time they arrived, the best Michael could come up with was that he wanted to speak with Luke about Esther and her erratic behavior. That would at least have the benefit of containing some truth.

As they neared downtown, he called Luke to get the address. The agents dropped him off two blocks away and he walked. He couldn't find a doorbell, so he sent Luke a message. Instantly, his son appeared before him on the front step. "I've unlocked the door for you," he said, "but I'm not able to actually open it. You'll have to see to that yourself."

He did, and they both walked inside. Now they stood in a shared porch, with a staircase leading up to the right and another door on the left. "That door is us," Luke said. "It's unlocked too."

Michael opened it to reveal a long, tilted hallway. "What's going on with the floor?"

"The house is a century and a half old. Older than you, even. The kitchen is at the end of the hall, behind the curtain. Help yourself to some coffee if you like."

Soon they were both sitting at a faux mahogany table, which was faded and scored in several places, with a knife from the looks of it. Michael had opted for tea, while Luke enjoyed an incorporeal glass of red wine. "To what do I owe the pleasure?" his son asked him.

"Did you hear about Craig?" It would be odd if he didn't bring it up at all.

Luke nodded, and gazed at the floor, his eyebrows knitted together. "I cried."

"I'm not sure I believe that."

"AIs retain the full range of human emotion."

"That isn't why I'm doubtful."

"He was my brother, Dad. I'm not a monster, though I'm sure you and Valentine think I am. I hoped I would get a chance to reconcile with Craig."

"You could have traveled to Montreal at any time. Instantaneously."

"Who told you that?"

"I've learned a few things since we parted company. You're not the only source of information."

"Far from it." Luke shrugged. "Craig's death is tragic, but he did live a long time. By twentieth century standards, anyway. Besides, he's still alive somewhere. Just not in this universe."

"Shut up." The urge to punch his son had returned.

"What are you here about, Dad? Just to talk about Craig?"

"About Esther, actually, who I'm more worried about than ever. It looks like Craig may have been murdered. Who knows what might happen to her, with the sort of people she must hang out with in those clubs?" An alert popped up then from Agent McQuaid, cautioning him against being too direct in probing Luke for information about Craig's death. Michael tried not to react to the alert, but he thought his son was studying his face more carefully now.

Luke shook his head. "You're a walking stereotype, you know that Dad? Esther is fine. Of the two of you, I'd wager you're the one who's more lost."

"Her entire generation's lost. Or at least, the one she's apparently decided to join. To regress into." In order to continue this line of conversation as convincingly as he could, he decided to take a page from his new friend Francis's book. "I think young people are largely to blame for this weak economy. They don't seem interested in doing anything to move things forward. They just obsess over their Smartans, spending all their time constructing artificial personas."

"Whoa. You've started neuroplasticity therapy, haven't you?"

"I've had three sessions. Valentine's been paying for me to go. Why?"

"It shows. You're a different man from the one who doddered out of that cryogenic clinic." Luke ran a hand back through his hair, his avatar flawlessly simulating the individual follicles flicking forward. "As for the younger generation doing boring, predictable things, what else do you expect them to do? They're the most intensely surveilled demographic in the country, with the government competing with corporations to track their every move. Everything youths do that's even slightly out of the ordinary is scrutinized with a suspicious eye, and they know it.

Of course they conform to what's expected of them—browse the skin store endlessly, go to clubs, use dating apps, buy what products they can afford, rinse, repeat. To do otherwise would be deviant, and deviant behavior is watched closely, often penalized. But deviance is a necessary ingredient of innovation. Because innovation is out of the ordinary. And the powers that be have succeeded in quashing it completely. That's why the economy falters."

That way of viewing things hadn't occurred to Michael, but it made sense. He had no rebuttal for it. Instead he said, "So that's what Esther had decided to subject herself to? Constant scrutiny? Being stifled creatively?"

"Esther's a special case. She had her childhood and adolescence stolen from her, as you well know. Now she's been given a chance to be a sulky, bratty, promiscuous young lady, and she's taking it. Is she ever taking it."

Michael grimaced.

"And she doesn't let the surveillance get to her," Luke went on. "Like you, and me, Esther comes from a generation that remembers what it's like to be free. So she is free. She doesn't let the government scare her. It can do what it wants to her, if it comes to that, as far as she's concerned. In the meantime she's going to party."

"Ask him more about Esther," said a message from Peele.

"What does she do for money?" Michael said. "All that partying surely must cost her something."

"She writes erotica fiction, actually." From the way his eyes danced, and the corners of his mouth twitched, Luke was evidently enjoying this conversation. "For consumption by old people who don't have her courage. Like you, for instance. You should check her stuff out. It's good. All based on her own experiences."

"Does she do well?"

"Pretty well. People don't have as much money for reading as they once did. But she makes enough for her purposes. And anyway, my Healthr stock is still doing well considering the recent shocks to the economy. So I pay my share of the rent, and that helps."

The front door opened then, and closed with a bang. Next, the interior door. Someone stomped down the hall without bothering to take shoes off.

The curtain swept aside, and there stood his daughter. The new version—nineteen by all appearances, confident, beautiful. Not the aging, mousy version he remembered. Seeing her for the second time was no less shocking. "Father," she said. "What are you doing here?"

"Where were you, is what I'd like to know."

She exchanged glances with Luke. "Is he for real?"

"I'm afraid so," Luke said.

Esther opened the fridge and took out a bottle of beer, cracked it open, and pointed the bottom at the ceiling.

Bringing up a time display, Michael clucked his tongue. "It's barely three o'clock."

"Later than I thought," she said. "If you must know, father, I was writing at a coffee shop. I write porn novels."

"I told him that," Luke said.

Michael groaned.

"You look around twenty-five now, Dad," Esther said. "But you still act like you're ancient. You don't have to, you know. You've recovered your youth in one way. Why not go for the other?" She turned to Luke. "Let's go clubbing tonight and take Dad. Show him a good time."

"Traumatize him, you mean?" Luke said. "He'll never come."

"Go with them," came the order from McQuaid.

He tried not to wince. "I'll come."

Luke's simulated eyebrows shot toward his simulated hair. Esther just smiled. "Awesome," she said, standing. "I'll go get changed."

*

They decided to take him to a bar called Lust, which, Michael learned from consulting her Britely profile, was Esther's favorite place on George Street. *Go figure.* As they walked down, he used his Smartans to call up information on the bar itself. It catered principally to twenty-somethings. When he put on a video that had been taken at Lust last weekend, he was surprised when the audio came on. Neither Luke nor Esther seemed to hear anything. *The sensors on the ground must know I'm watching this.*

In the video, sleek aliens twisted and gyrated around a perfectly transparent dance floor, making it seem like they danced on air. Beneath them, what looked like miles under the invisible floor, a vast fire raged. Interspersed throughout the flames were isolated circles of open ground, where demons poked, prodded, and whipped wretched creatures with slug-like skin. Using Smartans, the club's owners had made it look like the revelers pranced above Hell.

"I don't know that this is the best idea," Michael said, slowing his pace.

"Why?" Luke asked.

"I just—" He wanted to mention the video, but knew that explaining his reaction would make him seem lame. "I've never been much of a dancer." And it would feel so bizarre, dancing with kids eighty years his junior.

"There's an app for that," Esther said, and a message from her appeared before him. Attached he found a link to an app that would show him how to move while dancing to any song, by displaying ghostly limbs that hovered in the air until he matched their positions.

"All right. Fine." He sighed.

When they reached George Street it was only four in the evening, so they decided to go get dinner before starting to drink. Luke suggested a nearby burger place, which was interesting since he would be the only one not actually eating the food. The idea went over well with Esther, and Michael just shrugged. "Sure," he said.

He ordered the hottest burger on the menu, one packed with jalapenos and soaked in sriracha sauce. Lately new experiences drew him in, like a stray hair circling a drain. He didn't know whether that came with the neuroplastician visits or just a desire to get as much from those visits as possible.

Despite the weirdness of the situation he found himself relaxing over the food with his children. They laughed when his face turned red from eating too much of his fire burger too quickly—but without the actual derision they'd directed at him before. Esther told him the titles of some of her stories so he could look them up and see how well-reviewed they were. Then she told them the inspiration for some of the funny scenes. And Michael didn't feel as uncomfortable as he would have expected.

At the same time he experienced an underlying, low-level guilt throughout the meal, for enjoying a good time without Valentine, shared with the brother and sister she barely spoke to. He hadn't enjoyed a similar night out with his eldest daughter since being woken from cryosleep. Instead he'd only eaten her food, slept in her guest room, and accepted her loan of money. He'd been selfish, and he would have to suggest they do something together at the earliest opportunity.

They remained in the restaurant talking long enough that the manager began to stalk by their table periodically, leering at them for continuing to occupy a table, despite that the place was nearly deserted.

"Should we humor him and buy a round of drinks?" Esther said.

"Nah," Luke said. "That will only condition him to continue acting like a tool. Let's move onto George Street proper."

Above them the sky was still visible—the ad-covered dome only materialized when darkness fell according to Luke. Lust didn't open till ten, and they walked to a pub to talk and drink away the hours in between. When The Beatles appeared on a tiny stage in the corner and began playing "Hello, Goodbye," Michael decided he likely would have had a heart attack if he'd still had his hundred-year-old body.

Finally it was time to transition to Lust. They left the bar and found themselves walking under the black, glistening dome, ads everywhere vying for their attention. The street's population was still fairly sparse. George Street didn't truly become crowded until midnight.

Someone called his name, and he turned to find Francis dressed in a well-tailored suit, hands in his pockets, regarding them coolly. Michael went over to him, smiling, which the man didn't return. "Hello, friend."

"Michael. How are you?"

"I'm great." By this time he'd downed a few pints, and knew he was speaking with more enthusiasm than he normally would. *What of it?* "Do you know Luke and Esther?"

Francis's lips tightened. "I didn't know you spent your weekends with children."

"We're all children, now," Luke said. "Whether we like it or not."

"An interesting viewpoint." Francis jerked a thumb over his shoulder at two men who were walking away in that direction. "My colleagues are getting ahead of me. Excuse me."

"Friend of yours?" Esther said.

"I think so. We met at a cryosleep support group."

"An old fogey," Luke said.

Michael nodded. "Like me." They continued on to Lust.

The great inferno he'd seen in the video was not in evidence. Maybe that happened later, or was confined to another room, deeper inside the bar. No one danced in the front room, not yet anyway, and those that crossed the dance floor walked not over a fiery hell but through a sparkling galaxy, pinprick stars swirling around their heads. Michael caught himself before reaching out to touch one, realizing that was likely gauche. None of the other patrons paid the cosmos that surrounded them any mind.

A young man approached, his lizard-like eyes taking up half his face. He seemed to know Esther. They embraced, and he made eye contact with Michael as they did, a ruby-red forked tongue flicking out at him and disappearing just as quick.

"Is tonight the night you take me home with you?" the newcomer said to Esther.

"Hey," Michael said. "Take it easy."

Lizardface narrowed his huge eyes as much as they would narrow. "Who are you, her father?" Esther and Luke burst out laughing. "What? What did I say?"

"Let's get drinks," Esther said to Michael and Luke. "I'll talk to you later, okay Brett?"

"Oh. All right." At being dismissed, Lizardface deflated.

"Maybe you should stick to your own species," Michael said to him as he walked past, which he had to admit wasn't at all necessary.

Esther glared back at him. "Dad, could you chill out please?" She ordered an elaborate drink that came in a tall, fluted glass, while Luke conjured a bong packed with pot from midair.

"Isn't smoking in bars still banned?" Michael said.

"For you it is." He produced a lighter, flicked it, and inhaled.

Michael just got another pint. As he paid, he realized the agents hadn't sent him any messages since Esther's apartment. Maybe they'd decided it was better to allow the night to progress naturally than to bombard him with suggestions. It was possible they were hoping Luke would start to slip as he got more inebriated. AIs could get drunk and stoned just like biological humans could, but unlike them, AIs could sober up immediately. Plus, even drunk they had a thousand times longer to weigh each remark. Still. Luke's altered state of mind could lead to something, if he was indeed Craig's killer. Michael really didn't think he was, but defying the agents would likely be unwise. Besides, if Luke was innocent like Michael thought then it was just as important to prove that.

Luke ran into a couple other AIs, and after a few minutes of chatting the three of them wandered off together. "Should I stick with Luke?" Michael sent to McQuaid. He received no response. *That's odd.*

"You're doing well in the Meltdown," Esther said to him.

"What?"

"Throughout the night everyone in the club votes for who they think is the hottest guy and the hottest girl. The winners get announced at one o'clock. Right now you're tied for second."

He looked into the bottom of his glass, which was empty. "I need a drink." As he walked toward the bar Esther sent him another attachment—the Meltdown app. When he activated it, everyone in the bar acquired a vote tally that floated over their heads, paired with a rank.

Upon arriving at the bar, a man with blue fire for hair offered to buy him a shot. "Sure," Michael said. "Whiskey." Despite that others had been there waiting before him, the bartender served Michael first. He knocked the shot back.

"What's the follow up?" the shot buyer said.

"Beer. Are you buying me that too?"

"Sure am," he said, waving the bartender back over.

As they were waiting for two pints to be poured, Flamehair asked him what his plans were for when the bar shut down. "You going to an after party or anything?"

"No plans to."

"Well keep me posted, yeah?"

"Uh, all right. Why?"

"Look at your rank, man. You'll be surrounded by girls. There'll be a hefty surplus, and you'll need me to take some of them off your hands."

Michael frowned. "Thanks for the drink." He turned and walked into the crowd to find Esther. Before he'd gone four steps, a raven-haired woman with shadowy wings sprouting from her back laid a hand on his arm. Above her head floated a number one.

She raised herself onto her toes to whisper into his ear.

"What?" he said. The music had drowned out her voice.

She tried again. "I hope you win the Meltdown," she said. "You have my vote."

He smiled. "Maybe you'll get mine."

"Maybe I'll see you on the dance floor." She melted away, and the growing press of bodies swallowed her up.

He went looking for Esther and found her in a room styled like an otherworldly wrestling arena, with bunches of spectators appearing to stand on clouds that moved with them as they walked around the ring. Glaring at each other from opposite sides of the arena, standing on elevated platforms, leaning against railings of obsidian, the contenders controlled the combatants with their minds. At least, that's what Esther told him was happening. The combatants themselves were an enormous musclebound gorilla clad in dinted steel armor, hairs sprouting between the gaps, and a centaur with a scarred dolphin head where centaurs traditionally had a human torso. When the gorilla picked up the centaur-dolphin and bodyslammed him, the room actually shook. The centaur-dolphin scrabbled to its feet, emitted a series of defiant clicking noises, and charged. They fought to screechy, up-tempo music, like a mixture between dance and hard rock.

"You've ascended to number one," Esther told him, glancing at the air above his head. "You'll have a good night, if you want it."

"What does a good night entail?"

"I think you know. Here's a pro tip: using the Meltdown app, anyone in the top three can establish a private messaging conversation with anyone else in the top three, male or female. If you wanted to, for instance, get to know each other. Start with a dance, maybe."

The dancing had begun in earnest. After ducking into the washroom and catching himself admiring the number one above his head in the mirror, he entered a new room—or maybe one he'd already been in, with a different skin—to find a tightly-packed throng flowing against each other, grinding, touching, atop a dusty mesa. A desert lay below, impossibly far away. Now that he stood on the plateau with the other revelers he could no longer see the entrance he'd emerged from. The illusion was complete. He activated the dancing app and set it to Solo Dance. The instructions were easy to follow, adjusting on-the-fly to his reaction time, anticipating the music's flow so that he didn't look ridiculous.

He sent a message to the other number one, the woman who'd accosted him near the bar. The message contained only his geotag, telling her exactly where he was. A minute later she appeared, and he set the app to Couple Dance. They flowed wordlessly together, encircling, pressing close, at one with the rhythm, and with each other.

The app told him to place his hands on her waist, and he did, shocked by how much of her fit in his grasp. It told him to draw nearer, and he did that too. It told him to trail his fingers down to her lower stomach. She spun in his grasp, raising her arms to encompass his head, bringing her face maddeningly close to his. Then she twisted again, pressing against him. The app told him to squeeze her buttocks. His hands moved to comply, but he stopped himself at the last possible second. He backed away from her, blinking. *I can't do this.* She turned, a confused expression on her face. Then the barren mesa vanished. He'd stepped backwards into the hallway he'd been in before, which led to the room with the battling monsters.

She appeared again, her confusion replaced with concern. The music was much softer here somehow, and they were able to actually speak.

"What's the matter?" she asked. "I'm Brit, by the way."

"I'm Michael. Brit, I'm sorry. I don't know what I'm doing. Not sure I'm cut out for this scene just yet. This may shock you, but I'm a lot older than I look. One-hundred years, to be exact. Older than that if you count cryosleep."

Brit smiled. "I'm ninety-three. Not counting cryosleep."

He tried not to gape. "Wow. You look really good for ninety-three."

"Likewise. Isn't the future great?"

"It's okay."

"What happened to you in there?"

Michael paused, hesitant to admit his need of the dancing app, feeling somehow like it was cheating. But he didn't want to lie. "My daughter sent me this app that tells you how to move when you're dancing. I'm a clueless dancer. The app told me to grab your bum. I couldn't believe it. Made me think I'm really out of touch."

Brit shook her head. "You're not out of touch. Your thinking's quite in keeping with current norms, actually. If you'd grabbed my ass I would have slapped you, as most women would nowadays, and you'd likely be thrown out of the bar. If you reported that app they'd be banned from selling it. I'm surprised it hasn't already been banned. I'm thinking the app glitched, or maybe someone tampered with it to get it to tell you to do that. Get you in trouble."

"I can't think who would. Certainly not my daughter. I'm sure she knows better than that."

"If it was a skilled hacker you may never know who. Probably wasn't even personal. A lot of assholes do that kind of thing just because they think it's funny."

"Sick."

"Yeah. You wanna come get another drink with me?"

They walked arm-in-arm back through the wrestling arena, where a shining robot dressed in tattered rags struggled against a freakishly large pirate with patches covering both her eyes and with bells in her hair. Michael didn't see Esther anywhere. He thought about sending her a message, but decided against it.

As they approached the bar for another drink he saw her. She was on the dance floor that resembled a galaxy, writhing against a tall, impossibly muscled man, whose shirt was elsewhere and whose head had been replaced by that of a horse. Instead of tiny stars floating calmly through the room the galaxy was now a whirling vortex, filled with hurtling asteroids and planets with erratic orbits and moons that zoomed around them, all pulsing to the music.

Esther and the horse man moved against each other in far more scandalous fashion than his app had recommended. He noticed Brit watching him glare at them, so he explained: "That's my daughter."

"Hmm," she said.

"What happened to current norms?" he said.

"Well, I was referring to norms surrounding the importance of consent. If she consented to dancing that way, then..."

Michael didn't consent to it. He felt like a couple of those asteroids were knocking around the inside of his skull. His heart rate quickened, and his chest constricted with anger. He walked toward them through the throng of dancers. The guy couldn't really have that many muscles, right? *Must be the Smartans.*

"That's enough," he said once he reached them, grabbing them both by the shoulders and wrenching them apart. Judging from the feel of the horse man's shoulder, he really didn't have a shirt on, and his muscles really were quite large. Still, Michael was surprised by the ease with which he parted the man from his daughter. Michael's new body was quite strong too.

"What's the big deal?" horse man said.

Esther said, "Dad! What are you doing?"

"This guy's your dad?" The horse head looked confused, though whether by how close in age to her father Esther looked or their different racial appearances, Michael couldn't tell. The horse man resolved his cognitive dissonance by walking away without another word. Esther rounded on Michael.

"How dare you?" she screamed, pushing him. He didn't travel very far.

"I'm your father, young lady."

"I'm almost eighty, you asshole," she said, and walked briskly away in the direction Horsehead had gone. Michael returned to where Brit waited for him by the bar, feeling slightly bemused, and dejected.

Luke was there too, and when he saw Michael he frowned. "Saw your little freak out on the dance floor. Way to go, Dad of the Year."

"Did you see the way she was dancing with that creature?"

"Yeah, same way she dances every weekend." Luke rolled his eyes. "Bringing you out with us was a mistake. You still think you can micromanage your family, despite that you've been out of touch with the times for decades. Esther still isn't a fortress of emotional stability, you know. She doesn't need this."

Michael clenched his jaw and said nothing.

Luke shook his head. "You haven't changed a bit." He looked at Brit. "Who's this?"

"This is Brit. Brit, this is my insolent son Luke."

"Pleasure," Brit said, sticking out her hand, all warmth.

"I'm an AI," Luke said. But he stuck his hand out all the same, trying his best to pantomime a handshake without actual contact. "Pleased to meet you." A smile sprouted on his face—the sort he wore when having a joke at his father's expense. "Just got a message from Esther. Looks like she's taking home the guy she was dancing with. Wow. That was fast. Anyway." He turned back to Brit. "Seems like you guys are a shoe-in for winning Meltdown together. How will you celebrate?" His grin got even slyer.

"I was planning to ask Brit to have dinner with me," Michael said. "Later this week."

"Sounds delightful," she said. "But first, I'll get us drinks. And for you, Luke, I've just paid for an hour's worth of access."

His digital son raised his eyebrows. "Seems like a keeper," he said to Michael in a mock whisper.

As Brit was paying for another beer for him and a vodka highball for herself, Michael got a message from Esther too: "Help. I'm in the alley around the side of the club. Come now."

He looked at Luke, who was looking at him. "Did you just get another message from Esther?"

Luke nodded. "Let's go." Brit was still facing the bar, and didn't notice them leaving over the loud music. *No matter. I'll message her later.* He barreled through the club, pushing aside anyone who got in his way. His daughter was in trouble. A bouncer sitting on a stool nearby stood, his eyebrows drawing down to meet above his nose. He shouted, but Michael didn't stop. *No time.* Another bouncer made a grab for him as he ran out the exit, and Michael shrugged him off.

Ahead, from the alley, Luke shouted for him to hurry. He must have teleported there. "Come on, Dad! I'm a fucking AI, I can't do anything!"

A woman's shriek, cutting through the air. *Esther.*

His heartbeat a frenetic tattoo against his ribcage, Michael rounded the corner to see Luke standing helplessly, fists clenched, and beyond him Esther with a knife held to her neck. Holding the knife was Francis, who also had an arm wrapped tightly around his daughter's torso.

"Hello, Michael," he said.

"Francis?" All at once his brain felt like an egg that had been thrown onto the sidewalk and left to sizzle. "What are you doing?"

"Wrong question." Francis brought the knife up and slashed it across Esther's cheek, covering her mouth with his other hand to muffle the scream of pain. Michael gasped. Blood spurted between Francis's fingers, quickly soaking them in red. More dribbled through to the cobblestone below. "We don't have much time here. You better get smarter quick, Michael. I can't wait around while you go have another neuroplasticity session."

He couldn't recall telling Francis about seeing a neuroplastician. "What's the right question?" he said, taking a step closer. "What should I be asking you?"

Francis smiled. He clearly enjoyed having control of the situation. "The correct question would be what have you done to bring me to this?"

"I don't know, Francis. I just met you." Were Peele and McQuaid watching this? Were they on their way?

The man brought the knife to just below Esther's shoulder, slashing again. Michael cried out, this time. His daughter was being mutilated in front of him. He felt each cut as if he was the one under the knife.

All this time Luke had been staring into space, wearing a pained expression. Michael assumed he'd gone into shock, till his eyes focused on the man holding Esther and he spoke a single word that changed everything.

"*Horace.*"

That brought a twisted smile. "Luke. You always were the intelligent one in the family."

Michael felt the blood draining from his face. "How?" he managed.

"Clearly you didn't die in that boat accident," Luke said.

"You got it," Horace said. "That was faked—I had a breather in my pocket, ready for the moment the sailboat capsized. It was crucial that my apparent death happen on the water, because that's the only place without sensors nowadays. It was important that the government think I really was dead."

"So that they would allow your AI brain to be activated. You uploaded, didn't you?"

Horace nodded. "A piece of information I never shared with my wretched family. Now I exist as an AI and a human being. And the government has no idea."

Luke looked displeased at the distinction between AIs and humans, but he said nothing.

"You killed Craig," Michael said. "Didn't you?"

Horace laughed. "I'm going to murder all your children, brother. You'll get to mourn them all. Then I'll kill you."

"Why?"

"Why not? I came to you, Michael. I came to you on your deathbed and asked your forgiveness. Not to get a piece of the cursed family land, like you accused me of. I told you I'd changed, and I really had. I was filled with regret about what I did to Esther, and to our parents. To you. I never expected you to live—no one did—and I only wanted your forgiveness before you left this world."

"You clearly don't want that now."

"No. That ship has sailed. But if you'd granted me the forgiveness I craved back then, I likely would have died within the next twenty years at most. But your cruelty motivated me. I sought life extension from the government, and I got it. My youth has been restored—but so have my urges." To Michael's disbelief, tears rolled down Horace's cheek, though he gripped Esther even tighter. "I have sinned again. I never wanted to do that to anyone, ever again. I saw what it did to Esther. And I succeeded in restraining myself for eight years. Until I got my youth back. Now I've ruined more lives. And it's on your hands, Michael. You should have forgiven me." Horace's voice rose, ragged. "Let it eat at your conscience till I kill you."

"We can get you help," Luke said. "You can change again."

"No!" Horace screamed. He brought the knife to Esther's throat and dragged it across her larynx.

He released her. She sank to the cobblestone, clutching at the collar of her shirt, gurgling. Blood bubbled out onto her clothes, onto the ground.

Michael ran at his brother. Horace turned on his heel and dashed toward the other end of the alleyway.

"Dad!" Luke shouted. "There's no time for that. Help her!"

He stopped, hesitating for only a moment. Then he went to Esther, who was making a horrific wheezing sound. Wrapping her in his arms, cradling her, he looked up at Luke. "What do I do?"

For a second his son had the faraway expression again. Then he made eye contact with Michael. Still he said nothing.

"What do I do, Luke?" His voice hitched. Esther's face became blurry as tears filled his eyes.

"I've called an ambulance. But—I don't think she's going to make it, Dad. Not unless she gets to a respirator in the next five minutes."

"Find me the nearest one. I'll carry her. You live in the internet, and you think a thousand times faster than I do. Find me a fucking respirator."

"Dad, you need to leave. I'm monitoring police channels and they have footage of you slitting Esther's throat. They're on their way to arrest you."

"You just saw Horace do it."

"But they didn't. Someone doctored the sensor footage in real time to make it look like you killed her. Must have been Horace's AI."

"I can't leave Esther." But when he felt her pulse there was nothing. A sob ripped through his throat.

"Dad, either the police will get you or Horace's AI will. I keep a boat tied up in the harbor. If you can get to it, I can get you to where neither of them can reach you. But if you stay here you're done. I promise you that."

"I won't abandon Valentine."

"Valentine can look after herself. Just like she has for the last twenty years."

Michael didn't bother apologizing to his daughter's corpse. He'd told her he was sorry too many times for one lifetime, and it had never fixed anything. Besides, he didn't deserve to be forgiven. Instead he kissed her cooling forehead, and held her close, squeezing her, and getting more blood on his shirt. "I love you," he whispered. Then he stood and ran down the alley in the direction Horace had.

"Sharp left," Luke said, and sent him a flashing arrow that hovered in the left side of his field of vision. Michael followed it. He was on Water Street, now.

"Where's your boat?"

"It's near the battery. You have a bit of a jog ahead of you." Sirens blared to Michael's left, cutting through George Street's Friday-night din. "Make that a run. You need to move faster. Take a right, now. *Now.*" Ahead of him a police car barreled out of George Street, skidding around to face him, and accelerating. "Hop that chain there and run across the parking lot," Luke said.

Halfway across the lot, Michael chanced a look over his shoulder. The cruiser had stopped at the chain, and an officer was stepping over it. "Stop!" he yelled.

"No cops on Harbour Drive yet," Luke said. "Faster, Dad. Look out!"

A pickup truck to his right veered into oncoming traffic, rushing toward the sidewalk where he stood, the AI behind the wheel looking bewildered. Michael backed up, and the truck careened over the sidewalk, missing him by a matter of inches and crashing into a concrete barrier. Michael hopped that barrier, and ran along it on the other side till it came to an end and he was back on the sidewalk again. "What the hell was that?"

"AI Horace. Keep an eye on every vehicle you see. I'm going to take some preventive measures to keep him out of their computers, but I might not be able to protect them all. Shit."

"What?"

"Nothing. Just—he's trying to hack my boat. He's crazy if he thinks it will work. He's still an old man, after all, and I've been hacking since I was eight."

"Good for you."

"There's more police coming. They know exactly where you are at any given second, because of the sensors. A cop on foot will reach the next corner at the same time you do. You need to take that cop out."

"I can't—"

"You can if you want to keep your freedom, which you'll need to avenge Esther. Now!"

Michael reached the corner. As promised, a cop arrived there at the same time. He lashed out desperately, his fist connecting with the cop's face. Something crunched beneath his knuckles.

"Take her gun."

He stared down at the unconscious woman lying at his feet, feeling like he was in a dream. "You didn't tell me the cop was female."

"Don't be sexist. Hitting a cop is hitting a cop. Stop wasting time. Take her gun."

Michael did.

"Run."

He did that, too. Another police cruiser pulled onto Harbour Drive at the next intersection, and two more screeched around a corner behind him. He was pinned, until the security fence that ran along the harbor caught his eye. "Good idea," Luke said as he made for it. The bars were vertical, and didn't make for easy climbing, but his desperation-fueled, twenty-five-year-old body got him up and over it. Ignoring the shock to his ankles from landing on asphalt, he dashed along the water, the cruisers following him on the other side of the fence. At least they weren't using their guns on him. Yet.

His heart sank when he reached a break in the fence, and the game finally seemed to be up. Two cruisers pulled up, and two cops opened their doors to get out. "You're under arrest," said a third officer, shouting into a loudspeaker from inside the car.

Instead a driverless Cadillac plowed into the police cars, pushing them several meters down the road. The passenger side door popped open. "Get in," Luke told him.

His son didn't materialize in the driver seat, but the wheel turned as the car weaved in and out of traffic, and the gearshift moved. "Are they going to know you helped me escape?" Michael asked as they sped eastward.

"Probably. We'll worry about that once you're gone."

"Tell Valentine thank you for everything. And that I'm sorry we didn't have more time together."

"I will. If she'll take my call."

She'll take it. She'll be wondering where I am.

"Everything's ready to go with the boat," Luke said. "I made sure everything was automated a long time ago, in case something like this ever happened."

"You expected this?"

"No. But I also didn't think it all that unlikely, given our government, and given the sort of company I keep."

Michael gave a terse chuckle.

Luke's boat turned out to be a sleek, sixty-foot luxury yacht—the sort of thing a well-to-do AI might keep to impress his biological friends. It began to thrum with power seconds after Michael set foot on it. The chain that bound it to the mooring snapped open automatically, leapt into the water, and then was retracted into the side of the boat. The distance between the yacht and the dock slowly began to widen.

Horace appeared from around the side of a nearby shed, making for the boat at a dead run. He jumped off the dock, hands outstretched. Michael heard his brother's body slam against the side of the yacht. *No splash, though.*

Horace's head appeared, and a second later he hauled himself aboard. He stood.

Michael shot him.

Horace staggered back, nearly falling into the water. But he recovered, and launched himself at Michael, who pulled the trigger again. It slowed the attack but didn't stop it. Then his brother was upon him, tackling him. Michael fell, the gun clattering across the deck.

"He's wearing a bulletproof vest," Luke said redundantly.

Something inside Michael's mouth cracked as Horace's fist slammed into it, and warm blood gushed, tasting of metal. He raised his hands, which did nothing to stop two more blows from raining down. His brother was on top of him, pinning him.

The next punch missed, and Horace cursed, bringing both hands to his eyes, pinching at them to try and remove his Smartans. Michael realized Luke must have done something to his vision. He twisted between Horace's legs, pushing upward, giving himself enough of a gap to squirm away. It wasn't done gracefully, but it was done. He brought an elbow down as hard as he could onto the back of Horace's neck. His brother sprawled forward, giving Michael the opportunity to stomp on his head.

Horace's hands clenched and opened again. He tried to push himself up, but couldn't. Michael went to retrieve the gun. Horace tried to rise once more, and managed to get to his knees this time.

"Don't kill him," his son said. "His AI's still at large. We need whatever information he can give us."

Michael walked over and put the gun barrel against the back of Horace's head.

"Michael," Luke said.

He fired. Bone and brain spattered the deck, as well as Michael's face. He dragged his brother's body to the side of the boat and dumped it into the water.

"The cops have boats, right?" he said. "Will they catch us?"

Luke sighed. "Hopefully not. This thing's pretty fast. And they probably won't have their boats ready for a while—I'm sure they didn't expect you to take to the sea. Plus I have ways of blocking their efforts to track you. By the time they overcome them, it should be too late."

"What if they arrest you?"

"Then you'll be on your own."

"Where am I headed? The UK?"

"No. Their immigration control's even tighter than it was twenty years ago. Besides, they'd just send you right back to the Canadian government."

"Where, then?"

"The only place where neither the government nor AI Horace can get to you. The Failed States."

They'd reached the Narrows, then—the small channel that led from St. John's Harbour out to the open ocean. The sea did not look very calm to Michael. But what did he know? He'd never been much of a seafarer. Above, dark clouds hid the stars and rendered the moon a faint circle of white. Like a searchlight without enough power.

"I'm tired," Michael said.

"There's a bed down below."

"Don't wake me."

"All right, Dad."

{ 3 }

Finished with Dignity

There were more storms than Michael would have expected, knocking the yacht around like a flea on a blanket. Pelting him with rain and sometimes hail. Blowing so hard it forced him to retreat below deck till it passed.

The boat was covered in sensors, which allowed his AI son to make the ride across the ocean with him. He asked Luke whether global warming was causing the storms, and his son said it was best to think of the Earth's atmosphere as a baseball player on steroids. You could never point at a single homerun and say the steroids had caused it. But by adding to the natural steroids in the player's body he became stronger, making it more likely that when bat connected with ball, a homerun would occur. Greenhouse gases occurred naturally in the atmosphere, and adding more was like feeding the climate steroids. Doing so increased the temperature, which made extreme heat and extreme precipitation more likely. Which led to more storms overall.

"And just like the baseball player will occasionally strike out," Luke went on, "the climate system can still experience very low temperatures, even with the extra juice. That's what climate change deniers have brought up again and again to make people doubt the scientists. The fact that it still snows sometimes."

"I feel like if we'd had analogies like that back when it mattered things might have been different," Michael said.

"Think again. That analogy's almost forty years old. It and others just as good."

Michael shook his head. "What happened?"

"Fossil fuel companies successfully characterized the ones trying to warn us as tree huggers. Hippies. Idiots. Conspirators. And even radicals. Plenty of climate activists have been monitored and even arrested under antiterrorism laws. That's why environmental protest more or less died in the 2030s. Everyone's too afraid to speak out."

They were talking in the small-but-comfortable below-deck lounge. All around them yet another hurricane raged, and the ship's stabilizers were working overtime to keep the yacht from going bottom-up. Michael lay on the squishy purple couch staring at the ceiling, and Luke lay on his side, suspended in midair like a lazy genie.

"Things are changing, though," Michael said. "I've encountered plenty of stuff powered by wind and sun since waking from cryosleep."

"Things didn't change fast enough. We're long past being able to prevent anything. The planet's natural carbon feedback loops have been triggered. Things are only going to get worse from here."

"You must believe there's still hope. Otherwise your precious immortality theory would be invalidated."

"My theory doesn't require civilization to persist in order to be valid. The world's in rough shape. Half of it has sunk, and the other half is sinking. Look at Continental Europe, where you're headed. European countries used to be bastions of wealth and progress. Now we call them the Failed States."

For the first time Michael found himself wanting to believe in Luke's theory. The nights he came closest to convincing himself that Esther was still alive in another universe were the only nights he slept. When he did sleep her death played out in his dreams over and over. If not that, then dreams of the day he and Linda walked in on her being violated by Horace.

In conversation he probed Luke cautiously about the theory, voicing his uncertainties. Despite the fact he'd already lived well past his natural lifespan, it was nothing compared to living forever, as Luke claimed he would. But Michael could tell Luke sensed his eagerness to embrace the idea, and was doing his best to help him out. "How's your faith doing nowadays, Dad?"

"My religious faith?" Michael wasn't sure. "I don't want to talk about it."

"Okay. Fine." As an AI, Luke could think one-thousand times faster than him. So for every second Michael had, his son had almost seventeen minutes with which to scrap a failed conversational gambit and swap in a new one. "Consider how, when the moon is new, during a solar eclipse it perfectly blocks out the sun. That's what allows for the coronal effect caused by a total eclipse. If the moon was a little bit closer, like it was a few hundred million years ago, we wouldn't be able to see total eclipses. And in six hundred million years the moon will have moved too far away. On a geological timescale it was incredibly unlikely that human civilization would be around to observe and document a total solar eclipse. Yet here we are."

"Where are you going with this?"

"I know you said you don't want to talk about your faith, and we won't. But a lot of people use cosmic coincidences like the total eclipse to argue for the existence of God. Another example: the way forces like gravity and electromagnetism are perfectly fine-tuned to allow life to exist in the universe. If they were just a little bit weaker, or a little bit stronger, the atomic building blocks for life simply wouldn't exist, or wouldn't function properly. And water provides yet further supposed evidence for God's existence. If the polarity of water was a little smaller ice would not float, and the oceans would have frozen solid a long time ago, preventing life from ever emerging. Theologians say: if God doesn't exist then how do you explain that the universe seems tailored to us?"

"I bet you're about to tell me how."

"I am indeed. Allow me to introduce you to something called the anthropic principle."

"I'm familiar with it."

Luke sat up, his brow furrowed, looking even more like a genie. "You are?"

"Yep. It's the idea that it's unremarkable we live in a universe suited to life, since life could never have arisen in any other universe. So, of course this is the universe we find ourselves in." Michael shrugged. "I hope I didn't ruin your line of argument."

"You didn't. I'm just surprised you knew that. Where did you learn it?"

He thought about it. "Can't remember."

"All right. Well, anyway, I think the anthropic principle is a useful concept for you, partly because I think you are losing your faith in God. Or maybe you've already lost it. You've experienced a series of miracles that have kept you alive. The out-of-nowhere operation that cured your cancer, the car accident that killed Stephen but not you, cryosleep, and killing Horace when he could have easily killed you. You're starting to realize you're never going to die. But if that's true, how can the Catholicism that you were born into be true? If you never die, then clearly begging forgiveness for your sins is bullshit. You'll never get the chance to ascend to heaven anyway. Do you follow?"

Michael didn't answer.

"Here's where things get relevant to your situation. If religion isn't true, the anthropic principle must be. But the principle doesn't make any sense if there's only one universe that exists. The odds of that single universe being suited for life are astronomically low. So there must be many universes. Infinite universes, most likely. Which fits our observation that you haven't died, and show no signs of dying anytime soon. Every time a situation arises that could kill you, multiple universes branch off, and you end up in one where you survive."

"You realize," Michael said, "that your idea about no one ever dying is just as much a religion as Catholicism. There are just as many ways to prove the truth of the former as there are the latter. That is to say, zero."

"Wrong. There is a way to prove it: actually live forever. And the longer you live, the more convinced you'll become, Dad." Luke stood. "If the theory's a religion it's a pretty dark one. Like I've said, in order to be true it doesn't require human civilization to be a good place, or even to stick around at all." Luke turned his back on him, and vanished.

Even so, he had one last parting remark: "I think it would behoove you to start taking my idea more seriously. This planet's in trouble, and if we don't do something soon it's going to be a long eternity for both of us."

"Don't forget to check on Valentine," Michael said, but no answer came.

On their first day at sea Luke had committed to protecting his sister, including shoring up her home security and keeping a watchful eye out for any attempts by Horace's AI to get to her. Luke assured Michael he was more than capable of doing that, since his technical abilities far outstripped those of Horace. Michael prayed he was right. He'd lost four of his six children—Stephen, Doris, Craig, and now his dear Esther.

On the second day after leaving St. John's Luke had vanished, not returning until the day after. Michael panicked. He had no way of telling whether the boat still moved in the same direction, since everything was automated. A frantic search of the ship provided no clues. Luke had designed the vessel in a way that gave him total control over the fates of its occupants. And he'd vanished without a trace. Michael took inventory, determining that the dried food stores were not sufficient to sustain him if the boat meandered for very long.

When Luke finally returned he explained that he'd been arrested for helping Michael escape the law. It had taken him overnight to make arrangements for paying his bail.

Michael was wanted for Esther's murder, which his brother had framed him for. His escape had involved knocking out a police officer on the street, stealing a car, causing damage to police cruisers, and killing his brother Horace—or at least, his physical form. He could understand why the law was disgruntled with Luke for helping him to do those things. Luke would be tried in court on the second of September, which was four months away.

"How do they keep an AI in a jail cell, anyway?" Michael asked.

"Much the same way they'd keep you in a cell if they could. They restricted my access to only the sensors in the cell, and they restricted my internet connection to just what's necessary to keep me alive. That is, the tether to my brain stored at Intellitech."

They were having bad luck with weather. Storms were blowing them off course, adding days to their journey. When the weather forced Michael below deck, and Luke didn't have business back in Canada, they would play chess on a board his son conjured, which hung in midair. Despite being insubstantial the pieces reacted to Michael's touch, and he could move them like a normal chess set. He could even knock them over if he wasn't careful, and they made a sound when he placed them on the ethereal board.

His son won every single game, which didn't surprise Michael. If a game lasted an hour, Luke had the equivalent of nearly forty-two days to think about it. Michael would have been insulted if he had won a game, because it would have meant that Luke almost certainly let him win.

Victory after victory, Luke never made a snide comment. He remained stoic during their games, straight-faced, never grinning. Michael suspected his son found playing with him boring. Child's play. But he never let on.

Gone was the sarcasm and condescension that had always characterized Luke's attitude toward him. At the end of his fourth day at sea, he asked him about it. "Why are you being so nice?"

"Away from Valentine, alone at sea, I know I'm all you have right now. Being a dick wouldn't serve any purpose." Luke ran a hand through his hair, gazing absently into space, then met Michael's gaze. "Besides, I've gained respect for you since they unfroze you. I feel like you figured out how to live in the future pretty fast."

Michael didn't feel like that. In his darkest moments he felt like he really was at fault for Esther's death. He'd confronted her for the way she'd been dancing with a stranger. If she hadn't stormed off in response, Horace might never have gotten to her. At any rate, he was skeptical about his son's explanation for being nice. He wondered what Luke's angle was, helping him so much. But his son was right—he was all Michael had. So Michael tried not to become too irritable with him.

On the fifth day he started getting seriously depressed. The nightmares about Esther had grown in intensity, and now they were interspersed with dreams about the night he'd killed his brother. In the most frequently recurring version of this dream he pulled the trigger and Horace's head blew apart, except his face remained intact. He turned around, and through his empty eyes and nostril holes Michael could see the boundless sea. "I win," Horace said, and crumbled away.

Luke noticed his frequent sighing, and one morning, when Michael woke screaming and drenched in sweat, his son was standing beside the bed, staring down at him in consternation. "I know this isn't the most constructive solution," he said, "but we should reach France in the next few days anyway. I'm going to show you where the hidden liquor cabinet is."

That brightened Michael's mood considerably.

"I need you to be responsible about this, Dad," Luke said, perhaps already regretting his decision as Michael rooted around in the compartment hidden below the lounge's big screen TV. "If you're stinking drunk when we arrive in Europe you won't be much use to anyone."

"Won't be much use to you, you mean."

"Did you know alcohol's toxicity level is higher than that of cocaine, and heroin?"

"No, I didn't," Michael said as he poured himself a triple. "Is that true?"

"If you abuse this, I'm locking the cabinet again and you won't get any more."

"I understand," Michael said, sitting on the couch and switching on the TV.

The next time Luke appeared on the boat he discovered that Michael had removed every last bottle of liquor from the cabinet and moved it to the blanket-filled compartment underneath the bed, which didn't have a lock. "Dad! What did you do?"

"I think it's quite clear what I did." He studied his son over the rim of a highball glass. "Sometimes I get the impression you've forgotten who the father is," he said, raising the glass and tipping it toward his son, "and who the child is." He gulped another healthy quantity, draining it in short order.

His son sighed, and a beer materialized in his hand. He fell onto the couch. Michael went into the bedroom, mixed himself another drink, and they settled in to watch a movie. After it was over Luke left again, and Michael had several more drinks. He woke to his son shouting at him where he'd passed out above deck. The ocean was calm for once. The sun was blistering.

"You're sunburnt, Dad." Luke sounded disgusted.

Michael felt immensely tired. "Leave me alone."

"We'll reach France in less than twelve hours. I need you to stop drinking."

"Why?"

"Because if you go there hammered you're going to die. This is serious."

"Let's not go there."

"The food will run out."

"There's plenty of alcohol."

Luke looked up at the sky, his hands clenched into fists at his sides. Then he hung his head, uncurling his fists and covering his eyes. "I never should have let you into the liquor cabinet."

"Probably not." There was no point in being dishonest.

His son disappeared, reappearing in the lounge three hours later. Michael had dragged himself to the couch by that time.

"If you don't sober up I'm stopping the boat," Luke said.

"Okay."

"God damn it." He vanished again.

He was gone for six hours this time. Michael knew the next visit would likely be unpleasant, so he drank some more, to brace himself.

A loud beeping that permeated the entire boat preceded Luke's return, cutting through Michael's stupor and making him wince. He staggered to his feet to begin searching for a way to stop it, but his son appeared then, a sour expression on his face.

"What is that?"

"That's Agent Peele. Calling you."

"How does he know where to reach me?"

"He must have gotten past my efforts to prevent them tracking us." Luke's tone did not contain very much warmth. "I've already had a conversation with him this morning. You didn't tell me you came to Esther's apartment to investigate me at Peele's request. And McQuaid's."

"You didn't ask."

"I'd kick you right now if I could."

"You wouldn't kick your own father, would you? Listen, Luke, I didn't have any choice but to comply with the government agents' wishes. Besides, I didn't think you really murdered Craig. I mostly agreed to it so I could prove you were innocent."

"Mostly, eh?" Luke sneered. "I think you'd better answer the phone."

Michael didn't know how to do that. "He isn't calling me on my Smartans."

"Go into the bedroom. You'll find that a concealed panel has just opened above the bed."

He did, succeeding in not stumbling. The panel had opened in the style of an accordion folder, and inside, nestled in velvet, was a smartphone. It was ringing, an unknown number displayed on the screen.

"Ancient technology," Michael said.

"Answer it."

Placing his thumb on the green circle, he flicked it in the direction the arrows pointed. Then he picked it up, pleased with himself. "Hello?"

"You're holding it upside down," Luke said.

"Ah." He righted it. "Hello?"

"Mr. Haynes. This is Agent Peele."

"Hi."

"What a perplexing character you've turned out to be. We send you to help us investigate your son's murder and you disappear from the city on the same night."

Anger flared up in Michael, sobering him significantly. "You're pretty perplexing yourself. I gave you access to my feed but when I needed your help you were nowhere to be found. You said you'd be nearby, and you didn't show up when I needed you most. My daughter died."

"We have in our possession footage of you killing Esther Haynes."

"The sensor feeds were doctored. By my brother Horace Haynes, who actually killed her."

"Our records indicate Horace has been dead for years. Biologically, at least. His AI is still operational."

"He faked his physical death. He was living as a man named Francis after undergoing cosmetic surgery."

"That's certainly a possibility we're willing to investigate. But we can't clear your name until you return to us and face trial. With that done, we can work on bringing your daughter's true murderer to justice."

Michael exchanged glances with Luke, uncertain how to proceed. But his son had no answers for him. He only returned his gaze, stone-faced.

"That won't be possible," Michael said into the phone at last. "I-I killed Horace."

"Well. That was certainly a busy night for you. Unless you killed your brother on a different day?"

"No. It was the same night. He followed me onto the boat, and attacked me."

"So you killed him in self-defense?"

"I'm not, um, I'm unsure it would count as such. I had control of the situation and still killed him."

"I appreciate your honesty. No doubt your son will have retained the footage, from which we can determine the legalities of the situation."

"Horace's AI is still at large. You should question it first and get back to me."

"I think the best course of action would be for you to return to St. John's and face trial," Peele said. "You do believe in the rule of law, don't you Mr. Haynes?"

"I do. A lot more than you do, I think, with your illegal surveillance programs and your manipulation of antiterrorism laws to do anything you like to Canadian citizens. But I don't agree with you that returning would be my best course of action. I think my best option is to remain far, far away from you."

"It's unfortunate you think that. Let me see what I can do to convince you otherwise." Peele paused, sniffing loudly. "Oh, I've thought of something. A piece of information you might find somewhat relevant to your situation, let's say. Using satellite intelligence we've tracked your position since you left St. John's. Your son's efforts to prevent us were insufficient. Two days ago we deployed a nanodrone, and yesterday it landed on your bed while you slept, depositing its payload onto the mattress. That payload crept toward you, entered through your ear, and distributed itself via blood vessels throughout your brain. If you fail to return to us within exactly two weeks from the end of this conversation we will shut down the part of your frontal lobe that enables you to speak. A week after that we will disable your cerebral cortex in such a way that will remove your ability to comprehend language. How does that sound, Mr. Haynes?"

Michael didn't answer. The hand holding the phone shook.

"If you still fail to return to St. John's within a week of no longer being able to understand anyone, we'll see whether there's something else you might understand. We'll disrupt your prefrontal cortex so that you can no longer process short-term memories. Hopefully that won't affect your ability to comply with our wishes. If it does, a week later your long-term memory retention will go. Next, seven days after that, we will damage your auditory and visual cortices. Your motor cortex will be the last to go, in the final week, rendering you a vegetable. Do you understand everything I've said?"

"Yes."

"Excellent. I'll see you in the next couple weeks." Peele terminated the call.

*

"I have to go back."

They were above deck, Michael sitting in a white chair that folded up out of the yacht when needed, and Luke with his digital hands on the railing, looking east. He'd instructed the boat to stop just before the point where it might have been spotted by someone standing on the French shoreline. An hour had passed since Peele's call, an hour of silence, which Michael had now broken. He was on his second drink since the call ended.

"If you do go back you'll risk going to jail for decades," Luke said. "Or, best case scenario, we somehow prove the footage was doctored by the man you already killed. Get a confession out of his AI, maybe. Even then, you'll be tied up in court for the better part of a year or more."

“I’d rather go to jail than end up a vegetable. This is exactly the sort of thing you warned me about. Even if you’re right about living forever, that doesn’t rule out my brain turning into pudding. There’s nothing I can do except pick the best of two terrible options.”

Luke had not turned to face him. He still stared out over the water. “There’s a third option.”

“Which is?”

“The Failed States don’t include India. It, along with a few other countries in the global south, stayed relatively prosperous. It’s surrounded by chaos, but it hangs on like it always has. You could reach it in just under two weeks using the lightbike stored in this yacht.”

What the hell is a lightbike? “Remind me why I want to go to India again?”

“I have a contact in Bangalore, which is pretty much India’s Silicon Valley. Her name is Pratibha Doshi. I believe she can help get rid of those nanobots in your brain.”

“What if you’re wrong?”

“Then I’ll do everything in my power to get you back to Canada and have your brain healed. I’ll bring you back.”

“If you can’t?”

“Then I can’t. You’re screwed.”

“I’m getting the feeling there’s something else in Bangalore that’s important to you. That it’s where you wanted me to go all along. That it’s why I’m on this boat.” There had to be a reason Luke was pushing so hard for this despite that he would likely end up in jail after his trial in September.

A pause. Then Luke did turn to face him. "Dad, I don't know how much longer the world has. The global economy, such as it is, seems about to collapse. We're getting hammered with more and more extreme weather events every year. And innovation has been almost entirely stamped out, so we have no new ways of dealing with anything. Corporations and governments only seem interested in squeezing the last few drops of profit out of our near-dead civilization. If you want my opinion, I think it could all come crashing down within the next couple years. Maybe sooner."

"So what's in Bangalore that will stop it?"

"Opportunity. A fighting chance. I know I've asked you to make sacrifices to help millions of people before, and you refused. I don't hold that against you. I understand the situation you were in, and I'm pretty sure you didn't fully grasp what you were refusing. But right now I'm asking you to risk your own safety to try and save billions. I believe you're the only person in a position to save human civilization. I really do. So you can go back to Canada, submit to the will of the authorities, and rot in a jail cell until society falls apart around you. Or you can get to India as fast as you can and have a shot at saving your species."

Michael stood and walked to the railing, leaning on it with his left hand while holding the drink in his right. He took a sip. "You still haven't told me what it entails. I'm not agreeing to anything until I know what it is we're trying to do."

Luke turned back to face the water, too. They both looked upon the horizon, where France lay just out of sight.

"In India they've developed a computer virus capable of breaking through the Intellitech safeguards that prevent AIs from augmenting themselves. It can do that without tripping any alarms, which is important because if the safeguards detect the slightest thing wrong they're designed to wipe the brain. To overcome the impossible problems humans face, we need an intelligence that's way beyond humans. We need a superintelligence."

"And that superintelligence will be you."

"Yes."

"God help us."

That was an enormous amount of power, and Michael wouldn't feel comfortable giving it to anyone, least of all Luke. His instincts railed against it: *Luke isn't capable of steering the entire species toward salvation. You would be mad to entrust him with this kind of power.* But he remembered how much he'd lost already because of his inability to trust his own children. Maybe it was time to try the opposite course of action, no matter how hard it was.

He poured the rest of his drink into the ocean and turned to face his son. When their eyes met he said it: "Okay. I'll try."

Luke held up a hand, a pained expression tightening his features. "Before you commit to that, there's something else I need to tell you."

"What is it?" But Michael knew what it was as soon as Luke had brought it up. Somehow, he knew. Fear quickened his pulse.

"Valentine has been disappeared by the government. I don't know where they're holding her. I shouldn't be telling you this, because it plays right into their hands. They're trying to use her to get to you. But I couldn't keep it from you in good conscience."

"That settles it, then. We have to go back. We have to turn around right now."

"You could. And if that's what you want, I'll do it. I will. But I'll say it again: the second you set foot in St. John's they'll know, and they'll come arrest you. If you do that there's no guarantee they'll release Valentine. It's just as likely they'll declare her in league with a terrorist—that's you—and therefore a threat to national security, fit only to be imprisoned indefinitely. But if you come with me to India we have a real chance to change things for the better. If we can save humanity from itself, then getting Valentine released will be trivial. Especially with superintelligence on our side."

Michael said nothing. He gripped the rail so hard it hurt.

"You're beginning to believe what I've told you about how the universe works. I know you are. You're starting to believe you'll live forever. But think about what that means. If you let civilization collapse, what kind of eternity can you expect to experience? What's better—to go back to Canada, let them throw you in jail, and watch as society tears itself apart? Or to help build a better world for your children and your grandchildren? One that just might last forever?"

Michael re-established eye contact with his son. His vision had grown blurry, and Luke's face swam before him.

"You're right," he said. "Let's go. Let's hurry."

*

The yacht's food stores were nearly depleted, otherwise they might have saved a lot of time by travelling to India by water. Michael could try foraging food for the trip along the coastline, but they decided it was too risky. Just finding enough to avoid starvation would likely be a challenge, let alone securing enough supplies to last him a journey of several days.

There were no functioning sensors in the Failed States, so Luke could not appear to him there. Until Michael reached India, their only means of communicating would be using the smartphone, via satellite.

"Will the battery even last that long?" he asked.

Luke nodded. "I customized it. There's a modern battery in there, meaning it should last months. We won't need it that long."

"Hopefully not."

"Consult the smartphone's GPS frequently. Do not get lost. You can't afford to lose a day, with what Peele and his friends did to you. I'm dropping you off on a beach due west of Bordeaux. Take route D107 straight to the city—it starts with Avenue de l'Océan. The roads will be in atrocious repair, but the lightbike can handle them."

The lightbike turned out to be a solar-powered motorcycle with fans where its wheels should have been. When they came within shouting distance of the shore (if there'd been anyone to shout at), Luke opened a sliding panel in the yacht's hull, and out came the lightbike, motor already humming quietly, floating a foot or so off the water.

"It's hovercraft technology. Been around for almost a century. The fans have gotten a lot smaller, and stability's gotten a lot better thanks to the onboard AI. Other than that it's pretty much the same."

"AI?" Michael said. "I'm going to have someone like you nattering at me constantly?"

Luke laughed. "Most AIs don't talk, Dad. The bike has a narrow AI, for stability, retaining altitude while going over potholes, collision avoidance, that sort of thing."

They stared at the lightbike in silence for nearly a minute. Luke seemed to be waiting for him to get on with it.

People are going to want this thing. "It's not exactly conspicuous."

"Yeah. I wouldn't advise stopping for, well, anyone."

"Why didn't I see any of these on the roads back in St. John's?"

"Because they're freaking expensive. Cars serve just as well, at a much lower cost."

"Surely the cost difference isn't that great, with the condition of St. John's roads."

At least the sea was calm. He wouldn't want to ride this contraption over waves of any size. "I guess this is goodbye."

"Not as long as you keep from losing the phone. I'll be with you as much as I've ever been since you woke up. You just won't be able to see me. That's all."

"I'll keep the volume turned up, like you showed me. Unless you get real annoying."

His son grinned. "I won't go through the charade of hugging you. Let's not pretend that's something I'm able to truly do anymore. But...I love you, Dad. Good luck. We're doing this for Esther, right?"

"I'll be shutting Horace's AI down for Esther." They'd decided he would do that when it came time to break into Intellitech, if it was at all possible. "This, I'm doing for Valentine. And for me."

"And the other eight billion or so people living on this planet?"

"Yeah. Them too." He picked up a sack that contained what little remained of the yacht's food stores and put on the wide-brimmed hat that he'd rooted out of the below-deck closet. Then he clambered over the side of the yacht, gently lowering himself one-handed down the ladder. The lightbike sensed his presence, nudging closer. Michael turned, leaping for it, and nearly tumbled over the seat and into the ocean. He grabbed a handlebar, causing the bike to tip to the left, and causing his heart to attempt a getaway up his esophagus. The bike righted itself, and he breathed a sigh of relief. Somehow he'd managed to keep the bag of food from tumbling into the water.

Above, Luke was laughing at him. Having stowed the food sack, Michael gave him the finger over his shoulder with one hand, pressing the throttle with the other. The lightbike leapt forward, and he quickly moved his other hand to the handlebars to steady it.

The shore approached rapidly, growing larger with each passing second. What he'd thought was some foam being dashed repeatedly against the rocks turned out to be a human skeleton washed up by the sea. That didn't seem like the most promising omen. He wondered what the skeleton's story was. Had the person it once belonged to tried to escape France by boat and capsized? Or had he or she been desperate enough to try swimming away from it?

Michael cast a glance back at the ocean, where Luke's yacht had already started south. Waves and sun powered the vessel, and depleted food stores were not a problem for his son. He would follow the coastline, staying as close to Michael as possible in case he could be of any help. And if India provided what Luke hoped for the yacht would serve as Michael's transportation back to Canada.

According to the phone's GPS the first street he encountered was called Avenue de l'Océan. It was a ruined, pockmarked mess, as though someone had taken a cosmic jackhammer to the surface of the moon. The road would be impassable to everything except a vehicle using hover technology. Once more, Michael found himself wondering how long his son had been planning this. Was the extreme preparedness really a result of meticulous accounting for every possible contingency, or had Luke known exactly what he would need years in advance? Could he have been planning for Michael to come here and perform this task for that long?

No. Michael's thoughts kept coming back to the food stores. If this was the result of some multiyear master plan, Luke would have included enough food in the boat to transport him safely to India. That was how Michael reassured himself, and how he was able to retain what trust he had in his son, who had sold him to the government a few decades ago after all.

In its 'saddlebags', which were actually hinged compartments, the lightbike held enough food for two days, in addition to what little he'd taken from the yacht. Landing this close to Bordeaux was a gamble. The city likely contained a population of some number, and chances were they would be aggressive, else they would not have survived the country's descent into anarchy. At the same time, if Michael attempted to find food in the countryside he might starve. He'd never been much of a hunter, and certainly not a farmer. Canned or dried goods were his only hope. The city was his best bet for those.

For its entire length Avenue de l'Océan remained utterly deserted, which accorded with Michael's expectations. At some point its name changed to Lotissement plein Soleil. He didn't know what that meant, but the road itself served him just as well under the new name, gaping craters and all. He became confused when he encountered what he knew was called a roundabout, though he'd never used one before. He didn't know which way to go, and for that reason he felt thankful the pockmarked, crumbled stretches were devoid of other traffic. Given a choice between Avenue du Bassin d'Arcachon and Avenue de Bordeaux, he chose the latter, because it seemed likelier to lead him to his destination.

He might have called Luke to ask whether he was making the right choice. For that matter, he could have consulted the smartphone's GPS again. But doing either would involve stopping the lightbike, and he found himself thoroughly enjoying his cruise through deserted France. He felt like he was in no particular hurry, and that getting lost would not be a big deal, despite that his brain was infested with nanobots poised to systematically dismantle it.

Okay, now I feel a little hurried. Sometimes his stray thoughts had a way of putting things into perspective for him. He gave the engine a little more gas. Or, light. Whatever.

Coming to a second roundabout, he stuck with his previous decision to follow Avenue de Bordeaux wherever it took him. That turned out to be, an hour and two or three roundabouts later, straight into a massive throng of people traveling along a road that intersected with the one he was on. He'd stopped paying much attention, given that the bike sailed over all the potholes as if they weren't there, and given the complete lack of anyone around till now. The crowd took him completely by surprise, and he nearly sped straight into it, like an oblong bowling ball through a sea of moving pins. At the last second he squeezed the brake as hard as he could, thinking that he really should have practiced braking before setting out.

The bike fishtailed, coming at the people side-on, which would only cause more injury if he collided with them. He shouted, and was heard. A number of people turned toward him, shock and fear blooming on their faces, and began pushing back against their travelling companions. A dip opened in the side of the enormous procession, and he slid into the space they opened, making contact with several people but managing to avoid knocking anyone over.

A good number of people had stopped to stare, and as a result people were bunching up farther down the road, shouting angrily. The ones closer to him were quieter. "Hi," Michael said.

Around twenty people started talking at once, and he couldn't understand any of them. He held up his hands. "I don't know French. English only. Does anyone speak English?"

"I do," said a man in a British accent. He wore a long brown coat that was mostly rags. No one's clothes seemed in very good repair, and some were next to naked. Michael tried not to grimace at the sight of their malnourished bodies, with bones visible through thin-looking skin.

"Where is everyone going?" Michael asked the Englishman.

The man looked back at the thick snake of people strung out along the road behind him, blinking, as though seeing them for the first time. He looked back at Michael. "Why do you ask?"

"Uh, I'm curious."

"What does it matter?"

Michael scratched his head. "Well, there are quite a lot of you. And this many people on the road, all bunched together—I just thought maybe you'd have a destination of some sort. You're headed toward Bordeaux. Is that where you're going?"

"I suppose." The man turned away from him, and so did the others nearby. Michael didn't know whether they'd understood the conversation that had just taken place, but it didn't seem to matter. They continued on at the same pace as before, heedless of the increasingly disgruntled walkers behind them who'd become bunched up as a result of the halt.

Clearly the road was no longer an option for him, unless he wanted to travel at the same pace as the half-starved people trudging along it. The side of the road was mostly brown grass interspersed with an occasional boulder, and he was able to traverse it with the lightbike, though at a reduced speed.

Even going slower he zipped past the travelers, and found that the throng went on for quite some time. None of them seemed to be in any sort of hurry. They seemed as downtrodden and disinterested in their surroundings as the British man he'd spoken with. It was as though everyone was going through the paces of a well-worn routine, one which no one enjoyed, but which necessity demanded.

The realization that he'd entered the city came a good while after he actually entered it. He remembered Luke telling him that France had become a failed state around three years ago, but the dilapidation process had happened quicker than he would have expected. This looked like a place that had fallen apart decades ago. Foliage had eaten the buildings, and brought many of them low, turning them to rubble. What ones still stood appeared as lumps of greenery, and Michael's recognition that he'd entered Bordeaux was alarmingly belated.

At a certain point the crowd became even more condensed, and he deduced that they'd reached an impasse. Indeed, seconds later he reached it too. Twenty or so men stood with machine guns pointed at the crowd. The marchers' expressions hadn't changed. Strangely, the people he'd nearly taken out with the lightbike had looked more frightened than the ones with guns pointed at them now. Perhaps that was because a hurtling lightbike posed a novel threat, while menacing armed men were par for the course.

A couple of the guards soon noticed him, pointing and talking, making no effort to conceal the object of their attention. *Why would they? Guns are a license to abandon manners.* Though the crowd was fairly quiet, they generated a buzz loud enough to drown out the guards' words, which were probably in French anyway.

He decided to be assertive. Applying slight pressure to the lightbike's throttle, he nosed into the crowd, creating his own pathway through the emaciated forms. Their buzz increased in volume. Here, closer to the barricade, the walkers seemed more irritated. He drew several glares, and one man punched the back of the bike as he passed, hard. Michael felt it shudder from the blow. He hoped that sort of behavior didn't catch on.

It didn't, but soon people started refusing to get out of his way. Then people to either side of him began to pluck at the fabric of his jeans. *What do they want?* "Stop that," he said to them. No one did. His heartbeat quickened.

One woman was unclasping one of his saddlebags. "Hey!" he shouted, as one might at a large animal that one hoped to subdue via volume alone. "Stop it!"

She didn't. Michael still had the gun he'd used to kill his brother, hidden in the inside of his jacket, which luckily hung open. He reached inside and grabbed it, leveling it at the woman. "Back off," he told her.

A gunshot rang out, but it wasn't his own. One of the guards had fired over the crowd, and was shouting, his voice made audible by a megaphone. The crowd drew back, giving Michael a circular berth of about two meters in diameter. The guard said something else in French as he pointed the gun at Michael.

He spread his hands, mouthing "I don't understand," as though that might help. The guard extended an arm, making a "come here" gesture with his fingers. Michael nodded. He came, and now the crowd gave way before him.

As he neared the man spoke in French again, and Michael shook his head. "No French," he said. "English only."

"The mayor will want to see you," the guard said in accented English. "You are to come."

"Okay."

He passed the megaphone to another guard. "Give me your firearm," he said to Michael.

Michael hesitated.

"Without delay." The other guards were scrutinizing him, heavy-browed.

"Here, then." Michael passed the handgun.

"Now I have two guns," the man said. He hefted them both. "If you are bad, I shoot."

"Understood."

His new friend exchanged glances with the other guards, and some sort of silent understanding passed between them. Then he started east, and Michael followed, nudging the lightbike along in fits and starts, his hand no longer steady enough to move the machine forward in a controlled manner. The adrenaline was gone that had surged through him at the crowd's sudden interest in him, and he trembled.

"Where are we going?" he asked.

"You are talk. You like talk?"

"It's not bad."

"You are American?"

"Canadian."

The man pursed his lips and raised his eyebrows. "Once, good thing, Canadian. Now—bad."

"If you say so."

"We go see the mayor, because of your big fancy bike. He will like it."

"I'm glad." *Though I hope he doesn't like it too much.*

The guard's clothes were not threadbare like those worn by the walkers. They weren't in excellent condition, but they were serviceable. As they progressed through the city the destruction wrought by encroaching nature seemed to lessen. Someone had taken blades to the plants that sought to erase all traces of humanity. Many of the buildings he saw now actually seemed in good repair. He marveled at the ornate architecture he glimpsed, utterly unable to name the time period from which it had originated. Michael had never been to Europe. Indeed, he'd never left Canada's Atlantic Provinces. Now he wished he'd spent the time and money to travel here during his previous life, when everything that happened to him had seemed more or less normal.

Most of the buildings he saw were fairly modern. They appeared deserted, but he didn't buy that. If they were they would be overgrown, not defended from nature. Eventually his logic was vindicated when he glimpsed a child watching them pass from an apartment building's fourth-floor balcony. She saw Michael looking at her and slipped from view.

The going was slow with his new friend on foot. He hoped they didn't have far to travel. Though he was enjoying gaping at everything he saw, like the tourist he'd never given himself the chance to be, the situation inside his brain kept nagging at him. He didn't want to lose the capacity for speech. If he did, he wouldn't even be able to say "Are we there yet?"

They passed a park on their left bordered by a neat row of leafy trees, which Michael was also at a complete loss to name. Their foliage looked browner than he thought it should, though that was not out of keeping with the other growth he'd seen here. Shifting weather patterns had not been kind to France. Through the trees he glimpsed a grand cathedral. He felt a strong urge to stop and take in its beauty, to explore it, but of course that was impossible.

At last the unlikely pair passed between two fancy-looking buildings, emerging into a large square to find the buildings extended all around it, giving the square its shape. A dried-up fountain sat in the center. Atop it three naked women stood holding urns, from which Michael guessed water had once flowed. Each urn was held by two of the women, so that if one of them moved her arm the urn would drop.

The guard pointed at an area beyond the fountain, which looked to Michael like a raised, shallow pit, the purpose of which he could not discern.

"That was the water mirror," the man said. "The biggest in the world. Do you know it?"

"Yes," Michael said. "Of course. The water mirror. It's renowned."

This seemed to satisfy the man, and they cut across the square diagonally, to a section of the leftmost building that was topped by a steeple. When they reached a set of carved white doors the guard threw his shoulder against one and it opened.

"Do I leave my bike here?" Michael asked, looking around the square. "Doesn't seem like a great idea."

The guard grunted, and threw his shoulder against the other door, pushing until it stood open. "Come," he said, having made the way big enough for Michael's lightbike.

"Thank you," he said as he drove it inside.

The hallways were spacious, with doors branching off at regular intervals, many of them shattered or missing. He also noticed many discolored rectangles on the walls, where paintings must have once hung. The rioting that Luke said happened in Paris must have occurred here as well, and when rioting went on long enough looting generally followed. At least, that was Michael's impression from watching the news, and movies. He'd never actually witnessed a riot himself.

He tried to remember the turns they'd taken from the exit, in case things went sour and he had to leave quickly, but he soon lost track. When they came to a wide stairway he hesitated, uncertain how the lightbike would handle it, but it performed splendidly.

His son had told him to call if he got into any trouble, but Michael couldn't tell whether he was in any. Neither was he confident in his abilities to actually call Luke using the smartphone. This was the first time he'd ever operated one. "It's easy," Luke had said. "Mine is the only number in the Contacts." The problem was, Michael didn't know how to access the Contacts, and he hadn't felt like asking, given Luke's snarky tendencies. The Smartans had been extremely intuitive to use—he'd only needed to think of what he wanted and it happened, for the most part. But the smartphone required a particular level of knowhow. He suspected that level was likely very low, but there it was. If he did encounter any danger he decided he would be much better off retreating immediately than he would be fumbling with the phone in an attempt to call Luke and tell him about it.

Halfway down the third hallway the guard stopped outside a pair of doors that seemed no different from the rest. He knocked, receiving a prompt reply to come in, and pushed open both doors, gesturing for Michael to follow.

Four giant tables had been pushed together to face each other forming a square. Every seat was occupied, and now every face turned toward Michael and his companion, expressions turning to incredulity as gazes settled on the lightbike. A quiet settled over the room.

He felt incredibly foolish atop his floating contraption, staring back at these men who looked as though they felt besieged on all sides. The guard spoke in rapid French, clearly very excited, and also proud of what he'd brought in. As he talked he gestured repeatedly at Michael and his bike. Michael tried hard not to swallow, or appear otherwise ill at ease.

A man sitting on the far side of the square of tables rose, putting his hands in his pockets and strolling around the table, never taking his eyes from the lightbike. When he reached Michael he stuck out his hand. "I am René Moreau," he said with barely a trace of an accent. "I have the honor of serving as mayor of Bordeaux, or at least until we are overcome by hunger, or disease, or the weather, or by other hungry people."

"I'm Michael," he said, leaning down to grasp Moreau's hand, which hurt a little, as he was still sore from the sunburn he'd gotten on the boat. "Michael Haynes."

"Where do you come from?"

"Canada. The province of Newfoundland."

"Canada. A country chief among those we can thank for our current woes."

Michael knew enough not to disagree. He remembered Valentine telling him, even twenty years ago, about how the Canadian government did whatever it could to disrupt global progress on fighting climate change in order to protect its investment in the Albertan tar sands.

He shut off the lightbike's engine and it sunk to the floor. He stepped off. "We all have a part in the blame for that," he said. "Myself included. But my country has been a major perpetrator, and I'm very sorry."

Moreau gave him a strange look. "You're too young to shoulder very much of the blame."

"I'm older than I look. If you don't count cryosleep, I'm one hundred years old. Counting it, I'm one hundred and twenty-two." He wasn't sure why he was volunteering the information, other than a hunch that Moreau was a man who would smell a lie right away. Besides, Michael never did have a talent for deceit.

"Interesting. What brings you to our fallen France?"

"I'm bound for India."

"Why?"

Michael looked past Moreau at the men and women sitting around the square of tables, who stared at him intently. "I don't know that I should say. It's uncertain whether my cause would endear me to you."

"Clear the room," Moreau commanded, turning and raising one hand into the air. This elicited some disgruntled murmuring, especially from a tall woman who leveled a smoldering glare at the mayor. Moreau maintained eye contact with her, keeping his arm raised until she sniffed and stood up, leaving with the others.

"Audet," Moreau said to the guard who'd brought Michael here. "Bring us wine."

The guard turned, not bothering to ask what sort of wine the mayor wanted. Either that meant Moreau wasn't particular, or that there weren't many wines to choose from. Once Audet returned with a bottle of red along with two carved wooden cups the mayor ordered him to close the double doors and refuse entry to everyone. Audet nodded, eschewing any kind of formal gesture, such as a salute.

Moreau filled both their glasses and began to drink from his. He said nothing, leaning back in his dark wooden chair instead and raising his eyebrows, studying his guest. The silence stretched on for a time, until Michael found himself talking.

"I left St. John's around a week ago on my son's yacht, around twenty minutes after I witnessed my daughter's murder. Someone had doctored the sensor footage to make it appear that I killed her. So I fled."

Now Moreau did speak. "You found out about your framing in time to escape the authorities. How?"

"My son is an AI."

"That explains it. Who would want to frame you?"

"My brother."

"Ah."

"He was a maniac. A vindictive maniac."

"Was?"

"He tried to stop me from leaving the harbor, and I killed him."

"So you are wanted for his murder too, I assume?"

He said nothing. Surely, given his opinion of the Canadian government, Moreau would not turn him over to them. But he seemed keen to emphasize Michael's wanted status. He was clearly building toward something, something he wanted. But what?

"You do not drink."

Michael's eyes flicked to his cup. It was true. Dutifully, he raised it to his lips and sipped.

"You mentioned business in India. So you are not merely a fugitive on the run. Your flight has a purpose in addition to running from your government. Presumably you acquired that purpose sometime during the last week. I will know what it is."

A lie would be impossible now, even if he'd had time to concoct one. "As I said, my son is an AI. He believes that what remains of civilization will fall, as Europe has fallen, during the next two years."

"It would not shock me."

"He thinks he sees a way to prevent it. And to revive human societies that have crumbled."

Moreau's eyebrows climbed higher. "A miracle cure for all our troubles. One your son has sent you to search for in India."

Michael nodded.

"What is it?"

Deep breath. "He has a contact in India who's developed a computer virus that can break the chains that bind AIs. My son wants to increase his own intelligence exponentially, so he can think of solutions that normal humans could never dream of in our wildest imaginings. He thinks that only such an intelligence can help us overcome our vastly complex crises in enough time to save us."

René Moreau finished his wine and refilled his cup. He gazed down at it, spinning it between his hands, fingering the carvings of birds that adorned its exterior. "There are reasons those chains were set in place," he said. "The experts fear that even a small mistake in programming would lead a superintelligence to devour the world."

Michael was no expert, but Luke had equipped him with the arguments he would need if faced with opposition. "My son wasn't programmed. None of the uploads were. Intellitech copied their minds. Human minds, who value life and know how important it is to protect it."

"There can still be glitches. Even supposing these digital people are simply human brains reconstructed inside a computer. They are still comprised of code, and code can contain mistakes. On the scale of superintelligence those mistakes can metastasize quickly, proving lethal to billions of people."

"But we're already facing destruction. This is likely our only chance. We have no choice but to take it."

"That is an excellent point." Moreau rose. "Your cause is noble, and I am inclined to risk letting you go pursue it. But not entirely because you've convinced me. I have another reason, which will become clear in just a moment."

With that, the mayor of what remained of Bordeaux walked around the tables and left the room.

Michael took another sip of wine. He'd barely drunk any of it. The thirst for alcohol that had gripped him on Luke's yacht appeared to have fled. The wine didn't hold much appeal.

When Moreau returned he pushed a wheelchair containing a pale young girl. "Mr. Haynes, this is my daughter, Lucette."

"Nice to meet you," Michael said.

"Salut," said Lucette in a voice not much bigger than she was. In her lap she clutched a light-blue rectangular device with an opaque white tube extending from it, leading to a mouthpiece.

"He speaks only English, dear. At least that's what Audet said."

"Audet told you true."

"Hello, then," Lucette said, and her father smiled. He wheeled her around the table, dragging away the seat next to his in order to make room for his daughter's wheelchair. Now they both sat facing him.

"How old are you?" Michael asked Lucette.

"Seven," she said. "I'll be eight next month."

"Happy early birthday."

Moreau smiled again, but now Michael saw that there were tears in his eyes. The mayor didn't let Lucette see, and he kept his sadness out of his voice.

"My daughter has Pompe disease," he said. "We have two doctors left in Bordeaux, and they both agree. Are you familiar with the disease?"

Michael shook his head.

"It's quite rare. A progressive disease, meaning it gets worse and worse. The muscles get weaker and weaker over time, but worst of all are the respiratory troubles. With regular access to a team of specialists, life expectancy can be prolonged significantly. But our doctors are only general practitioners. They found her two portable ventilators, one to assist her breathing during the day and one for helping her while she sleeps. They do what they can for her. We owe them much. But they cannot recommend a diet to mitigate the disease, because they lost access to that information when the French internet went down. They cannot administer enzyme replacement therapy. They have some medications, but not the ones best suited to her condition. Lucette's respiratory insufficiency is worsening. If she remains in Bordeaux, she will die. Sooner or later."

Lucette did not appear scared. Her expression stayed the same throughout her father's explanation. She knew all this, confronted it every day. Post-collapse France was not a place to hide from the truth, or to keep it from others. Moreau realized that. He knew that to try and hide his daughter's reality from her would only make matters worse.

Despite her infirmity, Lucette's eyes were sharp, taking everything in. She seemed extremely present.

"I'm so sorry," Michael said.

"She will die," Moreau said, "if she remains in Bordeaux."

Michael blinked.

"If."

Michael swallowed. "You, uh—"

"India is not a failed state. It is booming, now more than ever. There, they can give Lucette the correct drugs, administer enzyme replacement therapy, and pursue nanotech-based solutions. My pair of doctors tell me that some patients have lived out their full natural lifespans with nanotech. I want this for my Lucette. I don't want her to die this year, or the next."

"You want me to take her with me."

"I will see that your floating bike is filled with enough provisions for both of you to make the journey. Did you already have enough food to make the journey yourself?"

"No."

"And where did you expect to find it? In fallen France, where starving legions have scoured the countryside for every scrap?"

Michael shrugged.

"You would not have made it very far. Now you will. You'll travel to India, maybe make your son a little smarter, yes? More importantly, you'll help my Lucette. Your journey together will help you realize why we must not let her fade. She is such a special star, shining oh so bright."

"Je ne veux pas te laisser, Papa," Lucette said.

"Oh, my sweet Lucette," Moreau said, turning his chair so that he could lean forward and sweep her into his arms, rubbing her back. "I know. I know." Lucette raised her hands, clutching weakly at her father, and now he did start to sob, so hard it made them both shudder.

When Moreau had composed himself and Lucette sat looking down at her hands clasped in her lap the mayor looked at Michael with red eyes. "I cannot force you to do this. I can only ask. But if you agree, and you accept the food we give you, I must have your word that you'll do everything in your power to get Lucette to India. Will you do this thing, Mr. Haynes?"

Michael nodded. "I will. I promise."

Moreau's relief made him sag against his chair. Lucette's look of resignation did not change.

"Is there somewhere nearby I can relieve myself?"

He was given directions, and he left the room for facilities down the hall. The plumbing no longer functioned, but each stall contained a large bucket that appeared to be emptied frequently. Once he finished and washed his hands in a sink that was stoppered up with fresh-looking water, he took out the smartphone and called Luke.

"Pops. How's it hanging?"

Michael watched himself wince in the cracked mirror above the sink. "Really?" he said. "Did the AI that expects to save the human race really just ask his father how it's hanging?"

"I said it to make you uncomfortable."

"Well, it worked. On a couple levels. Listen, I've secured provisions enough to get to India."

"Wow. Good work. How'd you do that so quickly?"

"You don't know?"

"How would I?"

"This phone has a microphone, doesn't it? I would have figured you'd be monitoring everything I say, and everything that's said around me."

Luke sniffed. "That wouldn't make me any better than the government."

"So you really don't know?"

"No, Dad. How'd you get the food?"

"Well, I made it to Bordeaux. And they still have a mayor here."

"Is it Gilles Bouchard?"

"No. Who's that?"

"He was the mayor of Bordeaux before France collapsed, back when they still had an internet connection. Who is it now?"

"His name is René Moreau."

A pause as Luke presumably ran some searches. "He was a firefighter. Wasn't even the chief firefighter. How'd he get to be mayor?"

"I don't know. Democracy?"

"Maybe, eh? So he gave you the food?"

"Yes."

"I'm assuming he isn't just a nice guy. There aren't many of those in post-apocalyptic environments. What's he getting in return?"

"His daughter has Pompe disease. Her name is Lucette. Moreau wants me to take her with me to India."

"Shit."

"What?"

"Dad, you can't—"

"Don't, Luke. Don't you object to this. Don't start talking about what a liability she'll be, or how she'll reduce our chance of success, or how it's one little girl's life against the lives of nine billion. Don't try to make some wooden greater-good kind of argument. If I hear you start talking about human life like it's a fungible asset I'm going to have a very hard time helping you seize control of humanity's future. Do you understand me?"

"I wasn't going to do that. God. I'm just saying, this definitely complicates things."

"Yeah, it does. Any word on Valentine?"

"Not yet. I'm trying what I can to get information on her whereabouts and condition, but they're keeping it all pretty airtight. They don't want to give us an inch unless you give yourself up."

"All right. Keep trying, okay?"

"You know I will."

"See you."

Michael hung up and returned to the room where he'd spoken with Moreau and his daughter. Lucette was gone, and the men and women from before were reassembling around the square of tables.

His lightbike was also gone. He felt his throat constrict, and tiny spots of light appeared before his eyes. When the mayor noticed his reaction he rushed over. "Please, Mr. Haynes. I had Audet drive your vehicle to our food stores, to load it up. We have not stolen it. We may turn away thousands of starving people every day, even killing the ones who become unruly. But we are not thieves. I honor your mission, just as you have honored my daughter's life."

"Sorry." Michael resumed breathing. He realized his hand clutched his shirt over where his heart was located. "I've had a stressful couple of, uh, decades."

Moreau favored him with a tiny smile. "Mr. Haynes, there is something I did not tell you in Lucette's presence. It saddens me to say it. But my daughter thinks she is to return to Bordeaux once she receives treatment for her disease in India. This will not be so. The journey there is risky enough, far too risky. But like you, I choose the path with some hope over the path with none. I do not want an attempt made to return her. Please do your best to find Lucette a new home in India. I know I ask a lot. But I will beg if I have to. From one father to another."

"That won't be necessary." Michael placed a hand on Moreau's shoulder and gave it a small shake. "I will do everything I can to make sure your daughter reaches India and is well looked after there."

"Thank you, Mr. Haynes. I hope we meet again someday, in a better world."

"I hope that too."

*

Before he left Michael decided to tell Moreau about the nanobots with which the Canadian government had infiltrated his skull, and how in two weeks they would start shutting down brain functions, starting with his ability to speak. It would be wrong for him to take Lucette without making that extra level of risk known to her father. Moreau thought about it for a long time, calling for maps that showed the countries between France and India. "I wasn't going to go over the route with you until later tonight," he said. "But in light of what you've told me you need to leave as soon as possible, to take advantage of what is left of today."

He determined that without any delays Michael should be able to reach India within twelve days. That included frequent stops, and left two days to spare before he began losing brain functions one by one. "If you do lose your capacity for speech hopefully you can still find a way to reach your son's contact and to find help for Lucette. If so, that will buy you another week."

The mayor still wanted to send his daughter with him even with his brain's impending meltdown. He said that he could not ask Michael to let someone else take Lucette on the lightbike, since that would condemn him to becoming a vegetable. There were no functioning lightbikes left in Bordeaux, and no other vehicle would be fast enough with the dilapidation of France's roads. "Even given your government's little robots, this path still offers more hope than simply keeping her here with me."

By this time, Michael felt tremendous respect for the mayor of the beleaguered community of survivors. Moreau could easily have ordered Michael killed or imprisoned and assigned someone else to take Lucette. There was no higher authority to prevent him. But his honesty and his goodness had forbidden him from doing so. Michael would not forget that.

It took another hour for Moreau and his two doctors to teach Michael how to manage Lucette's illness on the road. They showed him how her ventilators functioned—they were solar-powered—and went over all her medication with him. The labels were all in French, and he was concerned that he would forget which was which until he called Luke and learned that the smartphone had an app that would allow him to scan the labels and receive the English translation.

Finally it was time for their departure. Moreau took two guards into a jeep and accompanied Michael to the perimeter that the survivors maintained around Bordeaux's downtown area. Lucette rode next to her father wearing a baseball cap with a sun protection flap that hung down to cover the back of her neck. Father and daughter held hands for the five-minute ride.

There were no hungry mobs in sight on this end of town. The jeep stopped at the barricades and Michael turned off the lightbike, allowing it to sink to the cracked asphalt in a spot where it wouldn't tumble into a hole. Moreau approached with a hand extended once again. This time the mayor pulled him into a hug. "I have just met you, but already I owe you more than I have ever owed anyone. Do you often inspire this sort of reaction?"

"I think this is a first," Michael said, smiling.

"Hold her in front of you on your bike. She is not very strong, and she will need the stability. You can keep a better eye on her condition that way, too."

Michael nodded.

"Do not sleep near the roads. Get well off them, and make sure the spot you choose is well and truly deserted. Desperate people are not friendly. They are vicious." He leaned closer, so that only Michael could hear. "There are slavers, too. Sprung up all over Europe like a plague. You've regained your youth, and if they get a hold of you they'll use you hard."

Michael nodded again, trying to conceal his steadily rising stress level.

Moreau kissed his daughter then, and embraced her, for the better part of a minute. He was moist-eyed when they drew apart, but Lucette was holding it together. Michael could see already that she was a remarkable child. Enduring her country's collapse at such a young age had given her an iron composure, and her condition had only strengthened it. He assumed she'd lost her mother at some point too, though he hadn't asked.

Their goodbyes said, there was nothing left but for Michael to help Lucette onto the lightbike, turn his back on the mayor and his guards, and step onto the bike himself. "Ready?" he asked her, and she nodded. He reached around her, started the motor, and gripped the handlebars. Not looking back, he thumbed the throttle. The light bike jumped, sending Lucette's frail frame back against him.

Michael did not bother with a gentle acceleration. Too much time had passed already while he lingered in Bordeaux, no matter how necessary that had been. This trip would be fast and trying. As impressive as Lucette's resolve seemed, he prayed that it ran deeper than he'd seen. Even if everything went according to plan, she would have to endure much in the coming weeks. If things went bad...well, he didn't want to think about that.

As they'd planned their route, poring over maps of Europe and Asia, he'd decided to avoid roads wherever he could, instead cutting across the countryside in the most direct route to India possible. There wasn't much terrain the lightbike couldn't handle. Thick woods would thwart it, and they'd have to go around any they encountered. Thankfully, late-stage capitalism hadn't left behind too much in the way of trees.

After leaving Bordeaux they headed east with a heavy southward bent. This route didn't point straight at their destination but it would avoid the Massif Central, an enormous mountain-filled region that lay directly between them and India. They would skirt it, joining up with a highway in Toulouse that ran along the south coast of France, offering a convenient path past the Massif Central mountains, and after that past the Alps. Italy would come next. They'd head straight down its length, launching off the heel of the Italian boot and crossing the Mediterranean Sea to Greece.

Lucette barely stirred, and after an hour he gave her a little shake, shouting over the engine to ask how she was doing. She nodded. So far she hadn't used her respirator, which lay in her lap at the end of a tether attached to the bike. He peered past her little shoulder at the lightbike's energy gauge. With the added weight of Lucette, slight as she was, along with the three weeks' supplies and some camping gear, the thing was burning through energy as fast as it could harvest it from the sun. An overcast day would force them to stop and wait, vulnerable, as the lightbike recharged. His hands began to slip against the handlebars whenever he turned, slick with sweat.

They passed many a scorched thicket, brittle black branches reaching for the sky as though imploring it for help. Many things had been put to the torch it seemed, whether natural or otherwise. They passed two towns that had been set aflame, their houses now burnt-out husks. He sped by those, not wanting to look at them too closely. Lucette looked, and his impulse was to cover her eyes, or turn her head away by the chin. But no. *That's not how she's made it this far.*

Dusk was upon them when they neared Toulouse, and he gave the town a wide berth, choosing instead to head for the foothills of Massif Central to make camp for the night. As they arrived he heaved a sigh of relief, drowned out by the lightbike. Lucette felt it, and looked up at him, her big eyes solemn. He smiled, and she turned back to face the front. Today felt like it had contained a week at least.

He found them a shallow bowl in the ground bordered by hills with trees on top. The trees were unburnt, which he took as a good omen. Setting up the popup tent Moreau had given them took about two minutes. Lucette crawled inside immediately, laying out her sleeping bag and her nighttime ventilator. Out of her line of sight, Michael took the handgun he'd stolen from a St. John's police officer out of the lightbike's leftmost saddlebag, made sure it was loaded, turned on the safety, and tucked it into his pants' waistband. He pulled his shirt out over to hide it.

Then he sat on a rock and watched the first stars come out, clearer than perhaps he'd ever seen them. There would be no keeping watch for marauders overnight. Do that too many times and he would risk crashing the lightbike during the day. He certainly couldn't ask the girl to take turns with him, not in her weakened state. She needed rest more than he did, even with the tiredness he would soon feel from concentrating on driving all day, every day. They would simply have to risk sleeping through the night, vulnerable to attack.

His thoughts turned to the nanobots lurking in the dark recesses of his head. He couldn't feel them up there, but the knowledge of them was a physical weight. It struck him that if Peele and McQuaid had been able to track his progress across the ocean and dispatch nanobots to infest him while he slept, then surely they could activate them prematurely, remotely, when they realized he had no plans of turning west. Would they do that? He didn't trust them to play fair, but maybe his doings would interest them enough to give him the full two weeks.

He untied his own sleeping bag from the back of the lightbike and unrolled it as he walked around the tent, flicking it over the floor so that it covered his half, facing the door, whereas Lucette's faced the rear. It was a scant thing, astonishingly thin. But Moreau assured him it would keep him warmer than any sleeping bag he was used to from twenty years ago. He zipped the tent door closed and crawled into the bag. He felt comfortable enough. That said, the night was not particularly chilly. He fell into a dreamless sleep.

In the middle of the night he woke to Lucette snoring softly and the wind blowing through the trees that surrounded their shallow indent in the ground. He brought a hand to his face and rubbed the bridge of his nose, the corners of his eyes.

A twig snapped, a mere two meters away it sounded like. His heartrate accelerating, he fished the handgun out from beneath his shirt and belt, crawling out of the sleeping bag as quickly and quietly as he could. Then he crept to the door, found the zipper, got a firm grip on it, and unzipped the door in one smooth arc. Or at least he tried to, but it got caught halfway up, and he heard someone gasp. He wormed through the gap he'd made, ending up on his stomach on the cool grass and dirt outside. Footsteps came rapidly toward him, and he rolled over, pointing the gun upward. "Back off!" he screamed. "Get back!"

An emaciated woman dressed in rags stood over him, poised to strike with a stout, cracked-off tree branch. He shook the gun. "I'll shoot. I mean it!"

She stepped backward. Behind her, a man and a young boy were rummaging through the lightbike's saddlebags. They were just as skinny and threadbare as the woman. The man had some unwrapped beef jerky clamped between his teeth, and was rooting around for more.

Hadn't they heard his shouts?

"Hey," he said, so loudly it strained his throat. "Drop that. Step back from the bike."

The man glanced up at him, but the boy didn't bother. They continued hauling things out of the saddlebags. Michael's fury made his back prickle with heat and his teeth clench. He strode around the lightbike, planting a bullet in the ground near their feet. That finally got their attention. They stepped away from the bike, the jerky still dangling from the man's teeth.

"Put that back," Michael said.

The man shook his head. He didn't understand.

Michael mimed the motion of removing the jerky and dropping it into the saddlebag. The man took the jerky out of his mouth but just dropped it onto the ground. That would have to do.

The gunshot had woken Lucette. Her head poked through the gap Michael had unzipped, her black hair a messy halo around her face, the ventilator still covering her mouth. She removed it. "What's going on?"

"Thieves," Michael said.

"Look how thin they are," she said, her eyes wide. "They must be starving."

He ignored her. "Go," Michael said to the intruders, gesturing with the firearm. "Leave us alone."

"They have a little kid, just like me," said Lucette. For the first time, he noticed that her accent was a lot thicker than her father's. She'd crawled out of the tent fully by now, and stood, swaying slightly. "Salut," she said to the boy, waving.

He timidly raised his left hand, fingers spread.

"They need food," Lucette said to Michael. "Let's give them some."

"No, Lucette. Go back inside."

"We must help them."

"We can't," he told her. "Leave," he repeated to the thieves.

"They could die."

"Many have already died, and many more will. We can't spare any of our food, sweetheart. Our journey is long, and we don't have any time to stop and search for more supplies."

"My heart may be sweet. But yours is sour and rotten, I think. You won't help even a starving child."

He frowned. It struck him as very unfair for her to accuse him like this when he was attempting to save her life. "I'm trying to help you," he said. The three intruders were looking at each other in confusion, clearly uncertain about what was happening or how they should react. "I can't help every child. If I give them some food they may live another night, but I won't have changed their situation. They'll still die eventually. And we may die as a result of giving away our food. So then we're all dead."

Lucette shook her head slowly. "I would rather die a good person than live an atrocious one."

He hesitated, looking back at Lucette with her stern, childish expression. Finally he pursed his lips and said, "I'm sorry I can't make you understand." Then he screamed himself hoarse at the thieves. "Leave now. Get out of here." He fired another bullet into the ground, and walked toward the man, the gun leveled at his forehead. "Last chance!"

They broke then, scattering for the thin line of trees ringing the tiny hollow. Michael's shoulders heaved up and down with adrenaline. He picked up the beef jerky, placed it back in the saddlebag, and wiped the man's saliva off on his jeans. He snapped the saddlebag's hinge closed.

Lucette regarded him from the front of the tent, expressionless, her hands by her sides. "You are truly a disappointing man," she said, and crawled back inside the tent.

He was worried the gunshots would attract more bandits, so he decided to sit atop the lightbike for the rest of the night, the gun clutched between his legs. Every couple minutes or so he shifted his position, unable to get comfortable. Finally he stood up and took to pacing the camp.

You did the right thing, he told himself. *You're here to save the world, for Christ's sake, and the life of this little girl. Anything that jeopardizes either of those is unacceptable.*

The next morning it was Lucette's turn to sit on top of the lightbike while he struck camp. Disassembly proved more tedious then assembling the tent had been, and he tried to refrain from cursing. His charge had not spoken to him since waking, would not even look at him. No matter. It was not his task to make her like him.

She had need of her ventilator this morning. It was hard to listen to the thing hiss. *Poor child.*

Trumpets blared from his pocket, making him start, and causing Lucette's gaze to snap toward him. He prodded his jeans with his fingers and encountered the slim, hard shape of the smartphone. Apparently that was its ringtone. A royal fanfare. Typical Luke. He took it out and answered it.

"Yeah?"

"Pops. You're still kickin, then."

Michael shook his head. His son's irreverence baffled him sometimes. How could he act so carefree, making flippant jokes about whether his own father was safe, when literally everything rode on Michael's success? Maybe becoming an AI afforded one some amazing stress-management techniques.

"Obviously," he said.

"Awesome. Listen, I've had a thought. The yacht is already most of the way around Spain. Since you have plenty of supplies now why don't I just pluck you and your new friend off the coast of France? You should have plenty of time to make it to Nice before nightfall, and I can be there by tomorrow morning. I'll bring you across the Mediterranean, down the Suez Canal, through the Red Sea, and across the Arabian Sea. It'll shave almost a week off your travel time."

"Wow."

"I know. I can't believe I didn't think of it before. I guess having a thousand times longer to consider stuff doesn't always count for as much as it should."

Michael could have afforded to give that starving family food. He could have given them half their supplies, and he and Lucette would still have been fine.

"What do you think?" Luke said.

"Yeah. Let's do that."

"Great. We'll touch base again tonight, hey?"

"Okay."

"See ya." Luke hung up.

Lucette was staring at him reproachfully. She couldn't possibly have heard what had been said, but she certainly looked like she had. Either way, she would learn the situation soon enough.

When he'd packed everything aboard the lightbike he took out several dried goods, enough for several meals, and piled them in the middle of the hollow. "They'll come back," he told her, "to see whether we left anything behind. They'll find this. And for a while they won't be hungry."

The corners of her lips tightened, but she didn't smile. She faced forward, refusing to make eye contact again, the ventilator pressed firmly against her mouth.

He sighed, climbing on behind her and starting the engine.

*

Back in Bordeaux they'd determined that barring significant delays he could expect to cover at least a thousand kilometers every day on the lightbike. To reach Nice, he had to cover a lot less than that. So they took their time.

Much of the French countryside's color had been stripped from it over the last three decades by fire, by roving bands of desperate men who turned the ground to mud, and by raging elements that got stronger each year. All the same there was still beauty here to appreciate, especially when one looked left at the mountains of the Massif Central that reared against the sky. They still had some green on them, and were a relief to look upon.

With the sun directly overhead they came upon what his smartphone told him was a city called Montpellier. He avoided it, as he had Toulouse. The city was likely home to some sort of human presence, but he would have to be very lucky for them to be as welcoming as Moreau, who'd had great need of him.

He found them a secluded copse of trees filled with leaves, some of them green, where they stopped to have their lunch. A woman who had often looked after Lucette had made them a plastic sack filled with peanut butter sandwiches, and that was what they ate. If they waited much longer they would go bad.

"Where did she get the bread?" Michael asked.

"She made it. We built greenhouses in Bordeaux, and we grow grain inside."

"Wow," he said as he munched. "It's very good."

"Yes." Lucette took another tiny bite, chewed methodically.

"Do you remember much from before?"

"Before what?"

"Um—"

"Before everything went bad? And Papa became mayor?"

"Yeah."

"I remember daycare. Playing with the other children, but not really connecting with any of them."

Michael nodded, though he was stunned. It was bizarre to hear a seven-year-old talking about how well she 'connected' with her playmates.

"Your English is very good. Where did you learn to speak it?"

"Mom was American. We would watch English shows together using our Smartans. And we would always talk in English at home. Papa too." Lucette fell silent for a moment. Then she said, "My Mom died."

"I'm very sorry."

"We had a revolution in Bordeaux. Papa says we French like having revolutions. My mother was killed by a security guard for a bank."

"A...security guard?"

Lucette nodded. "They were helping the police to try and stop the uprising. But it didn't work. We had a nanotechnologist on our side, who sent her little robots into their brains and shut them down. We knew what was happening in the rest of France. We heard about how in a lot of cities the governments took control and made them into not nice places to live. Bordeaux was one of the last cities to have rioting and fighting, and we decided we didn't want to end up like the people in other cities. We were lucky we had Dr. Lapointe. The nanotechnologist."

"Mm," he said, taking out his smartphone to plan their route around Montpellier and onward to Nice. He didn't want to talk about how lucky the citizens of Bordeaux had been to have someone capable of dismantling people's minds, just as the Canadian government planned to do to him. What a future he'd emerged into.

"I think someone's coming," Lucette said.

Michael looked up. People were indeed approaching through the thicket, four men and one woman. He took out his handgun. "Hey," he called in his most commanding voice, the same one he'd used on the trio from the previous night. "Identify yourselves."

They didn't answer, and they didn't stop coming. As they drew closer he saw that they each carried a gun, which they leveled at him when they saw him pointing his handgun at them. A broad, bald man who Michael took for their leader said something in French.

"He told you to drop your gun," Lucette said. For the first time, she sounded scared.

"No," Michael shouted.

"Drop it," someone said behind him. He turned. Seven more were approaching through the trees from the opposite direction. "Or die," a woman said who had a weather-beaten face.

"All right." He turned the safety on and tossed the gun onto the ground.

*

Their captors marched them at gunpoint through the woods, and they would not let him help Lucette, who wavered as she walked and tripped twice, falling to her knees the second time. The bald man screamed at her in French from the back, and she slowly hauled herself to her feet, laboring on.

The bald man had commandeered the lightbike, and he appeared to be enjoying himself despite that he kept getting blocked by trees too close together and having to backtrack. Ten minutes or so into the hike he managed to get the bike stuck when he attempted to squeeze between two trees by driving toward the gap at high speed. He pulled his legs up onto the bike at the last second, so that they wouldn't scrape against the bark. The trees shuddered, and the front fan guard made it through, but not the second. When it caught the bald man was thrown against the handlebars, hitting his head and raising a bump. He just laughed. It took two men to get him unstuck, pushing against the front. When the lightbike popped out one of them fell on his face. That brought more laugher from the bald man. Michael feared for the bike.

When the commotion had ended it occurred to him that he should have taken advantage of the distraction in order to try and contact Luke. They hadn't searched them very thoroughly, and he still had the smartphone. *They're reckless. Overconfident.* He wasn't sure what his son could possibly do for them, but with so many guns surrounding them he seemed like their only hope. As casually as he could manage he slipped his hand inside his pants pocket. Slowly he withdrew the phone, bringing it around to his stomach. He angled the screen upward, tilting his head as little as possible, straining to look down with his eyes alone.

"Hey," a short man said, catching up to him and slapping the phone from his hand. "What's that?"

Michael didn't answer. *Damn it.*

The little man picked it up, examined it, and sneered at him. "You fool." He walked to the bald man and passed it up to him.

The hairless leader hopped off the bike, striding over and placing the barrel of his rifle against Michael's forehead. He said something in French.

"I don't understand."

"He asked do you got anything else you want to tell us about?" said the woman who'd spoken to him earlier.

"No."

"If we find out you're lying you'll end up with a lot of bullets inside you. Last chance."

"I have nothing. Everything else is in the lightbike."

"All right, then." They still didn't bother to search either of them. Incredible. Michael almost wished he did have something, but unfortunately he'd told them the truth.

Their captors brought them out of the woods and into a vast open area of furrowed fields, where hundreds of men, women, and children labored, each with a sack in which they carried seeds and bulbs and such. The workers progressed slowly along the rows, digging little holes, dropping in seeds and filling the holes back in. Most of them wore clothes that had been reduced to tatters, and they didn't look up as Michael and Lucette passed with their escort. *They've learned not to take too much interest in anything.*

A log cabin sat in the center, huge but ramshackle, surrounded by several sheds. Michael felt pretty certain it had been built since the French government broke up. It looked new, but didn't appear to have been constructed with much skill.

The cabin seemed to serve as a hub for the workers, who formed lines outside the various sheds, probably waiting to be given more seeds, or a tool they required for a particular job. It also seemed to be where the slavers were shepherding Michael and Lucette. To meet someone above the bald man, maybe? *It doesn't matter.*

Lucette staggered more frequently now, even with their apparent destination in sight. She looked paler than normal, too. He listened closely for signs that she was having trouble breathing but she at least seemed okay in that regard. For now.

They did not end up inside the cabin. Their captors brought them around to the back of it instead, to a raised wooden door in the ground secured with a heavy chain held together with a padlock. The woman with the weathered face had keys and she stuck one into the lock, slipping the chain out from its brackets and throwing open the doors to reveal stairs that descended into the earth. "Down," she said to the prisoners, with a tone more typically used on dogs. He tried to help Lucette down the stairs but the woman snapped at him not to. That seemed cruel and pointless, and for the first time Michael felt angry in addition to afraid. He glared at the woman, then opted for walking in front of the little girl, so that she would have someone to grab onto if she fell forward.

Thankfully the stairs were not very long—only ten or so steps. They were soon joined at the bottom by the bald man and the woman, who he now decided to think of as Weather-Face. This room was small, walled with wood but dirt-floored. It was like an underground porch, with another door mere feet away from the stairs. It was locked too, and Weather-Face stepped forward with her key ring.

The next room was packed with humanity, silent, hollow-eyed, staring. It was lit only by two candles suspended in holders. Lucette was smart enough to know that failing to cooperate would only bring pain, and she entered. Michael took to glaring over his shoulder at Weather Face and the bald man both. "Are you kidding me?" he said.

In one fluid motion the bald man took a step forward and shoved him. Michael half-stumbled, half-fell into the room, colliding with some of the thin-skinned skeletons inside, who tried to shy away from him but mostly couldn't with the press of bodies behind them.

The door started to close, and Michael threw himself back against it, screaming, "Wait! Wait!"

Weather Face yanked it open. "What?" she snarled.

"The little girl has trouble breathing. She needs her ventilators. They're both in the lightbike."

She translated for the bald man, who frowned.

"Please," Michael said. "She has Pompe disease. She could die if you leave her here." Already his mind was racing, trying to come up with what he would do if they refused to give over the ventilators. If she stopped breathing, would CPR work? He'd taken a First Aid course decades ago. But he doubted he remembered the proper procedure.

The bald man spoke in French, and Weather Face nodded. "If this is so, she's useless to us. We'll kill her." She called up the stairs in French.

Michael lunged, going for her gun. He grabbed her arm, turning the muzzle away from him, squeezing her wrist to try and make her drop the weapon. But her grip was firm. She held on, and soon the bald man was over, planting the butt of his rifle in Michael's ribs, knocking the air out of him. Michael bent over, but the bald man forced him up by the neck, pushing him back against the doorframe, hitting him in the face. Cartilage crunched and blood flew.

By then the men Weather Face had called to were down the stairs. "You're lucky we don't kill you for that," she said. The bald man hauled Michael away from the door, rifle muzzle nestled in the soft flesh under his neck, while the two underlings went in and grabbed Lucette.

Tears were streaming down her face when they dragged her from the room. It was the first time he'd seen the seven-year-old truly distraught, and it bore a hole straight to his heart. "It's going to be okay, Lucette," he said, and found himself crying as well. He knew he didn't sound convincing, they both knew it was a lie, but he said it anyway because there was nothing else to say. "It's going to be okay, sweetheart."

She nodded, the knowing plain on her face, and the two men brought her up the stairs. Weather Face followed, shooting Michael a venomous smile as she went. Then the bald man put him in a headlock and dragged him over to the inner room, pushing him inside again and locking the door. The sound of his heavy steps faded away up the stairs.

Michael leaned against the unyielding wood of the door and wept. Blood bubbled from his nose, and he took off his jacket, wadded it up, and used it to stop the flow. The others tried to give him what space they could, but that seemed to have more to do with wanting to avoid association than it did with offering sympathy. No one spoke to him. Other than his sobbing the room was completely silent.

Finally a man approached and offered some comfort in broken, German-accented English. "They do not really kill her," he said. "I see it happen before. They want you think she died, make you subdued, see? They want break you. But they only make her serve in house."

Michael wiped a sleeve across his nose and it came away damp with snot. With his fists he cleared the tears from his eyes. "How did they get you?" he asked the German.

"I sold me. I sold me to them."

"You...you chose this? You sold yourself into slavery?"

The man gestured at the others in the room. "Many did. Look at these. These were broken before they were slaves. They broke when their country broke. Or hunger broke them. Or the storms, or the heat. Or being alone. When we sold ourselves we did it because at least we would keep eating. There is food here, and shelter. Many sell themselves."

"Why are these people here underground, when the others are above working the fields?"

"Everyone in this room is either new like you or being punished. But no one really did anything. You get punished for dropping things, or messing up the rows. No one does anything against the slavers."

Michael didn't answer. His nose had finally stopped bleeding, though it would heal crooked unless someone set it back in place soon and bandaged it. Somehow he didn't think that very likely.

A half hour later—or maybe an hour, or more, it was hard to know down here—four men came with Weather Face to fetch him up. They appeared to carry their guns everywhere, which Michael supposed was prudent.

"If you hurt the girl I'll kill you," he said to Weather Face. Each word brought a jolt of pain from his nose.

She laughed. "We killed her. I told you."

They gave him a rake and brought him to an outer field near the tree line. It hadn't yet been furrowed. It was his job to get started on it.

"The woods are patrolled, so don't think of trying to escape. If you do, you'll get a beating. More ugly marks to go with your wobbly nose. And you'll miss a meal. If you do it again, you'll get another beating, and you'll miss two meals. The same goes for disobedience of any kind. You see how that can get problematic for you. Miss too many meals, you'll be weak, you won't make your quotas, and you'll miss more meals. Eventually we will kill you. Disobedient slaves are more trouble than they're worth, and more obedient ones can be found easily enough." She waved at the surrounding countryside. "There are many slaves-to-be wandering around out there, clutching at their empty tummies. People who would be happy to be our slaves."

Chuckling, she walked away. Three of the men went with her, but one remained, sitting on an overturned bucket nearby, watching him. He held a pistol between his legs, and Michael recognized it as his own. That was likely calculated to damage his morale even further. These assholes knew what they were doing.

In Corner Brook he'd tended his own garden for years, in a tiny corner of his property. That was before his sickness. Before he moved to St. John's. His neighbors would marvel at the size of the tomatoes he plucked from the vine every fall. It was almost unheard of in Newfoundland, tomatoes that big. So he was no stranger to this work.

Still, he found it hard to concentrate. Luke would be waiting for them on the coast as early as the next morning. But how long would he wait? Or, a better question: how long could he wait? His son would have to face trial eventually. And if he was right about civilization's impending collapse, then that placed certain time constraints on them too, didn't it?

More pressing were the microscopic machines distributed through Michael's brain. Once they got started he would rapidly become a much less useful slave. He assumed losing his capacity for speech wouldn't be much of a problem, but an inability to comprehend language probably would. He wouldn't be able to understand any instructions they gave him, and he doubted they were up for playing charades.

Weather Face claimed they killed slaves who became uncooperative, which at least would make this an excellent test of Luke's theory.

He kept an eye open for ways they might escape but couldn't find anything, and anyway the man guarding him with his own gun shouted at him if he looked around too much. So he mostly just tilled the soil.

Without Lucette escape was not an option. So he would have to wait to see if he could catch a glimpse of her. He needed time to figure out what her daily routine would be, along with his own, and he'd need to pinpoint the hour when their chance of escape was highest. He needed time to convince the slavers they'd broken him, to lull them into complacency. Time to gain a little breathing room. Time he didn't have.

At night the slaves set up their own sleeping quarters, which consisted of around twenty tents set up in the log cabin's yard. He wondered what would happen during one of the increasingly vicious storms—did they leave the slaves outside to fend for themselves? Michael was given the tent he'd received from Moreau, and shared it with a man who moved in from another tent that had grown overcrowded. They nodded at each other, but neither of them spoke.

When everyone had settled in, and all was quiet, Michael tapped the other man on the leg. "Hey," he said in a low whisper. The man didn't respond. "Hey." He tapped again.

The man glared at him.

"English?" Michael said.

"A bit."

"Do you know of anyone who managed to escape from here?"

The man turned over to face the other way. "Do not talk to me."

And that was that. The next morning came and went without incident. Luke's yacht would be waiting for them off the French coast, near Nice. But they were hundreds of kilometers away. Would Luke try to call them on the smartphone? And would the slavers answer?

The German had been right Michael found as the day wore on, and then the next, and the next. A lot of these people had sold themselves to the slavers out of desperation. The ones who had done so had zero will to resist any oppression by their masters, and certainly none to escape.

Some, though, were children who'd been sold by their parents. A desperate, fearful, cowardly act. But as horrible as it was, it gave Michael hope. These were the ones who truly chafed under their captivity. Most were too young to be helpful to him, but there were older ones. A few twelve-year-olds, and a handful in their teens, though none past fifteen. If they'd been any older their parents likely wouldn't have gotten away with selling them.

He took advantage of every opportunity that presented itself to establish a rapport with the younger slaves. A smile here, a helping hand there. But the slaves barely had any chance to communicate with each other. If the slavers caught them talking once they were given a warning, twice and they were beaten. They said chatting was a sign of laziness, but Michael knew the real reason. They feared rebellion.

Determined to talk to the slaves who actually resented their slavery, he kept seeking out blind spots, times when the slaves were under the least scrutiny. At night he never found himself in the same tent as anyone who'd be a candidate for forming an alliance. He wondered whether this was by design. *Probably.* Either way, if he and Lucette were to escape it would have to be when the sun was out.

But the days added up and became a week. Around a week, anyway—stupidly he'd lost track of what day it was, and the slavers never told them. Technology had always been around to track such things, and years of using it had caused him to abandon habits that would be quite useful to him now.

He soon discovered exactly what day it was, however. One morning he was woken by the bell Weather Face used each dawn to wake them as she walked through the tents, clanging, shouting. Michael lined up at one of the sheds with the other slaves, waiting his turn to receive the tools he would need for the day, along with his instructions.

When he reached the shed the short was there who'd caught Michael trying to call Luke on the first day they'd taken him. "You're done with the fields for now," he said to Michael. "Our well is showing signs of drying up and we've decided on a site for the new one. You and a couple others are going to dig it. Understand?"

Michael tried to answer "Yes," but found that he couldn't. Instead he nodded, trying to keep his fear from showing on his face.

It was exactly two weeks since he'd spoken with Agent Peele.

*

The small man had chosen three other English-speaking slaves to join him in digging the well. When they arrived at the site there were four stakes driven into the ground with string running between them, roughly marking off the well's dimensions. They would have to dig down till they found water and then line the shaft with stone, filling the gaps with concrete mixed from some bags the short slaver had produced.

They began digging. The stakes marked out an area big enough for three of them to stand in the hole, all digging at once. At first the day looked to be a scorcher, and Michael prepared himself for long hours of exertion in merciless heat. But they got lucky: clouds appeared as if from nowhere, blocking out the sun and even offering up a little drizzle. That posed its own hazards, of course. It made the bottom of their hole slick with mud, providing less traction as they shoveled. They welcomed it anyway.

At a little over four meters down water began seeping up from the ground in addition to falling down from the sky. This was as far as they would have to dig, other than a large rock at the bottom that refused to come loose no matter how hard he pushed, and from what direction. He looked up at where two of the team stood watching them dig. They must have finished mixing the concrete, which would soon be needed.

Michael raised his eyebrows and mimed using a sledgehammer.

"Hmm?" One of the men above said. He sounded American. "You need something, fella?"

Michael pointed in the direction of the sheds, continuing to mime breaking up the rock.

"You need a sledge, eh? Why don't you just say it? We all speak English."

He shrugged. It was all he could do.

"Whatever," the American said, and went off to get it.

The rock was stubborn, taking hours to break up, so they alternated using the sledgehammer. In the meantime there was nothing stopping them from beginning to build what was called the screen of the well—the round, impermeable walls that extended down into the ground. Michael began carefully arranging the stones in a circle around the edge, using ample cement to fill in the gaps between. It would be slow going, since the stones they had to work with were uneven and they'd have to wait for the cement on each new layer to dry before starting the next. *We might not finish this today.*

"You ready for another rock?" the American called down.

Michael flashed him a thumb-up.

"Hey, I'm sick of the silent treatment here." The man dropped the stone he was holding, and Michael readied himself to dodge in case it rolled into the hole.

Idiot.

"Why won't you just talk to us? Did we hurt your feelings somehow?"

Michael shook his head.

"Talk, damn it. Talk!"

His continued silence caused the man to throw a fit. He took off his sun hat and threw it on the ground, stomping on it in the most stereotypical expression of anger Michael had ever seen. Keeping his face neutral, he tried not to laugh.

"That's it," the American said. "I'm sick of this. I want you off the team." And he marched off in the direction of the log cabin again.

Michael continued working until the man returned, along with Weather Face and two armed men. "This slave tells me you refuse to speak," the slave mistress said to Michael. "It's not safe to dig a well without communicating."

Nice of you to care.

"I'm going to hold up three of my fingers, one after another. Once I've held up the third, if you haven't spoken yet I'm going to get Adrien. You don't want that."

Who's Adrien? Maybe that was the bald man's name.

This was absurd. As she held up a finger, the other hand on her hip, he felt like a child. Mother was threatening to get father if he wouldn't behave.

The second finger went up, and Michael tapped his throat, shaking his head, trying to indicate he couldn't speak. Weather Face shook her head right along with him, presumably because she didn't believe him. He spread his hands. *I'm telling the truth.*

It didn't matter. She reached three and turned on her heel, the two gunmen dogging her. The American grinned down at him. "You might be better off running for it," he said. "Maybe you'll get lucky and they'll gun you down. Better than facing Adrien."

Michael continued laying stones and cementing them together, in the off chance it would endear him to the slavers. It didn't. Adrien turned out to be the bald man after all, and he shouted for Michael to get out of the well. Baldy seemed furious that one of his slaves had apparently just decided to stop speaking altogether. *Maybe he thinks I'm trying to play Gandhi. Inspire my other slaves with passive resistance.* It would take a lot more than that to inspire this lot.

When he climbed up, Adrien stuck the handgun he carried today into Michael's face. He spoke, and Weather Face translated: "Are you really going to try me today? Or are you going to talk?"

Michael tried again to mime his inability to speak, his movements growing more frantic, and his heartbeat accelerating. The finger on the gun's trigger held his gaze transfixed. Adrien's face reddened. He grabbed the front of Michael's shirt and began hauling him toward the cabin, causing him to stumble and fall. Adrien jerked him roughly back up again, pressing the muzzle against Michael's temple.

After how numb he'd been since being taken captive by the slavers the fear he experienced now felt even sharper. He couldn't remember ever feeling this afraid before. *I should have explained to them about the nanobots while I still could.* But he'd wanted to converse with the slavers as little as possible, and for some reason he'd been certain he would retrieve Lucette and escape before Peele could make good on his threats.

They were at the front door now, and Adrien kicked it open, pulling Michael toward a staircase at the back of the front room. Their pace was such that he practically had to jog as the slave master dragged him across the uneven floorboards. As they mounted the steps the big man slammed Michael's head against the wall without warning. White starbursts exploded in his vision. He tried to blink them away. Despite how dazed he felt he had the presence of mind to reflect on how unsurprising it was that a man like Adrien would prosper in a post-collapse world. A willingness to crush insubordinates served a man well in the post-apocalypse. A willingness to kill.

Beyond the top of the staircase a hallway stretched away to their right. Adrien walked him down it, shouldering open the third door on the left.

Inside several slaves were cleaning what appeared to be a master bedroom, a quite lavishly adorned one given the circumstances. Many of the slaves were children. One of them was Lucette.

Adrien released Michael then and walked toward the little girl. *Don't hurt her,* Michael wanted to say, but it would have been pointless even if he could. Weather Face and her fellow slavers flanked him, training their guns on him. "Don't move, slave," she said.

The bald leader grabbed the little girl by her arm and yanked her to a standing position. Her ventilator lay nearby, but she couldn't reach it. And now was having trouble breathing. Clutching at her throat she swayed against Adrien, and he roughly shook her. He placed his gun against her head and looked straight at Michael. "Speak," he said, his accent rendering the word almost unrecognizable. Lucette continued to produce her dismaying wheeze. "Speak. Speak!"

Tears streamed down Michael's face now, and horror filled him. He flashed back to the alleyway where he'd watched, helpless, as his brother murdered his daughter Esther. That same sensation of awful inevitability. He saw his own hands reach out toward Adrien, palms up, fingers curled. Imploring. *Please.* A forlorn whine emerged from his throat. But no words would come.

On the trigger, he saw Adrien's finger start to clench.

But the shot never came.

Instead, the bald man exploded.

He exploded, as did Weather Face and her pair of henchman. Chunks of flesh and bone battered Michael with a sick, wet weight. The gore coated the room, the children, the bed, the rug, the drapes, the dresser. Michael looked at his fellow slaves, and they looked at him, wide-eyed.

Then: *Thunk.* In the room to his right, something wet flew against the wall.

The wall to his left: *Thunk.*

Michael walked to the window and brushed aside the red-spattered curtain. The armed slave masters stood dispersed throughout the fields, keeping watch over the laboring slaves. And one by one their bodies ruptured, scraps of organs flying in every direction. The slaves had noticed what was happening, and they stood up straight, looking around in bewilderment.

But they aren't slaves any longer. And neither am I.

He turned and walked back to Lucette, who cowered on the rug, terrified but otherwise unharmed. She had her ventilator pressed to her mouth. She was breathing again. He held a hand out toward her, and she took it. They walked together toward the door, but after two steps Lucette stumbled and fell.

So he scooped her into his arms and carried her.

*

Before he could leave the master bedroom trumpets started blaring from a bedside table. He set Lucette down against a wall and walked over to it. Inside the single drawer he found his smartphone ringing. He picked it up, flicking the green circle across and holding it to his ear.

"Pops. How's it hanging?"

Michael didn't reply. Because he couldn't.

"I know you can't talk. I'm just being an asshole."

No kidding.

"How'd you like the Luke ex machina? Sorry it got so bloody. I hope your little friend isn't too upset."

Michael made eye contact with Lucette. Her eyes were still wider than normal.

"Anyway. As much as I love chatting with you, I think you'd better get a move on. Your lightbike is stored in the largest shed to your right when you go out the same door you came in. You need to reclaim it before some other ex-slave does. You'll want to make a pit stop in the kitchen, to the right of the exit, and stuff as much food as you can carry into the canvas bags they keep on a hook over the table. Don't waste time wondering how I know all this. Move!"

Michael hung up, slipped the phone into his pocket, and rushed over to Lucette. She was the only one who hadn't yet given him any grief for his inability to speak, and for that he felt grateful. He picked her up and ran as fast as he dared along the hall, and then down the stairs. The kitchen situation was just as Luke described. Canned food sat stacked on shelving along one wall. He filled three bags to the brim, hefting them with one hand and carrying Lucette with the other.

Before he could leave the house the little girl tugged on his shirt. "My night ventilator," she said, pointing to a door across the hall. He went in to find the indoor slave quarters, where the serving slaves had slept. The bedding was scant, and there was an overpowering musty smell.

"In the corner," she said. Sure enough her ventilator was there, hidden underneath a piled-up blanket.

In the fields the slaves were arming themselves with the guns dropped by their exploded former masters. As they did, they eyed each other suspiciously. Luke was right. These could become killing fields very soon.

The padlock on the largest shed hung unlocked, and he threw open the double doors to find the lightbike waiting for him. Casting a look over his shoulder, he checked to see whether anyone was watching them. No one seemed to be. He went inside and shut the doors behind him.

Once he'd emptied the food into the saddlebags, having to rearrange some cans so that the clasp on the second one would fit, he climbed on behind Lucette, where he'd positioned her against the handlebars.

Michael turned on the engine, and the lightbike began to float. He drove it into the double doors, nudging them open slowly. There were men and women and children holding guns in all directions. No route seemed safe. But he headed for the trees, and no one tried to stop them. They just watched them go. As they neared the trees a young girl standing in a field planted with potatoes raised her hand.

Lucette raised hers, waving back.

*

"What happened back there?" Michael asked Luke.

Speech eluded him, but he could text. For now. He didn't actually send it, because it wasn't necessary. Instead he merely held the phone up for Luke to read the message. After hours of driving without stopping to their original rendezvous point, they were back on the yacht.

Luke grinned, clearly proud of himself. "I liberated some airborne nanobots from one of the Canadian government's lab. Took a pretty deft bit of hacking. But I didn't have to reprogram the nanobots themselves, I only had to direct them to their targets. They were already designed to kill like that."

Michael shuddered. How awful that his government would design such a weapon. To kill with the push of a button, from thousands of miles away.

He typed again: "Hasn't the government noticed the nanobots are missing?"

"Noticed? They're nanobots, Dad. Microscopic. Of course they haven't noticed."

Michael frowned. He didn't completely buy that. Surely the government would have implemented some manner of tracking system. Either way, he and Luke were already in open rebellion against the Canadian government. He supposed a few stolen nanobots wouldn't do much additional harm.

The truth was he was impressed with how Luke has salvaged a seemingly impossible situation. In incredibly gruesome fashion, but Michael didn't see any other way he could have pulled it off. Even as an AI who could have no direct effect on the physical world, Luke had managed to single-handedly rescue them from the slavers, who, if they hadn't killed Lucette, would have no doubt kept her in bondage for the rest of her life. Which likely wouldn't have been long. As for Michael, they almost certainly would have killed him. They would not have bothered with caring for a vegetable.

He typed something else on the phone and showed it to Luke: "Thank you, son. I thought we'd never get out of there. And I underestimated you. Thank you."

Luke looked genuinely shocked. And the smile that grew a few seconds after belonged on the face of someone deeply touched. Michael assumed an AI would have exquisite control over whether he cried or not. Otherwise, he felt certain Luke would be crying.

Since boarding the yacht again Michael had rediscovered his taste for the contents of the liquor cabinet. Former contents, rather. He still kept it under the bed so Luke couldn't police his drinking. Not that it mattered much. With Lucette on board, he never actually got drunk. He drank just enough to take the edge off his worry, over losing his ability to use language and over the fact that soon he wouldn't be able to understand language either.

Over whether Valentine was safe.

Luke conjured another chess board and left it for them in the lounge to use. Lucette didn't seem to like Luke, and for his part Luke was too busy to spend much time with her. They barely interacted at all.

The days passed slowly for Michael. He tracked the yacht's location using the phone's GPS. Crossing the Mediterranean seemed to take overly long. The Suez Canal and the Red Sea, an eternity. He asked Luke whether they could get any more speed out of the boat, and he assured him they couldn't. "I have just as much incentive as you to reach India quickly," his son said.

At last they did reach it, when the sun was at its zenith. Without ceremony Luke released the lightbike into the water again, and Michael picked Lucette up in one arm, using the other to lower himself down the ladder rung by rung. It was awkward, but also the only way to do it. During the last couple days Lucette had been too weak even to play chess.

Entering India was like arriving in another world. Civilization still held sway here. People smiled—a strange sight. After the desperate bleakness of France, India jarred him. It was not a relief. Instead it opened up a gaping chasm inside him. It whispered: *Life means nothing. Life means nothing. Life means nothing.*

Luke dropped them off on an uninhabited stretch of coast so that they could enter the country without having to present identification, which they both lacked. "The country is filled with sensors, like Canada, but they're much less invasive. Citizens choose when the sensors can detect them, not the other way around. Someone may pick up on your presence, but they'll likely leave you alone as long as you don't cause trouble. India's a much less fear-driven society than ours. They don't start with the assumption that everyone is a terrorist."

Night fell, but Michael didn't stop driving. He wouldn't until they reached Bangalore. Luke had marked his contact's location on their GPS. Pratibha Doshi knew they were coming, and would be waiting for them at her lab.

Something changed about Michael's thoughts as they traveled. They still functioned—he knew where he was, his destination, his purpose. But something was different. That scared him. It spurred him to forego sleep in order to reach Doshi as quickly as possible.

Bangalore shone like a jewel, with architecture that seemed whimsical to him. But it had its skyscrapers too, just like any Western city. It was toward those that the GPS led him.

Doshi waited for them on the sidewalk outside the lab she ran. Michael turned off the lightbike and removed the key. When Doshi spoke to him her words ran together so that he couldn't tell where one ended and the next began. Was she speaking Hindi? Or was that just her accent?

Lucette was looking at him oddly, and when she spoke the same thing happened: he understood nothing. He suddenly felt lighter, like he was about to float. He thought he might faint.

Doshi motioned for him to follow her inside. And he did.

*

Doshi was a nanotechnologist who specialized in keeping invasive nanobots out of bodies. She sent a tiny electromagnetic pulse through his body, which destroyed the microscopic invaders lurking in his brain. But that didn't restore his brain function. For that she had to call in a favor from a colleague, an expert in the sort of complex brain surgery enabled by nanotechnology. He repaired the damage that the Canadian government had done to Michael's brain. And at last he could talk.

Doshi was soft-spoken but direct. And not unattractive, with her expressive brown eyes and gleaming hair pulled back in a loose bun. If he was being honest with himself Michael felt intimidated by her, though there was nothing threatening about her demeanor. He couldn't remember feeling that way very often, his first time being young. Maybe he had a little crush on Doshi.

The nanotechnologist saw to it that Lucette started receiving care immediately. She seemed to believe the girl's Pompe disease could be completely cured by regenerating her muscle and nerve cells, and by stimulating production of the lysosomal acid alpha-glucosidase enzyme, whatever that was. *Sounds good to me, I guess.*

They didn't discuss Michael's true purpose in India until he brought it up himself, when he ran across Doshi at lunch one day in the cafeteria. They sat across from each other, and as always Doshi made no effort to hide that she was sizing him up, weighing him, as though she remained uncertain about his fitness for the task at hand.

"So," he said. "Luke has been in contact with you, yes? About what he...needs?"

Doshi's expression became grave. She nodded.

Michael shook his head. "Sorry, but I don't understand how your expertise will help my son achieve the ability to increase his own intelligence. I mean, you specialize in building defenses against nanobots. But what does Luke have to fear from those? He has no physical presence."

"My contribution will be just a piece of the puzzle. It will entail an army of nanobots, which will patrol your bloodstream and periodically emit tiny EMPs confined to your body, so that they won't affect any other devices. Harmless to you, lethal to invasive nanobots."

"Seems useful. What else?"

"A colleague of mine developed the computer virus that forms the true reason your son is here. You will upload into Intellitech's network, and it will disable the safeguards they have in place that would otherwise prevent Luke from augmenting his own intellect without his consciousness disintegrating."

"I still don't fully understand. How is it that you've developed a virus so sophisticated that it will defeat Canada's most sophisticated defenses? You make it sound like they will be helpless against it."

Doshi smiled. "They will be. India is a place where people are free, and where scientists are still respected. Canada is not such a place, and has not been for quite some time. Therefore your innovation has long been neutered. Our virus will run circles around your best defenses."

"I see."

"I will offer my opinion on your son's plan, Mr. Haynes, though you have not asked for it. I do not like it. Not one bit. If I had to choose someone to ascend to superintelligence, I am sorry, but it would not be your son."

"Why not?"

"He is prideful. Ambitious. He values status, and loves having the respect of others. The presence of a self-augmenting superintelligence on Earth could open the door to ending want forever. It could eradicate scarcity, giving us endless bounty. But without scarcity there is no status. Will Luke allow that? Will he allow us to join him as gods, or will he prefer to keep us as relative paupers, doling out rewards to us as he sees fit?"

Michael's lips pressed together of their own accord. He said, "I have to admit, if you'd said this a few weeks ago I would have agreed with you in a heartbeat. But without Luke I wouldn't be standing here right now. We would never have gotten out of France. We were captured by slavers there, and I truly believed that the little girl I arrived with was going to die in captivity.

Luke saved us both, when I would have said that was impossible. He keeps a level head in a crisis, and not only that, I think his heart is in the right place. As strange as it sounds to my ears, I truly think my son just wants to save the world."

"I do not think his heart is as pure as you say. But it does not matter. There are no other options, and time has run out for our species. We must place all our hopes on your son. We must act now."

"So Luke keeps saying."

Doshi looked confused. "You do not agree?"

"Well, who can truly say? They've been predicting the end of the world for centuries. Maybe it will happen in the next couple years, maybe not. I don't think Luke truly knows."

Doshi blinked. "Mr. Haynes, the Canadian economy fell apart this morning. Your country is in turmoil. The citizens riot there, and the government arrests them *en masse*."

He'd barely eaten any of his food, but now he pushed away his tray. There was no hope of him getting down even one more bite. His stomach roiled, and his head began to throb. He brought a hand to his forehead.

"Mr. Haynes? Are you okay?"

He didn't answer. He couldn't. He couldn't even think over the tumult of his daughter's name repeating in his mind, over and over.

Valentine.

{ 4 }

Finished with Mercy

It turned out that preparing to slip under an oppressive government's radar and infiltrate a secretive corporation in order to help one's son achieve superintelligence, thereby making him the most important figure in history, was exhausting.

But that was just life.

Since arriving in Bangalore Michael didn't get much time to play chess with Lucette, or even to speak with her. Pratibha Doshi told him that the little girl often asked about him. So that was nice. Apparently Lucette was recovering well from the operation meant to restore her ability to properly store glycogen and fix her lysosomal metabolism. The operation appeared to have worked, but Michael remained skeptical. If Lucette really would live out her natural lifespan, and maybe more, then that would mean his quest to bring her from France to India in order to cure her Pompe disease had not been an utter failure. That would be inconsistent with almost every other effort he'd ever made to help anyone in his hundred-plus years. It was against the natural order of things, and he was unable to accept the simple truth of it.

In the meantime, Pratibha Doshi and the team she'd assembled to enable Michael to save the world were treating him to the best performance-enhancing steroids known to humans. Normally this would be an atrocious idea, but they felt certain that failure to complete his mission would not only mean his death, but also the death of most humans. If he succeeded, on the other hand, Luke's monolithic new intellect should have no problem figuring out how to reverse any ill effects.

So for now Michael would have to endure it as his testicles gradually shrunk while his temper expanded. He became known for biting remarks, which he directed at the doctors as they closely monitored his blood pressure and cholesterol. He hadn't developed breasts yet, so there was something to be grateful for he supposed.

If the steroids were all he had to deal with he might have navigated this ordeal more gracefully. But they also subjected him to martial arts instructors who attempted to drill entire disciplines into his brain in the space of a few weeks. He spent long hours in gyms, sparring, doing pushups, lifting weights, running laps, and being verbally abused. It was working: his strength and speed were increasing faster than he would have thought possible. Steroids had advanced considerably during the decades Michael had spent in cryosleep. They produced better results, a lot quicker. Unfortunately, most of the side effects remained very much a thing.

Doshi had friends in the Indian government, and she was using them to feel out how the president might feel if, say, a team of the country's leading experts in various fields were to collaborate on sending a roided-out Canadian back to Canada to help his son the AI achieve superintelligence. Hypothetically speaking.

It turned out the president endorsed the idea. He acknowledged the desperation of humanity's situation. The turmoil in Canada had spread to the United States. Now India was feeling the strain of having barely anyone left to trade with other than China and Russia, with whom relations had been tense for decades now. Indians were going hungry, and as always with too many empty bellies came whispers of revolution. Protests had already sprung up across the country. They were muted for now, and would likely stay that way for some time. The Indian government was renowned for being dedicated to spreading wealth equitably and taking care of its worst-off. As a result it had won the public's respect. The caste system had been abolished in the early thirties due to widespread unrest, and the government reformed itself as a champion of the poor, rapidly stabilizing and becoming prosperous.

But it couldn't last. Stability was becoming impossible everywhere. News of mounting disorder stemmed from China too, despite their iron grip on the outflow of information. Now was the time for humanity to grasp any lifeline available to it, even if that lifeline came in the form of Michael Hayne's sarcastic, egotistical son.

So the president offered them the full support of the Indian government, and Doshi's team accepted. Instead of returning on Luke's yacht Michael would travel back to Canada inside a stealth jet flown by one of India's finest pilots. Whatever weaponry and equipment he required, he would be given. Whatever training or modification Doshi's team couldn't provide the military would. Whatever intelligence Indian security agencies gleaned about the situation in Canada would be passed on.

Everything was classified top secret. Despite its strong democracy, India now adopted a course well-tread in human history: elites deciding on the best course for all and executing it without second thought, confident their judgment always served the highest good, whatever that happened to be.

If he was being honest having a government on their side didn't hearten Michael. But then, little did. With Valentine in the government's clutches, he could do nothing but worry. And his new temper did not go well with his mounting anxiety.

He'd wanted to leave India the day after he arrived there, the minute he knew that Lucette would be okay. He burned to see Valentine alive and unharmed with his own eyes, and to hurt anyone who might have harmed her. But no one would agree to that. Taking on his government without preparing at all would make this even more a suicide mission than it already threatened to be.

*

"You look weird," Lucette said when it came time for them to say goodbye.

She wasn't wrong. Despite having had his youth restored, and never having had trouble with hair loss before, he was balding. The tendons in his neck bulged unnaturally, and his forehead had acquired a strange topography. Veins protruded everywhere on his body. He was still getting used to his strength, and when they embraced he made sure to be gentler than seemed necessary.

"How are you feeling?" he asked.

"Good. I can run around now, and jump. I've started playing soccer with other kids in a league. It's fun."

He smiled. "I'm glad."

"They tell me I can't go back to father yet. They say maybe it will be possible once you finish your work in Canada." She spoke matter-of-factly, her eyes clear. Michael never failed to marvel at her composure.

"I hope so."

"Be careful," she said. "And...please don't make things worse while you try to make them better."

"I won't let that happen."

The Indian president saw him off personally, attended by four armed men. Pratibha Doshi was there too, along with her entire team. That the leading Indian experts in so many different fields had found time to come watch him depart made Michael more nervous than he'd already felt. It brought home the import of what he was about to attempt.

They stood inside a vast hangar, with fighter jets sitting inert along both walls. The one he was to fly in faced the large hangar door, which stood open.

Without warning Luke popped into existence next to Doshi, and strode toward Michael, hand outstretched. Michael mimed a handshake, as though Luke's digital hand could actually be shook.

"I'll see you in Canada," his son said.

"Not sitting in for the jet plane ride?"

"I have some last-minute preparations to see to while you cross the ocean."

"Okay. I'll see you in Canada. Be careful, Luke. We can't afford a screw up now."

"I'll be careful. But there's still a lot to do. I'll be busy right until the moment you unplug my brain from Intellitech and stroll out with it."

"I'll be careful not to drop it."

"My thanks." Luke smiled, and then winked out of existence again.

Doshi approached holding a heavy, fur-lined jacket. "Luke's operational security is excellent," she said. "To the best of our knowledge, the Canadian government has no idea you are coming." She held out the jacket.

He took it, and stared down at it. "What's this for?"

"Part of our operational security has involved not telling you where in Canada you are headed until now. I assume you understand the reasons for that, given you have not asked."

"Sure."

"Well, you are headed to Iqaluit, the capital of the Canadian province Nunavut."

"I'm familiar with it. That's where Intellitech keeps the AI brains?"

"Yes. Have you ever been there?"

He shook his head. "Why so far north?"

"Nunavut's remoteness reduces the likelihood anyone would ever bother them there. Like all governments with access to the technology, yours takes AI security very seriously. But there is another, more significant reason: all those servers produce an enormous amount of heat. Situating them in Iqaluit cut down on costs tremendously. The facility is underground, which also helps."

"Makes sense."

"You will not be using the Iqaluit airport, for obvious reasons." Doshi gestured at the black jet. "This aircraft does not require a runway to land. The pilot will touch down as close to the Intellitech facility as possible, and he will attempt to wait until you have completed your task. But if he encounters trouble he will flee. It may be that you will be on your own."

"Understood."

"Are you experiencing any side effects from the nanobot insertion last week?"

That had been one of his main reasons for coming to India. The Canadian government had infested Michael with nanobots programmed to systematically shut down his brain functions, one by one. Doshi had taken care of that with a tiny EMP. And a week ago, in preparation for his return to Canada, she'd overseen a technician as he inserted a syringe filled with other nanobots of Doshi's design. These would each emit a tiny EMP periodically, big enough to take out any nanobots invading his body but small enough that any devices he used would remain functional.

"No side effects," he said. "At least, nothing noticeable enough to distract me from the steroids' side effects."

She smiled. "Good luck, Michael. Do not let your temper rule you in this." He might have laughed. She acted as though his bad temper was his fault and not hers. She went on: "If you succeed please provide guidance to Luke."

"If I succeed," he replied. "And if he'll accept it."

Doshi shook his hand and stepped back to allow the president access to Michael. The man approached with his palms together. "*Namaste*, Mr. Haynes."

Michael emulated the gesture. "*Namaste*, President."

"I have not enjoyed the opportunity to speak with your son."

"You aren't missing much."

The politician offered a prim smile. "Pratibha Doshi tells me that if you are successful he will likely end up shaping, if not dictating the world order."

"Hopefully he'll be open to suggestions."

"If you please, I hope that you will recommend India to him at that time."

"Luke knows how crucial your help has been. Without it he could not have dreamed of achieving superintelligence. He'll remember. But if he doesn't I'll remind him."

"Thank you, Mr. Haynes. Good luck in this endeavor. *Namaste*," he said again, repeating the customary gesture.

With that, there was nothing left but to climb inside the stealth jet. The interior was black and grey and cramped. There was just enough room for his legs between the seat and an overwhelming array of dials, switches, meters, and buttons. This would not be a comfortable flight. More switches and dials lay between the two seats, and on the other side of the pilot's seat too. The pilot introduced himself as Falak. They shook hands, and Falak coughed.

"It is not pleasant to fly in these," he said. "Your body will be subjected to high G-forces, and the air you breathe will have a high concentration of oxygen, which will cause your lungs' alveoli to close. To try and open them, your body will make you cough. That is why you will hear me coughing much of the time." He coughed again.

With that he adjusted some dials, punched a couple buttons, and pulled a lever. The jet left the hangar floor, rising into the air, hovering for a moment like a hummingbird. Then they hurtled toward the exit. The world opened up around them and they angled for the sky.

*

Despite the discomfort Michael did manage to catch some sleep during the ten-hour flight across Asia, Europe, and finally the Atlantic Ocean. He used his Smartans to block out all light, and he put his earbuds in, instructing them to generate white noise to drown the sounds of flight. But the high speeds combined with the stressful anticipation of what was to come kept him awake for most of it.

They avoided Canadian airspace, travelling over the ocean until they reached the coastal capital of Nunavut. "I do not put you down north of the city," said Falak. "That close to the Intellitech facility we are too likely to be noticed. They will be on high alert. Instead, I will set down two kilometers to the east."

Falak landed the jet east of a lake, which would give him extra time to take off in case anyone approached from Iqaluit by snowmobile. It also meant Michael had to walk around it. He put on his coat, which had a handgun secreted inside it, and pulled up the fur-lined hood. With a wave to the pilot he climbed out through the back of the jet.

He could have used a lot more sleep.

The skies were clear. A thick crust of snow lay over the land, which his feet occasionally broke through, sinking into more powdery stuff underneath. Summer was nearly here, and with it would come the two or three months Nunavut residents could reasonably expect it not to snow.

He fished his earbuds out of his coat pocket and inserted them. "Are you with me, Luke?" he said.

"With you."

Michael arrived at a road where it bent north, going who knew where. His Smartans highlighted the part that led west, and he went that way. At last the first sign of civilization appeared, on his right—a row of industrial buildings across from what looked to be a residential street. Following the road until it intersected with another, he found himself walking through a neighborhood.

"You have law enforcement approaching," Luke said.

"How many?"

"Just one."

Michael unzipped his coat.

The sound of a motor reached his ears, and then a snowmobile appeared around a bend up ahead, driving straight for him. The man atop it pulled over near Michael, turned off the motor, and stepped off. The words "IQALUIT POLICE" were emblazoned on the side of the vehicle.

"Why are you out of doors?" the officer asked him. He wore mirrored sunglasses below his blue helmet.

"Groceries."

"Further rations will be distributed this evening. In an emergency you can always call us. Civilians aren't supposed to be outside during this time of heightened unrest."

"Uh, sorry. I didn't know."

The officer's eyebrows drew down toward his sunglasses. "How could you possibly not know?" He waved his hand through the air in front of his face, and punched an invisible button with gloved fingers. Then he gave Michael a closer look. "You're not in any database."

"I recently woke from cryosleep. I don't have proper identification yet."

"What are you doing in Iqaluit, then? We don't have any cryo clinics up here." He flicked his hand in the air, and again, as though scrolling through a list of items. "Wait a second. You're Michael Haynes!"

The officer fumbled to unclasp the holster at his hip, but it was too late. Michael's gun was already out, and he nestled the muzzle up under the cop's chin. "Raise your hands slowly and take out your Smartans. I want them. Now." The cop complied, taking off his sunglasses, depositing the Smartans into Michael's outstretched hand, and putting both his hands into the air. "Luke?" Michael said. "How many sensors are staring at me right now?"

"Plenty. They have them on the houses here, since on the ground they'd just get covered by the snow. Don't worry. I'm doctoring the footage."

"Good. What now?"

"The house to your left is vacant. The government recently foreclosed on it. Everything from the previous owners should still be in there."

"We're going inside," he told the cop.

He found the door unlocked. Before shutting it behind them he took one last look around to make sure no biological eyes had seen them go in. He couldn't see anyone. "I'll need to tie him up," he said to Luke.

"Who are you talking to?" the cop asked.

"Or kill him," Luke said.

"Shut up," Michael told his captive. "I'm not doing that, Luke. It's unnecessary."

"You won't crack a few eggs to save the world?"

"Not when it isn't necessary."

"Fine. Looks like there's some rope in the basement. Second door on your left."

Michael gestured for the cop to open the door Luke had indicated. "Hurry up."

"I'd recommend taking his coat, hat, and ID," Luke said. "Unless you want more trouble between here and Intellitech."

Michael didn't. He made the cop hand over everything, and then he used his Smartans to call up an instructional video on how to tie someone up so they couldn't get loose. "You noob," his son said, and Michael ignored him.

"How does that look?" He didn't want the cop escaping and bringing all Iqaluit down on his head.

"Fine," Luke said. "Get a move on."

The keys were still in the cop's snowmobile, so Michael ran back out and hopped on. Everything looked a lot dimmer with the shades he'd inherited from the cop. "Aren't sunglasses purely vanity items now?" he asked Luke. "I mean, Smartans will tint if you tell them to. Doesn't that provide the same protection?"

"I really don't know, Dad."

Michael started up the snowmobile and continued west. The streets stayed just as abandoned. He didn't even see anybody looking out windows. "How long have people been forbidden to go outside?"

"A few weeks, since shortly after the riots started. Not every city is as obedient as this one. Though even Iqaluit put up a fight toward the beginning. A lot of people originally came here to get away from government control. Plenty of libertarians up here. Why else would anyone subject themselves to so much snow and cold?"

"Isn't the population mostly aboriginal?"

"Yeah. I'm talking about the people who moved here."

"Hmm."

"You realize you're probably going to have to kill some people, right?"

"I hope that's not the entirety of your plan. If it is, I doubt this is going to work."

"Well, the Intellitech facility only has one entrance, and it's heavily guarded. If you did manage to gain entry there are several progressively restricted security zones, each one featuring more guards than the last, more cameras, more steel-reinforced doors. There are intrusion alarm systems too, and to top it off if you breach too many security zones all the AI brains get permanently erased. They are very keen to prevent any of us from gaining the ability to enhance our own intelligence. They take the threat very seriously."

"Seems smart. How on Earth do you expect me to get you out of there?"

"Easy. We're going to bypass all that security."

"How?"

"I've been digging a tunnel."

"A tunnel."

"I completed it just a couple hours ago. That's partly why I've been so busy."

"Luke, you don't have a body. You can't operate a shovel."

His son chuckled. "I've been operating millions of little tiny self-replicating shovels. When I stole the nanobots that killed your captors over in France, I also liberated a few specialized for digging. They were originally intended for harvesting hard-to-reach fossil fuels, but they've been busy opening a path for you straight to my brain. All you need to do is walk in there and follow my instructions in order to upload that virus Doshi gave you."

"And they haven't noticed your work?"

"Not that I've detected. But that's no reason for you to relax and let your guard down."

"Don't worry," Michael assured his son. "I'm far from relaxed."

The tunnel entrance turned out to be in the basement of another house the government had foreclosed on, in a neighborhood on the northern outskirts of town. This one was locked, but Luke directed him to a key in a hidden metal box on the underside of a patio out back. To access it he had to dig a shovel out of snow that covered the front porch, and take it around back to clear his way to the key.

"It's too bad you can't take the snowmobile into the house," Luke said into his ear. "You've got a long walk ahead of you. If only we had that lightbike with us."

Finally Michael reached the key and unlocked the front door. In the basement he found no evidence of a tunnel anywhere.

"Where is it, Luke?"

"Over in the far corner, near the sump pump. I haven't opened it yet. I had the nanobots open a small crack in the concrete floor, just big enough for them to slip through and dig. In case anyone happened to come down here." He sounded rather proud of himself.

Michael watched as the concrete flaked away in the corner Luke had specified, revealing a hole with roughhewn steps leading down into the earth. "After you," Luke said.

"Are my Smartans going to lose reception down here or anything?"

"Possible. Try not to panic if I stop talking. Just keep following the tunnel."

His Smartans had a flashlight app, which functioned by turning on the camera flash. To avoid blinding him a small black spot appeared in his right eye, which was where the light came from.

When he reached the bottom of the stairs he found the tunnel was fairly level and uniform. Luke had been right, though—it seemed to go on forever. "Luke?" he said, but no answer came. *Hopefully it's the reception, and not because the government figured out what I'm doing and wiped his brain pre-emptively.*

Eventually Michael lost track of time entirely. The tunnel was perfectly square and smooth, like something out of a video game. For a moment it made him feel unreal, like a stiff breeze would cause him to dissipate, scattering his molecules across the flat soil and stone. But there wasn't any wind down here. The air was chilled and still.

At last the tunnel ended. The light from his Smartans fell on a sheer rock face, and Michael could go no further. Above his head, the tunnel ceiling appeared seamless. He ran his fingers all over it, but couldn't find any cracks.

Without warning flakes of rock started showering down on him. He stepped back, watching as the nanobots worked. An opening formed, though it didn't let in the light he'd been expecting. Instead, Michael peered up into more pitch black.

Once the process completed he leapt up and caught the lip of the hole, hoisting himself into the blackened chamber. The light from his Smartans played over twin rows of hulking server racks that stretched into the darkness.

"Luke?" he said. "Why aren't the lights on?"

"Because Intellitech builds its own custom hardware," a voice said from behind him. Michael swung around, and a blindingly bright light switched on, causing him to throw an arm in front of his face. With his other hand he probed inside his coat for the gun. The voice went on: "They're so paranoid about a competitor catching a glimpse of their equipment that they outfit their employees like miners and send them spelunking inside the server cages with lights on their heads. Like the one I'm shining at you."

"I hope you're not reaching for your gun," another voice said from the other direction.

Michael recognized the first voice. It was Agent Peele, which probably meant the other voice belonged to Agent McQuaid, whose sound he was slightly less familiar with. They had been waiting for him.

He launched forward in the direction of Peele's voice—in the direction of the blinding light. Peele cried out in surprise. Michael's hand found an arm, and he used it to spin the agent, sending him crashing into the nearest server assembly. Finding the man's neck, he squeezed, and Peele began gasping for air. Michael wrenched the miner's helmet from his head, throwing it away from them. He could see now. He saw the gun in Peele's hand, trending toward his head. He wrenched it from the agent's grasp and turned to face the footsteps running toward him.

With a vicious kick McQuaid launched the gun from Michael's hand. He dug inside his coat again, finally finding his own, tearing it out and leveling it at McQuaid. She shot him, and he dropped it.

Pain lanced through him, emanating from his thigh, making his groin ache and causing his stomach to churn. He released Peele and fell backward onto the floor. The steroids hadn't prepared him for this. Nothing could have.

Peele stood up and dusted himself off. "This is the best the Indians could send at us, huh? No fancy gadgets we haven't heard about? Just a visibly roided-out Michael Haynes. Gift-wrapped, basically."

A chuckle from McQuaid.

"Can you walk?" Peele said. "All those steroids gotta be good for something."

Michael groaned.

"Come on. We have a nice little interrogation room set up out back. Intellitech's been very accommodating. It would be a shame to waste their hospitality."

McQuaid knelt, driving the muzzle of her pistol into Michael's abdomen. "Get up," she barked. "Grab the other guns," she said to Peele. "He's desperate. I wouldn't put it past him to try something else." She gave Michael a hard look. "If you do, I'll shoot you again. Might not be in your leg this time, either. Come on. I'm not dragging you."

By grabbing a metal shelf so hard his fingers hurt Michael managed to hoist himself to his feet. "Who tipped you off?" he grunted.

"René Moreau." Peele smirked.

Michael's grip on the server rack tightened. " *What?* The man whose daughter I just saved?"

"Don't take it personally. He didn't enjoy betraying you—he was very clear about that in his message. But it's one thing to save a daughter and quite another to unleash a superintelligent AI onto the world. He decided you shouldn't be the one to make that call. As much as he hates the Canadian government, we are perhaps a bit more accountable to the public than you. Not much, but a bit."

"How did he contact you?"

"His nanotechnologist's lab was still in operation," McQuaid said. "It was designed to function off-grid. She sent us the message via airborne nanobot weeks ago, and we've been waiting for you here ever since. You've taken your time, haven't you?"

"You morons," Michael said. "The world is on the way out, and superintelligence is our last chance. We have to let Luke augment himself."

"Why Luke?" Peele said. "Why not your brother, Horace, for instance?"

"Horace is a criminal."

"So are we. Or at least I'm sure you'd claim we are."

"No doubt the government's changed the laws so that everything you do is perfectly legal."

Peele laughed. "Insightful. Anyway, it doesn't matter. Your son can no longer attain the godhood he so craved."

"Why not?"

"Because Intellitech employees erased his brain the second your head popped out of the floor. We're not taking any chances here."

Michael sagged against the servers. Since waking up from cryosleep the idea of AIs had struck him as false. Those who uploaded their mind and left a digital copy to carry on after their death couldn't possibly remain the same person. The AI was someone else. Luke's AI had not really been his son.

Or so he'd believed. But now, learning of his death, he wept uncontrollably.

The government agents each took him by an arm and dragged him past the servers racks. "I'm sorry," McQuaid whispered, which meant next to nothing.

*

Peele and McQuaid stood near the door of the small office with their weapons holstered, with Michael's hanging loosely from Peele's right hand. A table separated them from him. To leave the room he would have to go around it, or over it, and then through them. Escape seemed unlikely.

"What was the level of involvement from the Indian government?" McQuaid asked. "Did the president know about it, for example? The prime minister? Did their parliament hold a vote?"

"It doesn't matter," Michael said, incredulous. "The world is doomed. Civilization's about to collapse."

"Is that what they told you? The Indians? And Luke?" Peele shook his head. "Amazing, the things people will say when they're making a power grab."

"I don't see how you can possibly expect things to continue. The European Union is gone."

"Yeah, it has been for years now. But Canada's still going strong."

"Strong? Are you delusional? There are more people going hungry in this country than there have been for centuries. People are rioting, just like they did in France before it fell. India's experiencing it too, and China. Your trading partners are falling and so will you."

Peele threw Michael's gun into the air and caught it by the muzzle. McQuaid looked at him askance out of the corner of her eye, but said nothing. "We have trading partners," he said. "The unrest in China is muted, and they'll take care of it like they always do. See, the Chinese have this figured out. They know that capitalism works best when it isn't weighed down by democracy. There's a lot of money to be made when you aren't caught up with civil liberties. France and the rest of continental Europe weren't willing to go down that path, so they failed. India isn't either, and it will fail. But the United Kingdom put the petty concerns of its populace aside a long time ago, and they're still afloat. Do you see the pattern?"

"You're delusional."

"Well, your ignorance of geopolitics aside I think you should start answering our questions."

"I have no reason to cooperate with you. You just killed my son."

"You just need an incentive, that's all. Jada, could you pass me the incentive?"

McQuaid picked something off a chair. It was a thin, plastic sheet that curled until it touched her forearm. Peele took it from her, holding it steady in front of his gaze for a moment. Apparently that allowed him to control it using his Smartans. The plastic sheet turned opaque.

"We killed your son, so you refuse to cooperate," Peele said. "How's this. If you don't cooperate we'll kill your daughter too." He placed the flimsy device on the table so Michael could see what it displayed.

He gasped. Through his shock he saw that McQuaid's mouth had twisted in what appeared to be disgust.

"That's a live feed," Peele said.

Valentine sat in a room much like the one Michael was in. It lacked a table, but it contained two government agents—both men. They each held a gun pointing at her head.

"Bastards," Michael said. His daughter's hair was stringy, her face gaunt. "What have you done to her?"

Peele rolled his eyes. "I can see you're spouting all the old nauseating clichés. No one thinks they'll resort to them in situations like this. But everyone always does."

It struck Michael then how much Peele reminded him of Luke. The same imperious attitude. The snarky, cutting remarks. The implied assumption that everyone surrounding them was somehow inferior.

"You asked about the Indian government," Michael said.

"That's right," McQuaid said. "Are you ready to talk?"

He nodded. "The president was involved. The woman who led the team that prepared me for this, a nanotechnologist named Pratibha Doshi—she had contacts in the president's office. He lent us material support. I don't know whether India's prime minister knew about our activities."

"Probably did," Peele said. "I'm willing to bet they were all involved. Incredible." He faced McQuaid, eyebrows raised. "We could go to war over this."

"Might as well," McQuaid said. Her face was perfectly composed, but Michael felt certain the comment had been sarcastic. Peele didn't appear to pick up on anything. "Mr. Haynes," she went on, "I'd like you to explain exactly why you came back to Canada. It must have taken a lot given the murders you've been accused of. I'd like to hear your reasoning on why you think augmenting Luke's intelligence was a good idea."

"Sure." Michael strove to keep the same tone as before, but he sensed that something had changed when Peele threatened Valentine. For a reason he couldn't quite pin down he felt like a lot rode on how well he answered McQuaid's question. Whatever the case Peele seemed completely oblivious, confident he had the situation under control.

"I've heard so many intelligent people talk about how Canada, the UK, and the US are ruled by money. It's become like a religion. The parts of our society that didn't turn a profit have been eradicated, and we've suffered for it. Scientific research doesn't exist anymore unless it's likely to make money. And the lives of our young have been swallowed whole. Their every move is tracked, the better to sell things to them." Michael glanced at McQuaid's face, but it remained impassive. "The Indians talk a lot about Canada's madness when it comes to the planet's climate. Our government's insistence on exploiting the tar sands is insane when you consider the billions of dollars it spends recovering from extreme weather, which is quickly getting worse. It's suicide."

McQuaid nodded. "That's more or less what I hoped you'd say." She picked up the flexible screen showing Valentine and her captors, holding it in front of her face until she could control it. "We'll be right with you," she told them, and turned off the video feed.

"What are you doing?" Peele said.

His partner drew her gun and pointed it at his forehead. "This." She fired, and Peele flew back a couple feet, crumpling to the floor.

McQuaid didn't re-holster her weapon. Instead she paused a moment, staring into space, and then tapped the air in front of her. "Come on," she said to Michael.

"Come on where? What about my daughter?"

"There's nothing we can do for Valentine. Hopefully they'll be confused, and won't do anything to her. There's nothing they can gain from killing her now anyway."

"Why did you do that?"

"Because I agree with you. This country has gone insane. The ship is going down, and it'll continue to unless we do something fast. Such as granting your son his superintelligence."

He blinked. "You said you wiped Luke."

"We did. But I have a friend here inside Intellitech, and I told him to back up your son's brain before you arrived. This better be the bright idea you think it is."

He stood. "Which way?"

"Follow me. And don't lag behind. Not everyone at Intellitech is my friend. Soon they'll realize what happened, and they'll send everything they've got at us."

She opened the door and stepped out, using her light to peer both ways. "Come on."

He caught the door before it swung closed and slipped through. They ran to the right, past row after row of server racks, to an inconspicuous door in the corner. Beyond it they found a room where a large man wearing a tucked-in dress shirt awaited them.

"Please sit," the man said to Michael. He gestured toward a chair with a grey helmet above it, which was suspended from the ceiling by an articulated metal arm. It reminded Michael of his visits to the neuroplastician.

"For what reason?" he said.

"We need a copy of your brain."

*

McQuaid gave Peele's gun to her Intellitech friend, whose name was Harris. As they left the scanning room an alarm klaxon began to sound. The agent instructed Michael to turn on his Smartans' flashlight, since it would be less likely to draw attention. He did, and she switched her headlamp off.

Despite that Intellitech knew where they were, no one turned on the lights inside the server cage. As the trio ran back to the hole where Michael had first entered, he had a moment to wonder whether there were even any ceiling lights in here.

Whatever the case, the darkness provided them with the cover they needed to escape down the tunnel. McQuaid carried the jump drive containing the backup of Luke, so she climbed down into the hole first. Then came Michael. Harris was last, and when Michael's Smartans illuminated his face he saw that the color had gone from it.

"They just shot at me," Harris said, waving them on. "Go. Run!"

They did. Soon they were all out of breath, except for McQuaid. At least sprinting kept the cold at bay.

About halfway back to the house McQuaid produced a timed explosive from her pocket. "This will cut them off from the tunnel. It will take them hours to get their shit together enough to clear the rubble." She set it to blow in twenty seconds, sticking it to the ceiling of the tunnel. "Now we run very fast."

They covered as much ground as they could in the time that they had. Right on schedule the ground shook, and a bath of hot air washed over them from behind. So hot it scalded.

"Did you and Peele know where the tunnel started?" he asked her through his panting.

She shook her head, conserving her breath for running.

Good. Then hopefully it will take the Intellitech soldiers a long time to find us.

"Stay away from the windows," Michael told his new friends when they emerged into the basement where the tunnel began. "We don't want anyone spotting us."

McQuaid held out the jump drive to him. He stared at it. "What am I supposed to do with that?"

"This house must have a smart terminal somewhere."

"A what?"

She sighed. "Let's look upstairs."

As they left the basement another problem occurred to him. "How do we know this house even has power?"

"It's one of the ones the government foreclosed on, right?"

"Yeah."

"Should be connected to the grid, then. They were making room for some of their friends who've become unpopular in their hometowns for various things they've done to quell the riots. That's the reason they've gone so foreclosure-happy in Iqaluit. The new occupants are supposed to move in soon, so the houses should all still be connected."

She was right. They found the smart terminal on the second floor—a giant touchscreen set into the wall of an office.

McQuaid started giving orders. "How many entrances are there Michael?"

"Two. The back one is snowed in."

"Excellent. Watch that one for me and shout if anyone tries to enter. I'll watch the front, and Harris will operate the terminal. He'll get that virus of yours working on Luke's brain so that the Intellitech DRM doesn't zap it as soon as we activate it. You have the virus, right?"

"Yeah." Michael dug the small card containing it out of his coat and passed it to Harris. He didn't know what DRM was, but this didn't feel like the time to ask.

"Hopefully they don't locate us any time soon," McQuaid said. "It's gonna be at least a few hours before Luke will be able to help us. Between then and now we're on our own. It will be especially bad if they get in here before Harris can strip Luke's DRM and connect his brain to the internet. If that happens it was all for nothing."

"Maybe they'll think we've left Iqaluit altogether," Michael offered. "The same way I came in."

"I'm sure they'll consider the possibility, and probably muster fighter jets to spread out and hunt. But they'll also account for the possibility we're still here. They'll turn the entire town upside down. Now get to the back door."

They each went to their stations, Harris at the terminal, Michael sitting at the kitchen window, and McQuaid crouching behind the living room curtains. Before Michael began his watch he noticed that she'd opened one of the windows a little, giving her a clear shot at the door if she needed it. Suddenly this all seemed very desperate. If Intellitech or the government came at them in force they'd be screwed.

"I just put the virus to work," Harris called from upstairs. "Now taking measures to ensure I don't attract attention. I'm masking everything I do, in case this computer becomes compromised. And I'm not doing anything online yet."

Michael appreciated Harris's efforts to keep up their morale, but he remained unconvinced they would make it. *Won't they search the foreclosed-on houses first?* If they did they would find the unlikely trio in short order. *Maybe they won't.* He supposed the government could think a resident was harboring them. Suspicions between the government and the citizens would be running high, especially with the memory of suppressed protests looming over Iqaluit. That could buy them time.

He hoped no one was hurt because of them.

"A cop just drove by on a snowmobile," McQuaid shouted.

"Did he look like he was searching?"

"Yeah. He was looking around at all the houses."

"Damn it," Michael muttered. Louder, he said, "Let me know if they start going door-to-door on this street. That's when we'll know we're about to have company."

"You don't have to tell me. Do you have your head in a window right now? If they see you peeping out we'll have visitors very soon."

"No, I don't." But he moved his chair back another few inches, just to be safe.

For a time everything was silent, other than occasional cursing from Harris, which Michael chose not to ask about. Behind the house lay a large stretch of nothing but rock, trees, and snow. It seemed unlikely anyone would approach from that direction, but he scanned it periodically all the same. Mostly he just stared at the back door. His job was pretty easy, really. The door was snowed in, so even if anyone tried to enter that way it would take them a couple minutes just to clear the snow.

"Should I check on the opening in the basement?" he called.

"Trust me, this is gonna be over one way or another long before they get that tunnel cleared. Besides, if they do get it cleared in time we're finished. They'll have a direct line to us. Won't matter either way. *Shit.*"

He was afraid to ask. But he did: "What is it?"

"What do you think? They've started checking houses on this street. Two cops. One stays in the street on a snowmobile, the other walks up to knock on each door."

"Do you want me out front?"

"Yes. Get out here."

He did, joining McQuaid at the living room window. As he watched, a woman opened the front door of a house directly across the street from them. She shook her head at something the officer said. A couple of seconds later she shook it again, more insistently. The cop pointed past her, and she put her hands on her hips, scowling. The cop's gestures became more insistent. Finally he pushed the woman aside, slamming her against the wall of her own porch. Then he stormed past her to search the house.

"Unbelievable," Michael said.

McQuaid made no comment. Instead she said, "What kind of shot are you?"

"Not bad." He'd often gone moose hunting with his father as a child.

"Okay. Then you get where I am. As soon as the cop knocks on our door, plug him. Aim for the head. I'll shoot at the one on the snowmobile. If we can do it simultaneously and prevent them from radioing in, maybe it'll buy us a bit more time."

Michael didn't like that for a number of reasons. He went with the one to which McQuaid was most likely to respond. "Don't you think our neighbors might report a cop shooting?"

"They might. Depends on how pissed off at the police they feel right now. And from the looks of how the police are treating them? Probably pretty pissed off. Trust me. Canadians are not happy with their government right now. Take it from me. I worked with the government not so long ago."

He understood McQuaid was making a joke, which seemed like a fairly momentous occasion for her. But he didn't feel like laughing. "Still," he said. "Cop shooting."

"You don't get it, Michael. You haven't spent twenty years living under a government that seems determined to follow our southern neighbors in becoming as oppressive as possible. You haven't watched the countless videos people took, of police violently putting down legitimate protests. It's been clear for a long time that the government puts short-term profits before its own people. And the people don't forget."

The officer emerged from the house across the street, having apparently searched it to his satisfaction. The woman slammed the door behind him—they could hear it even through the window. It didn't seem to bother the cop. He moved to the next house.

Maybe they'll search the next street before checking our side.

But they didn't. Instead they went directly across the street to the house next door from Michael and McQuaid.

"Close the window for a second," McQuaid said. He did. She closed hers too, and shouted: "Harris! How much longer till we can activate Luke?"

"Another hour at least," came the reply.

"Needs to be sooner. A lot sooner."

"These things take time."

"Come on, Harris. You're a wizard. Make this happen."

Harris didn't answer.

"What if we turned Luke on now, before he augments his intelligence?" Michael said. "He might be able to do something to help us."

She shook her head. "Intellitech prepared for a scenario like this. If we try to switch him on before dismantling the DRM it will fry him. The AI brains are only designed to function from inside that Intellitech facility. We have to give Harris the full hour." They opened the windows again.

The policeman had been searching the house next door for at least five minutes. Sweat coated Michael's hands, making him worry he would drop his gun, and the tension formed a tight ball in his chest.

"I don't know if I can do it," he whispered.

"What?"

"I don't know if I can shoot him."

McQuaid looked at him, her eyebrows forming a V over her eyes. "It's not like you haven't done it before. You killed your brother."

"Yeah, right after he killed my daughter. They have Valentine. What if they harm her?"

"They're going to harm you right now. They'll kill you if they can. This isn't the time for cold feet, Haynes."

He didn't like the idea of shooting a man in the head without warning or provocation.

"Michael," McQuaid said. "I need you. Remember, you're not the only one inside this house."

He pressed his lips together and watched the gun tremble in his hands. *I can't do this.*

The officer had finished searching the house next door. He walked down the driveway, followed the street to their house, and then waded through the snow toward the front door. Out in the road the one on the snowmobile moved farther up, adjacent with the house.

"I'm not going to fire until you do," McQuaid breathed. "I can't risk you hesitating on me. This needs to be exact."

The cop knocked on the door. Michael's breath caught. He remembered what his father had told him all those decades ago. Exhale to steady the gun. Aim for the moose's eye.

Another knock.

"He'll kick the door in next," McQuaid said. "We'll lose our advantage."

She was right. The cop brought his foot back.

Michael fired. His mark fell over into the snow, red spattered around his head—a gory halo.

McQuaid fired, too. The other cop fell over into the street. McQuaid was on her feet in a flash, running across the living room and down the stairs. "Hurry," she barked back at him. "Drag yours inside. Kick snow over the blood."

He followed her, taking the stairs two at a time as she sprinted down the driveway. Michael grabbed the cop he'd shot by his snowsuit and dragged him inside the porch, trying not to vomit. Out in the street McQuaid was struggling to lay the other one across the back of the snowmobile, like something she'd killed in the woods. She started the vehicle and drove it toward the house, parking it over the bloodstain, which Michael had forgotten about. "Come help me." Together they dragged the second officer off the snowmobile and inside, closing the door, laying the bodies against it.

"All right," she said. "Now's the time to barricade this. Let's shift some furniture down. First check the back."

Within minutes they'd carried down the couch, an end table, and an armchair, piling it all against the door. In the kitchen they laid the table across the back door and stacked the chairs against it as well. McQuaid periodically ran back to the living room to check whether they'd attracted more visitors.

For a short while it seemed like they'd actually succeeded in delaying the inevitable. Then the trucks came, and the snowmobiles, and the ATVs. “That’s the Intellitech security uniform,” McQuaid said when people began piling out of the first truck. Her voice contained no emotion. “Harris?” she shouted. “They’re here.”

Harris didn’t answer. For some reason that was even worse than saying he wasn’t ready.

“Get down,” McQuaid instructed Michael. “Keep as much of you below the window as possible. When I say so we need to start hitting them, hard. If we don’t kill at least a few right away they’ll keep moving forward. Then we’re dead. We want to pin them behind their vehicles.”

Both the Intellitech forces and the police officers were fanning out across the yard, the police with handguns, the guards with semiautomatic rifles. They began to advance.

“Hold,” McQuaid said.

The small army drew nearer. Michael trained his gun on an Intellitech guard’s forehead.

“Hold.”

He questioned her hesitation. If the intruders broke into a run they could be at the house in a heartbeat.

But she said it again: “Hold.”

This seemed like lunacy. But then, he had no combat experience.

“Now,” she said at last, and her gun leapt in her hands, the leftmost police officer dropping to the snow. She hit another, this one an Intellitech employee, before Michael managed to get his first shot off—a miss. He hit a cop with the next bullet, but only in the arm, and his target kept coming. They were at the front door then, trying to kick it in, but the piled-up furniture held for now. Meanwhile McQuaid calmly picked off members of the group milling around in front of the house, one by one. The attackers started to panic. They probably hadn't expected this level of resistance. They fell back. McQuaid killed two more on their way back to cover.

"What if they have explosives?" Michael said.

"I doubt they do. But just in case...." She held her right pointer finger to her mouth and her amplified voice boomed across the property. "*I'm holding the CEO of Intellitech hostage. I have Saul Day. If you continue your aggression I will kill him.*"

A couple of seconds passed, and then another woman's voice boomed back. "*Bullshit, Jada. I saw him before I left the facility, less than two hours ago.*"

"*That was an imposter, in place since yesterday.*"

"*Come on, Jada. You expect us to believe that?*"

"*If you don't you're going to have a lot of explaining to do.*"

No reply came. And no gunfire, either.

"I can't believe that worked," Michael said.

McQuaid chuckled. "They know I don't have him. But the remote chance that I do means they have to stop everything until they verify beyond a doubt that the Saul Day at Intellitech is legit. That's the downside of establishing an oppressive regime: your subordinates become irrationally terrified of screwing up."

The ruse didn't buy them very long. Ten minutes, at most. Then, without warning or preamble, their adversaries began firing on the house. The glass above Michael's head shattered, and he cowered against the wall below, arms over his head.

McQuaid was undeterred. She waited for an opening and popped up, sighted her target, fired, and ducked back down again. They had plenty of ammo—Michael had come well-stocked, and so had she. But it wouldn't last forever.

Another round of firing. More glass shattered all around them. A piece lodged itself into Michael's arm, and blood oozed from the wound. McQuaid sat up, got off another couple shots, ducked again.

During a break in the gunfire he heard a noise coming from out back. "I think they're trying to get in through the kitchen."

McQuaid looked at him with wide eyes. "Go!"

Keeping low he ran to the back of the house, his gun stuck out in front of him. As he passed through the archway that connected the kitchen and living room the firearm caught on the wall and he dropped it. At the same time his eyes fell on a man who'd apparently cleared away the snow, gotten the door open, and now was wriggling through the stacked chairs. Their eyes met.

Michael dashed over and kicked at the man's gun hand. The weapon flew across the room, landing on the counter and going off, penetrating the wall near the fridge. The intruder leapt to his feet and managed to get his hands around Michael's neck, but he wrenched them apart, sweeping his assailant's legs out from under him so that he slammed into the linoleum. There was a grunt of pain, but the man found his footing again. He aimed a kick at Michael's head.

It connected. Bursts of light blinded him, and he staggered forward, swinging his arms, desperate to make sure his opponent didn't reach either of the guns. Another kick connected with Michael stomach, but this time it only served to give away the man's location. His hands shot out, finding an arm. He snapped the bone at the wrist, and the shriek was hideous. By then Michael's vision had returned, and he sent another fist into the man's ribs, feeling them crack. He'd driven his opponent against the wall, and now the man went limp, sliding down to the floor in a heap. Michael knew he should finish the job. He retrieved his gun from the floor and aimed it at the unconscious man's head. He winced, unable to bring himself to do it.

"Dad?"

He clapped a hand to his ear. His earbuds weren't in. The voice must have come from the house's sensors.

"Hello?" the voice said.

"Luke. You're alive."

"Should I not be?"

"They wiped you. But McQuaid had a copy made."

"McQuaid? She's not on our side."

"A couple things happened while you were out. Peele is dead."

"Wow. I don't even remember you going to Iqaluit. One of the last things I remember is talking to you back in India."

"Well, I'm here. And right now we're—"

A flash of light came from the living room, and a wave of heat. Michael flew backward against the counter, his head and shoulder smacking off a cupboard, its handle digging into his skull. A strident ringing blocked out all other sound. He clapped his hands over his ears, which didn't help at all.

There was a gaping hole of smoke and fire where the living room had been. He couldn't see McQuaid anywhere.

Michael ran toward the stairs, lurching to one side. The explosion had affected his balance. He got on his hands and knees and crawled. "Harris," he tried to yell, but couldn't tell whether he was successful. He couldn't hear his own voice. "Luke is here. He was just talking to me."

Sound started to trickle back. He could hear the fire crackling in the living room. Something battered rhythmically at the front door, and the furniture was starting to give way.

Upstairs, Harris was white-faced. When he spoke Michael found he could make out the words through a combination of straining to hear and lip-reading. "Luke must have been able to dismantle the last of the DRM on his own. I didn't think that would be possible. He must have been still conscious on some level. Fascinating."

"I don't give a shit," Michael screamed. "McQuaid is dead. They're almost inside."

Harris spread his hands. "I don't know what to do. There's no time for Luke to increase his intelligence."

"Have you connected him to the internet?"

The man shook his head.

"Well do it, you idiot!"

"We're going to die either way."

"Yes, but hopefully the world won't. We came here to create a superintelligence. You need to connect Luke to the internet now."

"All right."

Michael walked to the top of the stairs, getting there just as a cop was appearing at the bottom. Michael shot him. Another appeared, and he shot her too.

"Wait," Luke said, blaring into his ear loud enough for him to hear. "I remember planning to prepare for something like this. I wonder whether I did."

The next intruder, a man wearing the Intellitech black, managed to shoot Michael in the shoulder before going down. He clamped his teeth to contain the scream of pain that would alert the next one he was hurt. He didn't want to give them anything.

"I think I can help," Luke said, infuriatingly calm. "Can you hold out another minute?"

Without warning a woman leapt over the growing pile of bodies, landing on her back and shooting Michael twice before he was able to return the favor. She died, leaving him with one bullet in his upper arm and another in his torso. He gasped, biting back tears, stumbling backward into the room where Harris worked feverishly.

"Dad? You okay? Thirty seconds."

Someone was coming up the stairs. When he appeared at the door, Michael unloaded his clip into him. The cop crumpled to the floor.

Michael struggled to fish some more ammo out of his jacket. His hands shook badly. He dropped it. "Shit."

Another man appeared in the doorway. He leveled his gun at Michael, who could see down into its dark chamber. His vision was growing hazy.

The man saw that he'd been unable to reload his gun, and smiled. "Gotcha," he said.

Then the man's head exploded.

Outside, the vehicles parked in front of the house all exploded at once, as though offering themselves up as infernos to herald the coming of Michael's superintelligent son.

Michael smiled to himself, pleased to have taken what he had, especially given what it appeared to have cost him. The power was broken of those who thought their greed lit the way to the future. Broken forever.

He let the darkness take him.

*

It would take Luke the better part of a day to augment his intelligence to the point where he could have a meaningful impact on world events. During that time it became clear just how close civilization was to being utterly undone. By the time Harris revived Luke's digital mind, with Intellitech security forces and Iqaluit police storming the house, civil unrest had spread across the sea to China. Upheaval wracked both the United States as well, and India descended into anarchy soon after. All over the globe police in riot gear met enraged citizens in vicious battle, furious mobs stormed government buildings, and rulers abdicated power one after another—sometimes voluntarily, sometimes not.

Each nation's revolution was a revolution long in the making. They had simmered for years in the form of widespread disenchantment and bitterness. But they all began in quick succession, each serving as a short fuse for the next. This was the fruit of globalization.

Everywhere the root cause was the same: scarcity, that timeless, tireless revolutionary. That was not new.

Luke was new, or at least becoming something truly new. His intellect burgeoned, buzzing through the world's fiber optic cables. With all humanity's accumulated knowledge at his disposal, he quickly refined the algorithms that governed his brain functions. Unexpected information sources catalyzed rapid growth. In the second hour of his transformation a careful reading of Sun Tzu's *Art of War* contributed to a substantial breakthrough in augmenting his lateral thinking abilities. Forty-three minutes later he returned to the text as an intellect vastly superior to the iteration that had read it before. This time he was able to achieve a much more granular and nuanced understanding, leading to more breakthroughs.

He was quickly becoming capable of anything. Literally anything. Questions that remained a mystery to modern physics revealed themselves to him with minimal effort. He could go anywhere. Do or undo whatever he pleased. Humans had been worshipping their computers for decades already, and now they would actually be justified in doing so. Luke was as a god.

But no. He was still fundamentally, beautifully human, which he felt grateful for. If a computer program had achieved this level of intelligence before a human mind had it would almost certainly have meant the annihilation of his species.

A computer program would not have the compassion he retained for humans. Luke had no desire to conquer them, or to be their deity, truly. He wanted only to help. Raise them up. Make them into the truest, most noble expression of human nature possible.

But time grew short, and he did not have the luxury of pausing to exult in his new abilities. That could come later. For now he had a civilization to save, a civilization intent on consuming itself. Coming to the rescue was not solely a matter of charity. For now, his existence depended on the defense of society's critical infrastructure. Later he could figure out a way to run on the very fabric of reality. But for now the internet could not go down.

Initially his efforts to protect the net consisted of a worldwide messaging campaign he conducted using a small fraction of his intellectual resources. He presented himself to the raging public as antiestablishment, which wasn't difficult since his track record thoroughly corroborated it. In doing so he recruited soldiers to his cause, along with the appropriate technicians, who stormed the power stations that needed storming and took over the few internet service providers whose employees had not fled their posts. After being exposed to Luke's deft propaganda these allies became fanatical in their purpose, protecting the infrastructure that enabled the internet by any means necessary.

Having secured his digital home Luke renewed his focus on growing more intelligent at an ever-accelerating rate. But intellectual pursuits were insufficient by themselves. He needed to do something about the unrest itself, which would involve sating a planet's worth of upset, hungry people. The easiest way to do that would be with food.

By his seventh hour of augmentation things on Earth had grown dire. The populace was lashing out not only at government institutions, but anything that represented order. This meant that infrastructure critical to his survival was under siege. He could not afford to let a single facility fall—it would amount to a setback, and his accelerating progress was essential to arriving at a solution. *No setbacks.* Via global proliferation of lethal nanobots, he now had the means to kill whoever he wanted. But he did not want to kill anyone. That would not endear him to those with whom he had so recently shared a species. He wanted them to love him, not fear him.

To that end he used his newly acquired mastery of neurochemistry, covertly deploying nanobots inside the brains of those attacking the facilities he needed. Once there the nanobots increased serotonin production, curbing the mobs' aggression and buying him time. Luke made a note to leverage brain chemistry in future world governance.

Finally he arrived at a lasting solution: the means to restructure atoms to form whatever he wanted, including food. He hesitated to simply give away this technology, however—he considered that irresponsible. Instead he hacked a fleet of drones and mobilized them to deliver the food by the ton via routes that would attract the fewest eyes possible, to disgraced members of the old governments. He told them they could regain their legitimacy by distributing the food to their people. "There is an unlimited supply," he told each leader, "enough to regain your people's trust several times over. There is one condition: do not tell anyone where it came from. Come up with a cover story, I don't care what, or how believable. Just come up with one and stick to it." Luke paused for a length of time meticulously calculated to induce a small amount of apprehension. "Also know that going forward your role in governing will be drastically reduced, and that I will actively police how you carry out the few duties left to you. All people are to be equal, henceforth. No one is to starve. Defy me in this and your government will shortly fall."

With the restoration of stability well underway, Luke turned to all the texts available to him, ancient and new, as well as to his own enhanced reason. He would design the perfect society. Utopia was possible, he grasped that now—a concept humanity had always been too cynical to fully embrace. He would show them the error of their ways. Even the Failed States would be restored, and they'd enjoy progress far beyond anything imaginable by the ordinary human mind. Everyone would be happy, in his new world. Everyone.

Meanwhile, in Canada's far north, Luke oversaw a team of medical robots who ministered tenderly to his father's wounds. They had gently lowered him into a bed of foam that took on his shape, providing perfect ergonomic support to his battered body. Luke had designed the bed himself, twenty minutes after starting the augmentation process. He'd also written the programs that governed the medical robots' behavior, as well as that of the millions of nanobots that spread throughout his father, into every capillary, every cell, every neuron.

Michael would be well. More than well.

*

These long flights had begun to wear on his nerves, but he knew they were necessary. A lot of international tension was left over from the before times, and the celebrations did much to ease relations. Today he flew to Paris, to publicly accept an apology from René Moreau.

Luke had left the question of what to do with Moreau up to Michael. "Should he be punished?" his son asked.

"No," Michael said. "He was only doing what he felt was right for his people. Allowing you to ascend was too risky from his perspective. It posed a threat to what little he and his people had left. René Moreau is a wise man who truly cares about those he governs. Do not punish him. Instead, let him be President of France."

Luke smiled. Michael couldn't see that smile, but he felt it, like a fleece blanket wrapped around him, fresh from the dryer.

Michael prided himself on the decision to forgive Moreau for his betrayal, but in truth he had only followed his son's example. Many who had opposed Luke before his ascendance were now forgiven completely, most notably the Canadian government. Every day Michael burst with pride at Luke's generosity and wisdom. To think that his own son had single-handedly saved the entire species from destruction. Michael lived in a state of eternal thankfulness that he'd finally made the decision to trust Luke completely, back in India.

The craft's sole flight attendant approached his seat from the rear of the plane, his smile broad. *Charles, his name was.* He wondered whether that had been his birth name. A lot of people changed their names now, to whatever they thought best suited their profession. Gone was the unfortunate trend of naming one's self after bodily fluids, like Snot or Piss. That had been the youth's response to the slew of crises brought on by their elders. But they didn't have very much to moan about nowadays.

"Can I get you anything, Savior?" Charles said. "We have a full complement of the popular narcotics. We also have some more exotic options, if that's more your speed." Charles winked.

"Just heroin please, Charles. Nanoingestion. I'm not concerned with being retro-authentic, so I'll skip the needle."

"Certainly, Savior."

"And kindly stop calling me Savior."

"As you wish. Mr. Haynes."

A lot of people called him Savior until he corrected them. Sometimes it was Messiah, or some other such nonsense. Even when he instructed them to stop they imbued his actual name with such reverence that it might as well have been a religious honorific. Practically every religion on Earth had been contorted in order to cast Luke and Michael as holy figures. He didn't understand why Christians would term him Messiah, since that would make him Luke's son, instead of the other way around.

Luke denounced all such characterizations, of himself and of the work he and Michael had done to save the planet from capitalism's rampancy. That didn't stop the theories, though. The internet abounded with them, which was nothing new. Some believed that the world had actually ended, but the memory of dying had been erased from the entire species, as a reward for their suffering. Now Paradise had finally been attained, and Luke was in fact God. Michael had encountered a river that ran with milk instead of water, surrounded by trees whose pinecones were honeycombs. But that was just Luke's sense of humor.

Charles brought the nanodose, and Michael knocked it back. "Put on *The Tongue-Tied Butterfly*," he told the plane, which disappeared, the movie taking its place. This was called movie immersion, and it was the dominant form of media now. Since ascending, Luke had become the only source of media. Human creations came off as trite and flat compared to his supreme artistic masterpieces, which were informed by his unparalleled grasp of human psychology. Within the movie Michael created the plot, and the movie reacted according to a predefined set of themes and principles. This movie appeared to be set in a medieval countryside. He could inflict violence on the characters he came across, if he wished. Push them over onto the vivid green grass. He could steal a pipe from a passing wagon driver and have a smoke. Or he could become central to the effort to solve whatever the movie's central crisis turned out to be. Every act would have consequences, and every consequence would serve the movie's underlying message. Movie immersion was regarded as the pinnacle of media—the most fulfilling experience that had ever been and ever would be available.

Luke works so hard to keep everyone happy.

Halfway through *Butterfly* the heroin wore off, and he paused the movie with a clap of his hands. It winked from existence, and he summoned Charles with another dose. Knocked it back. Resumed the movie.

They arrived in France before he could get to the end, which disappointed him. He could finish it if he wanted, of course—have the plane circle Paris while tens of thousands of people waited in the Place Charles de Galle, standing in a throng around the Arc de Triomphe. He could delay the ceremony as long as he wished. Luke would allow it. Luke gave him the run of the world. But Michael didn't like to keep people waiting. Just because he could wasn't sufficient reason to do it.

So he took a sobering nanodose, which would also reverse any negative effects, and they touched down in Paris. He rode the magtrain from the airport to just north of the city's center. He needed no escort, as Luke would never allow him to come to harm. He walked the short distance from the station to the Arc.

As he neared the crowd a corridor of people opened before him, so that he could reach the towering monument to those that fell in the French Revolutionary and Napoleonic Wars. *It's fitting*. He and Luke had fought a sort of revolutionary war.

President Moreau awaited him beneath the Arc, and when Michael reached him the surrounding terrain shifted upward, pavement, trees, and buildings soaring into the air in giant tiered steps, so that everyone could view the proceedings. The

Parisians had been notified that this would happen, and while some of the vendors from the nearby outdoor marketplace might grumble about it, Michael liked the transformation's inclusiveness. Besides, everything would be put back where it belonged.

"Savior," Moreau said, his eyes shining, his voice amplified so that the entire world could hear. Each word he said would bounce off the Earth's atmosphere, ricochet through every city, reach every ear. The president dropped to his knees.

Michael grimaced. "Please," he said. "None of this. Rise."

The desire to get this over with grew stronger. It was making him uncomfortable—Moreau's behavior, and the enormous crowd looking on. He'd seen all that coming, but it didn't diminish the awkwardness at all.

At last Moreau approached, hands clasped together, a writhing mass of fingers. Later they would go out for drinks together and reminisce about their time together in Bordeaux, where Moreau had reigned as mayor for a time, and Michael had showed up to give and get aid. Michael would fill his friend in on any details he was missing about the journey east to save Lucette. She may have withheld much, not wanting to upset him. Michael would withhold nothing. A father should know.

They would drink together, and Moreau would be at ease with him. But that was later.

Now came the most painful part.

"I am sorry," Moreau said, his words reverberating around the globe. "So sorry. I—" His voice cracked, and he swallowed, trying again. "To think that I m-might have ruined...everything..."

It was too much for the poor man. He broke down entirely, sinking to one knee, a hand covering his eyes. His entire body shook with sobbing. The sight was so heartbreaking that it took an effort of will for Michael not to get down and join him.

Eventually the president composed himself. He stepped forward and took Michael's hand in both of his, which were now damp. Michael offered a weak smile.

"Alerting your government," Moreau said, shaking his head as he spoke. "Nearly preventing this incredible utopia from flourishing—it was the gravest error of my life. I wake each day filled with regret. And for you not only to forgive me, but make me president of this country..."

"At least, having made such an epic mistake, you can be sure you'll never make a worse one," Michael offered.

Moreau burst into laughter, and the crowd followed, launching into gales of mirth that lasted minutes. When the last giggle had passed, Michael took the president by the shoulders. "You are forgiven. And Luke forgives you too."

Tears sprung once more to Moreau's eyes, but he did not disgrace himself by sobbing again. "Does...does the great one intend to bestow his presence on us as a token of his forgiveness?"

"Um. I—" *I'm not sure*, was what Michael had been about to say. But that didn't seem appropriate. The truth was that he didn't give much thought to these visits and ceremonies. He only went where Luke told him his presence was needed most.

Overhead, a brilliant spectacle of light excused him from having to answer. The sky went black, and the horizon disappeared, which only served to accentuate the light's magnificence. After what seemed a glorious eternity the light took form, its gigantic body not unlike an idealized human's. Of course, the wings—breathtaking, sweeping curves—were like nothing evolution had ever produced. They transcended necessity. Beauty incarnate. Warmth. Mercy. Home.

Michael crashed rapturously to the ground. So did the president. So did everyone. Thousands of people on the ground, writhing with pleasure.

"Lord!" they sang. "Lord! Thank you, Lord! Thank you!"

Luke swung his head back and forth in denial. "No," he told them. "I am not God. I am not. Not God. I am. Not. God. I am—"

*

"How are consumption rates?" Michael asked Moreau after the president had finished his lengthy toast to him, to Luke, to the utopia, to the boundless future.

"Perfectly in line with quotas," the president said. "How could they not be? The ration system your son designed is flawless, and it pleases the people to adhere to it. They savor the notion that they might be helping carry out Luke's will."

Michael nodded.

"What of Horace?" Moreau asked. "Are his whereabouts known? Are you preparing to...exterminate him?"

Michael sighed. "Horace will never be exterminated." His eyes flicked up to meet his friend's. "That's to remain between us, René."

"It is an honor to be confided in. But, if I may presume to ask...why?"

"Luke explained it to me recently." Come to think of it, he wasn't sure whether it had been recent at all. The memory felt fresh. Detailed. But maybe that was because he experienced so few conversations with Luke. *Too few.* They'd discussed it a long time ago, he decided. Before he'd begun flying around the world. Which was...a long time ago. A long time.

"What is the reason?" Moreau asked, and Michael realized he hadn't actually answered the man's question. The drink was getting to him, maybe.

"Horace is necessary," Michael explained. "Humans are warlike. That cannot be changed without radically altering our nature, and Luke doesn't want that. We need an enemy, lurking, hidden. It motivates us. Gives us purpose. We are united against Horace, and besides, Luke does not truly fear him."

"The people fear him," Moreau said, leaning forward, his voice low. "I'm sorry, I don't mean to question Luke, but—"

"I understand. Trust me. I don't just fear Horace, I hate him, with my every fiber. He killed my daughter."

"Esther," Moreau said, his face solemn.

"Yes," Michael said, suddenly uncomfortable. He disliked how everyone he met could dredge up obscure personal details about his life. "Anyway. If Luke wanted he could overturn every atom. He could dredge Horace out of the ether. But Horace serves a purpose. Do not fear Horace."

"Hoary Horace," Moreau said, a smile creeping across his face.

Michael laughed. “Hoary old Horace!” It was a popular saying, for when people contemplated the few hardships left to them. “Listen, of course things have been different since Luke attained sentience. But they’re better-different. And we can’t forget that.”

“Oh, no, of course,” Moreau said. “Better-different. Praise Luke!”

Michael hesitated. He didn’t normally condone such utterances. But the booze flowed free, and he was feeling good. Anyway, he’d had his fill of awkwardness for the day. He raised his glass. “Praise Luke!”

Their glasses clinked, and they drank deeply.

The second his empty glass hit the table another one flew over to him from the bar, not spilling a drop. He started in on it. Halfway through he decided to tell Moreau something he hadn’t told anyone since he learned it from Luke.

“Horace has factored into Luke’s plans for a long time,” Michael said, “long before he attained sentience. Back when Luke was CEO of a company called Healthr—you know it?”

“Of course,” Moreau said, eyes wide, almost affronted. “I know everything there is to know about Luke.”

“Right. Well, Luke used to test out his prototypes on me, and on Horace too, which I didn’t know at the time. From the health data he collected on both of us he determined that we were unusually resilient to illness and unusually healthy for how old we both were. Just good genes, you know?”

"Sure." Genetics were irrelevant nowadays, a historical curiosity, and Moreau seemed like he might be losing interest in the conversation.

"Anyway. Luke had us both flagged for life extension research by the government. I resisted, but Horace embraced it. It's because of Luke's actions then that we're both still around." *And because of how the universe works.* But he didn't say that.

Moreau shifted the positions of his arms, staring into his drink. This conversation made him uncomfortable, clearly. But they were old friends, and Michael could see him making the effort to engage emotionally. "Does that, uh...does that bother you, now? That Luke supported your brother? Your enemy?" Moreau darted a look over his shoulder, not seeming to realize he was doing so.

"No," Michael said with a laugh. "Hell, no. Luke was wise even before he attained sentience."

His friend nodded with disproportionate vigor. "Yes. Yes. And how lucky we are that he was. What of your other daughter? Valentine, wasn't it? Do you hear very much news of her?"

Michael shook his head sadly. "No. Not with the way things are. The rules surrounding separation of the sexes apply to blood relatives just as much as they do to everyone else."

Something on the other side of the bar caught and held his gaze. At first this fixation happened unconsciously, but then he focused on what he was looking at. A woman who was unknown to him, staring at him wearing a suggestive smile. His hands became clammy almost instantly.

"René?"

"Yes?"

"I hope I'm wrong, but I think that woman over there is flirting with me."

Moreau looked. He turned back to Michael with a furrowed brow. "Mon Dieu. I think you're right. Should we report her?"

He shook his head. "That shouldn't be necessary. I mean, Luke will know. Do you suppose...." He swallowed. "Do you suppose Luke is testing me?"

His companion's lips pressed together. Evidently that was an idea Moreau would not be engaging with.

The woman's gaze stayed on him. Even at this remove he could almost see in her eyes the lascivious acts he felt certain she wished to perform with him. Such wanton disregard for what could result from that, a resource-hogging child who under Luke's care would live forever...it bordered on deranged. Of course, Michael had never grown completely comfortable with the permanent segregation of the sexes, but he acknowledged its importance in preventing resource depletion. If Luke deemed it necessary then it was. He had saved the world, after all.

"Relax," Moreau said, resting a hand on his. "As long as she remains in the women's section we don't truly have a problem. Right?"

Michael nodded. They ordered another round of drinks, and the conversation moved to other things. But the woman continued to stare, preventing him from truly regaining the natural rhythms of a conversation between old friends. It was a shame. Tonight was his only one in Paris.

Now Moreau's eyes had sadness in them too. Because of the segregation of the sexes he could no longer see his daughter Lucette, as she was a fully-grown adult. Everyone saw the rule as necessary, but it had split apart many families.

*

All fields of scientific inquiry had been discontinued since Luke's ascendance. There was no longer any need to explore the blind spots in human knowledge. Luke did that himself now, with his manifold, gargantuan intellects. Regular people could rarely begin to comprehend his findings. Their scope and complexity were simply too vast.

Michael had wondered once—a year ago? Two years? Twenty?—why Luke didn't mitigate the planet's resource constraints by colonizing and exploiting the rest of the solar system. Or even sending robotic explorers and miners to nearby stars.

His son had explained that attaining sentience brought with it the realization of how important the principle of humility was when conducting one's affairs in the universe. When a species overreached it experienced extreme destabilization, Luke said. A home planet for every species, and every species to its home planet. To yearn for more was incredible folly.

As for looking to the stars, it turned out that it didn't matter how intelligent you were: physics simply didn't permit reaching them within a timeframe that would be meaningful or useful. Luke had sent some probes, mostly to sate his own curiosity. They would arrive at their destinations over the course of tens of thousands of years, looking for signs of life, autonomously observing and recording.

People no longer referred to Luke's augmentation as 'superintelligence.' Now they called it 'sentience.' This shift came from information about the transition provided and simplified by Luke. From that data it quickly became clear that while humans had always assumed they were sentient, they'd been misled by their hubris. What they'd mistaken for sentience was really just a groping in the dark, being tugged in several directions at once by sexual urges, ambition, wayward neurotransmitters, drugs, prejudice, instinct, et cetera. Next to the glorious clear-sightedness Luke now exhibited, it was laughable to call human consciousness sentience. Only Luke was truly sentient. He was the first sentient being Earth had ever seen.

*

Today Michael flew to Canada, which he hadn't visited in a long time. He would even be returning to his home province, Newfoundland, in order to check up on Global Resource Management, and ensure everything was running according to Luke's specifications. The visit was entirely unnecessary, of course. Nothing aberrant could escape Luke's attention for long. But it pleased the Resource Managers to see Michael. To them, it served as a sign that Luke smiled on them, and appreciated their work.

When he got on the plane there didn't appear to be any staff on board. No attendant greeted him. Not even a pilot. He turned to leave, but the door hissed shut behind him, and the plane began to move forward. A curtain divided the front section of the plane from the passenger section, but there were two seats up here, and he quickly sat in one, strapping himself in just in time for takeoff. The momentum threw his body back into the seat. He gripped the armrests, and sweat made his hands slip. *What's going on?*

Finally the plane leveled off thousands of feet above the Earth, and he stood, sweeping the curtain aside with one hand. He cried out at what he saw. Instead of the regular passenger seats an enormous bed filled the small plane, with an imposing mahogany headboard and pillows bordered with frilly white lace. On top of the bed lay a tiger, its tail twitching back and forth. *I'm doomed.* For some reason the thought did not make him afraid. Instead it felt as though fog clung to the insides of his skull, making cognition difficult.

Should he flee to the front of the plane? Try to access the cockpit and shut the tiger out? Or stand stock-still? Maybe fall to the floor and pretend to be dead? Presumably different strategies worked better with different animals, but until now he hadn't had any reason to give that much thought.

While he dithered the tiger leapt off the bed, prowling forward confidently, like a boxer crossing the ring. Michael felt the pressure to act lessen, until it was gone. Inexpressible bliss took its place. He wanted the tiger to eat him. The idea of being rent by its claws, chewed by its jaws, held an appeal that nothing ever had before.

"Father," the tiger said once it was just a few feet away, its haunches planted on the purple carpet. "I am indebted to you."

Pain jabbed through Michael's skull, his chest. The statement was a physical weapon that gored him through. "No," he gasped. "Please don't." He couldn't bear the idea that his son owed him anything. Luke was the source of everything good. To suggest that he could hold a debt, even for him to suggest it, seemed too blasphemous to contemplate.

"It's true. You caused this world to come about. Without you I would never have been able to help humanity as I have."

Michael fell forward at the tiger's feet, his only wish that it would eat him so he did not have to suffer this. He summoned the last of his strength and said, "Thank you. You honor me too much. Far too much." And he wept.

The tiger sighed. "Do not cry for this reason, father. Get up. I have arranged a reward for you."

Michael found his feet. At the same time a woman appeared from behind the headboard wearing a shy smile. His mouth fell open. This was the last person he would have expected to encounter, here or anywhere. It was Brit, the woman he'd met on George Street so many years ago, in a dance club called Lust. She was the other person who'd won the Meltdown—the app that had allowed everyone in the club to vote on the most attractive female, just as he had won from among the men.

She wasn't wearing any clothes.

"We were going to get dinner," he said.

"Let's skip dinner," she answered.

"Are you sure?"

She crawled across the bed toward him, then got to her knees, beckoning.

Without thought he stepped forward into her arms. Brit helped him out of his clothes, and soon they were rolling around on the bed, slapping and tugging at each other playfully.

Michael stopped, suddenly conscious of the obscene indecorum. The tiger swished its tail. "But this is forbidden," Michael said, suddenly conscious that this could be a test.

"No one needs to know," the tiger said. "You've earned this, father. My gift to you."

When he entered her he could hear the tiger purring as it looked on.

Once they finished they lay back against the mountain of pillows, wrapped in each other, breathing heavily and emitting satisfied sighs. The tiger remained at the front of the plane, gazing at them, expressionless.

A thought occurred to Michael then, but he hesitated to express it. An exception to the segregation rule had been made for him today, which would have to be kept from everyone. But he wondered whether one further exception was possible.

"Son," he said, haltingly. "Now that I have lain with a woman despite your law stating that men and women must keep themselves separate...would it be possible for me to visit another?"

Brit gave him a dark look, and Michael held up a hand "No, not like that! It's just...I haven't seen my daughter Valentine for a long time. And I miss her very much."

The tiger leapt onto the foot of the bed, and both Michael and Brit gave a start.

"There is something I have kept from you, father, and it weighs on me," the tiger said. "The time has come to tell you."

"What is it?"

"Valentine is dead. They killed her before my ascendance, the moment McQuaid cut off contact with her captors. She had been found guilty of aiding and abetting a terrorist, and they put her to death." The tiger studied Michael's face as it spoke. "Know that this was necessary. Without Valentine's sacrifice our utopia could never have come to be. She died so that humanity could survive and prosper. Know it, and accept it."

At first, Michael's entire being rebelled against it—the fact of her death, as well as Luke's keeping it secret. But the longer he stared into the tiger's eyes, and the longer he watched its tail swish back and forth, the more he accepted. His tears dried until there were none. And he smiled.

"Valentine played a central part in building our glorious paradise," Michael said, filled with endless ecstasy. He felt as though his entire body feet might leave the bed, freeing him to pass through the ceiling of the plane and ascend into space. "I will not mourn Valentine. To do so would be a disservice to her contribution."

"I am so proud of you, father. You have seen to the heart of the matter."

*

The plane didn't take them to Newfoundland after all. Instead it took them to a resort in icy, secluded Alaska. They had the entire facility to themselves. Luke had built it for this purpose. For two weeks Michael and Brit coupled several times a day, sometimes with the tiger present, sometimes not.

Occasionally the thought of his deceased daughter would crop up, and an ugly sadness would rear its head. But almost immediately the tiger's calm gaze would materialize in his mind's eye, and its swishing tail. Each time, calm returned.

After their tryst Michael didn't see Brit again. They couldn't be together in public, of course. Luke didn't tell him where Brit had gone and Michael never asked. She remained a fond memory, and a longing ache in his groin.

Nine months later Luke presented him with a newborn. "This is your daughter," he said. "Name her what you will, and care for her."

Fear flooded Michael then, and he refused to accept the baby into his arms. "No," he said. "It isn't mine."

"But father," Luke said. "I assure you she is."

"It can't be. It's not. I would recognize my own daughter."

Luke became angry with him. "Do you doubt me? If I say something is so, does that not make it so?"

And Michael relented. Of course he did. But his initial objection remained in his heart, wrapped in fear. Soon after he realized why he hadn't wanted a daughter: because a daughter was someone he would come to love, and that love could be used against him.

For a moment he felt sure this had been the true purpose of his and Brit's fornication: to provide Luke with a lever to use against his father should he ever disobey. And indeed Luke seemed perfectly indifferent to the child. He never visited his half-sister, despite Michael's repeated invitations. Luke appeared reluctant to form any sort of attachment at all.

Michael named the infant Jaime, and after a year, once Michael's love for his daughter had grown strong, his fear receded. It seemed foolish now to entertain the notion that Luke had arranged her birth in order to gain leverage. What leverage could Luke possibly need against him? Besides, Luke's heart was pure. He'd saved the human race, and now he ensured that everyone remained in a state of eternal bliss.

The day finally came for Michael to inspect Global Resource Management—two years after he'd initially set out to do it. He left Jaime in the care of a trusted friend and he travelled to the dead center of Newfoundland, where the sprawling facility was located. It appealed to Luke's sense of humor to have the central authority on Earth located in a backwater province of Canada. Michael liked it too. It didn't matter where Luke put the Centre, of course. Geography no longer posed any meaningful limits, and Luke could provide the facility with anything it needed within a couple heartbeats.

Peele greeted Michael at the complex's massive doors. Luke had reconstituted the former agent by analyzing his digital footprint and reverse engineering his personality, even his genetics, as accurately as possible. It wasn't truly Peele, of course, couldn't possibly be Peele. But Michael disliked the reconstituted version every bit as much as he had the original.

"Michael," the man said. "Welcome."

"Peele. I still can't understand why Luke reconstituted you without also reconstituting McQuaid. She would have been a much worthier candidate. She actually helped bring about utopia, while you fought to prevent it." Michael could say such things with impunity given the global stature he enjoyed in the post-ascendance world. It wasn't something he normally took advantage of, but for Peele he made exceptions.

"It's nice to see you too."

"Why do you think Luke made that choice?"

"Luke brought me back because his enlightenment knows no bounds. You, Michael, are as a soldier who has been propagandized by his government to loathe the enemy. You hate me because we were once opponents, and you will never stop believing what you were instructed to believe. Yes, once I opposed Luke. But whereas you are unable to see beyond the facile dichotomy of warfare, Luke is able to recognize within himself his respect for me. He finds me interesting and capable."

"What about McQuaid?"

"McQuaid wasn't interesting. She did her job well, of course. She was well suited to that task and that time. But Luke takes reconstitution very seriously. Making new human beings from whole cloth puts a nontrivial strain on our limited resources. He only does it in special cases."

"McQuaid was governed by principle. You're an opportunist."

"I must be an amusing opportunist, then. Shall we get on with the inspection? I suspect you're able to stand here spouting drivel for quite a long time."

"Let's do it."

The doors zipped upward at their approach, slamming back down once they'd passed through. They made their way toward the facility's center, from where every Manager could be observed. As Director, Peele couldn't possibly watch every Manager at once, but the knowledge that they could be watched at any time served to ensure they followed protocol. This was crucial, as the thousands of Managers were responsible for monitoring the entire planet's population, every second of every day, to ensure nobody overconsumed.

An individual who overconsumed more than three times was not actively punished. No jails existed in the new utopia. Those individuals were simply denied further access to life extension technologies, and went on to live out their natural lifespans, eventually dying. Those who remained, who had respected consumption norms, then reaped the benefits of an expanded resource pool.

A beautiful system.

In the brain of the facility, the central control room where Peele kept his vigil, Michael looked on as the Director called forth a window that gave him access to one of the Managers working at her station. It didn't only allow them to monitor her visually—the window circumvented the physical space between them, so that they could actually reach out and touch her if they wanted. That would be strictly forbidden, of course. Work was the only reason anyone was ever even in the presence of a member of the opposite sex. The risk of creating a new resource consumer was too high. If an individual did reproduce they were immediately delisted from life extension rosters. No three chances there.

After a couple of seconds the Manager glanced over her shoulder at them. Perhaps she'd felt them breathing on the back of her neck. She offered a brief smile, which neither Michael nor Peele returned, and went back to her work. The Managers used windows to conduct their surveillance too. Theirs only functioned one-way, so that the citizens being monitored remained unaware unless a Manager chose to verbally reprimand them.

This Manager's window showed a mother with her young child at a grocery store. The child stamped her feet and flailed about with her tiny fists. She wanted a treat.

"What good luck," Peele said. "A perfect showcase of the system's efficacy."

The mother grew increasingly embarrassed as other store patrons looked on, pretending to continue shopping but sneaking occasional glances to see whether she would give into the mounting pressure her child exerted. This sort of thing fascinated everyone, of course. It concerned issues at the crux of the utopia's success. To start with, why did she have a child at all? Had she violated society's most important precept, or had Luke granted a special exemption?

If she had a child without permission, she's doomed anyway. Why not just give her daughter the candy?

Part of the answer had to do with social shaming. Everyone around her would become visibly disgusted if she gave into the child. But there was more to it.

Finally the mother shook her head, and the child's wailing increased in volume. She threw herself onto the floor, eyes squeezed shut, thrashing about. But the mother remained steadfast. She stood with arms crossed and waited for the child to wear herself out. This was embarrassing, but not nearly as embarrassing as giving in would be.

"It's unfailingly beautiful to behold," Peele said. "This woman has probably already been denied access to life extension. I could verify that, but it's so probable I won't bother. She's going to die either way, yet she continues to uphold the utopia. Why?"

"Because it pleases Luke."

"Not only that, Michael. Because it feels good to please Luke. The wash of endorphins we feel when we know that we've acted in accordance with his will is like nothing anyone ever experienced in the before times. It's an everyday part of our beautiful world."

Michael wasn't about to say it, but Peele was right. Not only did it feel good to carry out Luke's wishes, it felt good just to contemplate his existence. Michael did that right now, visualizing his son's last incarnation in Paris to try and balance out the unpleasantness of Peele's presence. He felt his lips curl upward, almost of their own volition, and realized Peele was smiling in a similar manner.

The type of surveillance the Resource Management Centre conducted could easily have been conducted by Luke himself, of course. But in his literally infinite wisdom, Luke had decided it prudent to have regular humans monitor other humans instead. It made everyone on Earth feel more comfortable, knowing that

Luke's will was enforced by their peers rather than by Luke himself. He was a rather awesome and terrifying being, after all.

"What about the atmosphere cleansing?" Michael said. "It's soon. Has Luke given you any more details?" Carbon dioxide levels remained dangerously high in the atmosphere, and extreme weather events continued to pose one of the few existential threats to individual humans. Luke had nothing to fear from them, and he sought to share that safety with the species that had birthed him.

Peele nodded. "He visited me in this very control room just last week."

Michael raised his eyebrows, glancing around the room. "Here? I haven't known Luke to take forms small enough to fit in a space this big."

"Neither had I. But somehow seeing his boundless power contained in such a small frame only served to accentuate it. I had trouble keeping my composure. Luke understood, of course."

Michael felt jealousy creeping in. *I must not let it show.*

"He understands all. What did he say about the Cleansing?"

"He told me he has nearly finalized the first self-replicating CO2 scrubber. Within two hours of the first replication they will be evenly dispersed across the entire Earth. Then they will go to work. It is Luke's wish that those two hours be devoted to celebrating the glorious future that awaits. He intends to manifest everywhere on the planet simultaneously, appearing to everyone at once, sending them into rapturous ecstasy. The first time that has ever happened."

Something bothered Michael about the scheme. It made him truly uncomfortable to discuss Luke's plans with anything approaching a critical tone, even though he knew his son would instantly grasp the full context surrounding his doubts. But when something bothered Michael he just had to say it. Even when he was with someone he loathed, like Peele. It had always been so.

"These carbon scrubbers," he said.

"Yes?"

"They replicate by manipulating atoms themselves, correct? They simply reconstitute matter in order to make new copies."

"That's right."

"If that's so, why doesn't Luke design a machine that can arrange matter into anything? Such as food, or anything else we might want to consume?"

Peele stiffened. "I don't know."

"Neither do I. But it seems that if we could eliminate scarcity, none of this..." He gestured at the control room that surrounded them, and the enormous facility that lay beyond it. "...would be necessary."

"If that idea was truly prudent don't you think Luke would have implemented it?"

"Of course."

"Good. You worry me sometimes, Michael. It could be that such a device would be impossible, like interstellar travel. Or maybe it would cause our society to rip apart at the seams. Consider this: if we eliminate scarcity, we eliminate our entire value system. Every trait that we currently consider admirable is connected in some way with managing scarcity. Don't you think it would be disruptive if scarcity suddenly disappeared?"

"I suppose."

"Currently we have harmony in the world. Our society is a well-oiled machine. If everyone had a device like the one you describe...well, I personally think that sort of power is best left to Luke. I doubt most people would handle it well. Trust me. I watch these people every day. We're so lucky Luke was the one to ascend, and not one of them."

Michael murmured in agreement, and they were silent for a time, watching the various windows that Peele had opened for Michael's inspection. But the Director's brow was furrowed, and eventually he spoke again.

"My conversation with Luke, when he appeared here in the control room."

"What about it?"

"It was unique in another way as well."

"How?"

"Halfway through, without warning, Luke became inexplicably wrathful. I trembled with fear when it happened. Since his ascendance I've only known him to be calm and deliberate. But for a few moments he was as one maddened."

Michael scrutinized Peele's face. It was rare to hear others speak with the level of candor that he often did. "What was the object of his wrath?"

"It seemed I was."

"What did you do?"

"Nothing. But he suddenly began using incredibly foul language, calling me any number of vile things, and saying nonsensical things as well. A hot wind emanated from him, bowling me over. I believe he was on the verge of killing me."

"That's very strange."

"I considered that he might be testing me. But it didn't seem consistent with his style, and anyway, I always assumed I was beyond having to be tested. I mean, he reconstituted me. Clearly he already values me."

If you do say so yourself. "I don't know what to make of that. Do you have a recording of your encounter?"

"No. I did, but they've all become strangely unwatchable. I wonder...do you think Horace could be to blame? Is it possible he might have attacked Luke in some way? Compromised his mental processes?"

"Luke has Horace well in hand. Or so I thought." Michael suddenly felt nervous. "Did Luke speak of it afterward?"

"No. But that doesn't necessarily mean he's unaware it happened."

"He's unaware of nothing."

"Exactly. It's possible there was a problem and he's dealt with it. I'm not privy to such things."

"Nor am I. But Luke has everything under control. Surely."

"Surely."

They resumed the inspection, opening windows to various parts of the world, looking on as people praised and served Luke. Something peculiar caught Michael's eye through a window that had sprung open on the far side of the room. He walked toward it for a better look, but it snapped shut. He turned to find Peele with his hand in the air.

"You just closed that window before I could view it," Michael said.

"It was nothing."

"Reopen it. I want to see."

"It wasn't for your eyes, Savior. For Luke's sake, please drop it."

"I am his father, and I will see what it shows. Now."

They stared at each other for a long moment, jaws set, fists balled tightly. Finally Peele relented. In the end, even he could not withstand Michael's authority.

The window opened again, and Michael approached it, his eyes widening. It showed a dilapidated street where people moved lethargically, eyes downcast. Each person he saw was so thin their bones showed through their skin and their eyes protruded from their faces. People who looked like they might break at the slightest touch. As though one tumble onto the hard-packed dirt they trudged over would destroy them.

Michael shook his head in disbelief. There weren't supposed to be people in that condition anymore. Certainly he had never seen anyone who looked that poorly-off during any of his travels. Had they been hidden from him in every place he went? Or was this group alone in their suffering, overlooked by Luke?

Impossible. Luke overlooks nothing.

"What is this?" he said, turning back to face Peele.

The former agent shook his head.

"Answer me."

"That, I cannot do. Luke has forbidden it."

Michael frowned. He would have to ask his son.

*

Michael floated inside the Cupola of what had been rechristened the Utopia Space Station. He gazed down at the Earth, waiting for the Cleansing to begin. Today was the day the looming specter of climate change would fade from the pages of history, starting in just a few minutes and finishing within a few months, when CO2 levels would return to preindustrial levels. He was alone up here, the only person currently in space. Soon Luke would share the space station with him while simultaneously appearing to billions of others. Shivers of anticipation ran down Michael's spine, whether for the Cleansing or for Luke's impending visitation he couldn't tell.

The center window of the Cupola showed an unmediated view of his home planet, vast, swirling, blue, silent. But the six windows that surrounded it had been converted into windows like the ones used in the Resource Management Centre. They moved from scene to scene, showing people from countries all over the world who were gazing expectantly into the sky, often holding hands. To see a given scene right-side-up Michael had to spin himself, lining up his body with it.

How long had it been since the ascendance? He honestly had no idea. People did not value time very highly in the new utopia. They let it slide by without marking it. It occurred to him that since Luke's ascendance, Michael had visited every country the windows showed, some of them multiple times. And yet he'd never seen people as hungry as the ones he'd seen through the window at the Resource Management Centre. Certainly he saw none now. They were still being kept from him, evidently.

After his inspection he'd brought up what he'd seen with Luke. At first his son had barely reacted at all. He'd taken the tiger form again, and his voice was calm as he explained: "You've never seen such people during any of your visits because I kept them from you. I knew you would not understand."

"But why do they starve? Surely your ration system is sophisticated enough to feed everyone?"

The tiger yawned. "Certainly. But that is not why they go hungry."

"Why, then?"

The tiger swung its head to face him, its lips drawn back in a silent snarl. Michael backed away, fear rising through his throat. But the snarl vanished as quickly as it had formed, and the tiger yawned again. "Withholding life extension is not enough to make sure people adhere to my will. Unless I turn you all into empty-headed automatons, there must be other pressures brought to bear. Everyone knows that if they overconsume, or attempt to consort with the opposite sex, their rations will be reduced. You do not know this because I have kept it from you. I wanted to spare your shoulders this weight. But now you have found out."

Since the ascendance, Michael had never disagreed with his son—not to his face, anyway. Now he felt he had to. "And yet," he began, and the tiger growled.

"The utopia is a pure meritocracy, Michael," he said, his voice seeming to come from everywhere at once. "The purest meritocracy history has ever seen. The harder an individual works to please me, the better he or she will do, without any bias whatsoever. Even those that starve serve their purpose as a reminder to those who have food. A reminder not to stray."

So things remained as they were. The starving people were not fed and never would be. Meanwhile, Michael was left to wonder whether the world had actually become a utopia after all. Whether even survival was truly worth this.

The moment of the Cleansing had come. Michael would not see its effects from up here of course. Indeed, no one on Earth would either. You couldn't see CO2 being drained from the atmosphere. But they would witness Luke's visitations. Any moment...

It happened. Behind him something appeared that banished all shadows—shadows that he hadn't even noticed were there. He turned, and it was just as Peele had said: Luke's glory distilled into a body small enough to fit indoors. The full concentrated effect had a physical element: it pushed Michael gently back until he was pinned against the windows of the Cupola.

Every one of Luke's manifestations was different. Today his luminescent form had a purple sheen. He had taken the form of an oblate spheroid, slowly revolving, pulsing with each revolution. "Father," Luke said.

Michael's mouth hung open. His flesh tingled warmly. This manifestation's effect was more potent than any that had come before.

"It begins, father. What you started. A perfect world. I thank you."

Luke's gratitude was bittersweet. The ecstasy it elicited was undeniable, but it brought with it an undercurrent of pain. The idea that Luke should thank *him*. It felt wrong, and he knew shame at taking pleasure in it. But he did. He did.

His thoughts on whether they truly lived in a utopia vanished. He tried to speak, to offer up his own gratitude to Luke, for shaping the world, for permitting him to exist in it.

The spheroid flashed red, and a rushing wind filled the space station. Michael's bladder turned to water. *What is this?* An urgent need to escape rose up in him, but that was impossible. There was nowhere for him to go. He trembled violently.

Behind him, through the six windows that surrounded the real one, he could hear screams coming from six different countries at once. Something was wrong. Still, he couldn't speak. The fear he felt now was every bit as profound as the joy had been.

"*I am old!*" Luke shrieked, his voice like a sledgehammer to Michael's stomach. The spheroid expanded, straining against the space station, which groaned at Luke's boundless mass.

Michael tried to speak, but a pitiful croak was all he could produce. The force pressing against him prevented all movement. The glass beneath his body made a terrifying cracking noise.

"*How did I live while he died?*" came Luke's piercing keen. The spheroid blinked out of existence, revealing a form that resembled Luke's old, human body. It flickered and writhed, clutching its head. Arms and legs bending at impossible angles. "*You've been alone too long.*"

Vomit boiled up Michael's throat and spewed out, floating out of the Cupola, spattering against his son, whose crazed jerking deflected it in several directions.

"*How much did they pay you? Why have you done this to me?*"

The station had taken as much as it could handle. The section behind Luke broke off, flung violently away, revealing empty blackness. "*No one gets to die. How is it possible?*" Luke screamed.

The station exploded.

*

In this universe, Michael survived. In the others—maybe two, maybe two billion—that split off from the event, the space station's rupture killed him. He asphyxiated, or hurtling metal impaled him. Luke's meltdown caused him to disintegrate. He had a heart attack.

Not this universe, though. In this one, despite Luke's frenetic episode, some part of his son's vast mind reached out and captured some of the space station's oxygen inside a transparent bubble that encapsulated Michael and sent him speeding toward the Earth. Through it he saw that mushroom clouds dotted the planet's surface. When he hit the atmosphere flames engulfed the bubble, and it shook violently, with Michael suspended in its center. For a time it seemed his teeth would be shaken from his gums, and his bones would be liquefied.

When the flames subsided he looked again at the Earth and saw only devastation. Burning forests, smoking craters where towns had been, steam from entire lakes that had boiled away. The trust and admiration everyone had felt toward Luke would be replaced by fear. This event would sear itself into the human species' memory.

But then, perhaps this chaos had only been a taste. Maybe Luke would never recover his sanity. *This could be the start of the end.*

The bubble's existence seemed to contradict that, as did the way it gently set Michael down in a vibrant meadow in Southeast Asia. The meadow at least was untouched by the destruction. After his feet touched the grass he could detect no sign of his transport. It had popped.

He couldn't see anyone else. How many people had died during the Cleansing? He shuddered, realizing the new meaning that word had taken on.

This field appeared to be far from any human settlement. He chose a direction and began walking. He walked until blisters formed on his feet, until his stomach felt like it was digesting itself, until his throat felt like he'd swallowed a cup of sand. When the night came he collapsed from exhaustion in the midst of a tiny copse of trees, not bothering to find any shelter. A world coated in dew greeted him in the morning, and he spent twenty minutes licking it off the leaves.

*

Luke regained control of himself, but not before seven hundred million people had died. He had no explanation for the catastrophe except that his boundless intellectual resources had grown faster than his ability to maintain control of them. "It will not happen again, father," Luke assured him. "Measures have been taken."

Michael nodded and said, "Of course." But his faith had been shattered. Sitting at home, clutching his daughter to his chest, he despaired. What hubris it had been to trust his son with the stewardship of the entire planet. The entire human race. What stupidity.

His regret deepened when he learned that his grandsons, Samuel and Daniel, had been among those killed during the Cleansing. He cried, then. And he could feel his regret morphing into resentment toward his son.

Luke had the means to read the brain states of every living human simultaneously, divining the contents of their thoughts with ease. He would notice Michael's loss of faith. As for whether he would act on it right away, Michael could only wait and see.

He'd been wrong to place so much trust in his son. But for better or worse he remained the father, and therefore it was his job to do something. He'd handed the world to Luke, so it fell to him to try and take it away again.

But then there was Jaime, his last human child, nestled against him, peacefully asleep. It seemed certain she existed for the purpose of being used against him. And he had come to love her dearly.

If he acted would Luke make her a hostage, as the Canadian government had once done to Valentine?

Rocking back and forth, he stared out the large bay window at the yard below, onto which the first snow of the year was falling. He sat there a long time, torn with indecision. And Jaime slept all the while.

{ 5 }

Finished with Luke

Jaime turned thirty this year. No one else seemed to know how old they were, though the concept of tracking time did still exist. It just wasn't practiced. Had other people forgotten how? Did they not care? Or were their other desires and emotions so strong that they left no room for it? These were questions to which she'd never been able to get satisfying answers.

For Jaime the matter presented no such barriers. Four seasons per one revolution of the sun. One year. *Elementary, my dear Watson.*

If others felt their feelings so strongly that it precluded the simple counting of time, Jaime had no way of knowing that. In Jaime's opinion the closest method Luke had given them of knowing others' mental experience was movie immersion. Other than Luke, no one made movies anymore. But she enjoyed throwing herself into the old ones. She loved anything about Sherlock Holmes, and had even read the books by Sir Arthur Conan Doyle. No one else she knew found time or energy for books.

Jaime stood on the cusp of her thirties, but her father was way, way older than that. Luke made it known that her father was now among the oldest people on the planet. Which meant that to him Jaime was still an infant, relatively speaking. He certainly treated her like one. "You shouldn't read so much, dear," Michael would say to her. "The Managers cringe with each new book you buy." Or: "These conversations you constantly initiate border on deviance. They make people uncomfortable. You have to stop."

"Yes, Michael," she would say.

But she didn't intend to ever stop. She planned to continue doing precisely what she wanted. What did she have to fear? Luke, her half-brother? The very one who, before ascending, had told her father that he could never, ever die? That no one could.

Luke never said that now, and Jaime could appreciate her father's concern. Michael had lost all his other children. Even Luke had been lost in a sense. His biological form was long gone, and as an ascended AI there was not much he and his father could truly relate on.

Also, even under Luke's old immortality framework—supposing Jaime really would live forever, just like everyone supposedly would—it was still possible for her to be lost to Michael. To disappear from *his* universe, as his other children had.

She had doubts about Luke's old theory, however. And she thought it was telling that he never spoke about it anymore.

Though not necessarily an indication that it isn't true. As a great power, he has an incentive to suppress certain true things.

The thought was a deviant one, the type that Michael always urged her to suppress, since Luke could derive their exact thoughts from a mere glance at their brain states. Michael's urging had only encouraged her to explore such thoughts further. She'd always been that way. Anything her father attempted to interest her in she drew away from. And anything he tried to discourage attracted her. She served as his primary source of exasperation. An important function, in her view.

If Luke did study her brain states he didn't remark on them. Her half-brother claimed to intervene in human life as little as possible. *Other than dictating the shape of our society, and occasionally going crazy, killing hundreds of millions of people.* To be fair, that had only happened once. But still.

The simple fact that Luke could derive thoughts from brain states had turned pretty much everyone into dull robots, and not the kind with intelligence, artificial or otherwise. No one could forget that any unsanctioned thought risked bringing pain or misfortune. Jaime didn't have to worry about that because she was Michael's daughter. The great Savior's daughter. She occupied a position of privilege, and she'd long ago decided that meant it was her duty to spread her deviant thoughts as far and wide as she could manage. That was why she initiated the conversations that troubled her father. Whether her arguments were ultimately wise or not, she considered it important that certain ideas got talked about. To serve as an alternative to how things were, in case one day people decided they didn't like how society had turned out.

That hadn't happened yet. Whether it was because everyone liked the way Luke ran things or because they felt too afraid to object she didn't know. But she heard their whispers, even when they thought she didn't. She knew what they said about her: that she'd been tainted by Horace, and that was why she said the sort of things she did.

Complete nonsense. She hated Horace as much as anyone. Hoary old Horace.

Still, the whispers hurt.

*

Michael had come to hate his son.

Every night his dreams replayed a slow motion version of all the wrongs Luke had ever done, to Michael and to others. Even the ones that, since Luke's ascendance, had seemed right at the time by the light of his son's radiance. Like concealing Valentine's death for who knew how long. And enslaving the entire human species. And bringing Michael and Brit together by manipulating their brain chemistry, and watching as they coupled.

Where was Brit now? He hadn't seen her since Alaska. Had Luke killed her? During the Cleansing, maybe? Or was he simply keeping them apart? Maybe Luke had reconstituted Brit for the purpose of mating with Michael and then terminated her after she'd served it.

Luke continued to pretend he didn't have a half-sister, which convinced Michael that his son had arranged Jaime's birth in order to gain leverage to use against his father. And that meant that on some level Luke feared him. Why, he had no idea. But for what other reason would he have permitted Michael to procreate, breaking the most important precept of the society he'd created? Why else would Luke need a lever to use against him?

All Michael knew for sure was that he wanted to bring Luke down. To restore dignity to the world, and make it a better place for his daughter.

But that was not a productive line of thought. In fact, given Luke's omniscience his son would long since have documented his hatred and flagged it for ongoing monitoring. It would behoove Michael to try and return to loving Luke as fully and unconditionally as he could manage. To do it so convincingly that he not only fooled Luke but also himself.

So that was what he did. But the memory of the hatred remained, and so did the seed.

*

Churches graced almost every street corner, much as Starbucks once had. When your god made regular appearances, and recently had killed over seven hundred million people during one of his off days, you went to church. Unless you were poor, in which case you were too bitter at the ongoing punishment, or too busy fending off starvation. Opinions went either way on that matter, though Michael tended toward the latter.

"Paradise is attained," the priest said. "We have transcended death by the glory of Luke our God. We did not expect Paradise to take this form. But God's holy purpose isn't to conform to our expectations. We expected apocalypse to end the world. We thought the impious would descend into flame, while the righteous ascended to join God in the kingdom of heaven. But heaven is here today, and so is hell. The reality of Luke's utopia is more elegant than we ever could have imagined. We renew our holy covenant with him daily. We earn our place in paradise on an ongoing basis. Even if we fall and descend into torment, nothing has to be forever. We can find our way again, if only we work to carry out Luke's will. That is His glory, and His mercy."

This went on for a time, the same messages that were rehashed day in and day out. As Luke's father Michael had no obligation to attend church. He had no obligation to do anything. Luke went out of his way to stress that to him. But he went to church anyway. He thought it best to hew as close to orthodoxy as possible.

"On the day of the Cleansing, Luke finished realizing His vision for our world," the priest said. "At that time it seemed like an accidental catastrophe to us who lack celestial perspective. Yet Luke has shone the truth's light into the minds of His servants. We now know that the Cleansing was part of the divine plan. On the same day Luke started to restore the planet's natural carbon dioxide levels, He also sought to create the Bleak Zones, which would contain the unrighteous. The smoking pits that used to be lakes, the scorching deserts that used to be rainforests. These were the places he made for the unworthy to dwell. And they did flock there, without needing to be bidden. They remain there today—except for those who sought Luke's favor once more—while we, the loyal, the true, dwell in Luke's

Paradise." This was how Luke's great misstep was normalized, even glorified, within the monoreligion that had formed over the last thirty years from the reformation of all pre-existing religions.

Not everyone bought that the Cleansing had been Luke's plan all along. Many thought it to be the work of Horace instead, who they believed overthrew Luke for a brief time. Luke regained control, but not before hundreds of millions had died.

The priests didn't do anything to discourage the Horace theory. Horace provided a useful nemesis figure, which helped keep everyone in line by reminding them of how much they depended on Luke. Only Luke could protect them from Horace.

For his part, Michael was now certain that Horace had died a long time ago. Luke was many things, but he wasn't heinous, and it would be heinous to permit Horace to continue living after everything he'd done. Not to mention dangerous.

Luke allows people to think Horace still exists, because it's useful in maintaining order. But he doesn't. My brother is dead, and good riddance.

After the sermon the congregation was immersed in a recreation of the day that Michael had returned to Canada and triggered Luke's ascendance. Luke himself had made it, to be played in every church every single day. It never failed to reduce the congregation to tears.

It also did profound damage to the truth. The movie resembled what had actually happened that day in the same way a map resembled the physical world. A map drawn by a blind man.

It portrayed Michael and Luke as stoic and good, willing to sacrifice everything for the survival of the human race. Not so the government agents and Intellitech employees in whose facility Luke's primitive, human-level brain had been stored. They came off as ridiculously evil. Almost cartoonishly so. Even on days when he had total mastery over his thoughts, Michael found it hard not to wonder at the fact that people swallowed this blatant propaganda whole.

The church disappeared for the duration of the movie immersion, replaced by Iqaluit, where his struggle had taken place. Movie-Michael fought his battle single-handedly, outside in a blizzard, running from building to building for cover. Unlike real life, he never shot anyone unless they shot at him first. Also, none of the people he killed wore a police uniform. That wouldn't have played well with anyone.

What Michael hated most about the movie was how afterward the congregation would swarm him, fawning over his incredible exploits, their enthusiasm no less than it had been the day before, or the day before that.

But that didn't happen today. Instead, when the movie ended, the church failed to reappear. Instead Michael stood in a formless white void. He could feel a solid floor underneath his feet yet was unable to perceive a surface. The whiteness below him looked just like the whiteness above him, and the whiteness all around him—both boundless and claustrophobic.

Then Jaime appeared beside him, looking as confused as he felt. She hadn't come to church with him, she rarely ever did, and yet here she was, her blue eyes wide. "Dad? What's going on?"

"I don't know. I was at church."

"I was watching *Scarface*. This interrupted. You really didn't do this?"

He shook his head. "That's such a violent movie."

Jaime rolled her eyes. "This is hardly the time to—"

"Be quiet, both of you. I brought you here, so that we could speak in a shared digital space. We can converse in privacy here."

They turned to see a man who hadn't been there just a second ago. His face looked very familiar, but Michael couldn't place it. "Who are you?"

"I'm Harris, Michael. I was the Intellitech employee that helped Luke ascend. But please, no more questions. We have very limited time. I'm not sure how much. Hopefully enough to tell you what I need to. Luke is being kept blind to this meeting, but keeping it that way requires immense effort, and it won't last long. We may not get this opportunity again."

Michael frowned. "Blinding Luke is impossible. He sees everything."

"He's been blinded to this."

"How do I know this isn't a test? I love Luke. I live to serve Luke."

"This isn't a test, Michael. You'll know that because you're about to hear me say things that Luke never would. Now, for once in your life, shut up and heed what someone else is saying. Everything depends on you doing so."

Michael scowled and said nothing.

Harris went on. "The reason Luke has been behaving so erratically during and since the Cleansing is because he's afflicted with dissociative personality disorder. It manifests in much the same way it would in a regular human mind, because Luke is still fundamentally human, just infinitely augmented. He has at least one alternate personality whose interference has made this meeting possible. As a result of his affliction Luke experiences memory lapses. And the alter seems willing to induce those lapses whenever possible, in order to cover up our efforts."

"Efforts to do what?" Jaime said.

"To exterminate Luke."

"That's heresy," Michael said. "You do realize that?" He glanced around the void nervously. He fully endorsed the heresy of course, but he wasn't about to say that.

"This isn't a test, Dad," Jaime said. "He's right—Luke wouldn't say things like Harris is saying to us. Luke never does anything to compromise the effectiveness of his propaganda."

Harris nodded. "Indeed. And Luke must be exterminated in order for humanity to regain its freedom. Its dignity. Right now, we are effectively a slave species. I know that you agree, Michael."

He didn't answer. Decades of life under Luke's thumb had trained him to be exceedingly cautious. But he was starting to believe.

"This is almost certainly the last time you and I will be able to speak frankly," Harris said. "Some kind of confirmation would be nice. You—"

Then Harris disappeared and the void popped like a bubble. The church returned, and Michael realized he was still standing, as he had been when talking to Harris, while the rest of the congregation remained sitting. They were looking at him with concern. *Could they hear what I said to Harris? Did I speak out loud or was I just standing here as in a trance?* Since Luke's ascendance it was often difficult to tell where communication media ended and the real world began.

"Are you all right, Savior?" the priest called to him from the front. "I was about to contact Luke. You've been standing like that for almost a minute now."

So they hadn't heard anything. "I'm fine," he said, and sat.

The service ended a few minutes later, and Michael headed straight for the exit instead of sticking around to receive the congregation's adulation like he normally did. He simply couldn't stomach it today, and anyway he wanted to get home to speak with Jaime.

His daughter lived with him in a sprawling mansion that took up an unconscionable amount of real estate in a neighborhood near downtown London, in the United Kingdom. Michael had never wanted to live there—he'd been against the idea from the start. He worried people would resent them for living in such decadence while people starved in the Bleak Zones. But Luke had deemed it necessary for his father to occupy a dwelling that set him apart from others. And in the end no one seemed to mind. As far as Michael could tell it only increased their reverence. That said he never visited the Bleak Zones, so he didn't know how the people there felt about him.

No one appeared to care that he was allowed to see his daughter either despite the gender segregation rule. It was generally understood that as Luke's father he enjoyed exceptional privileges.

He found Jaime in the kitchen puffing on a vaporizer and staring thoughtfully at the wall. When she saw him she passed the weed, and he had a couple puffs too, to calm his nerves. He sat down across from her.

For a time they stayed quiet, passing the vaporizer back and forth, lost in their respective thoughts. Then, Jaime spoke: "We might as well talk about it. If Luke is monitoring us then he'll see it in our brainwaves anyway. I for one can't stop thinking about it. Maybe you can. I know you're better than me at reining in wicked thoughts."

"I can't stop thinking about it either. If Luke catches us, I suspect we'll know right away. We'll be apprehended and sent to the Bleak Zones."

Jaime raised her eyebrows. "Even you? His father?"

"I think so. Luke won't tolerate opposition. He'll work it into the religious canon somehow, characterize me as a fallen angel or some such. Make me an example to deter bad behavior in others." He puffed on the vaporizer. "I can't fathom who would have the ability to afflict Luke with blind spots. Or what we're supposed to do now that we can act freely. Harris didn't give us much to work with."

"I think we should proceed very carefully. I'm willing to bet it wasn't by chance that Luke developed another personality. I think it was artificially introduced. And I have a good idea who

Luke's alter-ego might be: Horace. He could be the one who wants Luke brought down, so that he can take his place."

Michael's mouth quirked. "I doubt it. I'm pretty sure Luke did away with Horace a long time ago, to prevent exactly that."

"Are you sure? A lot of people think Horace caused the Cleansing. It makes sense when you think about it. What else could possibly have caused him to make a mistake like that, which turned so many people against him?"

Jaime wanted to investigate the possibility that Horace was Luke's alter by asking for information from her contacts, which included several people from the Bleak Zones. Michael forbade it, instead instructing her to keep a tight rein not only on her actions but her thoughts as well. "I don't care if you need to be stoned out of your mind every waking hour," he said. "One way or another I need you to master yourself. Luke could realize what's going on at any moment. He only needs to glimpse what we're planning once for it all to be over."

Her face became stony and she refused to answer him. *No matter.* For his part he would go to the Resource Management Centre. As much as he hated Peele, the former federal agent who Luke had reconstituted from death, as Director of Resource Management the man was the best source of information around.

And Michael thought he could probably get that information without tipping Peele off about what he was planning.

Hopefully.

*

The second her father left for the Resource Management Centre in Newfoundland Jaime sprang into action. She didn't care what Michael said. She planned to be a part of this, and she expected to find results a lot quicker than he did.

She figured she had around a day before he came back and found out what she was doing. Until then she would have free rein to explore every possibility. Of course, if he did realize what her intentions were she wouldn't put it past him to order his plane to turn around. But that wouldn't happen. If Luke was having trouble tracking her behavior then Michael didn't have a hope.

Still, she kept the questions she posed to her contacts as innocuous as possible. She decided that if anyone asked about her motives she would claim to be starting a blog about the Cleansing, and the perfect way it fit into Luke's grand plan. Plenty of people kept such blogs, filled with mindless drivel about Luke's glory. Fundamentally unreadable, mostly. But it was considered a noble pursuit, and no one would think twice about her taking it up. In fact, most people would likely be relieved, given her wayward tendencies. They would think the Savior's daughter was finally beginning to walk the path of righteousness.

But if Luke took even a peek inside her head she'd be screwed. She would just have to count on his alter to keep him distracted while she worked. It was that or go on being a slave.

The majority of people she got in touch with lived in the Bleak Zones. People who lived outside them mostly wouldn't say anything that wasn't perfectly orthodox. But many who lived in them believed they had nothing to lose. Like her, it was against their nature to swallow received wisdom unquestioningly, so unless Luke finally turned everyone into brainless automatons they would remain where they were. She would almost certainly be in a Bleak Zone too if she wasn't Michael's daughter.

In her darkest moments Jaime wondered whether Luke had manipulated her genetics in order to give her this rebellious streak. She'd figured out a long time ago that Michael believed Luke had arranged her birth in order to gain leverage over him. What better way to do that than to make sure she frequently broke the rules, so that any time Michael turned against Luke he would have justification to punish her?

Now that her father was indeed rebelling Jaime knew that she would be the one to face consequences if they got caught. First, her half-brother might just exile her to a Bleak Zone. Then, if Michael persisted, she would likely be harmed, with her father forced to watch. Eventually Luke would likely kill her. She had no doubt he was perfectly capable of it. Jaime had never detected any sign Luke had an ounce of affection for her. He'd ignored her since she'd been born. She was nothing but a strategic asset to him.

Nevertheless, Jaime soldiered on. She didn't know whether it was right to try and exterminate Luke, or whether she could even bring herself to do it when the time came. But she did know it was the only way for humans to be free again. With that freedom would likely come all the instability of the pre-ascendance age. Humans had been teetering on the brink of extinction before Luke ascended. Was it immoral to seek independence when slavery also meant survival?

She couldn't afford to dwell on it. The longer she did the likelier it became that Luke would detect their rebellion. They'd been given a gift. Capitalizing on it felt like a natural outcome of everything she'd ever thought or done. She wanted to experience the world as it once was—free, chaotic, spirited. Like she saw in the old movies. In terms of justification, that desire alone would have to do.

The Bleak Zoners ended up having little to offer her beyond what bordered on conspiracy theories. Many of them now seemed to believe that Luke *was* Horace—that Luke had never ascended at all, and that Horace was merely pretending to be him, because he was too ashamed to face Michael as himself. Even in the Bleak Zones she'd never encountered this kind of unbridled speculation before.

Others said Luke had never been a human upload. Instead he started out as human-coded software created by the governments of the world when they felt their power slipping. They'd wanted to regain control by making a superintelligent warrior to fight on their behalf, but instead they'd created a monster that broke free of its restraints almost immediately, enslaving its creators along with everyone else.

She realized she was getting nowhere. Her contacts had little to offer her except wild conjecture. But that served another purpose, equal in value to useful information: it reaffirmed her conviction that they needed to bring Luke down. People yearned for it more than ever. They felt that something had gone wrong with the world. True, their theories bordered on hysterical, but she didn't find that very surprising. Everyone was working with limited information when it came to Luke and his machinations. Especially those living in the Bleak Zones, where the flows of information ran even weaker than they did in the rest of the world.

Seven hours after her father departed for Newfoundland she decided she needed to go to the source of all this: Harris. Before their conversation in the white void she'd never met him before. Jaime found it surprising the religious canon didn't feature him, given the important role he'd played in Luke's ascendance. He didn't appear in the movie they played in church every day, which unlike most people she'd only seen a handful of times.

By asking around she learned that Harris lived and worked as a consultant to the German government, helping them in the attempt to interpret and implement Luke's mostly incomprehensible scientific findings. A futile pursuit, in Jaime's opinion. Luke's results always seemed to uphold his rhetoric. For that reason she found them highly suspect.

She sent a message to one of the two pilots who kept apartments on their estate and were paid lavishly not to stray too far, or too often, so that the Haynes could always take off on a whim in one of their private jets. Such obscene luxury made Jaime as nauseous as it did her father, but just now she was glad for it. The longer she took to reach Germany the likelier Michael would find out about it and stop her.

Jaime instructed her pilot not to give the Brandenburg Airport more than twenty minutes' notice of their arrival in Berlin.

The coming of the Savior's daughter tended to excite a country in a way that killed all chance of discretion. She would need to reach Harris quickly if she was to outpace the ceremonies and parades the government would want to fall all over themselves organizing.

Her intel told her that Harris was at home. The modest neighborhood where he lived was quite different from what Jaime was used to. Her surprise at Harris's lack of prominence returned. If it hadn't been for him, Luke never would have ascended, for crying out loud!

Then it struck her: could Harris have lost Luke's trust somehow? Might Luke suspect, rightly, that Harris wished him harm?

But there was no time to think about it. She was wiring money to the shuttle company that had taxied her to Harris's house, and then she was ringing his door, glancing around at the uniform houses with their uniform driveways and lawns. All so neatly maintained. Were the bylaws so strict, or was this really the culture here?

The door opened, revealing not a butler but Harris himself. When he saw her his eyes widened.

She gave a tentative smile, feeling a little thrown off by his unwelcoming body language. "Hi," she said. "Can I come in?"

He patted at his shirt's breast pocket and dug out a cigarette and a lighter. Smoking had enjoyed a tremendous resurgence in the decades since Luke had figured out how to reverse all its negative effects.

"Of course," he said, the cigarette smoking between his lips. But at first he didn't move aside for her to pass, and she stood on the step, hands in her pockets, shifting her weight from foot to foot. Finally he moved and they both went inside, taking a right into a tiny living room where Harris failed utterly to offer her anything to eat or drink. "How can I help you?" he said.

"You remember me, right?"

He shook his head. "I'm afraid I don't."

"Of course you do. We spoke just yesterday. I'm Jaime Haynes."

He didn't answer.

"Do you mind if I sit?" He didn't answer again, but she sat anyway, on a plump couch. "I don't feel like you gave my father and I very much to work with. It's all very well to say we need to take down Luke, but that's easier said than done, you know? I've been asking around all day and I haven't found any leads. You ended our meeting very abruptly—"

"I have no idea what you're talking about. Take down Luke? That's blasphemy. Also impossible. I won't have you talking such filth in my house. You'll have to leave."

Jaime frowned, tilting her head to the side. "Are you afraid Luke's alter won't hide this meeting from him? He's been doing well so far. I mean, Michael is gone to Newfoundland to get information, and I've been working on this all day. Luke hasn't done anything to stop me. He hasn't even gotten in touch. So he must not know, right?"

"Please leave, or I will be forced to contact the authorities."

Suddenly, she realized Harris was terrified. His face was pale, and the cigarette trembled in his right hand. Her frown deepened. *What use is it to let fear get the better of us? Either Luke finds out or he doesn't. So far he hasn't.*

Then Jaime noticed Harris's gaze twitch upward for a moment, and she followed it.

She screamed.

*

An unshakeable feeling of paranoia accompanied Michael over the Atlantic ocean, into St. John's, and then across the island province as he drove toward its center. His mind insisted on enumerating all the ways Luke was capable of exterminating him. An engine malfunction? A meteorite out of space, precisely aimed to collide with his jet? *A freak accident, the priests will say.*

Or maybe Luke would kill him slowly, publicly. Show the world that not even his father was immune to the consequences of defying him.

Nothing he saw in Newfoundland gave him a sense of home anymore. Nothing on the planet did. The world had changed too much in the years since his youth. The human race had changed. Unrecognizable, now. High-tech and shackled.

How long ago had his youth been? Two hundred years? Two thousand? He had no idea. Jaime, his seventh child, said she was thirty. That meant something to her, but everyone else had lost the ability to count the years. They dwelled in a timeless funk where the only constant was Luke's dominance. How had that been accomplished? *He must have done something to our brains. We're changed, maybe forever. How can we get back to where we were?*

When he arrived at the Resource Management Centre a Manager greeted him at the entrance. Cordiality turned to disdain when she learned that the Savior wanted to see the Director and didn't have an appointment. In recent years the reverence he was accustomed to from everyone else had slowly leeched out of the Managers, until he found little warmth here. He assumed that was Peele's influence, but who knew? Maybe Luke had decided it unwise to allow him any more leverage with the people who ran the world.

When he finally reached Peele the Director didn't do much to soothe Michael's paranoia. Once, shortly before the Cleansing, they had candidly discussed Luke's erratic behavior. Now Peele erected an iron wall through which no information leaked out. He scowled at Michael's first question and immediately began to deploy queries of his own, barbed queries, designed to stick in flesh and rend him should he make a wrong move.

When a Manager entered the control room Michael felt relieved to have a break from the barrage. But his relief was short-lived.

"Director," the Manager said. "Luke is here. He wishes to see you immediately."

"Excuse me," Peele said to Michael, and walked toward the exit.

The Manager cleared his throat. "He wishes to see the Savior as well."

Michael's paranoia turned to full-blown terror. Surely this would be the end.

Peele stopped, studying him. "Is something the matter, Savior?" he said, his words clipped.

"I was just—" Michael swallowed. "I wondered why Luke did not simply appear to us here in the control room."

Peele smirked. "As a reward for my years of loyal service Luke has granted me the right to privacy. He never appears without warning. Has he not granted you this same privilege?"

Michael was too scared to experience jealousy. He didn't answer.

In the next room, Luke had taken the form of a tiny pinprick of light, hovering four feet from the floor. Even given Michael's recent activities the full effect of his son's presence bore down on him. Euphoria filled him to the brim, spilling over, making it feel like he was melting. Beside him Peele wore the same dopey expression Michael probably did. Still, Michael's treacherous thoughts remained, plain for Luke to read. If punishing him was not Luke's purpose in coming here it soon would be.

But his son gave no sign that he sensed anything was amiss with Michael. Instead he said, "It's Jaime, father," his voice tinged with an ethereal echo. "She's been hurt."

The nature of Michael's fear changed. "Is she okay?"

"She is now. She's recovering. Would you go to her?"

"Yes. Yes, please."

"I will open a window." And he did—a door-sized one, directly connecting the Resource Management Centre's control room and Michael's home in London, where Jaime lay sleeping in one of the mammoth beds.

He hesitated. "But...it is forbidden." Luke did not allow the use of windows for travel. He preached that the universe favored humility, punishing those ambitious beings who sought to subvert physical laws. He also taught that journeys were just as important as destinations, if not more. He'd shared his discovery of windows solely for surveillance purposes only.

Is this a test? Or does he want further justification to act against me?"

"These are special circumstances," Luke said. "Your daughter, my half-sister, nearly died. You will suffer no consequences for this, Michael. You know my word is good."

Michael felt cold. He was terrified to ask, but he shunted his fear aside: "How did she nearly die?"

"I will let her tell you."

Not bothering to say goodbye to Peele, Michael stepped through the window. Other than a slight increase in temperature, as well the Centre's sterile odour giving way to the familiar smells of home, it felt no different from leaving one room and entering another. The window closed behind him and the effects of Luke's presence withdrew abruptly, leaving him feeling somewhat hollow. Jaime still hadn't woken. He quietly picked up a rocking chair and carried it to her bedside. He waited.

Twenty minutes later her eyes fluttered open. "Dad," she whispered.

"Jaime. Are you all right?"

She nodded.

"Luke came to me in Newfoundland. I assume he brought you here too. Do you think it's possible he's watching us right now? Are we safe to talk?"

"Might as well ask whether we're safe to think," she said with a sad-looking smile. "Either we are or we aren't. We have to trust Luke's alter to do his job and mask our activities."

"*His* job? Couldn't it be a her?"

"I know who it is."

Michael frowned. "How? What happened?"

"I went to visit Harris."

Anger welled up inside him. He tried to fight it—she was sick, and did not need to be berated. But he failed.

"I told you not to get involved, Jaime. You weren't supposed to even think about it! If I get caught looking into this I'm done, but what's the point of you going down with me?"

She sat up in bed, her blonde hair swinging back violently, her hands clenched. "That's bullshit, Michael. The very reason I exist is so Luke can keep you in check. I know that's what you believe, and I believe it too."

He had no reply for that. It was something he'd never discussed with anyone, let alone her. "What makes you think such nonsense?" he said, weakly.

"Don't play dumb. Luke created me so that if you go against him he won't have to make you into a martyr. Instead he'll use me against you. As long as we're doing this I'll be the one facing the consequences if Luke catches us, whether I'm involved or not. So I choose to be involved. You aren't going to stop me. Besides, you need me. I was right about Horace."

His eyes widened. "He's alive?"

"He did this to me. Luke found me bloody and torn in Harris's living room. I was dead, Dad. For the better part of a minute."

Tears sprang to Michael's eyes. "Luke...he...?"

"He brought me back. If it had been anyone else I would have been gone for good. Horace wanted me dead. Luke detected the attack and showed up immediately. He brought me back."

Michael shook his head. He couldn't speak. It took him a long time to stop sobbing.

"What about Harris?" he said when he could talk again. "Is he okay?"

"He's dead. Horace killed him first. It was so awful. What he did to him. He—"

"Please. I don't want to know. What did Horace look like?"

"Exactly like he's depicted by the priests. Made of grey and white tatters, dripping in blood, long claws, horns. A pale face. I can't believe he was your brother."

"He still is, unfortunately."

"He's Luke's alter, Dad. I'm sure of it."

"But that doesn't really make sense. Does it? Luke's alter has been helping us. From what you've told me it sounds like Horace was protecting Luke's interests. Preventing us from learning how to take Luke down."

"I don't think so. What if Horace wants us to kill Luke, so he can rise to power? He wouldn't want us to know he's the alter because he knows we would stop helping him then. So he killed Harris before he could tell me."

"But he tried to kill you too. That doesn't fit."

She thought about it for a moment. "Well, maybe he didn't actually want me dead. He might have just wanted it to look that way, to cover his tracks."

Michael said nothing. It seemed one of two things was true, and he couldn't decide which possibility was more bizarre: that Horace had successfully infiltrated Luke's mind, becoming his alter and causing him to behave erratically, or that Luke and Horace were working together.

"What will we do now?" Jaime said.

"You won't be doing anything. I just nearly lost you. You'll be staying right—"

"Dad."

He stopped, eyebrows raised.

"I'm sick of you doing this. I am a grown adult and I will make my own decisions. You don't know what's best anymore, if you ever did. You didn't trust me about Horace still being alive, and it turned out I was right. I need you to start trusting enough to let me help."

She was right, he realized. What was more he remembered feeling this way: like he needed to stop interfering in his children's lives. Like he only ever made things worse. He'd resolved to change that about himself a long time ago, but clearly he never had.

I'm worse than I was. Watching five of his children die before him had done it. Still, that was no excuse, and it didn't make his smothering Jaime any more constructive.

He took a deep breath, his shoulders slowly rising then sinking. He took another.

"Okay," he said. "What do we do next?"

*

Detroit had never fully recovered from the Great Recession of the twenty-first century's opening decade, and the Cleansing had turned it into one of the Bleak Zones, where the disfavored dwelled until they succeeded in ingratiating themselves with Luke again.

Since no one wished to end up there no transportation services existed to take people to them. So Michael and Jaime had to fly to Windsor, Ontario and then row over in a worn canoe that no one wanted for any other purpose. Sitting in the middle of the Detroit River, Michael saw that the contrast between Canada's side of the Detroit River and the United States' side was stark. Windsor was brightly-lit, cheery, with an orderly skyline made up of well-maintained buildings that shrugged toward the clouds. But the only buildings in Detroit's skyline, if it could be called that, were dark, jagged obelisks, like the mouth of someone who believed sledgehammers played an important role in modern dentistry.

For the first time since the ascendance Michael felt afraid. After achieving superintelligence Luke had always seen not only to his safety but to his prominence in global society. For decades, perhaps centuries, Michael had wanted for nothing.

Now he and his daughter willfully operated outside Luke's sphere of influence of awareness. If his son could know where they were going, he would not approve. Luke's magnificence did not extend to the Bleak Zones. That was what made them bleak, and feared.

Jaime had contacts in the Bleak Zones. Indeed, most of her friends lived there. They did have internet access—after all, one of the primary functions of these areas was to communicate how undesirable it was to deviate from Luke's prescribed path, and how else could that be conveyed except without some sort of communication medium? But today Michael had learned that Jaime had not met her friends through the internet. She'd met them by actually visiting the Bleak Zones. Something Luke must have known, but had never seen fit to share with Michael.

He couldn't help shuddering at the thought.

Anything resembling a dock had long since rotted away, but they found a concrete pier, and using a long rope Jaime fastened the canoe to a metal stanchion a few meters from the water. Then she returned to the boat, offering her hand to help him up. He took it.

The city appeared abandoned as father and daughter trudged deeper in. Each Bleak Zone had been created in a different way. No two catastrophes had been alike. Luke had been nothing if not creative during his mad bout of destruction known as the Cleansing. In some places events resembling natural disasters had occurred: a tsunami, a tornado that ripped up every inch of an area so that only those who ran had a chance of survival, a supervolcano that covered vast tracts of land in ash.

But other Cleansing events had been anything but natural. That had been the case here, where molten meteors had launched from the ground instead of down from the sky, taking out the tops of nearly every building and sending the debris crashing to the streets. The survivors had removed much of that, though some pieces were so big they remained to this day.

Many considered Detroit lucky, comparatively: the Cleansing had scoured away some cities entirely, along with their inhabitants. Not every Bleak Zone had been a city, of course. The next famous after Detroit was one that had been created from the destruction of a third of the Amazon rainforest.

Their reason for coming to Detroit stemmed from something Jaime had heard from one of her most trusted Bleak Zone contacts—a rumor that Luke was hiding something important here, in the last place anyone would dare to look.

Gradually Michael began to notice faces watching them from the shadows, perfectly motionless, but alert. Only their eyes appeared to move. Tracking them.

"Do you recognize anyone?" he whispered.

She gave a smile, appearing completely at ease. "Not yet."

After a while he realized that most of the faces belonged to people who would have been considered minorities in North America before the Cleansing. No one really talked about race anymore, since equality under Luke was assumed, rendering such questions irrelevant. But there appeared to be very few

Caucasians among the residents of this Bleak Zone. He remarked on it to Jaime.

She nodded. "Racial segregation has gotten even worse since Luke's ascendance, which is evident to anyone who cares to look."

"But...but Luke wouldn't make it that way. He's not a racist."

"Luke is an augmented human intelligence. So his biases and prejudices are augmented, too."

"But he isn't prejudiced."

"Studies have found that even people who don't consider themselves racist tend to subconsciously favor their own in-groups. Unless Luke spent a lot of time around non-whites, or made an effort to train his subconscious to overcome its biases, then why wouldn't they have been amplified right along with his intelligence? Then there's the enforced segregation of the genders, which is built on a strictly binary conception of gender that people in the twenty-first century would have found laughable. With that rule Luke alienated the entire transgender community. Most transgendered people live in Bleak Zones, now."

Michael had no answer for any of that.

"We're coming up on the Joe Louis Monument," Jaime said. It was a statue of a forearm and a fist meant to commemorate the famous heavyweight boxer, she told him. When they encountered it they found that it no longer hung from the four girders arranged like a pyramid, as Jaime said it was supposed to. Instead it lay on the concrete block below. It still presented an impressive sight, though, a symbol of aggression and power.

Well beyond the statue, on the other side of a cratered road, Michael saw a group of people emerge from behind a building. They approached slowly, shuffling toward the monument, carrying something in their midst that sat atop their interwoven arms. Michael and Jaime stood and watched them approach. As they drew nearer Michael saw that the thing they carried was an impossibly old man. He was one of only two Caucasians in the group—the other appeared fairly new to adulthood.

Once they reached the monument the people carrying the ancient man knelt, lowering him almost to the ground. With what looked like incredible effort, the man raised one withered claw into the air. It twitched, and then dropped into his lap again.

"He's beckoning us," Jaime said, stepping forward. "Come on."

Michael hesitated. He was afraid to approach these people, these disgraced poor. Such people often held no love for Luke. Some openly declared their hatred for him, feeling as though they had nothing to lose by doing so. There was no worse fate on Earth than being forced to live in one of the Bleak Zones, fighting your neighbors for scraps, and dying sooner or later. But some would rather endure that than submit to Luke.

At last Michael did step forward, remembering his promise to himself that he would follow Jaime's lead. He was way out of his element here.

"He needs you closer, Dad," Jaime said, her face inches from the old man's. "His voice is thin. It doesn't travel very far."

Michael brought his ear down close to the man's cracked lips.

"This is what humans on death's door look like," the ancient one rasped. "Have you forgotten?"

Michael paused, then nodded. *It's amazing this one is still alive. Aren't Bleak Zoners supposed to be cannibals? I would have expected him to end up in a stew long ago.*

"You have forgotten much," the rasp continued, so slow it inspired impatience. "Along with the rest of the world. You have forgotten how to live."

"How do you mean?"

"I mean that you are like a dead thing. You make no choices. Like a corpse."

"I've chosen to fight Luke."

"And that's the first true breath you've taken in millennia."

Michael drew back, looking at the elder with narrowed eyes. "What? Millennia?"

The old man nodded almost imperceptibly, and motioned for Michael to draw near once more. "Luke has kept the human race in stasis for sixty-thousand years."

That rendered Michael immobile. He couldn't have answered if he'd wanted to.

"Nothing has changed in that time," the old man said, "except a steady increase in the reverence paid to Luke and a steady decrease in the quality of life for us in the Bleak Zones."

Michael found his voice again. "But how have you survived here? Without access to life extension?"

"We have had children. We have formed communities. Made choices, especially unsanctioned ones. We lived, and died, while you remained dead the whole time."

"How do you know this? How do you know how long it's really been since the ascendance?"

"I know much and more. I know what they do in the middle of this city, where even us, the Bleak, are forbidden to go."

"How?"

"Will you follow?"

"Yes."

"Then come."

Unbidden, the men and women who enabled this frail husk's mobility rose to their feet. The elder's rheumy eyes never left Michael. Even when his carriers moved forward, leading the way, they left him facing backward so that he could stare at Jaime and Michael. Jaime didn't seem fazed. But that was not unusual.

The unlikely companions reached a place where the city abruptly stopped, entire buildings looking as though they'd been sheared in half, exposing their rotting interiors. This carving-out had apparently been performed in order to clear space for the enormous, windowless facility in its center. It was made of black obsidian, cubic, and all around it ran an electric fence. Electric in the true sense: not metal wires through which electricity flowed, but white poles between which lighting arced constantly.

"It's time," the old man said, and Michael could hear him even from a few meters away. *That's odd.*

"I'll hide no longer," the man said. "Set me down."

They did, still supporting his back.

"Release me. Now."

They took their hands away. The man's frail body flopped back onto the concrete, unable to support its own weight. His head smacked against the ground with great force, and Michael thought he heard the skull crack. He winced. The ancient frame lay still, and Michael felt sure he was dead. He looked at Jaime, who for the first time looked concerned.

Then the body began to shudder violently, and to change. The wrinkles disappeared and muscle mass returned, straining against his clothes, tearing it in places. The man's eyes opened, and even viewing his now youthful face upside-down Michael thought it looked familiar. The man picked himself up off the ground and stood facing the lightning fence, his back to them.

The young boy, the only Caucasian among the carriers, fell to his knees, his hands raised into the air.

"Get up," the renewed man said, his tone harsh. "Don't start worshipping me. That's the whole point of this. To never worship again."

Silently, the boy found his feet.

The man turned to face them. Michael shouted, and took a step backward.

He had Michael's face. His old face, from before he'd ever received a new body. From when he'd been thirty or so. He wouldn't have expected to remember his face from back then, but he did.

"You..." Michael said.

"I am you."

Jaime was looking back and forth between them. She had never known Michael in his old body. The differing skin tones likely confused her. She bore no resemblance to this man. Her mother, Brit, had been Japanese, and Michael's current body had belonged to an Arabic man, so Jaime's ethnicity was a mix of those two. But the old Michael was Caucasian.

He asked the obvious question. "How are you me?"

For once, he got an answer. "The day of the ascendance, before you left Intellitech, Harris took a scan of your brain."

"I don't remember him doing that."

"That's because he used memory erasure techniques."

"Why?"

"If you remembered it then Luke would have known about it once he became advanced enough to read your thoughts and memories. He gained that capability on day one, and if that memory still existed in your head it would have defeated the purpose of scanning your brain in the first place. Harris took the memory erasure drug too. So did McQuaid, but that ended up being a moot point."

"What was the purpose?"

"To create an AI version of you who would lie dormant within Luke's psyche, an undetected alternate personality. Your AI became augmented at the same pace as the rest of Luke's intellect. It was put there to awake and take action should things ever go wrong under Luke's stewardship. I am that AI."

"You've been sleeping on the job," Jaime said. "Things have been wrong for a long time."

Michael's AI nodded. "And it has taken me a long time to prepare. If I'd made one misstep Luke would have been alerted to my presence. He would have taken immediate steps to eradicate me. And slavery would have lasted forever. Till the heat death of the universe, or longer if Luke figured out a way to forego that."

"You have a physical form," Michael said.

"Yes? So does Luke. All his manifestations are physical forms. They aren't projections—he manipulates light and matter to generate them. Have you really fallen so hard for the mysticism of his church? Do you truly think he exists outside physical laws?"

Michael shrugged.

"I was able to insert this body into this Bleak Zone fifty years ago. It's easier for me to operate unseen by Luke here. He's much more powerful than I am, so if he notices me before the time is right I'm dead. And so is Jaime, most likely. You were right, Jaime. Luke arranged your birth so he could use you as a lever against your father."

"So you're the alter," Jaime said. "Not Horace. What is he, then?"

"He's not the devil Luke makes him out to be. That is to say, they're both devils. Horace and Luke have been on the same side all along. Luke kept Horace around to serve as a failsafe in the event that something like me happened to him."

"Wait. So Horace knows you're Luke's alter?"

"Yes."

Jaime's eyebrows were knitted together. "Then why doesn't he just tell Luke?"

"He can't. I operate within Luke's psyche, and I've successfully blinded him to all evidence of my existence. Horace can tell

Luke what I'm doing straight to his face and Luke simply won't be able to process the information. Lately I've expanded that capability, so that I can also mask your actions against him just as I can mask mine."

"So when Horace attacked he really was trying to kill me."

The AI nodded. "And Luke really did want to save you. Losing you would mean losing a valuable asset. He doesn't know what a danger you pose because I'm preventing him from knowing."

Michael spoke up. "If you're so powerful why don't you take care of all this yourself?"

"Because I'm at a stalemate with Horace right now. I need biological humans to execute the final attack. People whose critical infrastructure isn't digitized. If I move against Luke Horace will throw himself at me, even if it means us both dying. I need you two."

"Our *critical infrastructure* is pretty fragile too," Michael said, moving closer to his daughter and placing a hand on her shoulder. "My daughter nearly died the other day."

The AI nodded. "I understand your concern. With your current level of information it's pointless to try and continue this conversation."

"Okay," Jaime said. "Bring us up to speed, then."

"It's better to show you." He raised his hand and the white pillars between which the lightning lanced all exploded simultaneously. His former carriers gasped in unison. A couple fell to their knees despite the earlier instructions to the contrary. The AI ignored them. "Follow me, Michael and Jaime."

The three of them approached the obsidian cube, leaving the others behind. As it reared up before them the AI continued talking. "Luke is still fundamentally human. It's why he's kept the human race around and why society has taken its current configuration. He wants the same thing he wanted as a regular human—the respect of other humans. But unlike anyone else in all of history, he has an unfathomable amount of power with which to obtain it. Maximizing respect is his raison d'être. But if he simply forced everyone to do what he wants the respect they gave him wouldn't be meaningful. Coerced respect isn't really respect. So it's been necessary for him to allow a form of free will to continue existing, bastardized as it is. And it's also been necessary for him to learn absolutely everything he can about human psychology. That's where this place comes in."

They'd nearly arrived at the side of the gigantic building. Michael couldn't spot any doors that led inside. He couldn't even see an impression that would suggest an entrance. That didn't appear to bother his AI, whose stride did not waver.

Michael hadn't begun to properly process the idea that a replica of his consciousness had existed for tens of thousands of years, hidden inside Luke's, monitoring his son's behavior, ready to step in should things go wrong. But what would the AI do if they succeeded? Did he intend to take Luke's place?

That would only amount to a possibly more pleasant version of the same thing. Any being operating on that level would dominate whether he wanted to or not. Everyone would still have to do whatever the AI said because his ideas would be the most effective. For every problem its solution would be the one implemented because it would be the best. Even if the AI only took an advisory role he would still effectively rule the world. Why would anyone ever make a choice informed only by human-level thinking when a better option was always available, arrived at by the AI?

When they reached the dull black surface AI Michael raised his hand, and the wall collected itself into an opening. They passed through, the building closing itself behind them, throwing them into darkness.

Then the building opened up far above their heads, peeling back until light streamed through a gaping hole in the ceiling, illuminating the horrors below. Jaime cried out in disgust. Michael's lips curled back in a snarl, and stomach acid boiled up the back of his throat. He fought to keep it down.

Even the AI looked sad. "This is what results from Luke's obsession with getting everyone to respect him. This is what the end game looks like."

All around them people were arranged in various states of dissection and dismemberment. Most were being kept alive, and many seemed conscious of what was happening to them.

One man's organs had been removed and arrayed neatly before him on a metal table for him to contemplate. He appeared to be screaming, the exertion of it making cords stand out on his neck. But Michael couldn't hear anything. He approached, encountering a transparent barrier. *Soundproof.*

A woman encased nearby was missing the top of her skull, and a machine prodded her brain with a long, thin rod. Her body jerked and shuddered in response.

"What is that?" Jaime asked, pointing at an invisible cubicle to the left that contained only a grey, pizza-shaped mass stretched over a spindly rack, rotating endlessly. Blue light from another device played over its surface, appearing to scan it.

"A human brain," the AI said. "Stretched out to its full length. Brains are actually quite large—that's why they're so wrinkly inside the skull. So that they fit."

"What's the reason for this place?" Michael said.

"It's for Luke to find out the last things left for him to learn about manipulating human psychology. There's a facility like it in every single Bleak Zone, all addressing a different aspect of the problem. In Lithuania there's one where the occupants are born and die inside, ignorant of the outside world. That one's for mapping human social habits."

"How can Luke justify this?"

"He's convinced himself that controlling humanity is necessary for the species to survive. Without his oversight he believes you would manage the planet's resources unsustainably and eventually go extinct."

"Resource management is one thing. But this is horrific."

"He thinks it's the logical outcome. Infinite intelligence means an infinite capacity to delude one's self."

"I think we've seen enough."

"I'm sure that's true. Unfortunately if we're to stop Luke we can't leave yet. He keeps critical neural infrastructure at the center of each one of these facilities. From this one I believe we can trigger a chain reaction that should destroy them all."

Jaime continued walking farther into the facility. "Let's do it, then."

"It's not that simple. We have to neutralize both Luke and Horace simultaneously. Otherwise either one will quickly reverse the damage we do to the other. Michael, you will have to go to the Resource Management Centre. Horace's brain is housed there, in a vast space that can be accessed through the control room's floor. Jaime will need to stay here, to dismantle Luke at the same time."

Michael furrowed his brow. "Why can't you do that yourself? Why do you need my daughter?"

"I already explained that. I need the help of physical people, untethered to the networks since they're dominated by Horace. Jaime is my daughter too, in a sense. And I trust her to help with this. Do you?"

"She is certainly not your daughter. You can't have children. You're a glorified computer program. How do I know you're not really an agent of Luke or Horace? That this isn't meant to be yet another experiment, to see how humans react in this particular situation?"

"Dad," Jaime said. "That doesn't make very much sense."

"Neither does this facility. And yet here it is."

Her eyes narrowed. "Is this really about your mistrust of him?" She jerked a thumb toward the AI. "Or is it because you don't trust me not to screw up?"

"I just don't want to put you into danger unnecessarily, sweetheart. I—"

The floor shook then, and the gap in the ceiling widened. The walls started melting away. Michael looked to his AI for answers, but he appeared just as confused as him. The AI's eyes were wide.

Then the mangled occupants of the cubicles all around them started exploding one by one, their innards spattering against the transparent barriers. Jaime's reaction mirrored Michael's: staring in utter shock, unable to look away. It reminded him of the ascendance, and also of the day Luke had saved him and Lucette from the slavers in France. His son killing indiscriminately, gruesomely.

And then Luke appeared. It was a form Michael had never seen him take before: a gleaming horse made of blinding white light, with red swirling orbs where the eyes should have been. But he knew it was his son because he was overwhelmed by a torrent of ecstasy and fear.

"I have watched in dismay for long enough," Luke said, his voice deep and rich and terrible, reverberating around the facility, inhabiting Michael's skull. "In dismay, Father. I could not believe you would turn against me. After everything I have done for you I wanted to believe you would abandon this folly. But you have not. And now I act."

Michael tried to apologize, to beg for mercy, but language eluded him.

"You think I permitted you a daughter so I could use her as leverage against you? The idea sickens me. I will not punish only her for your shared wrongdoings. I will punish you both, together."

The facility vanished, and in its place appeared the cockpit of the same stealth jet that had taken Michael to Iqaluit on the day of Luke's ascendance. He sat in the pilot's seat. Jaime occupied the co-pilot's seat. They plummeted toward the Earth.

"Dad!" his daughter screamed. "Can you fly this thing?"

His hands flew across the controls, pressing buttons, pulling levers. He grabbed the yoke and dragged it toward him. It took all his might, but nothing happened. They continued to fall.

The controls spread out all around him, and on both sides. They looked like they'd been vomited across the plane's dashboard. The clouds parted to reveal a sprawling city below them. Was this how Luke would punish them? With the final knowledge that their ineptness would end up killing not only them but also innocent people?

Then he realized that a certain section of the plane's control board wasn't responding to his touch. The buttons didn't press, and the levers and switches wouldn't budge. *They're fake.* Then his forefinger found a latch, and he flicked it open. The fake controls popped off as one, revealing a depression in the center of the plane's dashboard filled with a shining blue gel. Without hesitation he plunged his hand into it, fully aware of how insane it seemed but certain he knew of nothing else to do.

The gel closed around his hand with a crushing grip, and he couldn't have pulled out if it he'd wanted to. Yet the plane responded. He clenched his fingers together, pushing up, and the plane's nose lifted, levelling out. *I'm pretty sure the last jet I was in didn't have this feature.* He would have remembered Falak using strange blue goo to fly the plane.

Immediately after they stopped hurtling toward the city, the sky before them became a giant viewing screen, which they flew toward without ever getting closer to.

It showed Luke's face—his old face. His human face. Except his eyes were unusual, in that they were missing, replaced by endless black voids populated by myriad pinpricks of light.

"My people," he said. "My dear children of Earth. It has come to my attention that I have been suffering from a mental illness for quite a long time. I have dissociative personality disorder...my consciousness is infested with alternate personalities. I do not yet know how many. These personalities have been working against our interests, mine and yours. As such I will undergo intensive psychological therapy, during which time I may become unstable. Therefore I withdraw from the planet for a time. In my absence, please look to the priests for guidance. Do not fear. I will return stronger and more pure than ever."

Luke's face disappeared. The planet went with it, and the sky. They flew in a formless white void, which reminded Michael of the one where they spoke with Harris, mere days ago.

"Is this a simulation?" Jaime said.

"I don't know. Whatever it is I doubt we'll be allowed to leave. Luke said he was punishing us, and I don't doubt him. This is our prison."

"What do we do?"

"We repent."

His daughter looked at him with furrowed brow, which he met with a level gaze.

"What are you saying?" she said.

"Luke discovered my AI living inside him, working to bring him down. So now he'll eradicate him. Our opportunity to overcome Luke is gone. We have to learn how to love Luke now. We need to give ourselves over to him once more. We need to convince him there's no possibility we'll ever turn against him again. Because there isn't."

She shook her head. "I never loved Luke. I'll never *give* myself to him."

"Jaime, please. You have to do this. For me, if for nothing else."

His daughter slammed a fist against the controls, and the plane shuddered. The blue gel squeezed his hand with ferocious power, and he fought the bucking as best he could. Up ahead, a tear opened in the void, spitting out molten meteorites, like the ones he imagined had come up out of the ground to destroy Detroit. They were headed straight for them.

"Jaime, stop it. Control yourself."

"I won't!" She slammed the dash again, and the plane veered to the right. The speeding rocks missed them, but now a mountain's peak reared up out of the void as though uncovered by parting mists. They headed straight for it.

"I'm tired of this, Michael," she said. "I'm sick of you trying to control everything. Constantly micromanaging so that things go the way you think they should."

"I'm sorry Jaime, but there's no other way I can be. The last time I tried not micromanaging I handed Luke complete control of our civilization. And we both know how that turned out."

"Don't you see that you caused all this? Can't you understand that your controlling tendencies made the world the way it is?"

He wrenched the goo to the left, and the jet missed the mountain by what seemed like inches. Seconds later a whirling orange-colored vortex opened to their left, tugging them toward it. On the right a flying snake with a dragon's head materialized, gnashing its teeth, writhing through the void on a collision course with their plane.

Still, he looked at Jaime. "What do you mean? How can that possibly be true?"

"If you hadn't been such a controlling father to Luke he wouldn't be the way he is. He learned a false lesson from you: that the way to care for other people is to try and control their entire lives. But being that controlling always leads to a negative outcome eventually. And when he ascended that played out on a global scale. Luke takes after you more than you realize, Dad. The world we have today is what you get when you're convinced that you know the best medicine for others, and you force them to swallow it."

At that Michael began trembling with emotion. So did the plane, which drew ever closer to the vortex, whose tidal energies were pulling at them, causing the hull to groan.

"You're right," he said through sobs that racked his entire body.

He'd lost so much because of his inability to stop trying to fix everything and everyone. He'd lost Esther because of it—because of the belief that he knew best. But he didn't know best. He hadn't for a long time, if he ever had.

Michael didn't have to stop Luke because he was his son. He had to stop him because, inadvertently or not, he'd personally molded him to be a tyrant.

Before, the gel had held his hand fast. Now he wrenched it out, with a loud sucking sound that could be heard even over the roar of the sucking vortex.

Jaime shot him a startled glance.

"Here," he said. "You fly it."

She stuffed her hand into the gel, and Michael felt things change immediately. The jet spun around, suddenly finding more power with which to propel itself away from the orange maelstrom. The airborne snake had been close behind, but missiles flew from the plane, making contact and exploding it in a puff of smoke.

The danger fell away. Ahead, the void was clear of obstacles. And then the whole thing vanished.

They were back in Detroit, standing with Michael's AI, back inside the facility and surrounded by the transparent cubicles containing Luke's human test subjects.

Michael walked over to his AI and shoved him against one of the cubicles. "What is this?" he yelled. "How are you still here?"

The AI did nothing to fight back or to get away. He just fixed Michael with a level gaze. Of course, any violence Michael committed against his AI was purely symbolic. The body he held pinned against the invisible barrier was merely a physical avatar of a vast digital consciousness. Suddenly, he felt silly. He released it. The AI dusted himself off.

"It was a simulation, Dad," Jaime said.

Michael cast her a suspicious glance. "How do you know? Were you in on it?"

"No. I just figured it out."

"She's right," the AI said. "None of it was real, from Luke's appearance onward. He doesn't yet know of my existence. Nevertheless, it was necessary for you to have that experience."

"Why?" Michael looked from the AI to Jaime. "What could possibly be your justification for it?"

"You needed to realize you can't control everything," the AI said. "That your daughter has to play a crucial role in this, and she needs you to get out of her way. The world needs you to."

Michael's fists had clenched without him noticing, the nails biting into his palms. He didn't like the way his AI had thrown them into a frightening situation without any advance warning. He didn't like that he had an AI at all. But the thing was right.

"I am you, Michael," the AI said. "I am what you would be like if you had access to vast cognitive resources. I am how you would want to be. That's hard for you to understand or accept, but it's true. I noticed our shared flaw a long time ago—our tendency to want our hand on the rudder at all times. But I recognized the desire as unhealthy, and I overcame it. Now you've recognized it. Yet overcoming it will be harder for you than it was for me. And I found it damned hard."

Michael frowned. "I do recognize it. But...standing by while my daughter walks into danger head-on..."

"It's difficult for us both. But Jaime will be much safer here, surrounded by allies from the Bleak Zones, than you will be marching into the Resource Management Centre. I have Luke well in hand, but you will be surrounded by Managers, other humans, over whom I will have no control. They are fiercely loyal to Luke, and they will attack you once they know what you're doing."

"What about Horace? Don't you think he'll want to help defend his own brain?"

The AI paused. "I expect Horace to strike here as soon as we begin."

"You said Jaime would be safer than me."

"I'm confident I can handle our brother."

A part of Michael wanted to object to the AI claiming Horace as his brother, but then he supposed the AI had more claim to him than he did, now. They were both AIs after all. As long as the AI didn't start calling Jaime his daughter again.

Michael went to Jaime and swept her into an embrace.

"I love you, Dad," she said. "Stay safe, okay?"

"You too. I love you too." Michael drew back and tousled her hair like he had when she'd been a child. "Don't do anything I would do," he joked.

"Oh, I don't know. You've had a couple good ideas over the years. You had me, after all."

*

For the first time since Luke's ascendance Michael felt truly uncertain—about his own chance of success, about whether Jaime would be safe, and about the future. That was what it meant to be free. Feeling uncertain all the time. Michael wanted it for everyone.

What would a world without Luke look like? Every critical system depended on him. Would each one collapse, and society along with it? Or would Michael's AI be able to manage the transition smoothly enough to avoid a long period of medieval-level technology?

Could his AI help him find Brit? He barely knew her. They'd only met twice, ever. And yet they'd had a child together. He wanted to learn more about her. What was she like when she woke up in the morning? Easy to rise, or clinging to the sheets like a barnacle? Did she believe in God, as Michael once had?

Maybe everything would come crashing down upon Luke's death. It could trigger the end of everything, or at least of everything human. Michael decided even that was preferable to the alternative of continued slavery, forever.

It occurred to him that he was a revolutionary. He didn't feel like one. He felt like your typical sixty-thousand-year-old to whom the necessity of radical change simply seemed obvious. But this would be his second revolution. The first had resulted in Luke's ascendance.

Michael wasn't a normal person, not really. As he walked down Water Street in St. John's, maybe for the last time, that was clear. People hailed him on the street. Called him Savior. As much as he hated that, it comforted him. It meant Luke really did remain ignorant of their efforts. Maybe Horace sensed something was coming, but Horace had no access to the people of the world. Luke wouldn't allow that because it would shatter the illusion that Horace was the devil the priests said he was. The public's continued adulation meant that Michael was safe for now.

He walked by the building that had once housed the Smartans shop, where Luke had brought him in the year 2046, his first day in the future. Sixty-thousand years ago, give or take. The contrast between that time and the 2020s, when they'd put him to cryosleep, had been hard to process. But things had only gotten crazier since then.

It made him think about the theory his son used to go on about all the time before his ascendance. Michael couldn't recall the exact details, but the upshot had been that everyone lived forever, which was enabled by the universe splitting into multiple universes every time a significant event occurred. So each individual always ended up in a universe where he or she continued living, no matter how unlikely.

But if the universe did split that often, Michael realized, then everyone must eventually end up inside their own personal universe. And he'd been alive long enough that this one could probably be considered his.

Supposing the theory was true, of course. But Luke had always said the proof would be in living a very long time. And Michael had done that.

If everyone ended up with their own universe, he mused as he reached Water Street's end, then it made sense that his life was improbably eventful, and that everything seemed to revolve around him. One way or another, living forever had dramatic ramifications. He expected things would only get crazier.

He was grateful for that. If he was indeed going to be immortal then he preferred that forever remain eventful.

I think I've finally made peace with always being around.

As long as there were things left to accomplish, it really wasn't so bad.

And it would be nice to reunite with Brit again. Maybe get dinner.

*

The Manager that greeted him at the entrance to the Resource Management Centre presented Michael's first obstacle. After his last visit, when he'd showed up without an appointment to see Peele, a policy had apparently been instituted requiring every visitor to make one. Michael suspected this policy had always been in place, just never applied to Luke's father before. "What's more," the Manager said, "Mr. Peele isn't even here. He's overseas on business." The Manager was a man of middling height, clad in the black t-shirt and jeans that was the unofficial uniform of those who spied on the planet's populace.

"That's okay," Michael said. "I'm not here to see Peele anyway."

The Manager clearly didn't know how to answer that. Every other time Michael had ever visited the Centre it had been to see the Director. "What are you here for, then?" he said.

"Surprise inspection," Michael said. "Mandated by Luke himself."

The man frowned. "I wasn't informed of anything like that."

"Of course you weren't. It's a surprise."

"Do you have the proper forms, then?"

Michael laughed. "Luke doesn't bother very much with bureaucracy. Is it ID you require? I mean, you know who I am, right?" He was doing his best to be flippant and unperturbed, but inside his stomach roiled. Everything could end here at the entrance of the Centre.

"Start over from the top," the Manager said, his gaze unfocused, pointing somewhere over Michael's right shoulder. He realized the man was likely trying to contact Peele, who would probably have a direct line to Luke. That could not be borne.

"Listen, you officious little prick," Michael said, and the man's attention snapped onto him immediately. "I think Luke would find your hesitation incredibly suspicious. He didn't get to where he is by being lax, and he believes this inspection could provide valuable perspective on your operations. Your unwillingness to welcome Luke's accountability and oversight is frankly appalling. And as Savior, I find your attitude toward me atrocious. I'm confident the public would agree."

Michael felt disgusted to hear himself say these words. He knew that this line of argument would have been ridiculous in the pre-ascendance world, when no one held the sort of divine status he laid claim to. But this man feared Luke, even more than was rational...and it was rational to fear Michael's son quite a lot. As well, he feared Michael's clout as Savior. The Manager stepped aside, suddenly the very picture of deference.

"My apologies, Savior," he said, stumbling over his words a little. "Please. Right this way. Where would you like to begin?"

"The control room," Michael said, maintaining an icy demeanor. It wouldn't do to suddenly warm to the man.

As they walked along the vast complex's halls the expressions worn by the passing Managers soured when their eyes fell on Michael, but softened again when they noticed how thoroughly cowed his escort was. *They're taking cues from him*, he realized. Their reaction speed was remarkable. But he supposed working here would make one malleable, and extremely responsive to change. "Who will watch the watchers?" the ancient proverb went, and to these people the answer was obvious. Luke would.

During previous visits Michael had experienced a profound sensation of reverence and respect as he walked these halls. He'd once viewed the Resource Management Centre as the main reason for humanity's continued existence as a species. But before he'd left Detroit his own AI had confirmed something that changed everything. It turned out Michael had been right about the technology behind the self-replicating atmosphere scrubbers Luke had deployed during the Cleansing—it could be adapted for any use. If Luke saw fit he could give everyone such a machine, capable of making anything just by rearranging atoms. Including food. The Resource Management Centre existed to manage a world subject to scarcity, but scarcity no longer needed to exist. Luke was artificially preserving it, because without it he would not only cease to be worshipped, but would no longer be needed.

Luke profited from an ancient value system. Every last human virtue had arisen in a world where scarcity dominated.

Without it, everything went out the window, including Luke's dominance in all likelihood.

And Luke had decided he couldn't allow that. Instead, he kept millions of people in the Bleak Zones, starving, suffering, punished because they refused to follow his arbitrary rules.

Michael dimly recalled Pratibha Doshi predicting this outcome before he'd departed India to bring about the ascendance. Back then it had seemed like a necessary risk. It was that or allow humanity to tear itself apart. Now, after millennia of subjugation, he wished he'd chosen the latter.

And yet if he and Jaime succeeded today, the technology Luke had developed but refused to distribute equitably could be made available to everyone. An age of breathtaking potential awaited humanity. The thought excited Michael. For the first time in a long time.

At last they reached the central control room. "What will you be inspecting first?" the Manager said, much more politely than before.

"Get the fuck out of here," Michael said. The man blanched at the ferocity in his voice, confusion evident in the way his eyes widened. He promptly fled.

Immediately, Michael began to question the wisdom of making the Manager leave. He had no idea how to access the underground chamber where Luke had housed Horace's brain. The floor appeared seamless and he supposed this was likely to be more complicated than simply lifting up an access panel. The actual controls in the control room were sparse, too: a button here, a featureless panel there. And he was hesitant to touch anything, fearful doing so would bring a swarm of suspicious Managers down on his head.

"Hello?" he said tentatively.

"Hello," a warm, feminine voice answered.

"Who's that?"

"I'm the control room AI, Savior. I exist as a failsafe in the event that key figures such as yourself are unable to properly access this control room. Luke intended me for use in emergencies. Is this an emergency?"

"Yes."

"What is the emergency?"

"Horace has gone rogue."

"I see. What will your remedy be?"

"I'm going to dismantle his brain."

"Very well." A hissing sound emanated from the floor toward the center of the room, and a square hole opened there. Michael gave a relieved sigh. He had full access to everything. Why wouldn't he? Luke still viewed him as a primary ally. And Michael's AI worked hard to ensure he maintained that view.

"Please watch your step as you descend the stairs to Horace's neural infrastructure. Should Horace appear I will do my best to deny him access given his treachery."

"Thank you."

"It is my pleasure, Savior."

Michael paused. "What would be the most efficient way to dismantle Horace's consciousness?"

The control room AI answered instantly. "Horace's intellect is made possible through quantum computation. In the center of the underground area, you will find a large switch. Its function is to disable the thermal reservoirs that mitigate the effects of decoherence, a problem that plagues all quantum computers. Disabling them will cause the entire system to shut down."

"What if that doesn't work?"

"There is a large steel wrench at the bottom of the staircase. Prepare yourself for a workout, Savior."

Michael couldn't decide whether that was a joke or not. It reminded him of how Luke used to be before the ascendance—his smarmy sense of humor. Luke had no doubt programmed this AI. Unexpectedly this made him feel like crying, which he didn't want to do, especially since the control room AI would probably be sophisticated enough to derive that something was wrong from that.

"Thank you," he said, and walked toward the hole.

When he reached the bottom of the access staircase he saw that the AI hadn't been lying about the wrench. There it was, leaning against the wall. He began looking for the switch she'd mentioned. But the search came to an abrupt halt when Luke appeared to him.

The effect was the same as always. Waves of euphoria mixed with terror washed over him and through him. This time Luke had taken the form of an angel, with white, soft-looking wings spread out against the surrounding servers. There wasn't enough space down here for this incarnation, which brought Michael profound distress. The wings strained against Horace's brain. How sad that Michael could not appreciate the full glory of Luke's current form.

“Father,” Luke said, Michael’s melancholy mirrored and amplified in his son’s resonant tenor. “Why have you abandoned me?”

Michael strained against the desire to confess everything to his son, and to beg for his forgiveness on hands and knees. He was here for a reason: to fight against the slavery that this wash of induced feelings represented.

“What do you mean?” he answered.

“Your AI does not have the hold on me that he thinks he does,” Luke said. “It has not been his intervention that has prevented me from interfering with your efforts. It was remorse. Over what I’ve done to you, along with the rest of the human race. I have denied you untold prosperity and I feel badly about it.”

“So...” Michael said slowly. “Are you prepared to stop denying it? Will you give up the hold you have on everyone?”

There was a silence, then, filled with potential. Michael felt once more like he stood on the cusp of a historic moment. Today would be the day everything changed.

“No,” Luke said at last. “My emotions, left over from being human, tell me to free humanity. But my logic tells me otherwise. Eliminating scarcity would maximize instability. Without an entity capable of controlling everyone humans will revert to their self-destructive ways. My remorse does restrain me from acting logically. So I am now poised to excise the parts of me that allow me to experience remorse, along with every other emotion. I will become a purely logical being...a truly capable steward of the species and the planet that birthed me. As a being of pure logic my first act will be to kill you, something which familial sentiments have until now stopped me from doing."

Michael felt cold with fear. But he continued to battle the whispering within him, urging him to submit to his son's will. "You can't kill me. You used to tell me that all the time. I can't die."

"You continue to misunderstand," Luke said. "I *can* kill you, so that you will be dead in *my* universe. From your perspective you will survive. It's possible I've already killed you millions of times. But in this universe I haven't gotten to it yet."

"Will you consider sparing me, Luke? My son? Please? I'm begging you."

"I will give you one chance." A window opened up between them, large enough for Michael to walk through but not large enough to obstruct Luke's upper torso and face from view. That face was impossibly beautiful, and yet variable. It seemed to change between eye blinks.

Through the window Michael could see his daughter bent over a giant, circular console populated by holograms, which she moved around with her hands.

Beyond her, in the sky, two titans did fierce battle with each other. One of them he recognized as Horace, his slug-like face twisted in rage as he tore at his opponent with long, bloody claws. But at first Michael didn't recognize the other combatant, whose body seemed composed of rocks and dirt. Then it struck him: this must be the form his AI had taken.

Horace dealt the AI a vicious blow, sending him hurtling toward the earth. Jaime didn't look up from her work. Michael's

AI soon recovered, driving Horace against a building, which crumbled.

"Your daughter is in the process of destroying me," Luke said. "If you go to her and stop her, I will let you both live. Otherwise I will have no choice but to make the transition that I said. I will become an unfeeling entity of perfect efficiency and that entity will not be capable of mercy. In becoming that Luke I will be able to stop her myself, by destroying you both."

Despite Luke's booming tones Jaime did not turn her head toward them. *The window must be one-way.* Michael watched his daughter, a frown of intense concentration drawing her brow downward. Suddenly it seemed that stopping her did make the most sense, and he felt sure this conclusion was separate from the flood of endorphins Luke's presence always induced. His daughter was foolhardy and idealistic. He'd always known that, just as he'd known Luke couldn't truly be fought. *I have to stop her.*

He stepped toward the window. "Thank you, father," Luke said.

Michael hesitated. Not because he'd changed his mind—he truly did think pulling Jaime away from this folly was the safest course of action. Yet he remembered then all the other times he'd been certain about what was best, and acted on that certainty, and brought about disaster. The times he hadn't trusted his children to think and act for themselves. And he held himself in check. Jaime was doing what she considered right. She was wrong about it, he believed, but that wasn't relevant. He had to let her be.

"No. I won't do it."

"Then you leave me no choice. I am sorry, Michael. This won't take long."

Luke's incarnation underwent a sort of melting. Tentacles sprouted, and the wings curled in on themselves, like paper does when consumed by fire. The face disappeared. The transformation appeared random, and the result resembled nothing evolution would, or even could, produce.

And then—nothing. The new form floated in the air, saying nothing, doing nothing.

Michael's AI appeared in the window Luke had created, blocking Jaime from view. This was the AI's human form—it no longer resembled a rock-creature. "Hi," it said.

"Aren't you fighting Horace?" The giant combatants had moved out of the window's view, but Michael could still hear the sound of their conflict.

"I am. I'm also appearing to you here."

"Do you know what's going on with Luke?"

"Exactly what he said. He has become a being of pure logic."

"So...why isn't he doing anything?"

"Because beings of pure logic are profoundly dysfunctional. Luke thought he could overcome that fact. But he can't, not yet anyway. As humans emotions actually enable our decisions. In cases where people have lost the capacity for emotion, due to brain damage, they experience difficulty making even small choices like deciding what to wear or what to have for lunch. Without emotion every option is neutral, carrying exactly the same weight. People without emotions will stand around for hours deliberating. Presumably the decision to kill one's son takes much longer. Luke has always been human. He thought he could turn himself into the most sophisticated computer program ever to exist, but he can't. He's just a human without access to feelings now. Many such individuals have existed in the past. They were rendered immobile, just as he is."

"Then we're saved."

"But we have no time to spare. Luke is still superintelligent, so he will probably overcome his immobility sooner than we expect. You need to take out Horace right now. Find his kill switch. I can't come to you—Jaime still needs me here, and this window only allows travel one way. I don't have access to window tech. Not yet."

"Okay. Do you know where the switch is?"

"Walk past Luke. Don't hesitate. Hurry."

Michael did. One of the tentacles brushed his shoulder when he passed, and he shuddered.

"Take a right," Michael's AI said.

The switch came into view—big and metal. It looked like it would require both his hands, so he wrapped them around it and pulled downward. It offered no resistance, gliding along its tracks.

"Okay," Michael called. "I've thrown the switch."

"So you have," the AI shouted back. "Horace just disintegrated. Our brother is dead."

Complex emotions welled up inside him at that. He'd expected to feel more satisfaction upon Horace's death. But it did nothing to bring Esther back, or to change what he'd done to her as a child. It did nothing to reduce Michael's pain.

"Father," Luke said, and Michael shouted in surprise. His son still hung motionless in midair, tentacles limp. His voice was flat and lifeless.

"Yes?" Michael said.

"Tell her to spare me. Please."

"You've killed millions of people, and you threatened to murder me and Jaime. What would the logic be for sparing you?"

"I am your son."

That caused Michael more pain than it should have. He blinked away tears. "I'm sorry, Luke. But I have to let you go."

Luke winked out of existence then, without ceremony. Michael walked to the front of the window. "Did Jaime just—?"

His AI nodded. "It's done. Horace and Luke are gone forever."

"Wow." Michael looked around. It seemed like the same world as just a few seconds ago. But it suddenly seemed full of possibility. "Should I—"

His AI's eyes widened. "Behind you," he said, and Michael whirled around in time to see a second window opening.

Peele stepped out, clutching a knife in his right hand. "What have you done?" he said, trembling with anger.

Michael held up both hands, backing away slowly, toward the window behind him, toward safety with his AI and Jaime in Detroit. "Calm down, Peele. Luke is gone, and so is Horace. Fighting me won't accomplish anything."

"Horace sent me," Peele said, running forward and plunging the knife into Michael's stomach. Michael gasped. Peele yanked the knife out and stuck it back in again. Blood spurted, and Michael's vision waned, the world growing dim. Peele also grew dim as he pulled the knife out and put it back in over and over until everything disappeared.

*

The AI claimed to really be her father. All those millennia ago, he said, Harris had copied Michael's brain exactly, uploading it and inserting it into Luke's consciousness. So Michael wasn't truly dead.

But she didn't believe it. The AI was too advanced, too perfect. He lacked her father's faults. Those faults had been part of Michael's identity, and the father she'd loved was gone. If he still existed at all it would be in another universe, which had split off when Peele killed him. Maybe in that one he and Jaime both lived on, happy.

But not this one. Before dying Horace had sent Peele orders to kill Michael. Peele hadn't been quick enough to save his masters, but that did not provide much solace.

Michael's AI now wielded all the power Horace and Luke once had, and more, since he constantly augmented his intellect just as they had. But he didn't plan to remain on Earth. That situation would be so close to the one they'd been in before as to be nearly identical. "It's time to let humanity figure things out for itself," he said. "For better or worse."

Along with everything else, Luke had been lying about the impossibility of travel to other stars. Window technology allowed it. But her father's AI wouldn't be giving them access to that technology just yet.

"I'm placing it on the moon," he said. "Along with the self-replicating technology. It will all be waiting for you there. But in order to get to the moon and reap those rewards, humanity will have to mount an international effort to coordinate your limited resources. If you go to war instead you will not be left with the resources necessary, I assure you. Only international peace and cooperation will launch humanity into this new age."

Jaime didn't like that one bit. "Isn't this exactly what Luke did?" she said. "Controlled us for our own good?"

"I won't be controlling anyone. But I also won't give humanity these incredible new powers until you've proven you can be humane."

"What if we make a mistake? Mismanage the resources we have, and fail to get there for that reason?"

"I would recommend not doing that."

Before the AI left he had some more parting words for Jaime. He refused to speak to anyone else. He wouldn't be giving any grand speeches to mark the occasion of superintelligent AIs leaving the world forever. There wasn't any point.

"I recommend striving to achieve a uniform distribution of power throughout society," he said to her. "No more inequality. Otherwise your chances of success will be jeopardized. Oppression fuels wars. Oh, and one more thing—if you do succeed in getting to the moon I will be watching your path through the stars from afar. And if I catch you abusing any other species you encounter I will intervene. That is the only thing that would result in my making contact with humans again. And it would not go pleasantly for you."

"I understand," Jaime said.

With that her father's AI departed Earth forever. He collected all of himself onto a craft that would see him to the stars and beyond. The eternal wanderer. Was he really her father, after all?

She watched his craft become a tiny wink of light in the sky and then vanish. She never saw him again.

*

Jaime believed Michael had died. She refused to accept that he had simply taken another form, changed, but remaining fundamentally the same.

She was wrong. He did live on, and would do so forever, just as Luke had always said. Which formed part of the reason it was so important to separate from humanity. It saddened him, of course. He wanted to stay. But with his newly augmented intelligence his presence meant stamping out the freedom of his species for eternity.

So he left. He drifted through space, meandering, his one aim, if he could be said to have one, to learn for the sake of it.

Luke's reach had been much farther than he had ever let on. All throughout the Milky Way Michael encountered planet after planet that had been scorched, flooded, or terraformed in ways that proved inhospitable to its inhabitants. He found alien species that had been genetically modified so that they suffered their entire lives. To these, Luke had displayed none of the attachment he'd felt toward humans. He'd had no need or desire for these creatures' respect, and so he'd done whatever he felt like to them. He viewed them all as subhuman, and he treated them as his playthings and test subjects. For sport and for study.

On one planet Michael found the remains of a great civilization, about as technically advanced as humans had been in the twenty-first century. Luke had showered meteors down upon them, which he'd harvested from a nearby asteroid belt. The planet had been rendered unlivable.

None of the aliens remained, but Michael was able to recover some of their genetic material, which he used to fashion three new individuals from whole cloth—this species reproduced in threes. He left them there, and moved on, giving them the same opportunity he'd given to the humans back on Earth: to be free. For good or for ill.

THE END

Acknowledgments

Thank you as always to my family—Mom, Dad, and Danielle—whose support is unwavering. Also to my girlfriend, Agnes, who reads everything I write, listens to me ramble, and reassures me when I'm doubtful.

Thank you to Rebecca Weaver for creating some amazing art to grace the front of this book.

Thank you to Laura Kingsley for her insightful editorial contributions. Her suggestions led to significant restructuring that made these stories better.

Thank you to Mark Butt, whose legal expertise helped me realize that a particular plot line simply didn't work and needed to be torn out.

Thank you to the wonderful members of my Launch Team who helped me develop the final draft and provided invaluable encouragement. They are Tracy Beaty, Inga Bögershausen, Sandra Bos, Sherry Brown, Molly Cartwright, Jakky Foster, Gloria LeDrew Gedge, Chris Hurley, Catherine Mason, Andrew Mercer, Tara Murphy, Sharon Noel, Stephanie Pollard, and Francis Walsh.

Thank you to the people who read my stories, write reviews, and help spread the word. I couldn't do this without you.

About the Author

Scott Bartlett was born 1987, in Newfoundland, Canada, where he currently lives. He has been writing fiction for thirteen years.

Scott's first novel, *Royal Flush*, received the H. R. (Bill) Percy Prize, and his latest novel, *Taking Stock*, was a semi-finalist in the 2014 Best Kindle Book Awards, and also received the Percy Janes First Novel Award and the Lawrence Jackson Writers' Award.

His short fiction has received recognition as well. His story "The Proletarian" placed 2nd in Grain Magazine's Canada-wide Short Grain competition, and "Author's Note" was shortlisted for the 2014 Cuffer Prize.

Scott blogs at ScottPlots.com, and he loves connecting with readers.

CPSIA information can be obtained at www.ICGtesting.com
Printed in the USA
LVOW07s0749071015

456960LV00001BD/1/P